MW00576620

the

CAUTIOUS
TRAVELLER'S
GUIDE *to the*
WASTELANDS

the

CAUTIOUS
TRAVELLER'S
GUIDE *to the*
WASTELANDS

Sarah Brooks

FLATIRON
BOOKS
NEW YORK

THE CAUTIOUS TRAVELLER'S GUIDE TO THE WASTELANDS. Copyright © 2024 by Sarah Brooks. All rights reserved. Printed in the United States of America. For information, address Flatiron Books, 120 Broadway, New York, NY 10271.

www.flatironbooks.com

Designed by Donna Sinisgalli Noetzel

Map by Emily Faccini

Library of Congress Cataloging-in-Publication Data

Names: Brooks, Sarah, 1980– author.
Title: The cautious traveller's guide to the Wastelands / Sarah Brooks.
Description: First edition. | New York : Flatiron Books, 2024.
Identifiers: LCCN 2023047378 | ISBN 9781250878618 (hardcover) | ISBN 9781250878625 (ebook)
Subjects: LCGFT: Fantasy fiction. | Novels.
Classification: LCC PR6102.R6646 C38 2024 | DDC 823/.92—dc23/ eng/20240213
LC record available at https://lccn.loc.gov/2023047378

Our books may be purchased in bulk for promotional, educational, or business use. Please contact your local bookseller or the Macmillan Corporate and Premium Sales Department at 1-800-221-7945, extension 5442, or by email at MacmillanSpecialMarkets@macmillan.com.

First Edition: 2024

10 9 8 7 6 5 4 3 2 1

For my family

CONTENTS

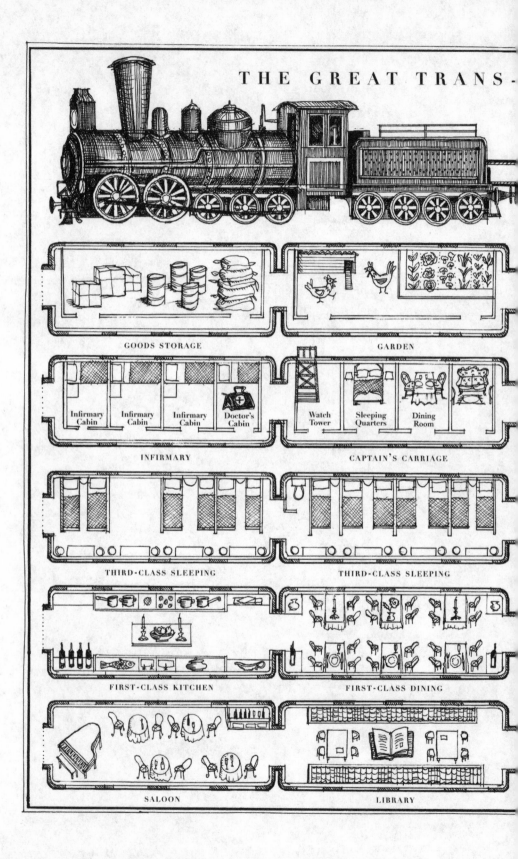

GOODS STORAGE

GARDEN

INFIRMARY

Infirmary Cabin

Infirmary Cabin

Infirmary Cabin

Doctor's Cabin

CAPTAIN'S CARRIAGE

Watch Tower

Sleeping Quarters

Dining Room

THIRD-CLASS SLEEPING

THIRD-CLASS SLEEPING

FIRST-CLASS KITCHEN

FIRST-CLASS DINING

SALOON

LIBRARY

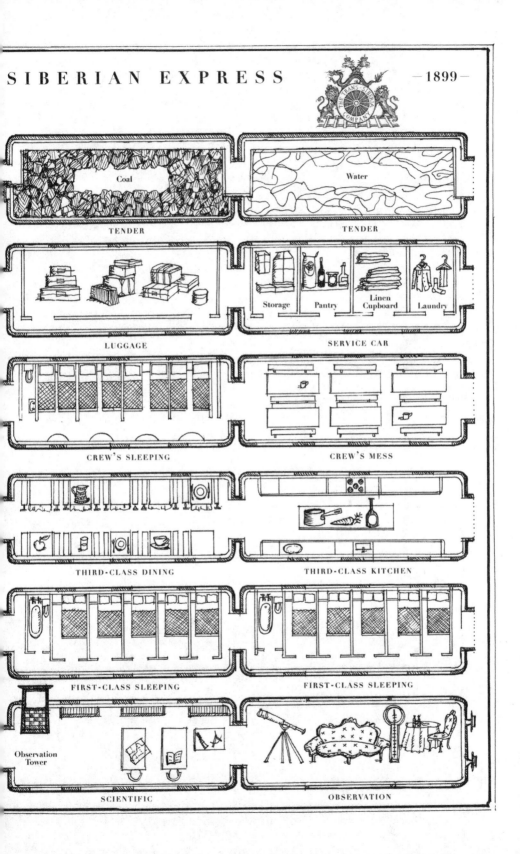

SIBERIAN EXPRESS

—1899—

Coal

TENDER

Water

TENDER

LUGGAGE

Storage | Pantry | Linen Cupboard | Laundry

SERVICE CAR

CREW'S SLEEPING

CREW'S MESS

THIRD-CLASS DINING

THIRD-CLASS KITCHEN

FIRST-CLASS SLEEPING

FIRST-CLASS SLEEPING

Observation Tower

SCIENTIFIC

OBSERVATION

the
CAUTIOUS TRAVELLER'S GUIDE *to the* WASTELANDS

The train itself—a marvel of the age, a monument to the ingenuity of Man and to his ceaseless striving for mastery over the earth. Twenty carriages long and as tall as the great gates of St. Andrei's Cathedral, with towers at either end; an armored fortress to plow the great iron road that must itself stand as one of the new wonders of the world, a miracle of engineering that lets us traverse once more these barely imaginable distances. The Trans-Siberia Company succeeded where so many others had failed, embarking on a project so fraught with danger that the greatest engineers in the land swore it could not be done. To cross land that has, since the end of the last century, been turning against its occupants; to face strangeness for which we do not have the language to describe; to build a railway to safely carry us over all those perilous miles.

The Cautious Traveller may balk at the very mention of the Greater Siberian Wastelands, at spaces so vast and unkind and stories so inimical to our sense of all that is decent and human and good. But it is the humble aim of this author to take the Traveller by the hand and act as a constant companion on their journey. And if I myself appear to falter, then know that I too am by nature and inclination, Cautious, and that there were times on my journey when the horrors outside threatened to overwhelm me; when reason trembled in the face of unreason.

I was once a Godly man and full of certainties. This book must stand as a record of what I lost along the way, and as a guide for those who follow, in the hope that they may better bear the strange days of their journey, and sleep a little sounder through the uneasy nights.

FROM *THE CAUTIOUS TRAVELLER'S GUIDE
TO THE WASTELANDS* BY VALENTIN ROSTOV
(MIRSKY PUBLISHING, MOSCOW, 1880), INTRODUCTION, PAGE 1

Part One

Days 1–2

I resolved to begin my journey in Beijing, on the one-year anniversary of the line's opening. It is four thousand miles to Moscow. The Company promises that the journey will take fifteen days, an extraordinarily short time, in comparison with the many weeks it has taken to cross the continents until now. Of course, the train itself has been long in gestation. The Trans-Siberia Company proposed the building of a railway in the 1850s, half a century after the changes were first recorded, and twenty years after the building of the Walls and the closing of the Wastelands (as they had already come to be called). Tracks would be laid, they decided, starting from both China and Russia, with special trains built that would allow for the laying of rails without exposing the builders to the dangers outside. There were many who doubted the Company's great gamble, and who criticized the hubris of such an endeavor. Yet while it would take two decades and the work of many hundreds of men, the Trans-Siberia Company eventually succeeded in reaching across the Wastelands and connecting the continents by an iron thread.

The Cautious Traveller's Guide to the Wastelands, page 2

1
THE LIAR

Beijing, 1899

There is a woman on the platform with a borrowed name. With steam in her eyes and the taste of oil on her lips. The shrill, desperate whistle of the train turns into the sobbing of a young girl nearby and the cries of the trinket vendors, hawking their flimsy amulets as protection against Wastelands sickness. She forces herself to look up, to stare at it face on, the train that looms above her, hissing and humming; waiting, vibrating with pent-up power. How huge it is, how implacably solid, three times the width of a horse-drawn carriage. It makes the station buildings look as flimsy as a child's toys.

She concentrates on her breath, on emptying her mind of any other thought. In and out, in and out. She has practiced this, day after long day these past six months, sitting at home by the window, watching the pickpockets and traders below, letting it all wash over her, letting her mind run clear as water. She holds on to the image of a river, slow-moving and gray. If she can just let it carry her to safety.

"Marya Petrovna?"

It is a moment before she realizes she is the one the porter is addressing, and she turns to him with a start. "Yes! Yes." Too loudly, to cover her confusion. Too unused to the unfamiliar syllables of her new name.

"Your cabin is ready and your luggage has been taken on board." Sweat beads his forehead and leaves a damp, darkened line around his collar.

"Thank you." She is gratified to hear that her voice does not tremble. Marya Petrovna is unafraid. Newborn. She can only go forward, following the porter as he disappears into the steam, broken by glimpses of green paint and gold lettering in English, as well as Russian and Chinese. *The Trans-Siberian Express. Beijing–Moscow; Moscow–Beijing.* They must have spent the last months painting and polishing. Everything shines.

"Here we are." The porter turns toward her, wiping his brow and leaving behind a dark, oily smudge. She is uncomfortably aware of her own clothes, chafing her skin in the heat, the black silk drinking up the sun. Her blouse claws at her neck and her skirt is tight around her waist, but she has no time to worry about her appearance because the porter is holding out his arm, stiffly, and she is climbing the high steps up onto the train, her hand taken by another bowing uniformed man, she is being swept along the corridor, thick carpet beneath her feet. She is on the train and it is too late to turn back now.

In front of her, a man with a beard and gold spectacles and the kind of voice that elbows all other voices out of the way, leans out of the window and shouts in English, "Where is the Station Master? Be careful with those boxes! Oh, I do beg your pardon." He squeezes himself against the window and attempts a bow as Marya approaches. She limits herself to a small smile and an incline of the head and leaves him to his hectoring. She has no wish for social niceties, nor the curious, appraising gazes of men, already observing her black mourning garb, noting her solitary state. Let them note. All she wants is to be alone in her cabin, to shut the door and close the curtains and gather a comforting silence around her.

But she is not to be allowed, not quite yet.

"Really, do stop fussing, I am perfectly capable of looking after myself." An elderly lady approaches from the other end of the carriage, dressed in dark-blue silk and followed by her maid. "Is this really First Class?" She peers at Marya, and then at the cabin door beside her. "I had been led to believe this train was the finest money could buy. I confess, I cannot see it . . ."

Hearing the familiar sounds of well-to-do St. Petersburg, thousands of miles away from its wide streets and tall houses, gives Marya a painful tug of homesickness.

"Your cabin, madam," says the steward, bowing to Marya but looking nervously at the elderly lady, who inquires, "Are you travelling alone?" while swatting away her maid, in her attempts to drape another shawl over her shoulders.

Marya sees a mixture of pity and reproach in her gaze, and flushes.

"My maid was unable to make the journey. It was too much of a strain on her nerves."

"Well, it is good that our nerves are made of stronger stuff. My weak-spleened nephews spent months trying to dissuade me from this journey with tales of all the terrors that may befall us, but I believe they only succeeded in scaring themselves." She gives an unexpected smile and pats Marya on the hand. "Now then, where is my cabin? If Vera here doesn't have me stuffed into an armchair with a cup of tea in my hand very quickly, I can't swear to her behavior."

"Right here, Countess." The steward gives a much deeper bow and a theatrical wave of his arm. The maid—Vera—opens the door at arm's length, as if afraid of the horrors within.

"Ah! So we are to be neighbors," says the Countess.

Marya gives a curtsey.

"Oh, we shall have none of that here. My name is Anna Mikhailovna Sorokina. And I will call you . . . ?"

Another catch of the breath, a lurch like the feeling of missing a step she hadn't realized was there, but the Countess seems not to notice. "My name is Marya Petrovna Markova," she says.

"Well, Marya Petrovna, I look forward to making your acquaintance further. We shall, after all, have plenty of time." And with that, the Countess allows herself to be guided into her cabin by her little maid, who has been regarding Marya from under her eyelashes.

"Will you require any more assistance?" The steward licks his lips and swallows. *He's afraid,* Marya thinks, and somehow this gives her more courage.

"No," she replies, more firmly than she expected. "No, I require no assistance."

Her bags have been neatly packed onto the rack above the bed, which has been made up into a couch for the day, padded with plump cushions. Everything looks new. The Company must have poured money into it, displaying its confidence in the gold embroidery on the cushions and the bright brass on the walls and the deep-blue carpet, soft beneath her feet. Everywhere there is the lettering of the Trans-Siberia Company, entwined around the flower vase and the light fittings and embossed on the porcelain teacups and saucers on the little table by the window. Her day case sits on the armchair beside it. The window is framed by blinds and blue velvet curtains. On the other side of the glass run two thick iron bars. She stares at them a moment, then walks over to the wall, where two doors are set into the polished mahogany. One opens into a wardrobe, where her dresses and shawl already hang, unpacked by unseen hands. The other opens onto a cabinet with a compact white porcelain sink, shining silver taps and a shelf holding a hairbrush and little pots of creams from Paris, and above it all a silver-edged mirror.

As a child she had been fascinated by the old gilt mirror in her mother's bedroom. Clouded with silver, she used to think it made her look like a spirit, emerging from the underworld or swimming up out of a lake. Whichever idea happened to catch her fancy, she would enjoy the feeling of being someone else, just for a while, before her mother called her down for tea with her grandmother, or her father quizzed her with mental arithmetic. She had thought that as she grew older she would grow more certain of herself and what she wanted to be. But now, this new Marya, what does she want?

She closes the cabinet door, not wanting to see. From her day bag she takes out a battered book, its cover threadbare and its pages creased with use. She knows every word, could copy every illustration from memory, but there is something comforting about its physical presence. Valentin Rostov's famous *Guide to the Wastelands*—her father's copy, that she would read in secret, dreaming of the train and the world outside its windows, imagining herself onboard. But not like this. Not alone. A sudden, sharp loneliness engulfs her. The train has not even departed yet and she has not followed the first piece of Rostov's advice: *Above all, do not attempt the journey unless you are certain of your own evenness of mind.*

Outside on the platform porters and stewards usher the final stragglers aboard and order tearful relatives back toward the gates. Mechanics with oil-streaked faces stride purposefully alongside the train. A gaggle of men with notebooks are kept back by a harassed-looking Station Master. A sudden flash of light, and she sees a man emerge from a black cloth behind his photographic equipment. It will be in all the newspapers tomorrow morning; a journey turned into a story before it has even begun.

A series of clangs proclaim the locking of doors and the dropping of iron bars. She focuses on breathing in and out, in and out. *Nothing outside can get in, nothing inside can harm us.* She bites her lip and tastes blood. *Iron to keep us safe.* The platform is empty now but for the small figure of the Station Master. She watches him raise his flag and look up at the station clock. Faces from behind the platform gates stare at faces behind the bars of the train windows. Some of them are weeping. Rostov's words swim into her mind: *It is said that there is a price that every traveller through the Wastelands must pay. A price beyond the mere cost of a ticket on the train.*

Rostov paid the price with his faith. With his life, some think. His *Cautious Traveller's Guides* had made him famous throughout Europe, directing the traveller to the most hygienic restaurants, the worthiest museums, and the cleanest beaches, noting the finest churches and enumerating their altarpieces and frescoes, their martyrs and saints, for wherever a traveller wandered in that continent, he could know that God wandered beside him. But his final book was a guide to a land which could only be seen from behind glass. No churches remain in the Wastelands of Greater Siberia; no galleries or fountains or public art to tell the familiar stories.

On the platform, a moment of quiet stretches longer than it should have done. Then the flag falls, and the Trans-Siberian Express, in a slow cacophony of steam and screeches and creaking wheels, begins to move. As the train drags itself away from the platform the photographer's flash goes off and for a moment the clouds of steam are filled with light.

Marya steps backward, blinking away the sudden brightness, and the train rolls out of Beijing Railway Station, toward the uncertain spaces ahead.

2

THE CHILD OF THE TRAIN

Better to be moving. That's what train folk say. Better to have rail beneath you, wheels to rock you, a far horizon to reach. On Leaving Day most of all, better for the wait to be over. And the wait has been so long, this time. Ten months of enforced stillness, it is enough to send the calmest of minds mad. Zhang Weiwei, sixteen years old, stands at the window in the little vestibule that leads through to the working end of the train. Here, in the carriages closest to the engine—the crew quarters, the garden carriage, the stores—passengers are not allowed; only the porters and stewards rush by, too busy to pay her any attention. She watches the solid stone buildings of the station recede. High walls enclose the track and groups of small children dash sure-footed along them, their faces covered by masks that turn them into yellow-horned, bulbous-cheeked monsters, waving and dancing their ritual of parting or warning or glee. On the other side of the walls, along the alleys and avenues, shutters will be slamming closed, water boiling on stoves will be thrown out as tainted, couplets will be muttered to ward off bad dreams. The city will be listening, and only when it can no longer hear the sound of the rails and the whistle of the train will it let out its breath and go about its business, content to turn its mind away from the nightmares that lie to the north.

She sniffs. How she has missed these acrid smells, the creaking mechanics of her train, the old familiar terror and excitement, the noise—so constant that she ceases to hear it until it is gone. How she has longed, these past months, for movement, for speed; she has craved it like the red-eyed men in Third crave liquor, gasping for the last drops from the jar, maddened to find it empty.

But now that they are moving again the air vibrates with tension. She has heard the whispers among the crew. *Too soon.* Too soon for the train to ride again, why not wait for winter and the safer passage through the snow, when the land is drowsy with the cold and danger cannot hide amidst the trees? In summer the land is wakeful, hungry. It is too soon to take the risk.

Not soon enough for her. But then again, she is too in love with risk, Alexei always says.

"And who on this train isn't?" she replies, and he has to acknowledge the truth of it; that they are—all of them—half mad with Wastelands sickness already, with a longing and fear that they would struggle to articulate but which beckons them to the Trans-Siberia Company. They are the ones who hear the Wastelands from the safety of their cities and homes, who cannot resist the call of the great train. They present themselves at the grand Company offices in their London headquarters, or on Baiyun Road or Velikaya Street, knock on the famous wood-paneled doors and stand before unsmiling, gray-haired men who regard them sternly and demand to know why they should be thought worthy. Most are turned away. The chosen few are tested and observed for any indications that they may be susceptible to a landscape that disorders the mind, that drives men to throw themselves at the windows of the train, to scratch their fingers bloody at the doors, desperate to reach the outside. Should no such inclination become apparent, they are given the dark-blue uniform of the Trans-Siberian Express, a contract, a handbook and a Bible on which to swear allegiance to the Queen. From that moment onward they are part of the crew—part of the Company that stretches halfway across the world.

But Weiwei is different. Weiwei is the child of the train. Born neither here nor there, in no country, under no emperor's star, she came bawling into the world as her mother left it, at the very midpoint of the Wastelands, on the floor of the Third Class sleeping car, on a night when phosphorescence turned the creatures of the plains into ghosts. She was swaddled in sheets bearing the Company crest, and passed between the porters and the cooks and a wet-nurse found among the passengers in Third. One week later, when the train stopped at the Russian Wall, she screamed, because until then she had only known movement and noise. Company officials in Moscow were at a loss for what to do with her, never having had to deal with an unexpected orphan before. (Her mother had disguised her pregnancy and had professed herself to her fellow travellers as being quite alone in the world.) But while the Company was inclined to frown upon such maternal carelessness, they decided the best course of action would be to return the child to Beijing on board the next train, and to deliver her into the capable hands of the Chinese state.

And so she was carried and fed and changed by her wet-nurse and whatever member of the crew happened to have a free hand at the right moment. But when the train reached Beijing, and the Captain came to take her to the authorities, the stokers said she'd brought them good luck, and that the coals had burned brighter on this journey; the kitchen boys said the butter had turned just right, for the first time, leading a passenger in First Class to compliment the Cook, something which had never been known to happen before. The night porters said they had liked her company, as she had listened solemnly to their bawdy stories and made barely a wail of complaint. And so the Captain said (at least, in the stories Weiwei was told), "If she earns her keep she may stay. But there will be no spare parts on this train—she must make herself useful, like all of us."

Her first job, then, was as a talisman, a good-luck charm. She slept in the warmth of the kitchen or in a nest of canvas sacks in the luggage car or sometimes in the engine box itself, where the stokers would later tell how she would regard the glowing coals gravely, as if she understood even then their importance in keeping her safe. Later, she was put to work carrying messages from one end of the train to the other, and by the time she was six years old she was a rail rat through and through; everyone's child, and no one's. No one's but the train's.

"You loitering, Zhang?"

Here he comes now, Alexei, only a few years older than her but already promoted to First Engineer, swaggering down the corridor with a railman's gait, sleeves rolled up to show the tattoos on his forearms—complex, congratulatory patterns that Company engineers give themselves after each crossing. Marks of brotherhood (she has never seen a female engineer), and of memory. They touch their arms, sometimes, when they talk of journeys past; of cranks that failed and shafts that barely held. Gears and cogs have turned into abstract patterns on their skin; into ways of remembering. She tries to see whether there is a new design, one to mark the last crossing, but he sees her looking and rolls down his sleeves.

She has barely seen him these last couple of weeks, though they have all been quartered onboard while in the station, preparing for departure; the engineers and the stewards and the porters and the cooks; the drivers and the stokers, the countless parts of the clockwork of the train as it grinds slowly back into gear. A little rusty, a little slower than before; there's an odd stuttering to once familiar routines, a new hesitancy, as if they are all afraid to move too fast in case something should break. The few times she has caught a glimpse of him he has been always moving, filled with a restless energy after their long months of inaction.

"First check?" she asks, to fill the silence. She glances at the clock on the wall. Two minutes before the hour.

"First check," he replies. The engineers' days are filled with checks and tests, a relentless schedule that scrutinizes every inch of the train's complex mechanics, the Company's much-vaunted proof of the train's safety measures. "They've doubled them . . . We're not going to have a moment to ourselves."

They speak in Railhua, the language of the train, a mixture of Russian, Chinese and English that began with the builders of the line, although the Company frowns upon it and tries to insist on the use of English.

"You'd think they didn't trust you," she says without thinking, then sees his expression darken. "I didn't mean—"

"It doesn't matter." He brushes it away with a wave of his hand and she is caught by a sharp pang of regret for an ease that has been lost. Another thing that the last crossing took away.

"Be careful, Zhang." He looks like he wants to say more but the clock has begun to chime the hour and he is too much of a railman to ignore it. "Just be careful," he says again, and she bristles at the implication that she is not.

She sets off in the opposite direction, toward the crew quarters where those workers not currently on watch can usually be found, playing dice or stretched out on their bunks or wolfing down rice and soup in the crew mess. It is as busy and chaotic as the rest of the train, but at the far end of the carriage, set into the wall, is a little shrine containing an icon of Saint Mathilda and a statue of Yuan Guan. A saint and a god to watch over travellers, and over rail people, who, while putting their trust in mechanics, in wheels and gears and oil, are also inclined to think that it can't do any harm to give polite recognition to the numinous, just in case. Which of them, after all, had not seen things in the Wastelands more impossible than these saints who were once said to have done miracles? Weiwei sees one of the stewards bend his head then place something on the shrine, a surreptitiousness to his movements. He straightens up slowly, glancing around him as if afraid of being watched, then brings his hands together and bows his head again, before hurrying off.

When he has gone she looks more closely to see what he left behind. A glint of bluish-green catches the light from the window; it is a small, perfectly round glass bead.

3

THE NATURALIST

There is a man watching birds from the farthest window in the observation car. Azure-winged magpies—*Cyanopica cyanus*—burst from willow trees as the train roars past, the long feathers of their tails iridescent in the afternoon sunlight. When Henry Grey looks at a living thing he sees it as a system of vessels, connected to each other in a pattern of infinite skill. He wants to get closer, longs to touch each quickening of sinew and twitch of muscle, to feel the pulse of life beneath his fingers. In his mind's eye he walks the corridors of a great glass building, each room filled with marvelous exhibits behind still more glass, eyes swiveling toward him. They are waiting for him to reveal their secrets. He feels their urgency. He has always felt it— the natural world waiting for him, challenging him. When he looks Heavenwards every bird is writing on the sky in words he longs to understand. Beneath his feet the earth is fat with promise.

He winces as a sharp pain stabs at his abdomen, and rummages in his pocket for the little bottle of pills made up for him at the Foreigners' Hospital. An ulcer, they had told him, he should try not to exert himself. "We advise against both physical and mental exertion," the doctor had said, a little Italian who had the manners of all the foreigners Grey had met in Beijing, a tendency to talk too loudly and too fast, as if their attention was always elsewhere. He returns the pills to his pocket and takes a seat on one of the couches that run along the center of the carriage, where passengers may sit back and observe the views through the wide windows that run along three sides of the observation car, the final carriage of the train. Even the roof is made of glass, though, like the windows, it is criss-crossed with iron bars. He watches as the low, ornate buildings of the capital fall away, bell towers and tiled roofs disappearing into the steam. He has found it a loud, tiresome city, excessively pleased with itself, and far too keen to empty an innocent man's pockets.

"Fifteen days," he says to himself. In fifteen days they will reach Moscow, and the Great Exhibition, and he will at last have the chance to redeem himself. His stomach twinges again but it is the sharp, almost pleasurable pain of expectation. It is the pain he feels when he is on the cusp of a discovery, when an idea is dancing tantalizingly within reach, or when he has found, beneath a rock or within a stream, some new and marvelous creature whose meaning he does not yet understand.

A sudden hearty laugh interrupts his reverie, and a young couple enter the carriage, speaking French. Of the man, he gains only a faintly disagreeable impression of too much hair and too many teeth, but the lady has a pale and delicate kind of beauty. He nods stiffly to them and turns back to the window. He is ill at ease in the company of fellow travellers and has no wish to cultivate new acquaintances. He has met many such travellers in the course of his journeys, at those hotels and inns in which European languages are spoken and the food—while a thin imitation of proper nourishment—can be eaten with familiar utensils. He has suffered too many tedious evenings, amazed at how they can speak so long about so little. Though they could be among the grandest of mountains or cities, their horizons remain barely wider than the walls of their own estates.

He takes another pill, glancing down at the bottle, which feels considerably lighter than it should do. He should have taken the opportunity to get more, but after months of inaction these last weeks have passed in a whirl of research and preparations.

Grey had reached China by a long and perilous route, sailing around the Cape and travelling slowly across India and then into the country from the south. After his humiliation in London (he should not think of it, even the barest mention makes the pain in his stomach flare up), funds had been tight, but he still had the proceeds from his book, and if he succeeded—well, he would not need to worry about money again. It had taken eight months of travel to collect the specimens he needed, but then disaster had struck—his entire collection of live specimens and most of his belongings had been washed away in a flood in Yunnan, after unusually heavy rains. He had finally arrived in Beijing, with his funds almost depleted, and nothing more to show for his travels than a few cases of insects pinned to felt, some pressed grasses and flowers, and his sketches, only to find, in a final insult, that the Trans-Siberian Express had been suspended until further notice. He had almost given up hope. But then God guided his steps to the man who would lead him to redemption. *It is proof,* he thinks; proof that God has a plan for him.

More laughter from the Frenchman. It is unbearable. Grey draws himself up to his full height and turns, ready to freeze them with a look, but the man has his wife's hand in his, and is drawing it to his lips as boldly as if they were quite alone. Henry feels his cheeks flame and tries to sink back down into the couch, but it is too late.

"Ah, my apologies!" the man exclaims, in accented English, and bows to Grey. "I hope a man may be forgiven for forgetting his manners in the presence of his wife. Guillaume LaFontaine, and my wife, Madame Sophie LaFontaine."

Grey forces a smile and allows for the smallest incline of his head. "Dr. Henry Grey," he replies, watching for any hint of mockery upon their faces. He has come to know the signs; the twitch of a lip, the sideways glance. How those long-winded buffoons from the Royal Scientific Society had enjoyed his humiliation in London, and even when he escaped the country he could not escape the stares and the knowing smiles. His fall had been reported in scientific journals around the world; had even made its way into the popular press, with its cruel little cartoons. But he sees nothing in the LaFontaines' expressions to betray any recognition at his name, and holds himself a little easier.

"I am sure we are to become friends," LaFontaine goes on. "I expect we shall have much to talk about. My wife knows that I have been bursting with impatience to meet our fellow passengers."

Traversers, thinks Grey, with some disdain. The wretched Rostov and his book had a lot to answer for—without him the train would have been left to the serious traveller, firm in purpose, not these foolish gamblers, so rich in money and time that they must find dangerous ways of spending it. They take the train only to collect an experience, like a pretty keepsake they can hang on their wall, to boast about to their friends. They will return home to their comfortable lives, their salons and coffee houses, barely touched by the marvels they have seen. He pities them, and finds it a pleasant feeling.

"I travel for study, sir," he says, "and fear I will have little time for the pleasures of conversation."

"Come, Dr. Grey," says LaFontaine, "surely there is time enough on this moving fortress for anything we like. When else are we to have so many hours and days released from the burdens of yet another art gallery, yet another museum, yet another statue by some long-dead sculptor which one cannot possibly leave without seeing? We are released from the tyranny of decision-making. What restaurant shall we eat at tonight, my dear? Ah, I know it already! What blessed relief!"

Grey gives a tight smile. "We may certainly be grateful for that. But we must not forget where we are. This is not a journey to be taken lightly."

As the morning draws on, other passengers begin to enter the observation car, though some take one look at the wide windows and the open sky and back straight out again. A cleric enters, holding an iron cross and rosary in his hands. He has a haunted look, and stands at the far window, turning the rosary around in his fingers and reciting a prayer, more loudly than is surely necessary.

Grey takes the language he is speaking to be Russian, and although he cannot understand a word of it the cadences of the prayer are as familiar to him as his own liturgy back home, a rising and falling of promises and pleas that wrap around him as they leave Beijing behind, travelling now through fields and scattered farm buildings. Those working in the fields stand still and stare. Some of them take off their hats and bow their heads. Some of them make signs in the air; arcane symbols to ward off ill-luck.

4
FELLOW TRAVELLERS

The child of the train is quick and clever. She has never grown as tall as she had hoped, so she can still squeeze into the smallest spaces and scramble up into the train's hidden corners. She has learned all the secrets of the train—how to duck through the kitchen carriages and steal a hot dumpling on the way; how to tiptoe through the garden carriage without disturbing the bad-tempered chickens; how to get to the pipework and wires when things go wrong (and they do go wrong—more often than the Company would like, or would ever reveal to their investors). She runs in time with the rhythm of the train, a rolling, lolloping gait, slaloming between the walls of the narrow corridors along the sides of carriages, dodging passengers still unsteady on their feet and leaving them spinning in her wake, pausing only to sneak into the Third Class kitchen and swipe a handful of dried fruits from underneath the nose of the sleepy kitchen boys.

"Zhang Weiwei, don't put on that innocent look with me, I know you're up to no good!" Anya Kasharina, the Third Class Cook, is ever-wakeful. Weiwei turns, spreading her hands and shrugging her shoulders. Anya gives one of her famous belly laughs and cuffs one of the kitchen boys over the head. "Who let rats into my nice clean kitchen, eh? You need to be more careful in the future!"

Weiwei makes herself scarce before the kitchen boys can take revenge.

Between the kitchens for First and Third Class is a cramped space known to the rail workers as the Divide, or sometimes, sarcastically, as Second Class. Weiwei has never managed to find a straight answer to why the train has a First and a Third class, but not a Second. In his book Rostov argues that the original architects of the Company overstretched themselves and ran out of money, but many of the crew claim that the architects of the train simply forgot. Whatever the reason, on the Trans-Siberian Express, Second Class exists only in this dividing space, where cooks and hands from both kitchens come to snooze or exchange gossip about the passengers. This gives it an unusual neutrality, above the class divisions among the passengers which tend to be replicated in the staff who serve them. And even though the First Class Cook states that the food in Third is not fit for street vermin, and even though Anya Kasharina maintains that the food in First wouldn't fill up the belly of a gnat, the two cooks have been known to sit on the narrow benches in the Divide, sharing a pot of tea and a slow game of cards.

It is also where the crew come for a moment's respite from the passengers, so Weiwei is accustomed to putting her ear to the door before entry, in case she should hear any of the gossip that oils the long running of the journey. She listens.

". . . but what's she going to do? Had her own way for too long, is what they think."

"She wouldn't run the risk of a crossing, though, would she? Not if she really thought . . ."

"What you're forgetting is, she don't see risk the same as we do. That's their mistake too, going along thinking she's as terrified as they are. That's not how her mind works, is it?"

Two of the stewards, both of them frequent inhabitants of Second Class. They are speaking of the Captain. They all speak of her like this, half-admiring, half-afraid.

"But to risk everyone, after last time . . . Even she wouldn't . . ."

"Wouldn't she?"

The stewards' voices fade in and out. Weiwei imagines them checking over their shoulders. The Captain knows when you're talking about her, say the crew. They say she's behind the door before you've had time to take a breath. They tell so many stories about her that it is hard to untangle what is real and what has grown into train lore.

This much they are sure is true—that her people had come from the land which is now just within the Wall, that they had grazed their cattle and ridden their horses over the grass, until they were driven away when the changes began; the skin of their animals turning translucent, birds falling from the sky, seedlings bursting through the soil like bubbles through water, too fast to make sense of, sprouting unfamiliar leaves. And so the Captain returns again and again to a lost ancestral land, she forces the train over the traitorous soil and she dares the Wastelands to rise up against her.

But the stories that Weiwei likes best are about the Captain when she was a young woman—when she cut off her hair and joined a train crew, disguised as a boy. Stories of how she worked her way up to become a driver, her secret so well hidden that nobody ever suspected. Stories of how she was one of the very first crew members on the Trans-Siberian Express, and of how the day she was made Captain she announced to the Company directors that she was a woman and they were so shocked (the story goes) that by the time they had gathered their wits she had already reached the train, and her ascent to the lookout tower had been captured by photographers from the world's press, so it was too late for them to go back on their word.

Weiwei checks over her own shoulder, half expecting the Captain to appear, having read her thoughts—something which she had seemed to do regularly during Weiwei's childhood, usually when she was sneaking about and listening at doors, just like this. But the corridor is empty, and she feels a twinge of disappointment. She would be happy, this time, to see the Captain approach.

"I tell you," one of the stewards is saying, "it's a bad sign. They should have let us hold the Blessing . . ."

A pause. Time for an awkward scuffing of a shoe, a worried scratch of the nose.

"Ill-omened, that's what this journey is." She hears one of the stewards spit on his palm and tap the iron on the windows. "And they know it, the Company, just like the Captain does, even though she's not saying anything. They know it to be true."

She turns away, not wanting to hear more. The Blessing sets them

safely on their journey. Each crew member takes their turn to scatter
water on the engine, using a sheaf of willow twigs, watching it sizzle
and steam. The water is in a vat containing the fruit and leaves of the
season, and soil from the station grounds, and so the train will carry
the earth of Beijing or Moscow with it, to help keep it safe from the
unkinder land beneath its wheels.

But not on this journey. This journey, the train has gone un-
blessed.

The Company had always disliked anything they perceived as
superstitious or backward, but until recently an uneasy truce had
existed. The crew could keep their small rituals, their icons and gods,
as long as they were discreet, as long as the passengers found them
charming. But now, they have been told, it is time for a change. A
new century is approaching—the passengers do not want *mysticism*,
they want modernity. There is no place for these rituals anymore,
said the Company.

And so the crew complain among themselves that the banning
of the Blessing is yet another sign that the dusty men in their offices
do not understand the needs of the train, and does it not bode ill
for this crossing, of all crossings? Have there not been other signs
and portents? Wasn't a white owl seen in the daytime at the Pinghe
Temple? Hadn't a turtle been caught in the river with two heads and
with markings on its shell in the shape of a bird in flight?

Two of the porters, recently hired, left for safer work on the
South-Eastern line. The Third Class under-steward handed in his
notice just the previous day. He had a newborn at home, he said, not
meeting anyone's eye; he had struggled with himself but couldn't in
all good conscience board that train again.

Weiwei has never known the Blessing not to be held. Its absence
feels like a weight they are carrying, pulling them back. When she
chews on her nails there is no earthy taste.

Third Class smells of sweat, anxiety, food already on the turn. There
are two sleeping cars, each holding thirty bunks, arranged in blocks
of three. Both cars are full, and stifling already. The Company has
lowered the price of tickets, fearful in case passengers decide to stay

away. But there are plenty who are desperate to make the journey, despite its dangers. As she passes through, they reach out to tug at her jacket—"Where are the bathrooms, where is the water, how does this work?" Their questions are as impatient and irritating as their grasping hands, though she knows what they are really asking: "*Is it safe? Have we done the right thing?*" and she cannot give them the answers they want to hear.

In the first of the two carriages passengers huddle alone or in pairs, as if holding their fears around them like a cloak. In the second, however, a little community has already formed: a woman handing around bright-red sugar plums; two traders dealing out bamboo cards and passing a tarnished silver flask between them; a young priest reading aloud from a leather-bound book in a language Weiwei doesn't recognize, a string of wooden beads between his fingers.

No one is looking out of the windows.

No one but a man with a mop of unruly silver curls, who has folded his long limbs onto one of the small seats that pull out from the wall along one side of the carriage, and who is staring outside so intently that he doesn't seem to notice the other passengers as they barge past, the dribbles of tea spilling down the back of his coat, the trays of food being whisked past his head.

"Professor?" she says, in Russian, touching his shoulder. He spins around as if scalded, but when he looks up at her his face splits into a smile, deepening its lines, and he enfolds her into an awkward, bony hug. She feels a flood of relief. Not everything has changed. Even after everything that has happened, some things remain in their place.

The Professor is not a real professor, though he looks just like her idea of one, and as soon as she was old enough he had taken her under his wing, determined that she should gain a proper education, "seeing as the crew of this train do not seem to be providing you with one." She had pointed out that the stokers and the engineers, the stewards and the porters and even the Captain herself all seemed determined that she should learn every last inch of the train and every last thing about it. "An education with *books*," the Professor had said.

He has never, as far as she knows, had enough money to pursue his own studies at a university, because everything he has earned, for all of his life, has been spent on tickets for the train, so that he could study the landscape outside. Members of the Society for the Study of the Changes in Greater Siberia—the Wastelands Society, as it is more commonly known—often travel on the train, and the crew have always felt a certain sympathy with them, recognizing a shared preoccupation, though they look pityingly on those scholars who explore Greater Siberia only in books, and who then insist on writing books themselves, so that their Wastelands are nothing but paper forests and rivers of ink, as insubstantial as the scholars themselves.

The Professor, though, is practically train folk himself, and unlike some members of the Society, has other interests to fill his time. He had taught himself Chinese, which Weiwei would sometimes help him with, and he could speak it adequately if unmelodiously, in an accent that always put her in mind of rusting pans rubbing together.

"Did you not want to study here?" she asked him once, as they stood in front of the great stone building that he had taken her to, on one of their stays in Moscow. When he told her that this was a place that men went to learn about the world, she was puzzled, because the walls were high and thick as though to keep the world out instead. They watched young men race inside, books beneath their arms, collars high and coats flapping, and she wondered how they were not afraid of being crushed, with all that stone above them. But the Professor just laughed and spread his arms wide. "What need do we have for those dusty classrooms?" It was what he always said when they were on the train—"All this," he would say, wonderingly, stretching out his arms to encompass the landscape outside. "We have all this."

"Child!" he cries, now, holding her at arm's length as if to get a proper look at her. "I wondered when we were going to be graced by your presence. 'Has she become too important for Third?' I asked myself. 'Has it been so long that she has forgotten her old friends?'"

"You have only yourself to blame," says Weiwei. "I am now so educated that I barely have a moment to spare from answering questions. Even the Cartographer insists on consulting me on his new maps."

The Professor coughs theatrically. "Ah, if only that were true."

Weiwei gives him a mock scowl. Despite all his efforts, she has never been a good student—always too restless, too easily distracted. "Well, it is true that I've been busy," she says. "Some of the crew haven't come back, and the Company is making us all work twice as hard. And of course, there are troublesome passengers to deal with, some of whom are particularly difficult."

"I am sure you will deal with them in a fair and just manner. Though of course, if you worked harder at your studies you could gain a promotion, and no longer have to be responsible for such troublemakers."

Weiwei ignores this, and the twitch of his lips. "And your work? Does it go well?" She says it in a conversational tone, but she watches him carefully.

He doesn't answer straight away, turning to look out of the window at the grasslands rolling past. "I think an old man like me deserves a rest now and again," he says, eventually. "After everything that happened."

He looks up at her. But before he can say more he stiffens. She follows his gaze to the doorway, where two men stand, surveying the carriage. They are dressed in black, in suits with tails that could look, if you saw them in the right light, like wings.

"Ah," the Professor says quietly. "Our very own birds of ill-omen."

They are heralded by the clinking of their shoes, polished black and in the European style, with buckles. It is their only affectation: from the feet up, they are as forgettable as the rest of the Company men, in their dark suits and wire-rimmed glasses and humorless smiles.

Li Huangjin and Leonid Petrov are, to use their official titles, consultants, but the crew call them Crows. Doubled, like all Company consultants—one from China, one from Russia; a balance that the Directors in London are careful to uphold. They speak in the dry, long-winded English of the Company, so that Weiwei has forgotten the beginning of their sentences before they get to the end. The Crows rattle their shiny buckles and they peck and peck at the train and its crew. Not even the Captain can keep them away, although

Weiwei can see that they do not like the way she fixes them with an icy politeness and an eye as cold as theirs.

Once, in the middle of a crossing, when Weiwei was racing down the corridors, trying to hold her breath between doors (pretending that the poisonous air of the Wastelands had crept its way into the train), she crashed straight into one of the Crows. She staggered backward and he caught her by the shoulder to steady her.

"And where are you running to so fast?" He seemed immensely tall to her, and she couldn't see his eyes through his glasses, which only reflected her back. She had always done her best to scurry away from the Crows. Their doubleness always frightened her, although she couldn't say why. But now here was just one of them, and she was struck by the sudden conviction that he would unfold his twin from his own body like another limb.

He leaned down, his hands on his knees, and he beamed at her, a smile that scared her more than any of the quick tempers of the stewards. "Well now, are you the child of the train or a Wastelands child, running wild like this? You are a member of the Company, and must behave like one."

She stared at him, speechless.

"What happens to those who do not maintain our standards?" He led her to the closest of the vestibule doors, the ones that open into a narrow space, before another door that opens to the outside. Taking out a heavy bunch of keys, he unlocked the inner door. The space between was just big enough for two people to stand, closing the door behind them before opening the one to the outside. He kept his hand on the back of her neck. Through the small window she could see the tundra flashing past, glimpses of bone white beneath the grass. He pushed her further toward the door and reached over to the handle of the outer door, and she let out the terrified squeal she had been desperately holding in.

He stood back from the door, but retained his hold on her neck, forcing her to look out of the window. "We leave them outside, where they belong."

There are times when she still feels that same clutch of fear when passing the doors, and is always relieved on those crossings when the Crows have stayed behind in Moscow or Beijing, rather than joining the crew on the train. Yet in recent years, as the Company has insisted the train make more crossings, their presence has become increasingly frequent. In spite of this, she notices that they still move awkwardly, unable to coordinate their strides to the movement of the train. You should let yourself work with the rails, not fight against them, any rail rat knows that.

Now, they walk past the rows of bunks, smiling and nodding at the passengers. Mr. Petrov (they insist on the *Mr*, as if their own names are too weak to stand up by themselves) even bends down to ruffle the hair of a small boy, who gazes back at him, impassively. Weiwei rolls her eyes. They do not stop for long, she sees. They will be on their way to First, to mingle with the passengers the Company prefers, who better fit their image of themselves.

"Try not to look *too* much like you're giving them the evil eye," murmurs the Professor.

But she can't smooth her features into the mask the Company likes.

When they reach the middle of the carriage she stands up straighter, feeling the Professor tense beside her. The Crows give her a cursory nod. "We are glad that our most loyal traveller has joined us again," says Mr. Li to the Professor. "We have heard that there have been differences within the Society of late. We do hope that these have been resolved?"

The Professor gives a vague smile and squints short-sightedly at them through his glasses, the very picture of a harmless scholar. "Ah, but differences are the life-blood of scientific discourse, are they not?"

"Indeed they are, indeed they are." The Crows smile back.

"What did he mean, 'differences'?" asks Weiwei, when they are gone, but the Professor just shakes his head.

"Not now," he says, quietly, looking down the carriage as if expecting to see the Crows swooping back.

Weiwei waits for more explanation, but the Professor seems disinclined to talk.

A crow is a sign of sin, the crew say. When the changes began, crows were the only birds that would fly over the Wall, eating carrion from the changed lands, returning with trinkets or bright stones clutched in their claws. This is why people in the north of China throw stones at them; they are tainted.

When she was small she would imagine the Company men flying. She believed that they had wings that unfurled from the black cloth of their coats, that they would take off into the air like the shadow birds in the Wastelands. That they would open their mouths wide and call to each other in clipped and cluttered English, and they would hold all the sins of the train in their claws like a stone, so hard and bright that it hurt to look at it.

5

THE WALL

The saloon car is hot and cramped with the press of bodies. Perfume hangs in the air and catches in Marya's throat. There is too much material here, too much silk and velvet. She is suffocating in fabric.

The First Class passengers have gathered to mark their approach to the Wall—as is traditional—with a toast. On clear days it can first be glimpsed a mere fifty miles from the capital.

She has heard that there are far fewer First Class passengers than usual, despite the Company's encouragement, but it still feels crowded, the ladies waving fans in front of their faces, the gentlemen buttoned into starched shirts, faces flushed with the heat and the fiery liquor that stewards bring around on silver trays. Marya takes a sip and winces.

"They haven't been able to import any real Russian vodka for months," says the Countess, ensconced on a throne of cushions like a small and irascible monarch in the court of a tiny nation. "So we must make do, I'm afraid." She shakes her head. "I fear we have a difficult journey ahead of us. I happened to catch a glance of tonight's menu and it was *not* a heartening sight. Poor Vera says her digestive system simply cannot take any more *peculiar* vegetables."

Vera purses her lips and nods in silent agreement.

Marya reaches for a suitable response but finds herself at a loss. It is too long since she has been among so many strangers. She is aware, for the first time, of the dullness of her dress, beside the bright plumage of these men and women. She cannot help feeling that her falseness must show on her face; that this other Marya will fall from her like an ill-fitting gown.

But Anna Mikhailovna is undisturbed, surveying her court with a critical eye, and her steady stream of observation is rather soothing, demanding that Marya do nothing but listen and murmur in occasional agreement. The Countess's late husband was a diplomat, she says. "Though it was his father who encouraged it. If he'd had his way we'd have lived forever in the Petersburg swamps. It's only now he's gone I can travel for the pleasure of it." Marya notes that she has retained many of the qualities essential to an ambassadorial life, including a jaundiced eye for her fellow men.

"And *that* gentleman with the newspaper is a silk merchant, enormously rich, thanks to this very train, of course. I forget how to call him, they are so strange, these Chinese names. And I heard that the other gentleman goes by the marvelous name of Oresto Daud, and is from *Zanzibar*, which I confess I would have taken for a made-up place if Vera had not assured me otherwise. Ah, and Herr Schenk, very round and red over there, banking or some such. I met him at the Embassy in Kolkata."

"Delhi," corrects Vera.

"Indeed. A very tedious man, you see. So unmemorable he makes me forget an entire city. Please stage a fainting fit if he approaches, Vera."

Vera inclines her head.

How calm they all are, thinks Marya, *these businessmen and aristocrats.* They do not look out of the window, at the approaching Wall, only at each other, or sometimes at the gilt mirror above the bar.

"But in his favor, Herr Schenk is also very rich," Anna Mikhailovna goes on, thoughtfully.

Of course, who else would make the journey? *The very rich do not only buy estates and fine trinkets,* thinks Marya, *they buy certainty.* They buy the conviction that this journey holds no danger for them. She envies them their confidence.

"Well, if he is very rich then he has no need to be interesting," she says, trying to ignore the false lightness in her voice. "And besides,

I have heard that an overabundance of imagination is a dangerous thing on this journey."

"Yes indeed," says the Countess. "And you, my dear? To be travelling alone, at such a young age . . ." She fixes Marya with a scrutinizing look.

"I am returning home to St. Petersburg. My husband and my parents died . . . a cholera outbreak . . ." She looks at the floor, her lies weighing her down.

"Oh now, I am sorry. There is no need to speak of it, don't upset yourself." The Countess leans forward to pat her hand. She reminds Marya of her grandmother's friends in St. Petersburg, those black-clad widows who took sustenance from misfortune, inhaled it like the fresh sea air that promised rejuvenation. "Do not feel you have to speak of such painful things."

Yet it is clear that the Countess longs for her to speak of it, so she says, quickly, "And that gentleman?" She nods to the man she had seen berating the porters during departure. He is speaking to a handsome young couple; or rather the two men are speaking, and the young woman looks outside, resting her chin on her hand.

"Ah, that is the infamous Dr. Henry Grey," says the Countess, dropping her voice further but speaking with a certain amount of relish. "Poor man, one cannot help but feel rather sorry for him. These scientific gentlemen do take embarrassment to their reputation terribly hard."

The story had been reported with some glee in the press, the Countess explains—Dr. Grey's famous discovery of a fossil inside the corpse of a seal on a beach in England, a fossil that showed a perfect representation of a child curled up as if in the womb and that proved, he had claimed, that animals contain within them the blueprints for their eventual evolution into the most perfect of forms, the human—it had all been shown to be wrong. What he claimed showed a human child was actually the curled form of an ancient sea creature, trapped in the limestone of the cliffs and then swallowed by mistake by the innocent seal. All Dr. Grey's claims came tumbling down, loudly and publicly. The Frenchman Girard, so proud of his theory of the evolution of forms, had mocked him on the stage of the Paris Institute. "Who could mistake a crab for a child? Only an Englishman!"

Marya feels a certain kinship with the man—she understands what it means to lose a reputation, and with it a livelihood.

"He is travelling to the Exhibition, I believe," the Countess goes on. "One can only look forward with lively expectation to what he might display. A mermaid, perhaps, to prove that we once breathed underwater?" She taps Vera on the arm with her fan, delighted by her own joke. Vera gives a dutiful smile. "Will you visit it yourself?" the Countess says to Marya.

"Visit . . . ?"

"The *Moscow Exhibition*, my dear." It is Marya's turn to be tapped with the fan. "An entire building, a *palace* made out of glass, which does seem rather frivolous to me, but then again one never knows what people will think of next, and I suppose there are worse ways to show off how clever we all are."

Marya bites her lip. "Yes, I look forward to visiting it." She is relieved when the Countess's attention is caught elsewhere.

They have drawn close enough now to the Wall to see it rising up out of the horizon, the crenellations along its top standing out against the sky as if it were the home of a giant whose castle spanned an entire realm. Guard towers stand even higher, tricking the eye into making the Wall seem closer than it is. The passengers raise their glasses.

"What a marvel!" exclaims the Countess.

There is no other word for it. And more wondrous still to think of the thousands of miles it stretches, and the six hundred watchtowers standing sentinel, always awake, always ready. Marya clasps her hands in front of her to stop them shaking. It crosses her mind that there is something prayerful about the gesture, and she almost laughs. Beside her, Vera really is praying, her lips moving in desperate pleas for protection. The Countess simply gazes, rapt, at the approaching Wall, an expression of child-like wonder on her face.

"Isn't it magnificent? Did you ever think you would see it?" The Countess looks up at her, and she thinks again, *Not like this*.

They fall into a reverent silence as the train slows and the tower looms above them and the Wall grows more enormous by the second. Early evening light illuminates the gray, pockmarked stone. She had grown up with the stories of the Emperor who commanded its building, over a thousand years ago, and of the men whose remains lay mingled with its stones. And of course the tales of Song Tianfeng, the Builder, who had engineered the second building of the Wall when the Wastelands began to encroach on the Chinese Empire; the moving of the original foundations one hundred miles to the north, the astonishing task of transporting thousands of stones from the quarries of the north, the reinforcing of the stone with iron, the journey across the great plains, to bring the news to the Russian Empire and to teach them how to build a wall of their own.

Marya thinks of all the men who gave their lives to build the walls. If not for their sacrifice, would the blight have spread to Beijing and to Moscow and far beyond? Would there be horrors prowling the countryside, slinking into the cities by night?

They slow to a complete halt directly underneath the tower, a huge arch of stone rising above them. And further above still will be guards stationed on the watchtower—ten looking toward China, and ten toward the Wastelands. She knows they wear iron helmets over their masks, hammered into the faces of dragons and lions, to say to anything that approaches—*We too have predators here.*

Other guards line up outside. How many other companies have a private army? But, of course, how many other companies have achieved so much? She knows the details well—who doesn't? That the Company's origins go back much further than the railway, as far back as the middle of the seventeenth century, when it was a trading company— English merchants who had coveted the abundance of the silk routes and the mineral-rich lands of Siberia. That from its headquarters in London the Company grew and grew, and so did the fortunes of its members, who bought influence and positions in Parliament and houses in the country. When the changes started, many thought they would spell the end for the Company. But what could have been a disaster ended up as an opportunity. It was the Company that provided the funds and determination for the building of the railway, for the iron thread that links the continents.

And yet, these Company guards seem so small, from the vantage point of the train, though they puff out their chests as best they can to fill their military jackets. With their masks—their blank eyes and breathing tubes—they look like a mockery of the human.

"Poor souls, they must have thought there would never come another train to salute," says the Countess. "What a punishment, to be sent here."

"They are told it is an honor, the soldiers." The Chinese silk merchant joins them at the window, and introduces himself as Wu Jinlu, accompanying his name with a little bow. "They are protecting the nation," he says.

But Marya has heard the soldiers from the city garrisons tell of visions and nightmares; returnees from the Wall who tell of voices in the night and inexplicable fevers.

"I believe they say that it is haunted, the Wall barracks," says the Countess.

"Ah, the garrison ghost." The merchant smiles. "I too have heard these stories."

His Russian is fluent, though tinged, thinks Marya, with a trace of the roughness of the Moscow textile markets.

"Of course, the Trans-Siberia Company won't approve," he goes on. "A ghost is certainly not modern enough for them, and I'm sure it refuses to pay rent. Ah . . ." He pauses, then nods toward the other end of the carriage. "As if they were waiting for their cue . . ."

Marya follows his gaze to where two dark-suited figures have entered, one European, one Chinese, stopping to shake hands with some of the men and bow stiffly to the ladies. One turns his head toward her, light glinting from his spectacles, and she feels a roaring begin in her ears.

"I take it those gentlemen are part of the Company?" The Countess doesn't trouble to lower her voice.

"Yes, we are indeed honored," says Wu Jinlu. "Petrov and Li, they are called. Merchants of probability," he goes on, with a little smile.

The Countess raises her eyebrows. "And what do you mean by this?"

"I believe their official title is consultant, but they are money men—advising the Company when to buy and sell; brokering deals and so on. They keep their beady eyes on what the ladies are painting their lips with in Beijing, what the gentlemen are drinking in the salons of Paris. They deal in what future they believe the train will conjure into being."

"How fascinating," says the Countess. "And there was I, thinking that we passengers are the most precious goods onboard."

"I am sure they will do an excellent job of making us believe that," he says. "Though it is normally the Captain who provides the welcome and warning routine. It is odd, in fact, that we have not seen her yet." He looks around, as if expecting that the mention of her name will call her. "But then again, this particular crossing is—" he hesitates, "significant."

Marya takes another glass of vodka from a steward and swallows it too fast. She tries to keep her expression calm but she can feel the Countess's gaze upon her. The shrewd old woman must be able to feel the racing of her pulse, her burning skin. She must be thrilling to the knowledge that there are secrets to be hooked and reeled in.

"Ladies and gentlemen," begin the Company men, in English, "if we may have a moment or two of your attention. On behalf of the Trans-Siberia Company it is our honor to welcome you onboard, and to wish you a comfortable and enjoyable journey on this most remarkable of trains. Of course, this journey is particularly noteworthy because it will end—for those of you who wish to join us—at the Moscow Exhibition, where this very train will form the centerpiece of our Company's display, a tribute to our work and a symbol of our confidence as we enter the new century."

Marya hears the Countess give a little huff. "One wonders if such hubris is earned," she says.

The silk merchant's lips twitch. He gives a conspiratorial smile and says, in a low voice, "Do you know what the crew call them? The Crows. A fitting name, I think."

Crows. Birds of ill-omen. Her father had returned from that last crossing with tremors in his hands. He had locked himself in his study, refusing all food. News of the train's misfortune spread across the city; rumors swirled and multiplied, it was all they spoke about in the streets, their housekeeper confided, but not one word of it would pass her father's lips.

Just days after his return the Company men appeared at the door, funereal in their dark suits. She stood hidden in the doorway as her mother coaxed her father from his study, as the Company men spoke to him in low voices. She heard only snatched phrases: "a flaw . . . a mistake . . . overwork . . ."

When they were gone, her father retreated back to his study, but her mother remained seated by the fire for a long time. When Marya finally approached her, she said, without looking at her, "Your father's carelessness caused this."

Marya remembers standing, frozen, as her mother went on. "They say it was the glass. The glass was . . . wrong. After all that time he spent on it, it was wrong. It cracked." She turned to her daughter. "It was meant to protect them, but it let the evil in."

Her mother was clutching her leather-bound Bible. She had been biting the chapped skin at her lips and there was a fleck of blood at her mouth.

"He is never careless," Marya said. "They are wrong, those men." She felt a fury that she had never known before, a rage so overwhelming that she wanted to bring her fist down onto the glass top of the table, to smash the mirror where it hung, reflecting her mother's blank expression, her own face, drained of color.

"I told him that there is no protection from that place," her mother went on, her voice dull. "He would not listen. He would not see that God has forsaken it and there can be no saving the souls that go there. All those souls, lost, damned. And he will be damned most of all."

She was right, as usual. It was barely a week later when Marya found him, slumped over his desk in his study. A heart attack, the doctor said—he had worked too hard, he had not looked after himself, and then the shock of what had happened—it had all been too much, there was nothing they could have done. She feels a wave of nausea. She can't bring herself to look too closely at the scene—not here, not now.

". . . And while we can assure you that the Trans-Siberian Company upholds the highest standards, we do remind you of the waivers you have all signed, attesting that you understand the risks associated with this long and ambitious crossing."

The passengers shift in their seats. It is one thing to sign a piece of paper when you are standing safely in the First Class waiting room, but quite another to think about it when on the train itself. *The passenger travels mindful of the risks. It is the passenger's duty to inform the train's doctor should they feel unwell at any point in the journey. The Trans-Siberia Company takes no responsibility for illness, injury, or loss of life sustained when on the train.*

No responsibility, she thinks. *How clear that is.*

The second time the Company men came to her home was in the days after her father's death, when she was curled up on the bed in her room while her mother waited in the parlor, surrounded by black crepe, for mourners who would not arrive. The housekeeper begged Marya to come down: "There are two men demanding to get into your poor father's study," she said. "Your blessed mother is too sad of heart to stop them. All his work—they say it belongs to them."

But Marya's head felt too heavy to raise from the pillow, too filled with fog to know or care what to say to strangers. She closed her eyes while the Company men took away what was left of her father's work and reputation, and she has not forgiven herself, she never will.

And now these men, these *Crows* are introducing the train's doctor, and he is speaking of the affliction they call Wastelands sickness—of symptoms and signs. She is familiar with them from Rostov's book— they may start with a lack of vigor, a feeling of lassitude, then develop into hallucinations. *The afflicted may be convinced they are pursued, or that they must immediately exit the train. They may forget themselves, their name, their purpose for being on the train at all. Although they may be brought back to themselves, with prompt treatment, not all are so fortunate.* There are no physical signs of the sickness; it is more insidious than that—a slipping of the mind, Rostov calls it.

"And what are we to do if we notice any of these symptoms in someone else?" asks a small woman who sits gripping her husband's hand and fidgeting with the pearls around her neck.

"Then it is your duty to report it to me just the same, for the safety of the train," says the doctor, gravely, causing the woman to grip her husband's hand even tighter.

"And now we will leave you to your drinks, and to getting better acquainted. We are sure that you will all become firm friends over the course of our journey." The Company men bow and smile, and there is a smattering of polite applause.

"Rather lacking in conviction, that last sentiment," remarks the Countess. "Though I can understand why." She gives the woman with the pearls a hard look. Then, before Marya can ready herself, the Crows are descending, making obsequious bows.

"I do hope that you have recovered from your recent troubles," says the Countess, without preamble. "It made things most awkward. I was quite worried that if we remained trapped any longer I would have to be buried in Beijing, and cheat my remaining relatives out of paying for a funeral."

The two men appear momentarily lost for words, but the Countess goes on, unconcerned. "I know there were naysayers, but I imagine that the Company can get anything it wants, in the end, is that not correct? Anyway, Marya Petrovna and I will hope that those doubters were wrong." She bestows a charming smile on them but Marya can't seem to arrange her face into the expression that she wants. She knew it would happen but now that it's here she feels she is not ready for the test—what if they saw her creeping in the doorway on that first visit to her home, what if they remember her face? Her false name and documents will not protect her then. She is finding it difficult to breathe. But the two men turn blankly polite gazes upon her, assuring her that the train is safe, and that they have every confidence in the success of their journey, before returning their attention to the Countess. There had been no curiosity, no suspicion in their eyes; she is just another young widow, returning to Russia to shrivel, and she thinks—no, they had not seen her that night, they had not thought to find out about the daughter of the man they had destroyed, to fear her anger, her grief. They had not thought about her at all.

A shudder through the carriage, and as they all turn to look outside the masked soldiers come to life, stepping backward as one, like clockwork toys. They raise their hands in salute, and then they are lost in the clouds of steam. With a jolt, the train begins to move again and they are out from under the Wall, emerging slowly into a fortified enclosure where tall poles stand, lanterns hung from their tops. To one side, a huge water clock.

This is the Vigil ground. The woman with the pearls gives a frightened squeak and flutters her fan in front of her face. Other passengers are turning away.

Marya forces herself to look.

"Would it really happen?" The Countess's voice is loud in the silence. "The sealing of the train, I mean."

Vera's lips are almost white. Someone drops a glass.

The Company men did not mention the Vigil in their speech, Marya realizes. Perhaps they feel that some things are better unspoken. Besides, it was made more than clear in the waivers they signed—surely every passenger is thinking now of the day and night they must spend at the Russian Wall before their journey would be safely over; or of Rostov's words, simple and to the point: *If after this time there is found to be nothing growing, either on the outside or the inside of the train, it will be allowed to pass through the gates. And if a trace is found of Wastelands life? Then the train will be sealed. All inside will sacrifice themselves for the good of the Empire.*

"It has never happened," says the Russian Company man, stiffly, his earlier obsequiousness vanished. "And we will see that it never does."

But it could, thinks Marya. Just because it has never happened doesn't mean it never will. The Company would do it, they would have no other choice—they couldn't risk the train getting past the Wall, bringing with it the taint of the Wastelands. Infection; blight.

"But the last crossing—" The silk merchant begins.

"The last crossing shows the efficacy of the protective measures within the train." The Company man raises his voice. "As you know, on that journey the Vigil was passed safely."

Though not before the deaths of at least three passengers, the newspapers reported. And her father— She stops herself, again. There will come a time when she has no choice but to look at it more closely. But not yet.

The train rolls out of the Vigil ground, through another set of tall iron gates. In the window's reflection she sees her own face, drawn and ghostly. There will be no stopping now until the Russian Wall, on the other side of the Wastelands. And the Vigil that waits for them there.

6

THE FIRST NIGHT

In Third Class, Weiwei helps the stewards wrangle passengers to and from the dining car, while trying to bring some form of order to the sprawl of belongings already spreading over the carriage. There are procedures to be followed, but she feels a sense of detachment from it all, an awkwardness, as if she has forgotten the steps to a dance that had once been second nature to her. She has lost the beat of the music.

She puts her fingers to the window. It calms her, the eager, hungry pull of the engine, the rhythm of the rails, as though the glass is charged with energy, dancing beneath her skin. She lets it drown out the clink of the Crows' shoes, the cracked, fragmented memories of the last crossing.

But it was because of the glass, the Company says. There had been flaws, cracks in the glass. That is what let the Wastelands in.

She snatches her hand away. The Company has replaced the windows now; has found a different master glassmaker to take over the glassworks, a better one, they say, though she cannot tell the difference. ("A cheaper one," says Alexei.)

But she thinks of Anton Ivanovich, masked in the railyard glassworks; bent over his lenses in the scientific carriage; alone in the crew mess; always frowning, unsatisfied, as if he could never meet the exacting standards he set for himself. She thinks of all the times she saw him checking and rechecking the windows. A man who paid more attention to detail than to the people around him. He hadn't been well-liked—he was like his glass, the crew used to say. Hard. Unbending. He rarely felt the need to speak to her. But she remembers him saying, once, standing here, just like this, "There is a certain pitch, a certain point where they all breathe together—the iron and the wood and the glass." She tries to feel it, but she doesn't know what to listen for.

"What's that?"

She spins around as a woman's voice, panicked, cuts through her thoughts. *What's that?* A refrain that echoes through every crossing. The crew have taught themselves not to react. A crawler, a specter; some familiar strangeness. They are accustomed to unpredictability, the dangers changing, warping from journey to journey, like the crossing a few years ago when there was a kind of yellow that caused an intense nausea in the observer; it appeared where it was least expected—in the branches of trees or in clear river water; a color that was *wrong*, that was where it should not be—and the crew had to spend much of the journey looking after those who had inadvertently caught a glimpse of it.

Weiwei follows the woman's gaze and sees movement outside—a shape, twisting toward her, and she jerks backward. But then the woman gives a shaky laugh, and Weiwei sees herself in the glass, her peaked cap turning her monstrous.

"Close the curtains, for goodness' sake," says the Third Class steward, appearing beside her. "People are jumping at their own reflections."

She has always hated the first night. The passengers are argumentative or clingy or drunk or often all three at once. On this journey more than ever, the train is wakeful and on edge. No one wants to close their eyes for fear of what they might see there—the thin fingers of nightmares crowding in at their eyelids; the stories, the rumors, and now the reality, that they are past the point of safety now; that the darkness outside is unbroken by friendly lights or open doors and welcoming fires; that they have unimaginable distances to cross.

A passenger is playing melancholy songs on a battered violin. "Play us something happy, for God's sake!" someone calls.

"Ah, but all Russian songs are sad," says the Professor.

He sits in his habitual place by the window, though she can't help but notice that he is quieter than usual.

"Why did the Crows mention the Society?" she demands.

"Oh, I don't understand all the politics involved," says the Professor.

She gives him a hard look. "That," she says, "is not true at all," and is relieved to see his lips twitch. But she knows him too well to push, so says, instead, "Do you have your usual bunk?"

It is a middle bunk, right in the middle of the carriage. From here, the Professor can survey all that goes on, while also keeping a comfortable distance. The lower bunks are used as communal benches during the day; the upper ones are uncomfortably close to the ceiling. The middle is best. She teases him for his predictability, his love of order.

"Yes, the same as usual," he says, standing up rather suddenly. But she has already seen what is different. He usually travels light, leaving spare clothes and belongings at the boarding houses in Moscow and Beijing where he stays between crossings. But here on his bunk there are bundles and bags, and an open case containing dozens of books.

"I should have spoken to you earlier," he begins.

"Are you—" She stops.

"I am getting old, child. I will have to stop travelling sooner or later."

"But there are plenty of crossings in you yet," she says, trying to hide the quaver in her voice.

The Professor smiles. "I am not so sure. I think it is time to return home to Moscow. To rest these old bones. I will still see you, fear not. I will be there each time the train comes in."

"Home? Your home is here." She hadn't meant it to sound so much like an accusation. "And what about your work, your writing? People rely on you . . ."

"My work," he begins, and she sees the tiredness on his face. He has aged, faster than he should have. "I have endeavored," he says, "over these past months, to make sense of what happened, but I cannot seem to do it, however hard I try, so what good will writing do? What use is it to theorize and pontificate when all that remains is empty space?"

"But . . . isn't that what the Society has always done?"

He bursts out laughing. "Ah, how little you think of us. Have I not always said that you should follow it more closely?"

"No, I didn't mean—"

"I know what you meant, child, and I take no offense." He wipes his eyes. "But you can see, can't you, what has changed?"

She thinks about the jumble of memories from the last journey—memories that she cannot put into order. *A man crying. Someone scratching at a window, scratching and scratching until there is blood on the glass. Someone calling her name.*

"Nothing has changed," she whispers. Everything she needs is on this train. Everything she cares about. Nothing has changed.

He shakes his head. "If only that were true."

The noise in the carriage is growing louder. The violin player has started to play a jig and a handsome man with yellow hair pulls his wife into a dance. Another couple joins them, and other passengers clap and shout encouragement, even the priest. It is always like this, on the first night. They think that the music and laughter and noise will keep the shadows outside at bay.

But Weiwei feels the shadows pressing in. She needs to get away from the noise and the nervous chatter of the passengers, from the Professor's sad smile. "*Nothing has changed,*" she had told him, but she had lied. For the first time in her life, she has begun to feel that the strong walls around her may not be enough.

Weiwei knows all of the train's hiding places. Some she has outgrown. Others she must share with kitchen boys looking for a quiet place to nap, away from the shouts of the cooks, or with the train's caretaker, who trails the scent of tobacco behind him, maddening the animals in the garden carriage where he stretches out for a smoke. It is hard to find a private place, sometimes, even on the biggest train in the world. But Weiwei is the child of the train, and she knows a hiding place that is hers alone.

The dry storage car is where the barrels of rice and flour and pulses are kept. It is cool and windowless, with rows of little wooden drawers along the whole of one of its walls, each one labeled in Russian and Chinese with the names of herbs and spices and teas, all waiting to be opened and smelled by a curious girl, and tasted; peppercorns that numbed her tongue, spices that set it on fire. Here too are the goods to be traded, teas from Southern China, much in demand in the salons of Moscow and Paris. In the dim light of the hurricane lamps the carriage appears as a mountainous landscape, perfect for climbing, irresistible to a child. It was during one of these expeditions that Weiwei discovered the trapdoor in the ceiling.

It was almost invisible, painted over to appear as innocent as the rest of the carriage. Only someone who happened to be clambering over the boxes below would notice it. She had been puzzled by it at first, then realized that the ceiling was lower than in other carriages. She eased it open and looked into the space above her, and it was only when her eyes adjusted to the darkness that she understood. Packed into the space between this false ceiling and the real roof of the carriage, barely enough of a space for a grown person to kneel upright, were yet more goods—barrels and sacks and boxes, bundles of silks and furs.

Secret, hidden. Smuggled.

She had burned with the pleasure of discovery. She had waited, and watched, and spied Nikolai Belev and Yang Feng, two of the porters, surreptitiously unloading the hidden goods in Moscow, through a skylight in the roof of the train, even more carefully disguised than the trapdoor itself. She had tucked this information away with all the other morsels she gleaned about her home for when she might need them, as currency or reward. But most importantly, she had realized that during the journey itself, no one approached this hidden space, either out of ignorance at its existence or out of a wish not to draw attention to it. And so it became her hiding space, somewhere to curl up amidst the furs, with adventure tales borrowed from Alexei, and where, in the warm circle of light from her lantern, she could be alone.

But on this journey the smuggling space is empty. Belev and Yang are two of the crew who have not returned, and it seems they had kept their secret to themselves. All that remains of their illicit trade are some empty barrels and sacks, and spilled peppercorns that crack beneath her knees. Now that it is empty the space seems less welcoming and, oddly, more cramped. She is more aware of how close the ceiling is to her head, how the light doesn't reach the far walls, making it seem as though the darkness is waiting to close in. But it is such a good hiding place, and she has found nowhere else so private or so good for thinking, when thinking gets difficult.

She crawls over to where she has stashed her box of treasures, safe from the prying eyes of the under-stewards and the kitchen boys. In it there is a copy of *The Cautious Traveller's Guide to the Wastelands*, given to her by the Professor when she was seven years old, and far too young to read it. On the first page he has written a note—*But not too cautious*. She runs her fingers over the faded letters and smiles. This was the first book she ever owned. She had told him, when she opened the brown paper it was wrapped in, that she didn't need a guide. He had looked her in the eye and told her that it was just for emergencies—for if ever he wasn't there. She closes it and screws up her nose. Blinks quickly. Beneath the book are yellowing newspaper articles; artists' sketches of her as a baby, then photographs marking her fifth birthday, then her tenth. "The Child of the Train, Under the Watchful Gaze of Her Guardian," runs the heading under one, which shows her wearing a tiny uniform and standing in the engine cab, trying to reach up to a lever. The Captain stands beside her, unsmiling. Yes, here is the perfect image of the Captain as her guardian—she is not helping her reach the lever, but simply watching as she works out how to do it herself. This has always been the Captain's way; undemonstrative, demanding, but always there. Present. Ready to catch her if she fell.

Then where is she now?

It had been a slow, almost imperceptible vanishing. During those first difficult weeks after the train had returned to Beijing, many of the crew had retreated to their own quarters near the station or into the city's song halls and inns. Their habitual discipline had faltered, the ties binding them together had loosened. The smooth clockwork had stuttered and come to a halt. When the news had come that the train would run again, Weiwei had been sure that the Captain would put everything back together. But she had barely appeared from her quarters since the announcement had been made, and even now that they are on board, she is just a disembodied voice over the train's speakers.

She sniffs and quickly folds the papers away, closing the box again, picking up instead one of Alexei's penny-dreadfuls from the flea-market in Moscow, and preparing to lose herself in the story of the pirate queen and the sea monsters. She moves the lamp closer, and startles as the shadows in the far corners of the roof space waver. "Don't be fanciful," she mutters. "*Fanciful thoughts lead to dangerous thoughts,*" they are told on the train. But she turns the lamp up higher, anyway, against the darkness.

—And the darkness moves, quiet as a whisper.

Weiwei freezes. The seconds pass. Perhaps she imagined it. This is what the first night can do—unsettle the mind, unleash its worst fears. You cannot trust yourself on the first night. It is not good to be alone. She starts to let herself uncoil.

And the darkness turns, and turns into a face, pale and framed by a deeper darkness. Two inky eyes stare, unblinking.

"Who's there?" she calls out, feeling foolish, poised for a kitchen boy to jump out at her, shrieking with laughter before running back to tell the others how he made the child of the train scream. She has done enough hiding and pouncing herself to know that among the younger crew you are measured by the steadiness of your nerves, your ability to meet a sudden, hideous, masked face with a blank, unimpressed "*Good evening*"; to not cry out if your bare feet should touch something crawling and damp in your bunk. So she stays still, stares back.

A long moment stretches out, congeals. Her breathing sounds unnaturally loud and there is a ringing in her ears.

And then the eyes are gone. There is no face in the darkness, no other breath, nothing moving at all. The carriage sleeps, undisturbed.

She sags against the wall, then scrambles back down into the carriage. There is nothing here, only first-night specters; only her imagination, skittering in panic.

When she finally creeps into her bunk she sleeps badly, falling hourly out of unsettled dreams.

7

IN THE MORNING

Marya wakes up to a discreet knock on the door, and a steward enters carrying a tray with a silver pot of coffee and a plate of warm rolls. He places the tray on the table beside her bed, then opens the curtains and withdraws. She closes her eyes. The smell of the coffee reminds her of mornings at home—her old home, in St. Petersburg, the call of the seabirds outside the window, the pale northern light reflecting off the water. Her father would have left already, he would be in his workshop, the heat of the furnaces reddening his skin. Her mother would not stir for another hour or so. If she listened carefully she would hear the maids going about their secret business, the rustle of mice beneath the floorboards.

Now she hears the clatter of the rails, footsteps outside in the corridor, the insistent voice of the Countess next door. It is strange to feel movement; to be lying in bed and knowing the miles are slipping away beneath her.

She is struck by the thought that, in a different reality, she would be travelling home now with her parents. That had been the deal her mother struck, when the Company had asked her father to open up a Fyodorov Glassworks in Beijing. As more crossings were being made, so the many windows of the train needed to be replaced more often, with the strongest glass that could be manufactured. "It is an honor, for our family," her father had said, and her mother had replied that she would give him five years. Five years and then Marya would have reached her majority and must be shown to St. Petersburg society. The years had gone by slowly, in the foreigners' enclave where her mother insisted they must live, far from the sound of the rails. Having taken the slow, southern route to reach China (almost as dangerous in its own way, though the dangers came from more human sources, and were therefore more acceptable), she could ignore the railway and the Godless Wastelands entirely. In her mother's eyes, the deal was binding. Marya had always wondered, though, if her father took it to be so. He would be evasive about his plans for their return. He would ask her if she wasn't happy here, among such cosmopolitan society. But her mother would purse her lips and tell her maid to close the shutters. "Our daughter is so pale and thin," she would say. "The air is quite spoiling her complexion." And her father would raise his eyebrows at Marya, and feign a coughing fit to hide his smile.

Though her mother forbade her to go near the railyard, Marya would find ways to sneak away, to stand at the railings and observe the huge beast as it returned from another crossing, pockmarked and scratched, as if the claws of great creatures had slashed at the carriages; as if unseen hands had etched patterns and spirals in the glass. She would watch for her father disembarking, watch him stare up at the windows, as if to assess the damage done. And she would watch too his expression change when he saw her, as if drawing a curtain over his worry and exhaustion. But she knew they were there, growing ever heavier as the years passed, and he spent longer and longer at the railyard, and made more crossings on the train.

Now hunger finally tempts her from her bed, and she falls upon the rolls and butter with more enthusiasm than manners. She stops herself from wiping her mouth with the back of her hand, then realizes—it doesn't matter. For the first time in her life, she is breakfasting alone. No family around her, no chaperone, no maid hovering at the door. Although she had kept on their small staff after her parents' deaths, she had bid them farewell the previous day, the housekeeper weeping, demanding to know how a young woman could think of travelling so far alone, on such a dangerous journey, and what was she going to do upon arrival in Moscow, and what would her blessed parents think, to see her so reduced? She picks up her cup. True, she will no longer have the life she has become accustomed to, nor the inheritance she had been brought up to expect. Fyodorov Glass collapsed, after her father's firing by the Company, its reputation in ruins. But still, after all the debts have been paid, she has some modest means. *More modest now,* she thinks, after the purchase of a First Class ticket. She will not have long before she must find a way of earning her own living. She takes too big a gulp of coffee and burns her mouth, putting the cup back down on its saucer with a clatter. Those thoughts would have to wait. She has no need for anyone else, not for the task ahead of her. It is better to be alone, with only Rostov to accompany her, as solitary in his travels as she is in hers.

Outside, beneath a pale-blue sky, the grasslands are unfurling into a shimmering, uncertain horizon. They look innocent, empty of everything, even shadows. *Be careful,* Rostov warns the cautious traveller; *no landscape is innocent. If your mind begins to wander, turn away from the window.*

But his own mind had wandered in the end, hadn't it? He had become an embarrassment, a man living in twilight. His family had tried to take the book out of circulation, but of course this had only cemented its popularity. Poor Valentin Pavlovich, where did you end up? Drowned in the Neva, some of the stories say, or in a poor house, or drunk in the gutter, still travelling the Wastelands in his mind.

"Madam, excuse me . . ." Someone is touching her shoulder. She starts, looks up, confused. A young Chinese man is standing beside her, his hair a little long, poking out messily from beneath his cap. "I knocked," he says in Russian, "but no one answered, and then I saw you were disappearing."

No, not a man, a young woman, a girl. She stands back and rubs her nose, and Marya wonders if she has fallen asleep and into one of those dreams where meanings slip away. "Disappearing?"

"It's what we say when someone . . . when they look like their mind is wandering. We have to bring them back." The young woman's tone is abrupt, though it might be down to her Russian, which is rough-edged and unplaceable and much older than she is, and as Marya starts to gather together her thoughts she realizes who this must be—the girl she has read about, the famous child born on the train; no longer a child, though she can barely be older than sixteen. Zhang Weiwei.

"I was just day-dreaming," says Marya, but she can't remember what she was dreaming of, can't remember thinking at all, and her thoughts now are clumsy and slow. She glances at the clock on the wall and is shocked to see that two hours have passed.

The girl follows her gaze. "It happens like that," she says. "It's like falling asleep but you are awake. It's why we have to watch carefully. People think it won't happen to them. You shouldn't stay in your cabin alone too long. It's best to be with other people."

She has an appraising look that Marya finds rather uncomfortable. "I have read the guidebooks," she says, and is annoyed by the defensiveness in her voice.

The girl shrugs. "They don't prepare you for what it's like. Not even Rostov, and he's quite good on most things. The rest of them are charlatans." She rolls the word around in her mouth in a satisfied way. "It's more dangerous if you've read their books than if you haven't."

Marya laughs, she can't help it. But the girl is still staring at her, and there is concern in her expression but something else as well, as if she can read the recognition in Marya's face and is wondering where it comes from.

"Thank you for your concern," Marya says, careful to keep her expression blank. "I will be more aware from now on." Though the old Marya has disappeared already, of course. A careful, deliberate vanishing. Perhaps this new Marya will find it too easy now to disappear, while she is still new, unfinished. While she is untethered from the present.

"There is a trick," the girl goes on, rather diffidently. "If you want to know it. It's better than the things they tell you in the guidebooks."

"Yes, please," replies Marya. "I would be most grateful."

"You should keep something bright with you," says Weiwei. "Something bright and hard that catches the light, like a piece of glass." If she notices Marya tense she makes no sign of it, but takes out a small marble from her pocket and holds it up to the window.

The sun catches a swirl of blue glass caught inside it. "It's the brightness that matters. People say that you should take something sharp and prick yourself with it, but I think what you really need is something that's sharp on your eye." She moves the marble and the light dances across and through it and Marya feels her chest clench. The aching familiarity of it.

"It brings you back," says the girl. "I don't know why."

"Glass is alchemy made solid. It is sand and heat and patience," her father would say, when he was feeling poetic. *"Glass can trap light, use it, shatter it."*

"But not everyone agrees with me. Lots of people don't." Weiwei purses her lips. "They say iron is better but I think that's just superstition." She looks at Marya as if she is daring her to challenge this assertion.

"People don't realize how strong glass can be," Marya replies.

Weiwei holds the marble out to her. "You can take this. If you want it. I have others."

She hesitates, then reaches out her hand. This is her father's work, she is sure, though she hasn't seen one since she was a child, crouched on the floor over her games. There was a certain technique he used, to make the twist of color inside seem to be always in motion. "Thank you," she says, and perhaps it is simply the power of suggestion but as she closes her fingers around it she thinks she feels her wits returning.

The girl is fidgeting again. "I was sent to see if you needed anything, because you're not travelling with a maid."

Marya bites the inside of her lip; tries not to let her expression change. She had known it would seem unusual for a woman like her to be travelling unaccompanied, but she had not expected it to be remarked upon so openly. She thinks of the Countess's shrewd eyes; of the stewards gossiping among themselves. Do they pity her, perhaps, or is there something more behind this gesture? Suspicion. Doubt.

"How kind," she says, carefully. "Was it the two Company gentlemen who thought of this?"

"It's what we always do, when guests are travelling alone." Another scratch of the leg, a rub of the nose. "Do you need anything, madam?"

Marya lets herself relax a little. She reflects with some amusement that she cannot see this girl making the most able of maids, with her crumpled uniform and hair escaping from her cap. "Thank you, but . . ." She is about to refuse when she thinks that surely there is nothing that this girl, this child of the train, does not see. She may come to be useful to her. "I have no need of anything at present. But if I may require your assistance later . . . ?"

"Please ask, madam," the girl replies, without much enthusiasm, and turns to leave.

"I wonder if I can ask you a question," Marya says, suddenly, and Weiwei turns back, but perhaps there is something in Marya's tone that puts the girl on guard, because she thinks she sees alarm flit across her face. She tries to keep her voice light. "Were you on the previous crossing? One has heard so many stories, you see, and of course, it is hard not to be curious . . . Is it true what they say, that you really remember nothing?" Though she says it with a little smile, this time there is no mistaking Weiwei's look of anxiety.

"If you'd like to ask any questions, please speak to the Company representatives, who will be happy to speak to you," says the girl, in the manner of someone reading from memorized instructions.

"Of course," says Marya. "I understand."

But before she leaves, the girl hesitates. "I'm sorry," she says, in a voice that sounds more her own. "I . . . I just can't remember."

When she is gone Marya sighs and rests her elbows on the table. She will have to be more circumspect in her questioning. She will be sly, and watchful, and all the things her mother taught her not to be. *"Don't stare, child, your eyes will fall out of your head . . . A lady doesn't listen at keyholes . . . A lady doesn't ask so many questions."* But Marya has always watched, and listened. She takes out her journal. As a young girl she had filled her pages with observations of the people around her; her family's unguarded words, the sparks of her grandmother's wit, the looks passed between adults. She had begun to understand that what people said and what they meant were not always the same thing. Over the past years, she has turned to writing about her new city, observing its quirks and novelties, the rhythms of its everyday life. When her mother thought her to be safe in her room, or visiting other young ladies in the foreigners' quarter, she had been pacing the streets to find those places Rostov's *Cautious Guides* did not deem worthy of mention. Now she will put it to good use, this habit of observation. She opens the journal to where a sheet of writing paper is slipped between two of the pages. The paper is blank but for the address of their home in Beijing, and the words, in English, *Dear Artemis*, in her father's handwriting. For the thousandth time, she smooths it out. Artemis, the Greek goddess of the hunt—the name of the anonymous writer whose column in the Wastelands Society's journal has become so famous. While the journal prints articles and letters on all manner of matters relating to the Wastelands and its history, geography, flora and fauna, this column is the reason that she—like so many people—waits eagerly for new editions. The column relates gossip about famous passengers, descriptions of outlandish sights, and rumors or scandals within the Company itself. It is said that the Company is desperate to find the identity of Artemis; that the criticism he—or she—aims has the power to make their stock rise or fall; that his columns have been debated in the Houses of Parliament in England.

What, then, did her father want to tell this mysterious Artemis?

She runs her fingers across her father's writing. This is all she owns of him. She found it, fallen behind his desk, missed by the Company men when they took the rest of his work. She feels the familiar flush of shame and anger at herself. She searched the house but found nothing more; none of the reports he had spent long nights writing; none of the notes he had always been scribbling, when struck at the dinner table by an idea, despite her mother's disapproval. She failed him. Failed to protect his legacy.

He had wanted to share the truth with Artemis, she is sure of it. Or had he written to him already? She wants to shout at him—at this scrap of him, this shade. *"Why could you not tell it to me instead? What were you hiding?"*

The answers must be here.

She will do what she has always done; she will watch, she will listen, she will record. This Artemis is a ghost, and perhaps he has vanished for good. But she might still find his traces—traces of what really happened on that last crossing—here on the train.

She rolls the marble around and around between her fingers. It will not shatter, this marble, even if you drop it from a great height. It is stronger than it looks.

She stands up so quickly that the unfamiliar rocking of the train almost makes her stumble. *She is stronger than she looks. Stronger than she feels.* She remembers the furnaces in the glassworks, the way her father plunged the glass into the burning heart of them. There, that is what she needs: the burning in her chest, her own furnace that she is carrying with her. She needs to hold her hand close to its flame, to feel the power that drove her to cast her old life off, that guided her toward this train.

8

ON FORMS AND CLASSIFICATIONS

Henry Grey has slept badly, the pain in his stomach waking him in the middle of the night. Breakfast has done little to improve his mood, with under-cooked kippers and weak tea. But the atmosphere of the library carriage is soothing; the smell of the books, the thick green carpet muffling the relentless sound of the rails, the inviting depths of the armchairs. The only other occupant of the carriage is an elderly steward, sitting beneath a large engraving of the train's route. Grey examines the bookshelves. He notes with approval the selection of volumes on natural history, mostly English and French, and he quickly searches, as he does upon entering any bookshop or library, for the volume that bears his own name. Yes, here, on a lower shelf—*On the Forms and Classifications of Mimicry in the Natural World*. He picks it up to feel its solidity, the weight of all those hours lying unmoving on the grass to observe the bees in his garden and to prove, for the first time, that some were not bees at all but *syrphidae*, hoverflies—the weak taking on the guise of the strong, the mimicking of a more perfect form. This mimicry gave them advantages over predators and it was proof, he argued, that creatures strived to better themselves, to move gradually toward God's own image. He had been praised, lauded, invited to leave his Yorkshire cottage and to lecture in London and Cambridge. He closes his eyes and remembers the feeling of those rooms, hushed with expectation; that eager attention upon him. Then he opens the book to the engraving of his name and sees that someone has defaced it with scribbled words—*A holy fool*.

He slams it shut. When he spies Girard's treatise on adaptation and modification he grabs it from its prominent place and moves it to the darkest corner of the carriage. The steward watches him without comment.

After a while the door to the carriage opens and Alexei Stepanovich appears. Clean-shaven, the engineer could pass for a schoolboy; surely he should be slouched at the back of a classroom, daydreaming his sketches of engines, not carrying the safety of the train on his shoulders. Grey feels a stir of unease and turns away quickly. He hears the engineer say something to the steward in that strange mix of languages they seem to speak on the train, then the clank of a toolbox.

Grey searches the shelves until he finds the book he is looking for—*A History of European Railway Bridges*. Carefully, he takes an envelope from his jacket pocket and places it between the front pages. No one ever borrows this book, the engineer had told him, it is the perfect place. Grey presses the book shut, feeling the envelope fattening the pages inside. This is almost the last of his funds.

God had guided Henry Grey to the young engineer. Five months ago, broken and exhausted, Grey had been cast upon the unfriendly shores of the Trans-Siberia Company offices in Beijing, tramping the corridors in a desperate attempt to speak with someone in authority—with anyone who would hear his case that the train *must* be allowed to run again, that it was unthinkable that travellers such as he should be left with no swift means of return to Europe. But the offices had been filled with all manner of rabble, with crowds pushing and shoving, and door after door had been slammed in his face. The best he had managed was a meeting with a minor official who had inquired whether he could not simply travel back the way he had come. "Surely you are a man of means," he had said, "to have come all this way for your own enjoyment?"

Grey had wanted to weep. He had wanted to take the man by his lapels and shake him, but there had been a pain in his stomach that had been increasing daily, and he had barely managed to stumble from the mean little office before collapsing onto the marble floor.

When he had opened his eyes he had found a young man in the uniform of the Trans-Siberia Company kneeling beside him with a glass of water and a worried expression. As a stream of people had pushed past them, oblivious to his plight, the young man had insisted on taking him to the Foreigners' Hospital, where he had fallen into a period of restless sleep.

In half-waking dreams the train had carried him far into the Wastelands before stopping amidst a vast ocean of gently swaying grass. There had been a door that had opened at his touch, and he had stepped out into a silence and a peace that he knew to be God-given; insects humming in complex harmonics, majestic birds slowly circling in the air, and around him, a thousand beating wings. *Eden*, he had thought. Its profusion of forms the key to the wonders of Creation.

When his fever had eased, and he was able to sit up in bed, the doctors insisted that he must take better care of himself. He agreed, eagerly. He would treat his body and his mind with care, he promised, because they were gifts from God, and because a new certainty now burned within him. The Wastelands were not simply a means to an end, he realized; not just a danger to be endured, but an *opportunity*.

Over the next weeks, as he convalesced, he submerged himself in as much scholarly research on the Wastelands as he could find. Of course, much of it was the work of the Society, whose amateurish methods were all too apparent—a mere matter of speculation, for the most part; poorly referenced articles, and letters from rural clergymen. But more scientifically rigorous data was simply not available. Of course there had been expeditions, in the early days of the changes, far into the interior. It was human nature, after all—the desire to map, to collect, to understand. But none of the explorers ever returned, and soon all expeditions were halted. After that, it was only the Company that had access to the Wastelands, through their so-called Cartographer, and they guarded their findings jealously, doling out miserly snippets in an academic journal owned by the Company themselves. *What discoveries must we be missing?* he thought. *What opportunities for learning, for understanding? What good is this secrecy to scientific progress?*

A plan began to form in his mind. At the same time, he tracked down his rescuer, who turned out to be an engineer on the Trans-Siberian Express, earning his trust over bottles of sherry and discussions of the mechanics of the train.

What he had come to believe, explained Grey to Alexei, was that within the Wastelands he would find proof of his theory of mimicry—that within all things there is a striving toward a more perfect form. It was this striving that was behind the changes. The Wastelands, he explained, trying to keep his language simple so that the engineer would understand, can be understood in only one way—as a vast canvas for the illustration of God's teaching. A new Garden of Eden.

It had taken time, of course, to persuade the engineer of his way of thinking, and longer still to convince him of what needed to be done. How loyal the young man was, to a Company that saw him as no more than a cog in their machinery, who took his talent for granted—wasn't there so much more he could do? Couldn't he see the contribution he could make? That together, they could change the understanding of the world. "Our names will be remembered," he had said to the engineer. Isn't that what everyone wanted? To not be forgotten. To be more than a line in a ledger, the sum total of your life adding up to little more than the strength you wasted to make other men rich.

Grey had him then—he had seen the awakening in his eyes. The next day Alexei had come to Grey's rented house, brimming with excitement, saying that he had worked out a way that it could be done—that he could cause the train to stop for just long enough to give Grey time to slip out and collect the specimens he needed. And that very day was when the Company announced the line would open again, and that the train would arrive in time for the Moscow Exhibition. More proof, if any were needed, that their plan was blessed.

Grey puts the book back on the shelf and wanders over to one of the tables, careful not to look up as he hears the engineer packing away his tool box and walking over to the bookshelf, as if wishing to browse the books himself. A door shuts. When Grey finally looks over, he sees that *A History of European Railway Bridges* has gone. He lets a warm, triumphant glow suffuse him. *It is done.* Yes, challenges lie ahead, but he will deal with them when the time comes. He will be guided. He has faith. He ponders upon the name of his theory. *Grey's Natural Philosophy* . . . No, no, too self-serving. *New Edenic Thought* . . . Yes, perhaps . . .

Grey comes out of his reverie to see that the young widow—Maria?—has entered the library and is asking questions of the steward, who stands eagerly to attention.

". . . but how can you be *sure* it is safe?" she is asking. "Can the doors really be so strong? And the glass, can you know for certain that it will withstand . . . everything?" She flutters her fan in front of her face and the steward draws himself up even taller. Grey tuts.

"Nothing gets in through those doors, ma'am, you can depend on it, not the strongest creature what ever lived nor yet the cleverest lock picker. This train is better armored than all the bank vaults in all the world . . ."

"*Nothing gets in or out without two sets of keys and a combination that changes every crossing,*" the engineer had said. "*But I might know a way to get hold of them . . . On earlier crossings, not a chance. But now? Now I think there is a way.*"

Of course, getting out of the train is only the beginning.

". . . and can guarantee that this glass would not shatter in an earthquake, ma'am."

"But there was a problem, wasn't there, on the—"

"Not going to happen again, ma'am. It was discovered who was to blame, very sad, he wasn't well. Now, new protocols—"

Grey coughs, pointedly. This is a library, after all.

"I do beg your pardon," says the young widow, and Grey waves his hand. He is inclined to be gracious this morning, now that his future is beckoning him from down the line, waiting for him. He steeples his fingers together and gazes out of the window at the grasslands. How filled with promise they are, beneath such a wide blue sky. He can almost feel the ground beneath his feet, the breeze in his hair, and all the wonders at his fingertips, about to be discovered. He takes a notebook from his jacket pocket and flicks through the pages of hand-drawn maps, copied meticulously from charts the engineer procured for him. All are carefully annotated, but only one is starred and marked with a red circle. *Here.* Out of all the miles of track, after careful consideration, here is the place he has chosen.

"Look! What's that?" At the opposite window the young widow makes no attempt to lower her voice. Grey sighs in exasperation, but of course cannot help but look. A pale-pinkish outcrop of rock, he thinks, at first, just beside the track, but it is moving—no, its surface is moving, as if it is alive with . . . He stands abruptly, and strides to the window where the widow is pressing her hands to the glass.

"It is a train," she whispers.

No, thinks Grey, *it* was *a train,* the shapes of its engine and carriages, though overturned and decayed, still recognizable. But now it is something else, beneath the lurching, scuttling mass of crab-like creatures, a whole colony of the things, their pale bodies clambering over one another so that the wreck seems oddly alive.

"It's best to try not to look," says the steward. "Or if you can't help yourself, keep hold of something while you do."

"What happened to it?" Grey wraps his fingers around the iron crucifix he keeps inside his breast pocket, next to his heart. The longer he looks at the wreck the more he thinks there is an order of sorts to the creatures' movements, like a hive of bees that revolve around their queen.

"The first crossings weren't always successful. There were accidents, derailments . . . And they had to just leave the engines there, of course, and now, well . . ."

"How do you bear it?" The widow's voice is unsteady. "Working here, being forced to see it. How do you keep coming back?"

The steward scratches his chin but he doesn't look out the window. "You get used to it," he says, unconvincingly.

"It is strange," says the widow; "though I have read about it so much, the Wastelands, I hadn't expected . . . It is the reminders of the human, of ourselves that . . ." She trails off.

Reminders of what can go wrong, thinks Grey.

9

SHADOWS

Weiwei's day is a whirl of chores and shouted demands. There is always another task to be done, a floor to be cleaned, brass to be polished, lost belongings to be found, passengers to wake and harry. Unlike the stewards and porters, the stokers and drivers and guards, the boundaries of her role on the train have never been well-defined, which can be irksome, when the tasks are never-ending, but useful too, allowing her to slip in and out of any part of the train, and to always be able to claim that she is running an errand for someone else. Her mind wanders. *What had she seen last night?* Nothing. A trick of the light, a symptom of the passengers' jumpiness. *Or a trick of her own mind?* There are more trays to be carried to First, more dirty dishes to be cleaned. *Eyes in the darkness.* She crashes into a steward in the dining car and spills tea on her uniform and forgets to pick up the clean linen from the service carriage. The stewards curse her and even Anya Kasharina scolds her for her lack of care, chasing her out of the kitchen with a ladle.

A large poster hangs in the crew quarters, a picture of a cheerful young man in the uniform of the Company saying, "*Do you feel strange? Are you having difficulty remembering? See the doctor!*" Weiwei hurries past it with her head down. "Oh, be quiet," she tells the poster. But Marya Petrovna's words from that morning echo in her head: "*Do you really remember nothing?*"

There have been other crossings where her memories were muddled and unreliable. Once a sleeping sickness came over the whole train; passengers laying down their heads on their dinner plates, crew members asleep at their posts. For days it was only the stokers who stayed awake, feeding the insatiable engine. The doctor hypothesized to the Captain that the heat protected them from whatever afflicted the rest of the train. But the rumors among the crew were that the Wastelands *knew*. It kept the stokers awake because they fed the train, and the train is as hungry as the Wastelands. Like knows like. "An affinity, that's what it is," said Anya Kasharina, who inclines toward the mystical—though she would never say it within earshot of the Crows. The sleepers on that journey had all shared the same dreams. They had walked in the snow without leaving tracks behind them. They had been watched by eyes in the dark. On another crossing, the inhabitants of the train had been taken over by odd compulsions, drawing pictures on the walls of remarkable creatures that they swore they had never seen. The Company had worked hard to ensure the stories did not get out. They dealt swiftly with crew members found to be speaking out of turn.

But this last crossing had been different. *Do you really remember nothing?*

Only an absence where the memories should be. And then, as if waking up from a dreamless sleep, to find they had arrived at the Wall and the Vigil yard; to find every mirror on the train shattered, the polished wood of the walls scored into spirals and lines. She rubs at the raised scar on the palm of her right hand. Some of the passengers never recovered—their minds fragmented, like the kaleidoscope the glassmaker once made her, its shifting patterns impossible to hold in the mind's eye. By the time they had reached Beijing, three passengers in Third had died.

She stops in her tracks and glares at the smiling figure on the poster. No. There is nothing wrong with her mind. There had been something there in the storage car, something hidden and out of place. *Someone.*

On other crossings, she would have gone to find the Professor at times like this, knowing that even late at night he would be awake, bent over his books beneath the last lamp still lit in his carriage. Knowing that he would give her his whole attention; listen without interrupting her or sighing or looking at the clock, and as she spoke, whatever it was that was worrying her would evaporate like incense smoke. He would not tell her, she thinks, that there is nothing hiding in the roof space—he would offer to go with her and make sure of it.

But she doesn't go to find him, not this time. If he is leaving her then she needs to get used to it, to prepare herself for when he is no longer there.

Shaking the thought from her mind, she takes a flask from the crew mess and fills it with water. *Just in case.* She grabs a piece of bread left out on one of the tables and slips it into her jacket pocket. As she does so, she feels a pressure at her ankles, and looks down to see Dima, staring up at her hopefully with wide amber eyes.

"Cats don't like bread," she says to him, though she knows he will happily try to eat anything. She crouches down to stroke his thick gray fur and feels the reassuring rumble of his purring beneath her hand. *Our stowaway,* she thinks. They had found him here in the crew dining car, five years ago, just after they had left Moscow. He had been all skin and bones, gobbling up food left on the floor. It had been a difficult crossing—storms on the line, shadows on the horizon, but the cat had padded calmly through the train, unconcerned and quite at home. And although the Captain had not been pleased that an animal had been allowed to come aboard, even she seemed taken with him, and his habit of chasing lights down the corridor. One of the cooks named him Dmitry—Dima—after her great-uncle, saying the greedy look in his eyes reminded her of him.

"Do you want to make yourself useful?" Weiwei asks him, and he rubs his cheek into her knuckles.

The Captain—at least, the Captain they had all known—is careful about stowaways. There had been those, in the past, who were desperate enough to take their chances, though the penalties were so high. Those who thought the risk was worth it. Once, when Weiwei was only five or six, she had been playing in the luggage car at the beginning of the journey, before the train had reached the Wall. It was a winter crossing, snow freezing the tracks, ice making patterns on the windows.

There had been a man in the luggage car, crouched beneath a pile of tarpaulins. The man had smelled of liquor and sweat, which was how she had found him, rummaging beneath the layers of cloth to get to the thing that was different, that she knew, even at that age, didn't belong. She remembers his fingers curled around her wrist, she remembers the stink of his breath. *"I'm not here,"* he had whispered. *"You understand? I'm not here."* And he had opened his jacket and tucked there she had seen the glint of a blade.

She had run straight to the Professor. She might have only been small but she knew when a person was there and when they weren't. She knew that a knife couldn't make a man invisible. The Professor had picked her up and stormed to the Captain's quarters, demanding to know why a child had been put in such danger.

The crew had made a fuss of her, after that. The stewards had told her she was a brave girl; the cooks had given her extra helpings of sweet custard. Anya Kasharina had enfolded her in her arms and told her she had to learn not to take risks.

They didn't want to tell her what happened next. He was a bad man, they said. Hiding away on the train, not paying for a ticket, was as good as stealing. He was nothing more than a thief.

It was only a long time later that she learned the truth. They had not waited to reach the Wall, but had pushed the man out into the snow. It was Belev and Yang, the smugglers, who told her, one evening when they were between crossings, their bellies full of liquor, when the waiting made them boastful and nostalgic. They told how they had opened the carriage door just to scare him, to teach him a lesson. In winter the train moves slowly, shoveling aside the snow as it goes.

"But how did you open the door?" She was never sure how much of the stories to believe. "No one else has the keys."

Belev laughed. "Little sister, you know better than anyone that you can get anything you want on the train. If you want keys there are ways to get them."

She looked from one to another. "What happened?"

"We saved time and effort. We administered train justice," said Yang, wiping his mouth. Belev grunted. "The Captain knew about it."

And that was that. It was train justice that sent the man with the knife out into the snow in the dark, miles from anywhere. And it was train justice that made him vanish from the logbooks and reports, vanish as completely as if he had never boarded the train at all. She shivers to think of him, out there in the snow with only his patched jacket. She has thought of him on every crossing since.

Dima is not usually allowed in the main area of the storage car, so it is several minutes before she can coax him away from all the new smells and hiding places, and in the end she picks him up and carries him awkwardly up the makeshift ladder to the roof space. She puts down her lamp, and waits. There is a damp feel to the air, despite the heat. Gone is the customary stillness, replaced by the feeling that movement has just stopped, that something is waiting to happen. Her muscles tense. She feels Dima go still, his claws digging through her uniform into her skin. His ears flick back and his nose twitches. And then he begins to growl; a deep, warning noise that seems to rise up from his belly.

Slowly, she sets the cat down. "What's that?" she whispers to him. "What do you smell?" All the fur on his arched back is standing up, and his ears are flattened against his head. He is as disinclined as she is to go further into the shadows.

She is the child of the train—she is not frightened of anything. She doesn't need to run to the Professor like she did when she was small. If there is a bandit here she will expose him. A stowaway is no better than a thief. A stowaway must face train justice. She moves forward, slowly, holding the lamp in front of her, watching the pool of light grow.

There is definitely something there, at the far end of the carriage, where a few old barrels still sit. There is a darker shadow that holds itself poised, a tension in its bearing just like Dima's, as if it were a cornered animal.

"You can come out," she says in Chinese. "I . . . have bread, and water. If you're hungry . . . I can help . . ."

Silence. She repeats the words, in Russian this time.

"It's got seeds in it, the bread . . . It was made fresh yesterday."

The shadows are still, they are nothing more than shadows. Weiwei lets out a sigh. She is thankful that she has said nothing to Alexei. He would never let her forget this. She leans forward to retrieve her lamp—

—and the shadows move. A slithering sound, a smell of damp and rot, and the picture she has held in her mind of a bandit, of a knife in the dark, warps and shatters, but she cannot put the pieces back together in a way that makes sense, she cannot convince her legs to move, though Dima has begun a steady, high-pitched keening, a noise she has never heard him make before; she can only crouch helpless as it readies itself to pounce, her breath catching and coming out as a whimper—

—and the shadows rearrange themselves into arms and legs, the face into high cheekbones and watchful eyes, the slithering sound into the rustle of silk.

Not a bandit nor a wild animal but a girl. Dressed in blue silk, her hair loose and tangled around her shoulders. A vision so unexpected, so far from anything Weiwei had imagined that she stumbles backward and hits the floor.

With a hiss, Dima vanishes down the trapdoor. Weiwei and the stowaway stare at each other. Her dress makes her seem older, but when Weiwei looks closer she thinks she must be about her own age, though it is hard to tell. She tries to focus on her face but it is surprisingly difficult—there is something in the way the girl is regarding her that makes Weiwei's skin itch beneath her collar. She is not used to such close attention; she is used to watching, not being watched back.

The stowaway says, in Russian, "Are you going to run away too?"

Weiwei says, more defensively than she means to, "Why should I run away? I belong here. You're on my train."

The girl nods, solemnly, and touches the floor with the palm of her hand, as if to acknowledge Weiwei's right to it. "You have brought water," she says. Not a question, a statement. As if she had expected nothing less.

Weiwei hands her the flask, which she grabs with both hands and drinks noisily. "You should have thought about this before you stowed away," says Weiwei, after a moment.

The girl regards her, unblinking, and Weiwei has to admit to being a little impressed—she has never been out-stared before. Finally, she takes the bread out and the girl snatches it from her hand then scrambles further back into the roof space. When Weiwei raises the lantern she sees a kind of nest.

"Are you alone?" It is the first thing she can think of to ask. All the other questions will not put themselves into words in her head.

The stowaway nods, the expression on her face unreadable.

"Are you—" She stops. It is all too far removed from her expectations to make sense. A man with a knife and threats on his tongue can be understood. Danger that comes dressed in a blade and a snarl can be faced and fought. But this—a girl, alone, this is a different kind of danger. There is a line here that she must not cross.

"How did you get onto the train?" she asks, instead. "How did no one see you?"

The girl hesitates. Then she says, "Because I am careful and quiet and still. Because I was not what they were looking for."

There is something odd about her Russian. A little stiff and old-fashioned, as if she is searching for words that are hard to reach. "But you need food, and water," says Weiwei. "You'll have to find them somehow. You must know how long the journey is. Didn't you think about the danger? What will happen if someone finds you?"

The girl shrugs, a gesture that Weiwei finds unsettling, though she cannot say why. "You can help me."

Weiwei folds her arms. "And if I don't?"

The stowaway gives a sudden, unexpected smile. "I think you want to help. I think you are good at lying and I think you are clever, because you brought a cat to find out what I was. Those men, they would not think of that."

"Those men—" Weiwei stops. The stowaway has been watching, she is not as unprepared as she seems. She doesn't take her eyes from Weiwei's face.

This is madness. She should run straight to the Captain. She shouldn't even be thinking about it—they all know the rules, they know the punishment for any crew member found aiding a stowaway—confinement to quarters, then immediate dismissal upon reaching their destination. Absolute loyalty to the train—to the Company—that's what the rules demand. *But where is the Captain's loyalty to the train now?* Why should Weiwei run to her when she has closed her door to the crew? When she is vanishing, absent?

"I can bring more water," Weiwei says, slowly. "And more food, but I will have to be careful not to bring too much, or someone will notice. And you have to stay here, hidden. You have to promise."

The stowaway tilts her head to one side, as though she is considering. "I will stay here," she says.

Weiwei nods, as all the other questions she wants to ask crowd into her head. So she chooses the most simple one. "Will you tell me your name?"

The stowaway doesn't reply.

"It doesn't have to be your real name, not if you don't want. I'm Weiwei," she says, putting a hand to her chest, as she has seen adults do when they speak to children, as adults have spoken to her, many times.

The girl looks away. "Elena," she says, eventually, and Weiwei thinks, *That is a lie.*

She leaves the lamp behind when she goes back down the trapdoor. "I'll come back soon," she says, and the girl nods, watching her go, her arms wrapped around her knees.

Weiwei walks back to the crew quarters quickly, certain that her guilt must show on her face. The stowaway is not dangerous, she tells herself, she is just a girl. She is frightened and alone. And surely she would not run the risk of hiding on the train unless there were some terrible circumstances compelling her. No, there is no disloyalty here—just as Weiwei herself has been sheltered by the train, so she will help in her turn. She will give the girl time to tell her story, to reveal what she is running from or to.

She is so deep in thought that a thump at the window beside her makes her spit out a train curse and jump backward, colliding with a passing kitchen boy.

"Crawlers!" he yells, pointing to the window, where a creature the size of a dining plate clings to the iron bars, its legs tapping wildly at the glass. A shell covers its body but not its pale-pink underside, from which mouths gape, opening and closing at irregular intervals. The kitchen boy grabs Weiwei's arm as another one falls onto the bars, and another, until the whole window is a mass of tapping legs and gaping mouths.

"They must be on the roof . . ." Though they are usually only on the wrecks, never on the train itself.

"I'll call for the gunner!" the kitchen boy shouts gleefully, scampering away toward the speaking apparatus.

Weiwei takes a step closer but the sheer number of creatures has caused them to lose their grip on the bars and they are spinning away from the train, their legs curled into their shells. Moments later she hears gunshot and other pale bodies fall from the roof, clattering against the glass. By the time she reaches the sleeping carriage the under-stewards are betting noisily on the numbers falling from each of the windows.

"Want to take your chances, Zhang?" one calls to her, but she shakes her head and clambers up to her bunk. It is the image of the creatures at the windows making her uneasy, she thinks, not the stowaway in her space beneath the roof. But she can't helping thinking of Rostov's words: *What else is hidden from our view?* She is already taking her chances, she thinks, though she is aware of it only in a distant way, like a change in the weather, the importance of which is only understood much later.

Part Two

Days 3–4

Three days' journey from Beijing, one of the marvels of
the natural world appears on the horizon, shimmering
like a mirage in the last of the evening sun. Lake Baikal,
four hundred miles long and—some say—five thousand
feet deep. The most ancient lake known to mankind. For
hours the train runs beside it. The moon rises and the
water turns to silver. It is hard not to think of the darkness
beneath it, and what may be living there, in the depths
where the light never shines. I advise the cautious traveller
to limit the time they spend observing it.

On the great lake once were enormous engineering
projects, to harness the power of the water to run the
mines. When the gold began to disappear in the late 1700s,
the workers spoke of changes in the water, of sightings of
shadows beneath the surface. But they were not believed,
nor were those elsewhere, who noticed oddness in the behavior of their animals; a strange scent on the air. There
were reports of swarming insects; birds hovering closer to
homesteads. A peculiar brightness in the reflection of the
sun upon water.

It is said that so much had been taken from the land
that it was always hungry. It had been feeding off the blood
spilled by the empires, and by the bones of the animals
and people they left behind. It gained a taste for death.

The Cautious Traveller's Guide to the Wastelands, page 23

1

THE LAKE

There is a John Morland poem Henry Grey is trying to remember. It goes something along the lines of: *Let it be revealed in the water and the sky / the glory of His mind.* No, that isn't it, a reflection comes into it, the water mirroring the sky . . . He'd had it all memorized at one time, it had kept him company on walks across the moors. *A mirror of the glory of His mind,* he thinks. No, still not quite right. But it will do for now, while the sky is a bowl of pale blue and the great lake lies ahead, fading into a cloudy haze in the distance. Grey watches it greedily, wishing he could get closer. He watches a gathering of winged insects, seeming to form themselves into circles turning lazily around and around in the air just outside the window. A hunting formation? He takes out his battered notebook to jot the question down, flicking through pages of questions already written. Sketches crowd around the words, as if he never has time to even turn to a blank page. He raises his binocular telescope, bringing the birches near the shoreline into sharp relief, the eye-shaped lenticels in the pale bark seeming to stare back at him, as if following the train's progress. One blinks, he is sure of it, but when he keeps the telescope trained on them all the eyes are open wide, unmoving. He shakes his head, but makes a note in his book: *Are they watching?*

He had hoped to be alone to watch for the approach of the lake, but a group of gentlemen recline in armchairs by the far window, cigar smoke wreathed around their heads, obscuring the view outside. They are talking loudly and incorrectly about the depth and length of the lake. Grey angles his chair away from them, but it does no good.

"Doctor Grey, you look lost in your thoughts. Come and share some of them with us, for we have none of our own, I am sad to say!" It is the young Frenchman, the one with the beautiful wife, already making space for Grey among the smokers. "I was just telling these gentlemen that we have a man of science and learning in our midst, and now here you are. Perhaps you can lend us your wisdom. We were observing a . . . what is the word . . . a metaphysical paradox."

"The kind that are much beloved of the Russians," says a Chinese gentleman—large, bearded, and with surprisingly mellifluous English.

"We are discussing whether a thing is less beautiful if one knows that it is also dangerous. This lake, for example." LaFontaine gestures out of the window, without looking at it. "It is worthy of our greatest painters, and yet it is also poisonous, infected . . ."

"We do not *know* that it is poisonous," someone objects.

"Isn't everything out there poisoned?"

"Well, it depends on one's definition, and unless we really believe that the Company has sent someone out there to test it, we cannot definitively say—"

"The landscape, then," interrupts LaFontaine. "The landscape, *in general*, we can agree, is threatening to us. And yet it can also be a thing of beauty." He spreads his arms wide, and the gathered gentlemen hum their agreement. Only the cleric, whose name Grey has learned is Yuri Petrovich, refuses to give obeisance, sitting hunched in an armchair.

"But then does this threat lessen its beauty? Is the swan more lovely than the eagle, the placid whale more magnificent than the warlike shark?"

A paradox barely worthy of the word, Grey thinks, but nonetheless steeples his fingers together and makes a show of giving these platitudes thought.

"Beauty is subjective, of course," he begins. "But all of God's creation must be seen as beautiful, from the most humble, commonplace creature to the most rare. As a scientist and a man of God I say that neither familiarity nor danger should change the fact of their miraculousness. This lake—" He looks out of the window and catches a flash of silver, the silhouette of a tree thrown into relief upon it. "This lake may be fatal to human incursion but who are we to say there are not creatures who swim and thrive within its waters?" *A mirror of the Heavens*—is that it? The lines are on the tip of his tongue.

"But what purpose can this chaos serve? This absence of order, of meaning."

"But that's just it." Grey leans forward eagerly. It gives him a shivery feeling at the base of his spine when he is doubtful and certain at the same time, and that is how he knows he is moving closer to God. "Meaning. Why must we think that an absence of order equates to an absence of meaning? Is it not meaning enough that we should wonder? Is that not what God demands of us?" He feels his voice grow loud and strong. "It is not an *absence* of meaning that surrounds us. It is an *excess* of meaning! You ask, young man, whether beauty and danger can be seen to cancel each other out. Why do they need to? They give us meaning upon meaning which we may read, study, *wonder* at." He notices that while some of the gentlemen are nodding thoughtfully, others appear amused. "There is a poem," Grey goes on. "A poem by John Morland, perhaps you know him?" The gathered gentlemen stare back blankly. "No matter. He writes—"

"*And so reveal in water and in sky, the mirror of the Heavens and the window of His eye.*" Yuri Petrovich's voice is rich and strong. He doesn't turn around.

"That's it," says Grey, a little taken aback. "I see that you are familiar—"

"Greater Siberia," interrupts the cleric, enunciating each word carefully, "reveals nothing but the absence of the Lord's eyes. It cannot be *studied*, you cannot hope to look for *meaning* in that which is an abomination."

The carriage has fallen silent. Yuri Petrovich's gaze is fixed outside, his back stooped. Grey has seen his type before; those members of the clergy who are weighed down by their beliefs yet grasp them ever more tightly; who wish others to see how they suffer, so that they may suffer too.

"And yet, sir," says LaFontaine, "you choose to travel through this, as you call it, abomination." He leans back in his chair, his tone careless.

"My father is dying," the Russian replies, his expression unchanging. "I cannot afford the months that the southern route would take."

"I am sorry," says Grey, into the silence.

"You have nothing to be sorry for. He will be with God soon and no longer troubled by the decay of this world. You should save your sympathy for yourself."

The other gentlemen exchange glances. Cigars are lit again and the space around Yuri Petrovich grows. "And yet he travels First Class," Grey hears someone say, in an undertone.

Grey says, "All things on this Earth are God's creation, as strange as some of them may seem. There is a place for each of them."

The cleric gives a twisted smile. "Here only the Devil walks, and leaves ruin behind him."

"My goodness, it is lucky we attended confession before we left," remarks LaFontaine, to appreciative chuckles.

Though loath to walk away from an argument, there is something in the cleric's demeanor that makes Grey turn back instead to his notebooks and observations. Still, he cannot help but feel energized by the challenge posed. The Devil? No, he is wrong, this man, and he, Henry Grey, will prove it. He writes out the lines from Morland's poem. He would have remembered them himself in the end, he thinks.

When Grey returns to his cabin later in the afternoon, and opens the wardrobe to dress for dinner, he finds that his clothes have been pushed aside to make way for a suit and helmet, thick gloves and boots. The engineer has begun to fulfill his part of the bargain. Grey touches the thick brown leather of the suit, the strong glass at the front of the helmet, and feels a shiver of anticipation.

2

THE CAPTAIN'S QUARTERS

In her cabin, Marya finds a card propped up on the table. In neat copperplate it tells her that the Captain requests her presence at a soiree that evening.

8 O'CLOCK.

DRESS, FORMAL.

RSVP TO THE HEAD STEWARD.

Though it is a precious chance to get close to the very heart of the train, she feels a knot of anxiety. The Captain, of all people, must know a thing or two about pretense; in such close quarters will she see right through the fantasy that Marya holds around herself, to her father's ghost etched in her face? Perhaps it is too soon, she thinks, to stand up to such scrutiny.

No. This is why you are here, she tells herself, fiercely, though the card shakes in her hand. *It is what you wanted.* To clear her father's name, her *own* name, because without it, what future does she have? The life of a governess, perhaps, hiding like a shadow in the homes of the rich, barely more than a servant, whereas once she might have sat at their tables like an equal. She feels a stab of guilt that her motives are not more selfless, but these are things she must think of, now that she must earn her own living in the world. There is no possibility of regaining the fortune—the life—she has lost, but at least if she regains her family's good name then she may hold her head up high while enduring it. Anyway, to refuse the Captain's invitation would only draw attention to herself; there will be talk of a snub. It is difficult to find a plausible excuse here on the train, in the absence of other engagements, and there will be questions raised. Does she think herself above such niceties? What is she hiding? Already she knows that gossip is the currency of the train, that in the face of the dangers outside the passengers have turned their attentions inward, away from the implacable hills, the uncanny movements in the grass. They chatter together, heads turning, stories gathering, growing, taking on a life of their own. She knows because she sees the Countess doing the same; she luxuriates in speculation, observing her fellow passengers and weaving pasts for each of them. The Countess has an eye for the absurd and takes great delight in others' foibles. Vera sniffs in disapproval. Marya wonders uneasily what the Countess says about her. She accepts the invitation.

After all, she is eager to meet this Captain, this woman in the role of a man. Marya has read the breathless articles—The Trans-Siberia Company's "Lady of the Rails," one writer called her; another questioned whether she was really even a woman. Each article was marked by a certain scandalized fascination. *Of course, while one cannot help but question the ethics of a woman giving orders to the brave men of the train, the Trans-Siberia Company has always followed its own path.* Despite the stories, the uniqueness of the Captain's position makes it difficult for Marya to picture her; there is no comparable frame to set her against.

And she has been marked, above all, by her absence, although at the same time she is everywhere. "The Captain wouldn't like it"; "The Captain always says"; "The Captain understands." Her title is always on the lips of the crew, and of those passengers who have made the crossing before, who evoke her as one might a benign but powerful deity, yet she herself is unseen, locked away in her quarters. "Working," the stewards say, placatingly. *Hiding,* Marya thinks, with a hardening of her resolve.

Her father had admired the Captain, she is sure of that, despite his reticence to speak of his work. "She has iron in her bones," he said, once, which was the highest praise she had heard him give. But this hiding away in her quarters, this withdrawal from the life of the train, does not fit with her father's portrait.

She puts on her best silk, a formerly pale-blue evening dress dyed mourning black, and fastens a thin string of pearls around her neck. The stark black and white make her feel as though she is an illustration in a melodramatic novel. She goes to a box on the table and takes out the glass marble. It glows with warmth in the evening light. She tucks it into her bodice, the glass cool against her skin. What was it that the child of the train had said? It brings you back. She needs to remember who she is, tonight. To remember why she is here.

The other guests on this occasion are the naturalist Henry Grey and the Countess. There will also be members of the crew, her invitation informs her, though it will be a small gathering.

They are escorted there by two stewards. As they pass by the final cabin in First the door opens and the Crows appear. They bow stiffly, and behind them Marya glimpses shelves tightly packed with boxes and files. The Company likes to keep its secrets close, she thinks, and stores this information away for later. The Captain's quarters are near the front of the train, and they pass through Third Class and the crew quarters before being shown into a reception room. Unlike those in First Class, furnished in opulent textiles and colors, this cabin has a striking simplicity. There are wood-paneled walls with framed maps and pictures of the train from the past thirty years. There is a polished parquet floor. There are curved wooden chairs and a drinks cabinet. The ubiquitous Company crest is missing, she notices, along with the other flourishes and swirls of decoration found everywhere else, invoking an unfussy calm. Music plays on a phonograph in the corner—a ghostly string quartet providing an incongruous descant to the percussive bass of the rails.

"The Captain's pride and joy," says a man beside her, gesturing at the phonograph. "Ordered from Paris." He is slim and dark-haired, with a neatly trimmed beard, dressed in a Western-style suit and wire-framed spectacles. She knows at once who this must be— Suzuki Kenji, the train's Cartographer. A man her father had liked, one of the few whose names he had mentioned.

"I wonder if those musicians ever imagined that their music would be heard so far away," says Marya. "Where no concert hall exists for a thousand miles."

"An unexpected audience, but a discerning one," says the man, with a smile. "My name is Suzuki Kenji," he says.

"It is a pleasure to meet you," she says, then clears her throat. "I have read a lot about you and your work." His name had appeared many times in articles about the discoveries the Company had made. She has seen reproductions of his maps hanging in drawing rooms, seen his likeness depicted in the popular press. And she had heard her father refer to him as his friend. She knows he commands an entire carriage, complete with observation tower. Her father must have spent time up there; he had spoken proudly of making lenses to help the Cartographer refine and improve his telescopes, to better observe the landscape outside.

"Would you like a glass of wine?" Suzuki's voice brings her back to the room.

She had intended to abstain from any alcohol, for fear that it may cloud her thinking, but decides that she needs to settle her nerves. While Suzuki pours the wine, she watches him closely. He is different, she thinks, from the other crew members she has met. More self-contained, more his own person. She wonders how much he knows. His job is to watch, to observe, to record—surely he must know what happened on that last journey; he must know if what the Company claimed about her father is true. Unless his eyes were drawn too much to the outside to notice what was going on in the train itself.

He catches her looking and she drops her gaze, her cheeks burning.

The Countess descends on them and insists that Suzuki show her one of his marvelous maps that she has heard so much about.

"Of course, there is one right here on the wall, in fact," he replies, offering his arm, and giving Marya a little smile over the top of the Countess's head.

The other crew member present is the First Engineer, Alexei Stepanovich. He is much younger than she would have expected, but holds himself with a confident swagger. Behind the boldness, though, she sees that he is awkward, darting glances around the room.

"Will the Captain be joining us?" she asks, thinking it odd that they have been invited here only to be left to their own devices.

"Oh, yes, I'm sure she will . . . soon." He falters a little, and glances at the closed door. "There is always so much to do, at the beginning of a crossing."

"Yes, I have heard that she is very busy."

The engineer bends over to adjust the needle on the phonograph.

"And I'm sure she was much affected by the sad events on your last journey."

His fingers slip, and the needle scratches. "The train and crew are stronger than ever," he says, with the same air of parroting the Company line that she has noticed with Weiwei. *How well they have all been taught,* she thinks, but whether they are unwilling or unable to talk about what happened, she cannot tell. She had thought her father had chosen not to speak—that he had closed himself off deliberately. But now that she is on the train she is not so sure.

She is about to push the engineer further when he stiffens and stands to attention. The room stills, as if a switch has been flicked off.

"Good evening," says the Captain, in English.

This, thinks Marya—this is the famous Captain, about whom she has heard so many stories? A small woman, about sixty years old, her gray hair pulled back into plaits wound around her head. She wears the uniform of the Trans-Siberia Company, with nothing to distinguish her from the rest of the crew except the gold stripes on her sleeves. And the fact, of course, that she is a woman. But Marya is sure that she can feel the Countess beside her deflate a little. *What had we expected?* thinks Marya. A warrior woman, a figure from an adventure story, tall and fierce and proud? Yes, all of that.

A steward enters, pushing a trolley piled with food and trailed by kitchen boys holding platters aloft. The Captain steps aside to let them pass, then gestures that they should all enter the dining room.

Marya is seated between the Cartographer and the engineer and opposite the English naturalist. The Captain sits at the head of the table, speaking no more than is absolutely necessary, though the Countess more than makes up for this, speaking with the ease of one who knows she will always be listened to.

The first course is a mousse of smoked fish, each serving presented in a little fish-shaped silver mold, followed by a course of cold meats and pickled vegetables, then chicken, steamed with red-hot peppers, swimming in oil. The Countess, on the other side of the table, looks dubious, while the Cartographer piles more food onto Marya's plate each time he takes some himself.

"You must eat," he says, "or later our cook will come to me wringing her hands and begging me to tell her what was wrong with her food, and I will get no peace from her until I have eaten every morsel she makes."

"I confess, the food is much better than I had expected," says Marya. "Though I had only Rostov to prepare me."

"Ah, our culinary delicacies have improved greatly since his guide was written. Our cook curses him constantly for the stain on our reputation."

"I'm sure much of his guide is exaggerated."

"It is not, in fact. He was a skilled draftsman and captured the scenery better than most professional artists who have tried. I think that the stories of what happened to him, the stories of his own life, I mean, have obscured the work itself, have twisted it into something it is not."

"Yes." She is oddly pleased to hear him praised, and it gives her confidence to ask Suzuki about his own work, and he listens to her questions and answers them thoughtfully. She finds that she is almost enjoying herself.

"Forgive me," she says, eventually. "You must be tired of explaining your work to passengers."

"Actually, no. I am rarely asked anything at all."

"Oh! How strange."

He smiles. "Perhaps not so strange. The answers I have to give will not please everybody."

There is something crouching behind his words, she thinks, and she has the sensation that whatever it is, it is not meant for her. The Captain is watching them, and she catches, for the first time, a glimpse of steely intensity, of a cold, hard intelligence. She feels the confidence she has built up begin to waver. She has a story ready, about her late husband and his interest in the Society and its members, yet somehow she cannot bring herself to launch into such an elaborate lie.

Instead, before she loses her nerve completely, she says, "I have heard that the Wastelands Society also undertakes impressive work."

The conversation around the table falls silent.

Then Henry Grey sniffs. "For housewives and retired clergymen, certainly," he says. She sees the engineer look up at him quickly, then back down at his food.

"I have always thought them admirable," says the Countess. "To do so much with so few resources. I read a fascinating article the other day about *phosphorescence*. Is that the right word? By a gentleman who seems to have had to turn quite nocturnal during his journey, to have observed so much. A great contribution to scientific understanding, as I see it."

In the months since her father's death Marya has read everything she can about the Society, hoping that she will find a path to Artemis. Of course, she knew already about its beginnings, among the amateur natural scientists who, frustrated at being shut out of the conferences and lectures being held in the great universities of Europe and Asia to discuss the changes, began their own discussions instead, in dining rooms and church halls and public houses. These discussions grew into a Society that was open to all, that required no invitation nor academic membership, and that from the start had published long and polemical articles, pointing out the dangers of the Company's proposed railway, the damage it would do to the land.

"And yet perhaps there are things that cannot be understood. That should not be."

Everyone at the table turns at the sound of the Captain's voice.

"They look for meaning in the landscape, for reason," she goes on. "Yet who is to say there is reason to be found?"

"God's reason, surely," says Henry Grey. The Captain says nothing.

"What about Artemis?" says Marya, taking a sip of wine to ease the dryness in her mouth. "Whoever he may be. Does he really understand the train, or is he—or she, of course—simply a charlatan who peddles gossip? I have always longed to know."

There is a strained silence.

"A charlatan," says the Captain, unsmiling.

"It seems that lately there have been disagreements within their ranks," remarks the Countess. "A schism, even. Since the unfortunate events of the last crossing." She has the air of one who is simply making a throwaway remark, but Marya sees the beady look in the old lady's eye. Oh, she knows exactly what she is doing. And Marya has seen the same cartoons in the newspapers—just the other day, one depicting the Society as flies in clergymen's collars or ladies' hats, attacking each other with pens while a grotesque, bulbous spider in a top hat crouches on a map, in the center of a web stretching between continents, baring its teeth in a wide grin. *Theater before dinner*, read the caption. Yes, the Company must be delighted to see a schism form.

"There have always been conflicting ideas about the Wastelands among the Society," says Suzuki. "One need only read their journal to understand that. And it is understandable that recent events have made certain of their members believe that it is no longer possible, nor indeed *right*, that the Wastelands should be studied at all." Marya sees that he is carefully avoiding the Captain's gaze. "And it is of course only healthy that the work of the Company is challenged and scrutinized."

"Then perhaps you should share your own research more widely, to allow for more of this, as you refer to it, 'healthy scrutiny,'" says Henry Grey, pointedly.

Suzuki inclines his head. "You must, I fear, take this up with the Company."

"One cannot help but notice that the mysterious Artemis has been absent these past months," the Countess goes on, as if this exchange has not happened. "I have missed him." She pauses. "I had rather hoped to be the subject of his pen one day."

"Since the last crossing," says Marya. "There has not been one column since then." Did this mean, she wondered, that he was one of those who believed that the Wastelands should no longer be studied?

As the stewards begin to clear the plates away and bring in bowls of jellies and sugared fruits, the conversation grows more expansive. The blinds have been drawn down on the windows and the lamps lit. If it weren't for the constant motion of the train they could be in any reception room in any city, a little party passing the time. If it weren't for the odd ripples of tension between the Captain, the engineer and the Cartographer; if they weren't working so hard to appear normal.

It is late by the time the party breaks up. Henry Grey offers his arm to the Countess to walk back to First Class, though Marya notices that he is more intent on observing the Captain, deep in conversation with the engineer. A frown wrinkles his forehead, and she wonders what he is thinking, and if he too has reason to doubt the Captain. But of course it is not surprising that a scientist should observe closely.

"May I escort you back?" the Cartographer asks Marya.

"Thank you," she says. He does not offer his arm, but only walks beside her, his hands clasped behind his back. She supposes it is the custom, in Japan, and wracks her brain for what else she has read about those islands, though she cannot seem to bring anything to mind, finding herself distracted by the way he smells of metal polish, as if he is as clean and gleaming as the instruments of his craft. It is difficult to tell his age, but she thinks he cannot be much older than thirty. He is slim, and just a little taller than she is. She frowns, and finds that she is glad that he is keeping his distance.

"Marya Petrovna, have you—" He stops. "Forgive me, I was going to ask—" He shakes his head. "I thought perhaps we had met somewhere else . . . You seem familiar, somehow."

She tries to keep her composure, but she is sure that he must be able to read every expression on her face. "I'm sorry, I cannot recall—"

"My mistake entirely," he says, quickly. "I must apologize, it has been too long since our last journey and I have got out of the habit of appearing civilized."

"Not at all, you have been most polite all evening, and have not once yawned, despite my incessant questions." She should take her leave, she knows. After all, the more she speaks the more chance he has to work out why she seems familiar. But she finds that she doesn't want their conversation to end. It has been a long time since she spoke with someone freely and easily.

"I think you have had to rely on our friend Rostov for too long.

For all his admirable qualities, there are limitations to what he can tell you," says Suzuki, with a smile.

"Indeed! For all that I love his books, I do wish he were not quite so insistent on the dangers of knowing too much. Surely it is better to understand *everything* about a place one visits, not simply the parts that are deemed suitably comfortable or correct. I have a secret wish to write my own guides and include all the facts and places that have been hidden from the poor cautious traveller." She stops, feeling her cheeks reddening. Why would she share this with him, when it is something she has kept from everyone? Wary of laughter, condescension, disapproval. Only her father knew, and quietly encouraged her.

But Suzuki nods and says, "I hope you will write them. A traveller should know the truth of where they are going, or they should at least be allowed to see for themselves." She hears the sincerity in his voice, but something else, as well; a faint echo of words left unsaid. "I think perhaps that is what Rostov wanted, in the end."

She can't think of how to respond, and there is a moment of awkward silence. "I hope I did not speak out of turn, mentioning Artemis," she says, eventually. "I know he has often been critical of the work of the Company. I did not mean that I agree with all his writings, and I certainly did not want to upset the Captain."

Suzuki lowers his voice. "There are those of us on the train who always enjoyed reading the mysterious Artemis, though we must keep this hidden from the Company, of course."

"Your secret is safe with me," says Marya. An idea strikes her, and she looks thoughtfully at the Cartographer. But no, if he were Artemis then surely her father would have known.

At her cabin door he gives a polite bow. "Thank you for a fulfilling evening," he says. "I enjoyed our conversation."

"And I too," she says, truthfully. As she watches his retreating back, she thinks—she would like to trust this man. She likes the calm way he talks. She likes being listened to. But she wonders what it is that he is hiding.

3

NIGHT WANDERINGS

The rules of the train are very clear. Crew members caught aiding a stowaway will face train justice themselves. "There is no order outside," the Captain always said, in the brief, unemotional talk she would give the crew before each crossing, looking at each crew member in turn, so that they felt she was talking to them, and them alone. "And so we keep our own order within. That is why we have rules. If we follow the rules and maintain the order of the train, we will be safe."

The stowaway has put a crack in the order of the train. *Too many cracks and it will shatter.* It is too fragile, haven't they all seen that now? "Stop it," Weiwei says to herself. "Just stop it." If the stowaway stays hidden, who is to know? Could one girl really pose a risk to the train? But what if she is found, what if she falls ill, what happens then? Weiwei doesn't like to think of it. If she tells the Captain now, she would be helping Elena. Yes, that's right, she would be helping her—she would make sure the crew did not take justice into their own hands; they wouldn't, not against a girl so young, barely older than Weiwei herself. She would be fed and looked after. Order would be restored.

By evening, she has made up her mind. Through the carriages she goes, squeezing through the Third Class dining car, where they are still queuing to get in, to sit six to a table and join in the clatter and curse the cooks. Through the sleeping cars, where passengers gather in little knots of men and little knots of women, one small child running between them like a ball kicked from one to another. Through the crew carriages, where off-duty crew members have their heads lowered over bowls of noodles, wreathing them in steam. All the way to the Captain's quarters, moving too quickly to think and raising her hand to knock sharply on the door.

She is surprised when a steward opens the door and there are voices and music and the sweet smell of dessert. An orchestra plays on the phonograph, a scratchy, ghostly sound.

"Yes? What is it, Zhang? I need to get back to this, they'll be demanding coffee any moment."

"I . . ." She stops. "Is she . . . entertaining?"

He leans on the door. "Unless it's urgent, or in other words, unless there is fire on the line or alternatively a fire on the train, then come back later. No, come back tomorrow, at a decent time to be knocking on someone's door."

"But . . . I don't understand." Behind the steward she can see into the Captain's dining room. The Cartographer is there, and the passenger she gave the glass marble to, Marya Petrovna, she is smiling at something that someone has said. It must be the Captain, out of sight at the head of the table. The Captain who has been missing this whole time, who has left them all to their own devices, here she is, as if everything is normal, drinking wine with First Class.

"Come back tomorrow, Zhang," says the steward, firmly, closing the door before she can argue. Just before it shuts, she sees Marya Petrovna look up at her then away, with no sign of recognition. Just another servant in a uniform.

Weiwei stands in the empty corridor, staring at the closed door as if her gaze could burn right through it, just as when she was a child, convinced that if she just *wanted* hard enough, she could bend the world to her will.

She had thought—as far as her thoughts had taken her—that she would knock and knock until the Captain had no choice but to let her in, and she would share the secret of the stowaway, relieve herself of the burden. She would be a good, loyal Company member. But now this. She could wait until morning and try again, but there is an angry little voice in her head that is saying, *Why? When the Captain is feasting yet leaving the train to the mercy of the Crows?* Why should she be the one to follow the rules?

Once, she asked the Captain why it was that she had allowed an orphaned baby to stay on the train. "Didn't I disrupt the order?" she asked, knowing even then how important order was to the train—for everyone to have their role, for everything to be in its place.

The Captain thought for a moment or two. "There were some who said," she began, "that I only allowed you to stay onboard because I was a woman. I think they were relieved, to know that I was just as they expected, after all. It nearly made me change my mind."

"Then what made you change it back again?"

The Captain tapped her fingers on the iron rail around the look-out tower. "I suppose," she said, "it was the thought that human life could triumph even here, even in the midst of such chaos. You would be a symbol of our success, an act of defiance against the Wastelands."

An act of defiance, thinks Weiwei now. *Yes.* She sets off, away from the Captain's quarters. The corridors in this part of the train are empty, all the crew are busy with their evening work, she does not need the excuses that are ready to trip off her tongue. An insistent, irresistible urge is rising inside her. She can feel the release, the relief of giving in, like dropping the precious object you have always been so afraid of smashing.

Into the storage carriage and up over the piles of goods, pushing open the trapdoor in the ceiling and squinting into the shadows above.

"Hello?" she whispers. Now that she is here, the thought of climbing into the darkness where the stowaway waits makes her uneasy. "Hello?" again. "Elena?"

But the darkness doesn't answer back. She climbs in further, groping on the floor for the lantern she left. The same musty smell, but the lantern illuminates only an empty space. The stowaway is gone.

A panicked stumble through the roof space, just to be sure, to be absolutely sure that it is true. Why has she gone? *Where* has she gone? She wants to wail, *Why would you take the risk?* She, Weiwei, might pass through the train unnoticed, but she is the child of the train and she knows its rhythms and workings; holds it in her head like a complex mechanical puzzle, what times the shifts change, and when the porter is likely to sneak to the kitchen for a sip of wine, and where the under-stewards can be found napping, and when the First Class passengers dress for dinner. The child of the train can slip through it like a ghost, but a stranger will be noticed, the alarm will go up. And what will she say, the stowaway, when she is caught, interrogated? When she is asked if anyone helped her?

Back down into the carriage itself, also empty, then out into the corridor, where she notices the smell, the patches of damp on the carpet, faint footprints, as if someone has just walked barefoot through a muddy puddle. Now where would that person go? The footprints are too faint to follow easily but she keeps catching a glimpse, keeps catching that musty dampness hanging in the air, as her ears stretch and she tenses, expecting at any moment for shouts to ring out—a stranger onboard, an intruder, a thief of space and resources. But all is quiet. The nighttime train is different from the daytime train. You can feel its movement more, somehow, when the corridors have emptied, when the noise of the rails fills in the silence and creeps into your bones. The nighttime train creaks and whispers. It grows bigger, as though it is breathing out all the distances of the day.

She opens the door to the garden carriage. The air feels lighter in here, cleaner. Lettuces and herbs grow in neat tubs, and chickens strut in a fenced-off enclosure. There are cabinets where mushrooms grow in the dark. Weiwei comes here, sometimes, when she feels the walls of the train begin to close in on her. "Elena?" she calls. But the chickens just look at her quizzically, and there is nowhere for a stowaway to hide.

On, then, to the Third Class sleeping carriages. The lights go out at eleven, so the carriage is dark but for the one small light above the doorway that burns all night. There are the sounds of conversation but no hint of a disturbance—the stowaway must have passed through unseen—and Weiwei allows a grudging admiration at her stealthiness. She moves on to the dining cars, convinced that the girl must be looking for food. But the locks on the Third Class kitchen are untouched, and in First the under-cook is baking bread for the next day. Weiwei looks inside, carefully, the smell reminding her that she hasn't eaten this evening, and it takes all of her self-control not to sneak in and try to steal a roll. Luca, one of the kitchen boys, is leaning sleepily against the oven, a brace of utensils in his hand to wake him up with a clatter if he falls asleep. But no trace of the stowaway. Where else would a stowaway go, if not to find food?

And then she thinks—*Water.*

She creeps on, quickly now, through the empty dining car and into the First Class sleeping carriages, all the way along until she reaches the bathrooms.

The First Class cabins all have sinks and water closets, and when the train was first built they even had their own baths. But this had taken up too much space and had put more pressure on one of the most complicated aspects of the train's engineering—its provision of water—so special bathrooms had been put in, to be shared among the passengers.

On any steam train, water is a constant, pressing need. On the Trans-Siberian Express it is an obsession. The train is always thirsty. It gulps down water in an endless, bottomless greed. It drinks and drinks, and the largest tenders made could not hold enough to see it through the long spaces of the Wastelands, so the surveyors and scientists and engineers of the Company had built a labyrinth of pipes and pumps and tanks, to reuse the water and send it around and around the train itself. Pipes for the engineers to listen to and coax, stores for the drivers and stokers to watch and measure and guard, taps for Weiwei to polish and marvel at. She is always annoyed that the passengers barely seem to notice the gleaming pipes that run along the corridors and into the cabins and kitchens and bathrooms (except when they make clunking noises in the night, when there are complaints that a person can't get a good night's sleep with all this racket). They don't seem to think it miraculous that water pours out at the turn of a tap, or that they can sink into a bath, on a moving train, days from anywhere.

There is water seeping out of the bathroom, staining the carpet around the door a deeper red. She hesitates, then pushes open the door, just a crack, to slip inside.

A cloud of steam surrounds her. You can't move fast, in the steam, it slows you down too much, sticks to your hair and your skin. All she can see is a yellow glow above the mirrors where the one lamp is burning, all she can hear is water running from the taps. Water pools around her feet, soaking her shoes, it runs over the sides of the white porcelain bathtub. Somewhere down the corridor comes the chime of a clock. Midnight.

"Hello?" Slowly, through the water, pushing the clouds of steam aside, to the bath, the black and white tiles of the floor shimmering with each step.

There is a drowned girl beneath the water. Her hair surrounds her like weeds, her skin almost translucent, her lips slightly apart.

Then she opens her eyes.

Without really thinking about what she is doing, Weiwei rolls up her sleeve, and plunges her arm into the bath. She reaches for the stowaway's hand, feels strong fingers close around her own and Elena is pulling her down toward the water, and Weiwei thinks—there are stories like this; stories the passengers tell her on slow evenings, that they bring from their homes and their grandmothers, stories of faces in the depths and of the border places where you should not go. She has time to think all this, even time to think, *How strange to think so many things so quickly* . . . And she is close enough to the water to feel its warmth on her face, to feel that they are suspended in time, she and the stowaway, as though they have become reflections of each other, one above the water and one below. If she lets herself be pulled in, she thinks, she will not come back out, or she will be changed, like the people in the stories, who cannot return to the lives they left behind. So she tugs harder, she grips the side of the bath with her other hand and she pulls and pulls and the stowaway rises from the water, breaking the surface and sending a wave sloshing onto the floor as Weiwei staggers backward.

The girl's hair is plastered to her head, her eyes an inky blue. Only her head and shoulders are above the water. She looks like a child, annoyed at being disturbed from her private games.

"What are you *doing*? Why on earth would you . . ." Weiwei is at a loss for words, not a state she is familiar with. She waves a hand, frantically, in the direction of the door. "What if someone else came in? What if someone had seen you? You're not . . . you don't even have decent . . ." She looks around and spots the blue silk dress in a damp pile on the floor. "What were you thinking?"

Elena tilts her head to one side, as Weiwei has seen birds do, when they are eyeing a juicy meal, calculating distance and speed and probability. "I wanted the water," she says, as if wondering why anyone is making a fuss.

"We need to leave," says Weiwei. How long have they been here? The steam is vanishing, and so too is the way it softened everything around them. Now all the sharp corners are coming back into focus, reality reasserting itself. Now they are just two girls somewhere they shouldn't be, and she listens for footsteps in the corridor, for shouts of surprise at the water staining the carpet outside. The dripping water echoes loud enough to bring the stewards running.

"Here." She picks up the blue dress, turned darker blue by the water.

The girl stands up and takes it, making no move to cover her nakedness, so Weiwei looks away, more shocked than she would want to admit.

She hears the slosh of water as the girl steps out of the bath, and frowns. It should be draining away, not flooding like this. Weiwei crouches down to poke at the drain in the corner of the room, which leads to an underfloor tank, from which in turn the water will be taken and reused, passed into the giant tenders to feed the engine. It is clogged with what looks like soil or mud, a wet earthy smell making her cover her nose and look back at the stowaway, who is wriggling into her dress.

"I should find you some other clothes," says Weiwei, poking at the drain again.

"Why?" Elena tugs the short sleeves over her shoulders, where they fall down again.

"Why? Because if you're going to sneak onto the train illegally it might be a good idea not to be found wandering the corridors at night looking like—"

"Like what?"

Weiwei hesitates. "Like a . . . a . . . I don't know, if you're going to do something as wrong, as, as *dangerous* as this then you have to be *careful*." She can feel her temper rising at the sheer madness, the sheer stupidity of it, though whether it is the girl's or her own she isn't sure.

The girl gives her that tilting look again. "I'm sorry," she says, and sounds so insincere that Weiwei can't help it, she starts to laugh.

"Most people would just run a bath, you know, not flood the whole room." She imagines Alexei's face if he were here and laughs even harder, and it has been a long time since she has felt a release like this, despite the absurdity of it all, despite the Captain locked away in her quarters, despite the Wastelands and the Crows and the scattered fragments of her memories. It feels like walls breaking.

Their luck holds, the corridors are empty. Where there should be crew members patrolling, there is no one in sight. The part of her that is loyal and good feels a shiver of unease. The part that is conspiring to protect a stowaway lets out a sigh of relief.

Elena pads beside her silently. As they slip through the darkened sleeping carriages Weiwei imagines passengers waking, and, upon seeing two small figures hurry past, convincing themselves that ghosts stalk the train.

They do not speak. Midnight is no time for social niceties. They have reached the vestibule before the store carriage when the stowaway stops abruptly.

"Look," she whispers.

Weiwei looks, but now that night has fallen all she can see is their own ghostly reflection in the glass.

"Not outside, on the inside." Elena points and Weiwei realizes what she's looking at—a moth, on the inside of the window, half the size of her hand, its folded wings patterned in black and gray tracery.

She leans closer and the moth opens its wings to reveal a pair of black eyes, wide like a nighttime bird's. Weiwei steps back in surprise but Elena laughs and with a swift movement catches the moth in her cupped hands. When she opens them a crack Weiwei can see the moth sitting still, unconcerned. Two thin fern-like strands emerge from its head, waving slightly.

"Another stowaway," says Weiwei. It must have traveled with them since Beijing, folding its wings out of sight. "It's beautiful." Though the eyes on its wings are disconcerting, staring back at her.

Wordlessly, Elena raises her hand and places the moth on the side of her head, like a hair ornament. She twists her neck to admire her reflection in the glass.

"All the ladies will want one," says Weiwei. "You will be the toast of Moscow. You may need a new dress, though."

Elena looks down at the damp blue silk then smooths the fabric and inclines her head—*like the elegant French lady in First Class*, thinks Weiwei.

"I have never had clothes that are new," she says. "I would like them."

The moth opens its wings and settles on her hair and Weiwei feels a sudden flash of desire. She wants it. Not to place on her own hair, but to treasure and keep, to own a thing for itself, for its brightness. For its wide pale-ringed eyes. There is almost nothing she owns that does not belong to the train—her only clothes, the uniform of the train crew; her only possessions, a few books and pictures that she hides from prying eyes. She wants something beautiful, something that is hers alone.

"Here—a gift." As if reading her thoughts, Elena lifts the moth down, letting it crawl over her fingers, the fern-like strands on its head moving up and down, as if trying to taste the moisture on her skin. Weiwei holds out her hand and the moth crawls onto it, so light she can barely feel its feet, the brush of its wings. As it walks across her hand it leaves a trail of what look like scales, silvery and dry.

4

THE TIDES

Past the lake, they enter a wet, marshy region. Marya finds her gaze held by the sheen on the surface of the pools, thick and oily and changing color with the light. The other passengers in First hide their unease beneath brittle conversation and arch comments, as if they were watching the *demi-monde* of Paris go by in their pleasure gardens.

"Quite soothing, really. I could watch it all day," remarks Guillaume, in the saloon car. He and his wife have the best seats, the ones in the middle of the carriage, optimally positioned to survey all that is going on. A certain hierarchy, an order, is developing in First, and the LaFontaines are at the top. They wear their glamour so lightly they affect to be unaware of it, but their table is the loudest and liveliest at dinner, and in the saloon car in the evenings the other passengers turn toward them like flowers seeking the sun. Although it is Guillaume whose laughter you can hear, who leans back in his chair to tell another story, while Sophie LaFontaine dips her head over her needlework. Guillaume and the little court of First Class do not seem to notice or mind. *She looks sad,* thinks Marya, although she is rich and beautiful and loved. She shines, in her fine dresses and golden hair, but it is a brittle, fragile shine, as if she has no confidence in it herself.

Just beneath the LaFontaines is the Countess, on account of her age and wealth and her lively conversational style which, although Vera rolls her eyes, is generally agreed to be charming. Then the silk merchant, Wu Jinlu, who spins tall tales and flirts outrageously and has even been seen to make Vera smile, and Oresto Daud, a trader from Zanzibar who has made his fortune in the spice trade. He is seen as interestingly exotic by the denizens of the train, all of whom—in First Class, at least—are from Asia or Europe, and therefore his position is elevated, though he is a quiet, unassuming man.

In the middle tier in the hierarchy are the Leskovs, a couple from Moscow returning from a diplomatic posting. Galina Iva-novna speaks a great deal and her husband speaks very little and they seem, to Marya, to have in this way found a happy existence together, although they are made nervous by the slightest commo-tion from outside the window. And then there are those passengers Marya has come to think of as the scholarly bearded gentlemen: Henry Grey and Herr Schenk, who the Countess found so tedious, and a serious Chinese man. They are gentlemen respected for their positions and their learning, but who are not encouraged to share this too much.

Her own status is unstable. She has been taken under the Count-ess's wing, which grants her a certain elevation. But her widowhood separates her. She sometimes notices a space being left around her, as though there is something infectious about her grief. This suits her well.

Yuri Petrovich, the cleric, is at the bottom. He is not invited to sit in the little circles that build up in the saloon car in the evenings, and at mealtimes he eats alone at a table for two. The Countess finds it amusing, and is working on cultivating Yuri Petrovich, although so far her efforts have yielded only a number of sermons on female immorality and the decay of the aristocracy.

"He tells me that it is not too late to repent of my decadent ways, though I fear that he is underestimating my advanced years," the Countess confides to Marya, over a pot of tea. But Marya can't help but find his presence unsettling. Perhaps, she thinks, it is because, unlike the rest of the passengers in First, he makes no effort to pretend to be unconcerned by the landscape outside, but glowers at the dead trees rising from the marshes, as if he could hold back the changes with the sheer force of his disapproval.

By now a routine has developed to order the days in First. Mornings are spent in the observation car or the library, playing cards or conversing idly. There is a preference for the crowd, sees Marya, a reluctance to find oneself alone. After lunch there may be a recital by the dour musician, hunched over his violin or the piano in the saloon car; or a talk by one of the crew members about the history of the train. Today it is the turn of the Second Engineer, a Mr. Gao, to talk about early railway architects. This, she has decided, could be her chance. She will plead a headache and take the opportunity to slip away into Third Class, where she might have the opportunity to seek out members of the Society. Here, her imaginary husband will finally be put to use—a young widow looking for an acquaintance of her late husband would surely be forgiven for her disregard of social mores.

But when the doors open it is not the engineer but Suzuki who enters, carrying a bulky projector.

"Mr. Suzuki! We didn't know it would be you improving our minds today," says the Countess.

The Cartographer puts down the projector and bows to her. "Mr. Gao has been called away on another matter. I hope my presence in his place will not be too much of a disappointment."

"Certainly not," says the Countess, turning a meaningful smile on Marya, which she studiously ignores. But perhaps she will stay after all, to hear about the Cartographer's work and take the opportunity to observe him more closely.

Suzuki has set up his projector and a screen at opposite ends of the carriage, and the armchairs have been arranged facing him. He is to speak on the topic of "Mapping Impossible Landscapes." He has closed the curtains and dimmed the lamps and now images whirr and click into place on the screen, showing in sepia the same landscape they are travelling through, each with a handwritten date in the bottom corner. When he began his talk there had been questions and light-hearted chatter, as if shutting away the outside had lifted the general mood, but now the carriage is silent as they watch the images click past, year by year, crossing by crossing. Marya finds that she is gripping the arms of her chair. Here is a weeping willow, its branches trailing in the water, the picture taken three years ago. And here again, but the branches have twisted into skeletal shapes. And again, but it is half missing, as if swallowed up by the air around it. And again, months later, but its branches are raised, splayed apart, as if it caught in the moment of an explosion.

At the sound of a door opening she looks around to see that the Company men have entered the carriage. She expects them to draw up seats, but they remain standing up near the door, their lips drawn into thin lines.

"As you can see," says the Cartographer, looking over briefly to where the Crows are standing, "by taking photographic evidence at set points along the journey, a visual mapping is taking place that will provide valuable insight into the speed of the changes." There is a new deliberateness to his voice, thinks Marya, as if he is reading from a carefully written script. As if he is saying two different things, to two different audiences. "Since their beginnings the changes have been unpredictable. Growth and decay and rebirth and mutation—a cycle that is much faster than any we should see in the natural world. I hope that these photographs, taken over the past three years, will make up part of the Company's exhibit at the Moscow Exhibition, showing the contribution the Company makes to the scientific understanding of the Wastelands."

She risks another glance at the Crows. They are staring at Suzuki with an intensity that makes Marya's skin prickle, but when she looks back at the Cartographer he is perfectly composed. They do not want these photographs to be seen, she realizes. Not by the crowds who will surely come to the Exhibition and not even, she thinks, by the passengers in this carriage. They start clapping, though Suzuki has not finished speaking, and the passengers look around, puzzled, then begin to clap too. Mr. Li opens the curtains while Mr. Petrov thanks the Cartographer for his fascinating talk. Suzuki bows, but Marya can't read his expression. She would like to speak with him, to find out if her suspicions are well-founded, but the Crows are already guiding him away.

Afterward, most of the passengers turn their chairs inward, to talk or read or play cards. *The Crows did not need to worry,* thinks Marya—these passengers don't want to see the landscape that Suzuki spoke of, they don't want to think about the changes. Only Sophie LaFontaine glances outside, then down at the sketchpad on her lap, though when Marya looks over at what she is drawing, she tilts the paper away.

The change from First to Third is palpable in the cheap wood paneling on the walls, the floorboards underfoot, the smell of boiled vegetables from the kitchen permeating the air. The tables in the dining car are packed full of passengers but none of them pay her any attention—they are looking outside or shouting at the flustered stewards. She hesitates at the door to the sleeping carriages. She has passed through here before, on her way to the Captain's quarters, but she had been accompanied by other passengers from First, and by stewards. What will people think of her now, running unchaperoned into Third Class? Ridiculous, that such things might still matter, here where the landscape itself should make a mockery of human order. And there are no rules to say that passengers from First cannot go where they wish. She straightens her back and pushes open the door. But she is at once uncomfortably aware, amidst the mass of humanity in the carriage, of the fineness of her mourning silk, the careful tailoring of the bodice; aware that it will be taken as obscene, to care for the latest fashions as much as for the representation of grief. Heads turn toward her. Obscene, to care for any luxuries at all, here.

"Where are you off to so quickly, my darling?" calls a voice from an upper bunk. "Climb up here and I'll give you reason to forget your sorrows."

"You'll give her sorrows anew, you scoundrel," cackles someone else.

"Don't mind them," an older woman calls to her. "They have as few manners as they have brains."

Marya keeps her head down and walks on, her cheeks burning. She had thought herself stronger, after everything she has done these past months; after finding the man in the tiny, tucked-away workshop in the mean little alley, who would provide—for a price—the documents needed to become someone else. She had felt like an imposter, a character from a story. She had felt as though she had fallen out of one world and into another, where there were men who worked in the shadows, people whose names were not their true names, places where rats scuttled across a floor where children were playing, oblivious to the darkness and dirt. It had been there all the time, it was just that she had never looked, and she had thought herself better for knowing it, for seeing beyond the boundaries of her own privileged life. But now, she feels foolish and exposed. And what for? Most of the windows have their curtains closed. There is no one looking out, no sign of a likely Society member.

But she can't face walking straight back the way she came, under those amused gazes, those eyes weighing her up like goods to be bought and sold. She forces herself on through the second of the sleeping carriages and lets out a sigh of relief when she is through the door into the vestibule on the other side.

A voice says, "Are you looking for some peace and quiet too?"

She gives a start. The vestibule is dimly lit, and seems to consist mostly of cupboards and boxes, creating a space beside one of the windows where a person could sit almost unobserved. A tall, elderly man with unruly gray hair unfolds himself from where he had been sitting on a low bench. "I didn't mean to alarm you," he says.

"Oh no, you didn't, I mean, I just didn't expect anyone to be here." She hopes she doesn't look as flustered as she feels, but the man doesn't seem to think there is anything strange about her sudden appearance.

"It is my hideaway," he says, conspiratorially. "The other passengers don't come here, and the crew leave me alone. Of course, I am more than happy to share," he adds.

"I don't want to disturb you," she begins, then notices the pair of field glasses in his hands.

"Ah. Goes against all the advice, I know," says the man. "But I always look." He nods at the window then looks down at the field glasses, turning them over and over. "I always look," he says, again, and she thinks she sees his eyes becoming misty.

"Are you looking for something in particular?" she asks, turning to look out of the window, but before the words are out of her mouth she realizes what he is looking for. She can't believe she hadn't noticed where they are, when she has read Rostov's description of this landscape so many times. "*Oh,*" she breathes.

"You will think me a foolish old man," he says, smiling.

"No, not at all."

It is one of the most famous passages from his guide: *A waterfall cuts through the rock . . . It was here that I saw a figure emerging from the pool below the falls, her eyes dark, her hair falling like weeds around her face. A child, though she observed me in a manner quite unchildlike. A girl, but as unformed and as wild as the water around her. A not-quite-girl.* His words had been studied and argued over ever since. Marya had seen illustrations in magazines—some depicting an innocent-looking child, some a savage; some, most disturbingly, an alluring woman. But no one had ever seen anything like it since, and it was generally agreed to have been a trick of the light, or a sign of the growing disorder in Rostov's mind.

"I know what is said," says the man, "but still, I have always hoped . . . And I thought, perhaps this final time." His smile grows sadder.

"You have been on many crossings?" Marya asks, feeling a stir of excitement.

"Oh yes. Many crossings. But it is time to give these old bones a rest."

"The last crossing—were you on board when . . . ?"

He turns the field glasses over again. "I was."

It is clear that he doesn't want to speak of it, any more than the crew do, but Marya pushes anyway, even though she knows the words hurt them both. "The Company say that it was the glass, that it was faulty, but I have heard that there are those who don't agree." She tries to sound like nothing more than a gossip, like the old ladies in black in their parlors, exchanging news of recent deaths. "I have heard that the Wastelands Society believe that there is more to it. If only Artemis were still writing . . ."

Alarm flickers across the man's face, before being replaced by a polite blankness. "Ah, my dear, I am too old a traveller for all that. Is it not quite ordinary for the Society and the Company to contradict one another?"

He knows something, thinks Marya. She hadn't mistaken that look of alarm. "Yes, of course, that's right. I'm sure it is just a malicious rumor." She gives what she hopes is an empty-headed smile, but the man's attention has been caught by something outside. His brow furrows, and when she follows his gaze she sees a ripple in the reeds, as if a great wave were pushing through them, then another, and another, and it can't be the wind, because there is a lone tree on the horizon, and its leaves and branches are utterly still.

"What is it?" she says, frustrated at the interruption but unable to tear her eyes away from the waves.

"The tides." And then, almost to himself, "But surely it is too early." He pats his jacket pockets until he finds a well-worn notebook, and flicks through the pages.

A shudder rocks the train, and she feels her stomach clench. Her father had spoken, once, of the tides, how they seem to taunt the train, how they follow no pattern, no rule. *"We will have no ungodly talk at this dinner table,"* her mother had declared.

She holds on to the handrail to steady herself. They began in the last few years, her father said. No one knows why. The train must outwit them, slowly, carefully. He said they were getting stronger. Another shudder, stronger this time, and she grasps the old man's arm. His wrists are so thin the bones seem to protrude from the skin like the gnarled knots on a tree.

"We should go back into the carriage," she says, guiding him through the door.

She sees Weiwei approaching from the opposite direction. "There's no need to worry," the train girl shouts, but the train jolts and panic skitters through the carriage as objects roll off bunks, falling in a succession of thuds to the floor.

"Can I have your name?" Marya asks the man, but as he opens his mouth to reply, a wave hits them.

It is hard to describe, after it has happened. It is as if the air folds in on itself, like a fan; as if the side of the train has been shoved by hands that are impossibly strong, and Marya has enough time—in

that way in which a moment stretches out, suspended—to imagine
the train's huge wheels lifting from the rail, the train toppling to
land helplessly on its side. All the fittings and the lights and the walls
shake and rattle. Several wall panels fall to the floor with a crash
and blankets and parcels pour out from within as though the train's
innards are made of cloth and brown paper. *Smuggled goods,* thinks
Marya, distantly. This will be annoying, for the smugglers.

Then it's over, and the train is still on the rails and the passengers
are sobbing, and the man is crumpling, sliding to the floor like a
puppet whose guiding hands have fallen still.

She stumbles from Third as the doctor is arriving, clearing a space
around the stricken man. Back in her cabin, she tries to slow her
breathing, but her usual tricks are not working, she can't find the
deep, slow river to calm her mind, and she feels as if her lungs are
being squeezed, as if her heart can't find the steady rhythm it needs
to beat.

Her father's body, slumped over his desk. The doctor, his hat in
his hands. *"A heart attack. Nothing that you could do."*

But there were things the doctor hadn't seen. Had she really seen
them herself? Overwrought, the doctor had said, prescribing a sleeping draft. Understandable, in the circumstances. And when she had
woken, and the body had been taken away, and the bureaucratic
rituals of death had begun—could she really be certain of her own
memories? *Water pooling beneath her father's face, grains of sand on
his cheek. Where were they from? Cleaning it all away, before alerting
the rest of the household, before letting herself think about what she was
doing. Closing her father's eyes so that no one would see the patterns
within them, like cut glass, washed of color, as empty as the windows he
had made.*

5

THE NOT-QUITE-GIRL

The crew tidy up, as always. They tidy up and try to keep the passengers calm as the train continues its halting way through the tides. Weiwei sees Alexei and another engineer hurrying past, their lips set, their faces pale. The train has been hit by waves before, but never one this powerful.

The train is the strongest ever built.

It is safe, it is safe.

But she is not as sure as she once was. They had all known, even before the last crossing, that the train was being pushed too hard. But they had always believed their own boasts; they had built their own myths of the great armored train. They had been so sure that it would run forever.

"How is the Professor?" Anya Kasharina heaves herself to her feet when Weiwei enters. The kitchens and dining cars are a chaos of smashed crockery, soup spilled on the floor, salt scattered across tables. Weiwei steps gingerly, broken glass crunching underfoot.

"He's with the doctor," says Weiwei.

"Is it—"

"He wasn't physically hurt, but they think that the tides were a strain on his nerves." They don't say *Wastelands sickness* out loud. It's best not to think of it too much, though all the stewards carry tranquilizer darts, in case any passenger or crew member is overcome by it.

The cook wipes her hands on her apron. She has a soft spot for the Professor, always giving him extra portions and telling him to eat up and get some flesh on his bones. "Well," she says, too brightly, "aren't we always telling him he needs to get his nose out of those books. Over-tired, if you ask me."

The train slows, suddenly, and Weiwei looks out of the window to see another wave go past; the air shimmering, the grass flattened. Anya touches the little iron icon of Saint Mathilda at her neck. "It'll make the butter turn, what's left of it," she mutters. The tides upset the delicate balance of the train. They sour the wine and make the kitchen boys clumsy at their chores. They keep the crew from sleeping and cause even the most placid of the stewards to lose their tempers.

When a semblance of order has been brought back to the dining cars, the cook presses a seed cake into Weiwei's hands, wrapped in muslin. "For the Professor," she says. "His nerves won't get better if he doesn't look after his stomach first."

But Weiwei's feet take her toward the storage car. She will go and see the Professor afterward, she promises herself. It's likely the doctor won't let her in, anyway, and the Professor will need his sleep, no point disturbing him for nothing. She pushes away the twinge of guilt, tries to ignore the weight of the seed cake nestled in her jacket pocket. Rest is what he needs, time to remember what the rails mean to him. *Nothing has changed,* she tells herself, fiercely. They will keep riding the train forever.

When she nears the Captain's quarters she slows down, as she has become accustomed to on this crossing. If she walks slowly enough, if she times it just right, the door might open. The Captain might emerge. *No. She will be in the watchtower,* thinks Weiwei. She and the Cartographer will be watching the tracks of the tides, sending orders to the drivers; when to slow, when to wait, when to plunge onward.

Weiwei has just passed the door when she hears it open, and she spins around. But it is Alexei, hair plastered to his forehead, smears of oil up his arms. She feels a wave of disappointment, then the look on his face makes her pause. "What's wrong?" she demands. "Is something damaged? You fixed it, didn't you?"

"For goodness' sake, Zhang . . ." He looks down the corridor, then gestures for her to follow him. As they reach the door to the vestibule three repairmen hurry past them, nodding to Alexei as they go. Each has the same set expression.

She turns to watch them. "Where are they going?" Weighed down by tools she doesn't recognize. "What's happened?"

He pulls her into a corner of the vestibule and lowers his voice. "You can't tell anyone. We don't want to cause panic."

"I won't." She swallows.

"When the wave hit, it must have dislodged one of the water pipes to the tender, but that's fixable, it should be fine. The problem is that it's knocked the whole system out of joint, somehow; it's caused leaks."

This is the horror of the train crew, the creeping fear that haunts each crossing, that something has shifted, deep in the bowels of the train, amidst the pistons and pipes, that something might rattle loose despite all the care and attention lavished upon it, and might rattle something else loose in turn, and that the tiniest of faults might escalate into something unstoppable.

"Leaks? But . . . how much water have we lost?"

He doesn't answer, but she can see the answer all too well in his wet hair, in the bottoms of his trousers, soaked a darker blue. "There's a well coming up, further down the line," he says, finally. "We can refill some of it at least, but until then we're going to have to use it carefully."

"But isn't it still days away?" She remembers them having to use a well only once or twice before. The train has to slow down so much in order to lower the water scoop that it is a risk only run if absolutely necessary.

"Yes," he says, unhappily, "and we're going to have to slow down, to conserve what's left."

A shiver of anxiety slips down her back. "So it'll take longer to get to the well."

"There's nothing else we can do. We'll just have to hope it lasts and ration the drinking water. And pray to all the gods of the rail that it will rain."

She doesn't know why her first thought is of the stowaway. Why the image of water leaking from the pipes, drop by precious drop, makes her so afraid, not for the endless thirst of the train but for a girl she barely knows. She thinks of her staring out at the moonlit lake. Thinks of her rising from the water in the bathroom, a drowned girl, coming back to life. She walks unsteadily toward the storage car. The train is already slowing down, but the clatter and thud of the rails seem somehow louder, more insistent, as if to mock them with a reminder of how far there is to go, the well and its life-saving water vanishing into an unreachable distance.

But the stowaway is already an extra mouth to water and feed, already taking what was not hers; now that there will not be enough to use thoughtlessly, now that every drop must be measured, she will be a burden the train cannot carry. Weiwei starts to feel sick. She quickens her steps as she enters the service car and more porters hurry past her, too preoccupied to ask where she is going. Others are still tidying up the mess where cupboards have flown open, scattering their contents across the floor. Through the garden carriage—where all she can see in place of the greenness of the rows of vegetables are the withered stems to come—and into the storage carriage. She hopes Elena has stayed out of sight. She hopes she has not been scared by the erratic movement of the train.

But the stowaway is not hidden away in the roof space. She is out in the open corridor, standing by the window, her attention so fixed on the landscape that she doesn't notice Weiwei's presence, so that Weiwei sees only her reflection in the glass—her lips slightly parted, her hair framing her face, her eyes large and dark—she sees her shimmering, ghostly, against the birches, her fingertips pressed to the window, as if in communion with her double outside. Then the Elena in the glass looks right at her, and for a moment it is as if the outside is looking in, before, almost imperceptibly, she alters the way she stands, mimicking Weiwei's own posture again, changing back into the Elena she knows. But it is too late—Weiwei has seen her, for the first time, as she *is*, not as she pretends to be, and hasn't she known it all along? Hasn't she been hiding the truth from herself? Not a scared, lost stowaway, in need of protection, but a Wastelands creature, a not-quite-girl.

Part Three

Days 5–8

When the changes began, there were those in Greater Siberia who were pulled toward the forests and marshes, who spent longer and longer away from home. There were some who never returned at all. We can only speculate, of course, as to what drove these fathers and mothers, these sons and daughters, to leave their families and their lives behind. Perhaps they wanted to be closer to the water and the soil. For the Cautious Traveller, accustomed to careful navigation through unfamiliar cities and lands, this may seem mysterious. But I confess that my encounter with the Wastelands creature made me curious, and I began to suspect that she may be a link to these lost men and women. Who is to say, indeed, that there are not more like her, who watch us from the safety of their wilderness?

The Cautious Traveller's Guide to the Wastelands, pages 35–36

1

ELENA

They stand, frozen in place, Elena still facing the window so that her features half vanish into the landscape outside. But her eyes are fixed on Weiwei's, and the moment draws out, into its own, suspended time, as the rattle and crack of the rails seems to fade, and now Elena is letting go of her clever disguise, she is stepping out of the role she's been playing, simply by holding herself in a different way—a way that makes her limbs seem stronger, more angular, her gaze more wary and piercing. Everything about her is poised to flee, and if Weiwei makes a move, if she speaks, the moment will crack open and whatever remains between them will be lost. She doesn't move. No hiding now. No pretending. Outside, the reeds have given way to swaying forests of ferns, with eel-like creatures slipping through the leaves, trailing silvery paths behind them, and Elena's gaze leaves Weiwei's and follows them, and she is not just a curious passenger anymore—there is recognition there; she is not looking at an alien landscape but at her home. Weiwei can't stop herself from an audible intake of breath at the thought of it, and Elena's attention—vivid and forceful—crashes back into her.

Weiwei still doesn't move.

Elena says, "I thought you would be afraid."

Weiwei says, "Are you going to hurt me?"

"No."

"Then I am not afraid." Although she is, and she is sure that Elena knows it, but after all, they are both good at pretending.

Elena turns to face her, and looks, for the first time since Weiwei met her, unsure of herself. She keeps one hand on the brass of the handrail behind her, the other flat against the wooden panels of the wall, as if she is holding on to the train for support.

"It must feel strange to you," Weiwei ventures, nodding at the wall.

"Alive and not alive," says Elena.

Yes, it is a good description of the train, one that Alexei would recognize, she thinks. She has caught him and the other engineers speaking to the train, sometimes; other times swearing at it, or coaxing it on, as if they secretly knew that it was alive in a way that goes beyond mechanical ingenuity.

"Is that why you wanted to ride on it?" There are so many questions she wants to ask: What are you? *Why are you here?* But she is horribly aware of how stilted she sounds, as if she is being forced to make polite conversation with someone she barely knows.

Elena, though, seems to hold herself a little more easily, the tension in her limbs easing. *She is not going to flee,* thinks Weiwei. *Not now. Not yet.* But still, there is a new wariness in her expression. She must keep her talking.

"I wanted to know what it was," Elena says. "Why it made the ground tremble and the air taste wrong. I wanted to know where it was going and why it kept coming back, why its breath was a dark-gray cloud and why it needed so many eyes."

"Eyes?" Then she realizes—the windows. The eyes of the train. "So what did you do?"

"I followed the iron road to where a wall higher than a forest swallowed it up. I lived in the reeds beside a pool. I watched the men who came out of the wall. I learned from them about the train, how they feared it and worshipped it. I learned that they did not want to ride on the train, because they were afraid. But I wanted to know what it felt like, to be carried over the earth so quickly. I wanted to know where it went. I learned that there was a way into the train—a secret way."

"You saw the smugglers—you saw them use the skylight."

"They were very clever, very quick. You could only see them if you were watching carefully. A soldier would be on the roof, tapping and testing and saying yes, it is all safe and sound, and then, when no one was looking, he would use his stick to open a door and up came parcels and down went bags that clinked."

"So that was how they always had so much money," mutters Weiwei.

"I thought—this is how I can get in, how I can make it carry me to wherever it is going. But I was scared—"

"You?" Weiwei exclaims.

Elena wafts a hand in front of her face in an exact copy of the dismissive gesture that the Third Class steward uses, and Weiwei smothers a laugh.

"I was scared *at first* but I watched and I learned and I knew I was ready. But then the train stopped coming, and the soldiers started to speak of leaving, they said it was never coming back."

She stops, and Weiwei thinks there is something she isn't saying. "Then it came back after all," Weiwei says. "And here you are."

"Here I am," echoes the stowaway.

"And is it . . ." She thinks about what to ask, "Is it what you expected?"

Elena purses her lips. "I did not expect it to be so loud, as if the train is in your head."

Weiwei nods. "I don't really notice it until we stop." And then its absence makes her feel hollow and exposed, as if she is not wearing enough clothes. "And out there?" she asks, though it gives her a jittery, anxious feeling. "What does it feel like out there?"

Again, Elena thinks for a moment, then she takes Weiwei's hand and places it on the window, holding her own hand on top. "Like this," she says, and Weiwei feels the familiar hum of the rails beneath her palm, running through her bones; feels the rhythm of the train below her feet; remembers Anton's words, *There is a certain point where they all breathe together—the iron and the wood and the glass.* A point he was always looking for, where he knew the glass would hold. She hadn't really understood, not then. But now, between the movement of the train and Elena's cool touch on her skin, she thinks she can feel what he meant.

"It is beating," Elena says, "like a heart. That is how it feels. But not just one thing—many things. Everything, together."

"Everything connected," says Weiwei. Isn't that what Anton had said? And she can feel it; the train and the rails and Elena and her own small hand, she can feel them all, beating together.

At that moment the clock on the wall behind them strikes the hour, and Elena snatches her hand away. "You have work to do," she says. "You should be in the dining car."

Weiwei opens her mouth to demand how Elena knows this, then thinks better of it. *I watched and I learned.*

"You should be hidden," she says, instead.

Time turns to liquid. Though she winds the clocks in all the carriages, Weiwei cannot seem to keep the minutes and hours from stretching and contracting, she does not trust the rails to keep her anchored to the ground. At each window she passes she seems to see the stowaway, flickering at the edge of her vision. In the face of each crew member she thinks she can see suspicion, fear—*you*, they seem to say, their brows wrinkling, we can sense something on you, the taint of the outside. *What have you done now?* they seem to say.

What has she done? She had told Elena that she wasn't afraid, but it isn't true. She is terribly, terribly afraid.

She is sent to Third Class, to help the stewards oversee the rationing of the water. They tell the passengers that the train's slowing is normal, that water rationing is just a precautionary measure. Most are afraid enough to want to believe them, and there is a meek acceptance of the meager cups doled out for drinking, of the shared bowls for washing, despite the layer of grime that soon builds up on the water's surface.

The more she tells the passengers that there is no need to worry, the more her own throat itches with dryness. And all the time, as she works and cajoles and reassures, she is thinking of the stowaway, she is thinking about how to ask the question, *What are you?*

There are some questions that are easier to ask in the dark.

"What am I?"

Past midnight, and they are lying in the roof space, the lantern blown out. Weiwei thinks she can hear Elena turning over the words in her head. "What I *was*," she says, "belonged to the marshes and the reeds, the water and the soil. But no, before that . . . Before I was anything, there were humans who were drawn to the water. When the land began to stir, they heard it calling. They changed. They started to talk in clicks and gasps. Their skin silvered and gills opened on their necks. They thrived."

She is quiet for so long that Weiwei wonders if she has fallen asleep, but then she says, very quietly, "They had all that they wanted. But I wanted more."

"More than the Wastelands? But it is so big." Weiwei tries to imagine what it would be like, out there, amidst all that space, that huge sky.

She hears Elena turn over. "Why do you call it this?"

"What?"

"This name you have given to it. As if there is nothing out there. As if it has been emptied, left behind, when it is full of living, thinking things."

"Well, because . . ." Weiwei begins, then trails off. She has never questioned it before.

"Everything out there is alive," Elena says, "everything is hungry, everything is growing, changing. We feel it like this." She reaches out to find Weiwei's hand again, to lie it flat on the floor, so that the rail travels through them both.

Weiwei lies there, her eyes open in the dark, thinking about what Elena has said, feeling the beating heart of the train, though it is slower than it should be, more careful, since the tides. "But what are you *now*?" she says.

She feels Elena shrug. "I don't know," says the stowaway.

2

OBSTACLES

Henry Grey wakes, unrested. All night the train had crept and jolted, tipping him out of successive dreams. There had been no more strong waves, but he had felt his body tense in expectation each time.

In the dining car there is a strained atmosphere. Several passengers have kept to their cabins; those present are red-eyed and subdued, and the stewards are clumsier and slower than ever. Breakfast is unsatisfactory. There are stains on the plate his smoked kippers arrive on, and when he asks for more tea he is refused point blank.

The Countess, seated at the next table, demands more coffee. "There is barely a dribble here, has the price of coffee risen in the night?"

The steward wrings his hands. "It is a temporary measure, madam, if you would have patience."

Grey allows himself a small congratulatory glow that he is not one of these passengers who complain at the slightest discomfort.

"We must all have some forbearance, madam," he cannot resist saying.

"Must we, indeed?" she replies in a needlessly ironic tone. She and her washed-out little companion both regard him coolly. Others in the carriage, he has to say, seem more inclined to her way of thinking. The young widow, Marya, is silent and pale. Her hair, he notices, is unbrushed, and there are ink stains on her fingers. He butters him-self another piece of toast. It is a sad tendency of other nationalities, he thinks to himself, to fall apart at the slightest provocation.

After breakfast he retires to the library, where he expects to find Alexei. The red circle on his map is approaching—they should reach it on day eight of their journey—but there is a new tentativeness to the train's progress. He aches, as if by stretching every sinew he could will the train forward, faster. He is so close. Every evening has been spent in his cabin taking notes on the Cartographer's charts that the engineer has given him, and the other articles and books he has collected. He has practiced getting in and out of the clumsy suit and helmet Alexei provided, and handling his collecting jars with the thick gloves. He is ready.

After an hour, though, there is still no sign of the engineer, which, considering the amount he is paying the man, seems unacceptable. Frustration builds in his chest, making the ulcer in his abdomen twinge all the more painfully. It is this reliance on others that is unbearable; this helplessness in the face of incompetence and idleness. But these are not good, Christian thoughts. Should he not have forbearance? He is being tested, that is all.

After the clock on the wall chimes another half hour, he resolves to take matters into his own hands, which necessitates walking through the Third Class carriages, a handkerchief covering his nose. Nutshells crunch beneath his feet and there is a certain stickiness to the floor. So many bodies in here, so close together. The passengers look him up and down as he passes but he merits no comment nor glimmer of recognition. There is a dangerous edge to the air, as if even a small flame could ignite everything.

Over the door to the next carriage hangs a sign stating, in a num-ber of languages, that entry to this part of the train is forbidden to passengers, but he ignores it and walks through to what must be the crew's mess. The tables are set with plain white tablecloths, and they run the length of the carriage, with backless benches on either side of them. A scattering of crew members are shoveling food into their mouths, and don't look up when he enters, so he strides through the next carriages, along a wood-paneled corridor and a series of closed doors.

He is just beginning to think that the engineer must be deliberately avoiding him when he spots him at the other end of what seems to be a service carriage. He is balanced precariously on a ladder, jumping down when he sees Grey approaching.

"I have been looking for you," Grey begins, as he gets closer. He turns to make sure no one is in earshot. "Did we not have an arrangement that we would meet today?"

"You shouldn't be here, who let you in?" The engineer speaks low and fast, wiping his hands with a dirty cloth. "Passengers aren't allowed back here."

"Well, nobody stopped me, and frankly, there seemed no other way to reach you—"

The engineer doesn't wait for him to finish but bundles him into a store room and shuts the door. Around them, pipes rattle and wheeze, moisture gathering on gray metal. "Look, I need to tell you, I can't do it."

Grey stares at him. "But we had an agreement, you accepted my money. You know how much this means."

"I will return the money, but I can't go through with it, *we* can't go through with it, it's too dangerous, especially now that—"

"What? Especially now that what?"

The engineer rubs his forehead, leaving behind a greasy mark. "There's been a . . . complication. After the tides."

"Yes, I know there has been some disruption, but why should this affect our plans? We have been over this, it is natural to feel anxious at the start of a great project, ambition is never easy—"

"Dr. Grey, I understand your frustration but I agreed to this only when I believed there would be no danger to the train."

"And there will not be—you know that I would never risk the lives of others."

"It is not your risk to take."

And the engineer tells him, with much hedging and many caveats, and technicalities he cannot follow, that there is a problem with the water system.

"But you can mend it."

"Yes, but—"

"And we will take on more water, so really it need not hold us back from—"

"Dr. Grey, you're not listening. We will be low on water until we reach the next of the wells, and that will not be for at least three more days. And even after that, though we have patched up the problem, there is still a weakness, which will remain until we can deal with it properly in Moscow."

Grey tries to control the frustration he feels rising within him; a frustration he has not felt since those terrible weeks in Beijing, fruitlessly tramping the corridors of the Trans-Siberia Company offices, feeling all possibilities slipping away from him. The pain in his stomach sharpens and he tastes bitterness on his tongue. He must not allow his emotions to get the better of him—the doctor at the Foreigners' Hospital had been most insistent on this point. *Regulation in all aspects, that is the key to your health—the regulation of diet, of behavior, of emotions.*

"But surely, with all your ingenuity, there is something that can be done? I have come to appreciate it already, even during these few days onboard. It is quite remarkable." He watches the engineer's face and is pleased to see a flash of pride. "Although," he continues, carefully, "it would seem that your work is not always appreciated by those representatives of the Company itself."

Alexei's expression darkens. "And I will not be like them," he says. "They have no understanding of the train, the delicacy needed to ensure its safety. They think they can push and push with no consequences." He stops, and takes control of himself. "I am sorry," he says. "There is nothing I can do, we must end our agreement."

Grey watches him walk away and feels the pain in his stomach intensify, making him so dizzy he needs to hold on to the handrail. *No. Nothing is ending,* he thinks. Not when he has come this far.

3

THE GAME

It is the morning after the tides, and Elena is thirsty.

"We'll reach the well soon," Weiwei says, when she has returned to the storage carriage, her back aching from a morning spent carrying flasks and water buckets. "The rationing is only until then. You just can't have any more midnight baths." She tries to keep the worry out of her tone, forcing herself to hold Elena's gaze, though the stowaway is too close, her attention too vivid. It makes the roof space seem small and enclosed. Does she regret it, leaving the freedom of her home? What will she do, without the water she needs? The questions hover on Weiwei's lips but she can't bring herself to ask them. Elena licks her lips. "When is soon?"

"Three days," says Weiwei. "Only three days."

If the train holds. If there is enough water left for them to reach the well.

"There is a game," Weiwei says, after a while. A game of silence and stealth, of watching and waiting. "You will be good at this. But I must warn you, for all your stalking through the marshes, I am good at it too."

It is a game of distraction, because she does not know what else to do.

It has only one rule. *Don't be seen.* Weiwei has played it since she was old enough to explore the train alone. Before that, even, if the oldest stewards are to be believed; they claim to have lost her on several occasions, when she took advantage of a moment's distraction to crawl away, and they would find her curled up beneath a bunk in Third or in a nest of blankets in the storage cupboard. Then later, when Alexei joined the train as an apprentice, the game grew into a complex system of points and faults, a competition to prove who was the quickest, the most skilled in squirming out of the way of the stewards, of tricking the passengers into looking elsewhere, of finding the most unexpected spaces to squeeze into. But when Alexei was promoted to Engineer, he had made it clear that such games were beneath him.

"Only because I win more often," Weiwei had said.

Alexei had shrugged. "I let you. You were just a child."

After that, Weiwei played alone.

She finds a change of clothes for Elena from the lost property box—a plain blue dress and pinafore of the kind that some of the younger women in Third wear. Elena holds it up without much enthusiasm, making Weiwei laugh at the expression on her face. "If you're wanting to blend in you can't go around in silk in the middle of the day. Where did you find it, anyway?"

"There were ladies who came to the garrison, who looked like summer flowers. I wanted to touch them, I took their dresses from the floor. They called me a ghost, but the soldiers didn't believe them, so I hid the soldiers' medals and I threw their shoes into the water, and they were more afraid than the ladies had been. They lit candles and left me sweet rice and peaches, and after that I did not steal any more shoes."

The garrison ghost, thinks Weiwei. Would those soldiers have been more afraid to know that it was a Wastelands creature haunting them, not an unquiet spirit? "You scared them," she says. "They tell stories about you."

Elena looks rather smug. "But I didn't scare them as much as the train did," she says. "They were scared every time it arrived from what you call *the Wastelands*. They kept it trapped, they watched it as if it were a creature with claws and teeth and hunger, come to rip them apart. When it was gone they would wash and wash themselves, they would say, *How I fear I will never get clean.*"

They begin with the crew quarters; creep into the garden carriage then hurry out when the chickens begin to squawk; slip into the storage cabins and the laundry and the linen cupboard. As Weiwei had guessed, the crew are busy with the passengers, and those few they see hurrying through the corridors are easy to avoid. But it is still a foolish risk to take, a mad, sickening risk. She shivers, despite the heat, as she and Elena crouch behind a moving panel in the wall—one of the many that have been used for smuggling—having dived out of sight just before two porters make their way through the carriage. Elena is alert, every muscle poised. *As if she is hunting,* thinks Weiwei; patient and slow and ready to spring.

Yet she would be lying if she said she didn't feel the thrill of it, the joy of having someone to share the train's secrets. She feels more awake, more alive, than she has done since the last crossing, despite the risk, despite the fear of the loss of water, despite all the rules she is breaking. She feels proud of the train's power, its ingenuity, seeing it anew through Elena's eyes, trying to answer all her questions. She hears her humming to herself, and it is not so much a tune, Weiwei thinks, as an attempt to feel the same pitch of the train; to sing in time with it. But sometimes she sees the stowaway frowning, as if she can't find the right pitch, and she hurries to show her some new wonder, to pull her back.

"The furnace," she says, tugging at Elena's arm. "You wanted to see the furnace."

They get as close as possible; Elena has been desperate to see the furnace, to see how the fiery mouth of the train opens and swallows down coal. She is still puzzled by how so great a thing as the train can move of its own accord and has let Weiwei know that her explanations are inadequate. But it is the one part of the train never left unattended, the stokers always watchful and alert. The best Weiwei can do is to take her through the narrow corridor in the final carriage before the cab—one of the two coal and water tenders—and let her look through the little window in the door, though it is difficult to see through the thick glass to the deep orangey dark, where the stokers, in their goggles and thick protective suits, tend the furnace like acolytes to a god.

The game is more difficult in the passenger carriages, though in Third Class there are enough passengers for one more to go unremarked on.

"It's impossible not to be seen at all," says Weiwei, "so the rule is, if anyone speaks to you, you lose a point."

Elena nods, but it is Weiwei who loses point after point, even though she is practiced at slipping past groups of passengers as they are occupied with food or with arguing.

"No one seems to notice you at all," she grumbles, as they hide in a corner of the Third Class kitchen car.

"Will we go to First Class now?"

Weiwei shakes her head. "They'll know you're not one of them, and the stewards are more careful, they're scared of getting complaints."

"But I want to see it. And no one notices me. They will not complain."

"You don't know what they're like, they complain about everything."

"Not about me," says Elena, and she grabs Weiwei's hand, pulling her out of their hidden corner and down toward First.

"Oh, piss and iron," curses Weiwei, "no, Elena!" But though the stowaway is slight she is strong, unnaturally strong, and she pulls her forward, through the kitchen carriage and into the dining car, mercifully empty, then into the sleeping carriage and straight into Marya Petrovna, throwing open her cabin door.

The widow looks distracted, her hair uncombed. "Weiwei!" she exclaims. "How fortuitous, I had wanted to see you."

Weiwei freezes, aware only of Elena beside her, pressing herself into the carriage wall.

"What is the name of the poor gentleman who was taken ill yesterday?" the widow goes on. "I had hoped to send my best wishes for his recovery."

"His name is Grigori Danilovich Belinsky," Weiwei replies, slowly. "Though most people just call him the Professor."

Marya Petrovna seems to be looking vaguely in Elena's direction, but then rubs her forehead as if she has a headache beginning. "Thank you," she says. "I shall . . . I shall certainly send him my regards," and she walks off toward the saloon car without a backward glance.

Weiwei watches her go. "She didn't see you," she says, in amazement. "She looked but she didn't see you."

Elena is smiling in a rather self-satisfied way. "I told you so," she says.

Weiwei is torn between jealousy and excitement. The game changes. It is not that Elena is invisible, it is not as simple as that—it is more that she is able to trick the eye into simply *not* seeing her.

"But how does it work? Do you change something about yourself? About the backdrop? Why can I still see you?" It is Weiwei's turn to ask questions and Elena's to be patient, and a little proud.

"I told you, I am good at being silent and still."

"But I could see you . . ."

"You know I am there. I can't trick you."

"But how does it *work*?"

They test it in the saloon car, though Weiwei is tense with nerves as they enter. The beautiful Frenchwoman looks up sharply as Elena flits past, but then the stowaway freezes, and it is as if she vanishes entirely into the background. The Frenchwoman frowns, but goes back to her reading. Weiwei lets out the breath she has been holding.

The husband, of course, notices nothing. *A typical Traverser,* she thinks; too busy thinking about how he will brag to his friends at home to notice anything.

"Are you quite well, child?"

Weiwei realizes that the Countess is regarding her quizzically.

"Ah, perhaps she will be able to tell us when we may bathe again?" demands the Frenchman, looking up. "It is quite too much to expect us to neglect our health in this way."

"Really, LaFontaine, there is much research to suggest that too much bathing can be equally harmful," says another of the European gentlemen.

"But not for those of us with sensitive noses," says the silk merchant.

"One usually stands with one's mouth closed, my dear," says the Countess.

Weiwei closes her mouth. She tears her gaze away from the wall, where Elena is trying not to laugh.

What power! What possibilities! Beyond anything Weiwei could have ever hoped for—a pair of eyes on the hidden parts of the train; a pair of ears to listen to the stewards' gossip. Secrets to collect and hoard away. Back in the storage car, Elena mimics the Third Class steward's puffed-out chest, Vassily's charming smile. Draped in discarded sacks, she grows into the fearsome Countess; she raises her eyes to the heavens in a perfect imitation of the pious Vera.

But Weiwei has a question that is bothering her. She waits for the right time to ask it, when the train has quietened for the evening and they have returned to the storage carriage, when Elena has sipped the water Weiwei has managed to horde from her own rations.

"There was a man," says Weiwei, "who wrote that he once saw a girl from the window of a train, and the girl haunted him; she haunted his book. Afterward, he never wrote again. It was twenty years ago he wrote it, soon after the railway was built. But do you think the girl could—" she hesitates, "could it have been you?" It seems impossible, but time works differently here, that's what the Cartographer says, though she knows that he has found no pattern to it.

"I remember a man," says Elena, slowly. "Among all the men I watched, there was one who watched me back. He pressed his hands to the window. He opened his mouth as if he would speak to me."

"But how did he see you?" This is the question that has been tapping at her mind ever since she realized what Elena can do. "If you watched for so long, if you can hide yourself so well, how did he manage to see you?"

Elena doesn't answer right away. "I don't know," she says, eventually, and Weiwei lets herself smile at the annoyance in her tone. "Maybe some people look more closely," Elena goes on. "Not many. People like you, who are looking for something. Who are not satisfied with what they have."

Weiwei frowns. "I'm not looking for anything." *Everything I need is on this train.* It has always been enough for her, and nothing has changed, despite what the Professor might say.

After a while Elena says, "His book is famous?"

"Yes, the most famous book about the . . . about the train, and the landscape. Rostov, he was called. He wrote a guidebook for passengers on the train, so they would know what they might see. So they could be . . . careful. But on the journey, he lost his faith. Some people say that he lost his mind." *Not satisfied,* she thinks. *Perhaps that is right.* She has read his other books, his *Cautious Traveller's Guides* to Beijing and to Moscow and to other places she has never been, and in all of them his own certainty is emblazoned on every page. See this, go here; this is the history, the meaning, the truth. But the guide to the Wastelands is different; his certainties fall away; the more he looks, the less he understands. No wonder he could never find his way back to who he was before.

Then in a different tone Elena asks, "What happened to him?"

"To Rostov? Nobody really knows. After he wrote his book, he . . . well, people say he went mad, he vanished."

"What do you say?"

Weiwei pauses. "I like to think that he decided to try on a different life, to leave caution behind. That he carried on travelling."

"Carried on travelling," echoes Elena, though Weiwei can't help thinking that it was more probable that he fell into the Neva, or ended up unrecognizable in a Petersburg gutter. *That's what happens,* says the whispery voice in her head, *to those who lose themselves to the landscape. To those who aren't satisfied.*

4

THE CARTOGRAPHER

The second morning since the tides, and Marya leaves breakfast early, finding the grumbles of her fellow passengers to be even less appetizing than the food.

"Are they seeking to poison us with this coffee?" the Countess demanded. "Or perhaps to keep us from ever sleeping again?" They were served strong, short cups, with more assurances from the stewards that it is just a temporary measure, just until they take on more water, which will be soon, very soon, they were told.

Outside, the tundra stretches into the distance, though at breakfast the stewards had advised them not to look too closely, for risk of nausea. *The landscape may appear to be wavering,* writes Rostov, *as if it has been painted upon a screen of the finest gauze, and another painting, not quite identical, has been laid on top of this, and then another, and at times it may seem that all can be glimpsed at once, producing a most infelicitous effect upon the observer.* Of course, being told not to look makes her want to stare at it all the more, though she finds that Rostov is quite correct.

She had attempted to visit Grigori Danilovich—the Professor—but had been turned away, just as Weiwei had predicted. She tries not to let the frustration show on her face, but it is hard, when she is so sure that there is something he knows, something he did not want to tell her. Was it the mention of Artemis that he had reacted to? Or what happened on the last crossing?

In her cabin she closes the curtains and sits at the little table by the window to write in her journal, trying to resist the temptation to use the word *infelicitous*. She has always found it reassuring to see a narrative emerging, her thoughts finding an order as words on the page. She stops, and rubs at her fingers. The water rationing has meant that it is difficult to get them clean. It reminds her of when she was a child—however hard she scrubbed there would be a last, accusing spot of ink, leading her mother or governess to wonder why she could not pick up her embroidery or music—more suitable pursuits for a lady than writing.

She is already lagging behind in writing down the events of the past days, only just reaching Suzuki's talk, and her pen slows as she tries to describe the feeling of seeing the landscape's changes flash by, slide after slide. She had felt a sense of vertigo, a slipping of her certainties. How must the Cartographer himself feel, helpless to do anything but watch and record? She puts down her pen, trying to remember what he said about the changes, and scientific understanding; trying to read the expression on his face as he watched the Crows. She pushes her journal away and stands up. She needs to see him again.

A corridor runs along one side of the scientific carriage, and there is a window into part of Suzuki's workshop, but the blinds are down. She straightens her shoulders and taps on the glass door. When there is no answer she tries the handle, and finds that it opens easily.

"Mr. Suzuki?" As she steps inside, she has the sense that there was movement from within, only moments before. But all is still, and there is only a faint, damp smell.

She looks around the room; the laboratory, she supposes it should be called. What does it tell her of the man? Only what she knows already. On the tables are instruments that he had spoken of in the Captain's quarters; instruments for meteorological and magnetic observations, clever machines that tick away taking measurements of atmospheric temperature and humidity and barometric readings.

Along the far wall of the carriage stretches a bookcase, holding books in a number of different languages—Japanese, but also Chinese and Russian and English and French. She has never been able to resist the lure of a bookcase, and wanders over to it, running her hand over the titles until she sees one she recognizes, and smiles, despite herself. She takes out the familiar gray volume and sees that it is well read, its pages stained with thumb prints, some turned down at the corners.

"Please, feel free to borrow anything you like. Though I'm sure you have your own copy of that particular one."

She startles, almost dropping the book, and sees the Cartographer descending the spiral staircase.

"The door was unlocked." She suddenly feels guilty, intruding into his private space yet surprised, as well, by the flare of happiness she feels at seeing him.

"I should know better than to disturb a reader at their task," he says, reaching the bottom of the stairs. "I hope one day to see your own books sitting on shelves like these, and learn of new places."

She laughs. "You will have to be patient, I fear. My mother thought it unseemly to even think of visiting anywhere that hadn't been thoroughly approved of by the right people. Writing about it would be considered even less acceptable."

As would venturing here alone, she thinks, into this unfamiliar space, speaking so freely to a man she does not know.

"Even as we are about to enter a new century?" he asks.

"I believe she would have tried to cling onto the last one. But I should apologize, I did not mean to interrupt you in your work."

"Not at all, you are more than welcome. I have been too much alone with my charts and my notes and am happy for the company. I remember that you had mentioned your interest in the work done here. Let me show you, and please stop me if I become tedious. The Head Steward once said that if I spoke one more word on compasses and magnetism he would drive a fork through his own eye."

Marya smiles. He is more at ease, here in his laboratory, than among the passengers and crew, and she finds that she can breathe more easily too. He speaks warmly of the advances made in observation and measurement, showing her instruments for the recording of rainfall and pressure and temperature, showing her the charts and graphs with such care that she can't help but become caught up in his enthusiasm.

"What brought you to the train?" she asks, after a while.

"I wanted adventure," he says, slightly apologetically. "Though perhaps that is something you can understand." Then he says, "And the position of Cartographer has always been held by an outsider."

"An outsider?"

"Someone with loyalty to neither the Russian nor the Chinese empires."

"Oh, of course." The famous neutrality of the Company. "Yet Japan . . ." She tries to remember what she had heard about the country, closed to foreigners for so long.

"Though we can't travel the world, we can still be curious as to how the earth is shaped. I learned cartography from a master who had never left the small island of his birth, barely ten miles across. 'Everything you need,' he used to say to me, 'is here beneath your feet, but it will take ten lifetimes to understand it.' Yet I was impatient, I wanted to fill my lifetime with what was new, uncharted. I thought it was worth the sacrifice."

Yes—this is what she has read. That those who leave may not return. That Japan closed its doors at the end of the last century when the changes in Siberia began. That the sea alone was not thought enough to protect it.

She doesn't ask him what he left behind. What it was he sacrificed. She feels suddenly that for all his friendliness he is very alone, even in the way he holds himself—as if keeping a protective space around him.

"Perhaps I might see the observation tower?" she asks, if only to try to chase away the odd, hollow expression on his face.

"Of course," he says, his composure returning, and she follows him up the winding steps, which open into a circular room with a domed roof and glass all around, criss-crossed with iron bars. Despite the iron, the view is astonishing, as though they are flying across the landscape, untethered from the ground. The room itself is no less remarkable, filled with telescopes and magnifying glasses built into the windows, and neat piles of maps covering a large table. Suzuki stands as she looks closer at the maps' intricate detail—always the line of the rail, then around it, every rock and gully and rise labeled, and she realizes that there are maps drawn over other maps, again and again. *Ghostly records,* she thinks. Records of what has been changed or lost as the Wastelands make geography untrustworthy.

"It is important that it has been seen, and acknowledged," he says. "Even if it has vanished."

She sees the past overlaid with the uncertain present, as if Rostov's description of the landscape has found form in the Cartographer's maps. "There is a clergyman in First who believes that the changes are a sign of moral degradation," she says. "That we have brought this on ourselves through our godlessness."

"A common belief," says Suzuki, his brow wrinkling, "though not one I share. Ah, let me pour you some tea, I have saved a little water."

As he passes her the cup she notices ink stains on the backs of his hands, though he pulls down his sleeves to cover them. Unexpected, for a man so neat and precise, and she wonders, watching him, why he should have chosen to work here, in the midst of all this change and uncertainty. He is so self-contained, so controlled. Everything in the tower is in its place, deliberate. But perhaps that is just it—that by mapping the changes he can pin them down, impose a sense of order, even if it is lost before the ink is dry. She can understand the compulsion.

She sips the tea—it is strong, and bitter—and looks around at the telescopes and lenses set up around the circumference of the tower. There is only one covered by a heavy cloth.

"What's this?" she asks.

"Just a faulty model," he says, and she notices his hand twitch, as if he wants to stop her from looking, but she has already pulled on the cloth, giving in to the contrary streak that compels her to want anything she is told she cannot have. It reveals a compact brass device with a shining casing. She remembers seeing it in her father's workshop; he had been working on it constantly in the years before he died, and she has to fight to keep the recognition from her face. He had been so proud of it, and of the new techniques to make lenses specially adapted to the speed and movement of the train, with a mechanism small enough to make the telescope portable. But it was just a prototype, he had said. If all went to plan then the Fyodorov Glassworks would expand into the manufacture of lenses. It was not enough to simply see *through* glass, he told her: "We have to see *with* it, use it to expand our vision, to make the train a travelling observatory."

"It has never worked properly, I must get it looked at when we reach Moscow," says Suzuki, but there is a forced casualness in his voice, and Marya sees that there is a lock on the eyepiece. She tries not to let her frustration show, wishing that she could look more closely at this tangible link to her father. But Suzuki is already gesturing to another of the scopes. "This one gives a clearer view," he says, beginning to explain its use.

This scope faces the front of the train. She puts her eye to the lens and there, a dozen or so carriages ahead of them, she sees the watch tower. It is a mirror image of the Cartographer's observation tower, but alongside the scopes there are what she knows to be guns, there is a man with his finger always close to the trigger, watching the sky, waiting to shoot anything that threatens the passage of the train. And near him, she recognizes the small, neat form of the Captain. It is only the second time that Marya has seen her, and she wonders how much of her time she spends up there, away from the passengers and the bustle and the everyday tedium of the train. She looks stronger, more grounded here than she had done at dinner. She stands with her hands on the railing, looking straight ahead, as if she is urging the train onward, driving it over the plains.

"If you adjust the dial you can see farther." He reaches out to show her, though he is careful, she sees, not to stand too close. She uses the dial and what she first sees as a greenish, blueish blur, as if looking through a steamed-up window, resolves into a clear blue sky and below it a forest, where she can make out individual branches, silvery and thin and reaching upward as if to carry their leaves further toward the light.

A soaring, wide-winged bird appears, so suddenly that it feels as if she has conjured it into being.

"It's so clear . . . so close." Close enough to see the iridescence on the bird's reddish-brown feathers, a sudden shimmer of copper when they catch the sun. A bird of prey, its wingspan must be as wide as her outstretched arms. She thinks about the two-headed eagle, the imperial emblem, looking to the West and the East at the same time, one pair of eyes always open, always watchful.

From up here, she can see another line, branching away from the one they are on. She tries to follow it but it is swallowed up by the trees. She knows that other lines had been built back when the Company had grander ideas about exploration—visions of research stations in the interior, of trains travelling the length and breadth of the Wastelands. But the lines were soon abandoned, along with all those ideas, when it was decided the risks were too great.

"Do you ever imagine what it would be like," she asks, not taking her eye from the lens, "to follow those lines?"

"I try not to. The crew call them ghost rails. A rather dramatic name, I know, and the Company would rather we did not use it, but it seems to have stuck."

"And of course I know Rostov's thoughts about the dangers of the imagination."

"Ah yes, that it is best to think as little as possible. Advice I try to take, of course."

Advice that she had been expected to take all her life—don't think so much, don't ask questions all the time. Don't *imagine*.

In the distance a shadow is filling the sky. A moving, pulsing shadow, like an inkblot forming and reforming, twisting and turning in midair. Suzuki says something in Japanese that sounds like it might be a curse.

"It's beautiful." She can't help it. Birds. Hundreds of birds; no— thousands. The lone bird she had seen against an empty sky has become a rushing, seething mass, turning one way into a shadow then another into a gleaming, iridescent jewel.

"Is this normal?" she demands.

He looks through another of the scopes. "We have seen murmurations before, a relatively common phenomenon among this mutation, but a gathering in these numbers is . . ."

Mutation. A bird becomes another bird, a species changes behavior, color, size. How did Rostov put it? *Rapid and geographically restricted transformation.* It is hard to take her eyes from the birds. "What is it doing? *They*, I mean." But she's not sure anymore whether the birds are many or one.

"There's nothing to worry about," says the Cartographer, quickly, though he doesn't take his eye from the telescope. She has seen it before, this absolute concentration, when she had visited her father's workshop; when she had glimpsed the excitement he felt. She feels a wave of grief so strong that she has to clutch the scope for support. The pulsing cloud of birds moves across the sky, elongating then contracting then tumbling down like a drop of water, only to catch itself in midair and open like the wings of a butterfly. *How do they know how to move, these birds? As if they are one mind working together.* She imagines herself within it, her own wings spread wide, moving in a dance she only partly understands.

And the room darkens. At all the windows, feathers and eyes and sharp beaks. Beating wings on the glass. She and the Cartographer are at the heart of the murmuration.

"Look away, now!" Suzuki shouts to her, but his voice seems to come from a great distance, and she can't look away, there are bright-yellow eyes watching her, countless eyes, but all one; that same guiding mind, so utterly, utterly unfamiliar and yet irresistible. She can't look away; she doesn't want it to look away, and she is dimly aware of him stepping in front of her, his arms stretched out as if to encircle her without touch, but she doesn't want to be sheltered, she wants to *see*. Even amidst the confusion of feathers and claws she thinks of her father saying, *Look closely*, and she darts out from the Cartographer's protecting arms. She puts her eye back to the scope.

A single yellow eye looks back.

Then there is the sound of an explosion, from above them, and the movement of the birds changes, swirls away, as if the tower is a plaything the murmuration has held in its grip for a moment, then dropped. Light floods back into her lens and smoke drifts into the air from the gun tower and the dark shape of the birds twists and stretches off to the north. She feels Suzuki's hand on her back, guiding her away from the scope, his voice in her ear, but she can't make any sense of it, she can't make sense of anything but the eye in the lens. A mind, watching.

5

THE SKYLIGHT

When the birds arrive, Weiwei and Elena are stalking the Crows. They have tried to follow the Captain, but even Elena has found it hard to get close to her, locked away in her quarters. The Crows, though, flit from carriage to carriage. The Crows listen at doors. They know the names of all the passengers, they keep their sharp eyes on the crew. Wherever Weiwei and Elena go, they hear the clink of buckles, see the flapping of black coats.

Elena has already taken against them. "They do not say what they really mean. Their faces do not match their mouths." She has seen them taking water for themselves, far more than the rations allow, and Weiwei has had to stop her entering their cabin to steal it back, as much as she would like to herself.

"Why do you call them this name?" Elena demands. They are in the vestibule near the Captain's quarters, waiting vainly, once again, to catch a glimpse of the Captain.

"Crows? Because they bring bad luck. And how they dress . . . because their suits are like black feathers, like crows." It feels foolish, saying it out loud to Elena.

"Bad luck?"

"Well, yes. Crows are . . . bad . . ." Weiwei trails off, scuffing a heel on the floor.

"Crows are just themselves. These men are bad."

They are about to give up their waiting when Elena turns to the window. Birds. Swirling patterns in the sky, a mass of feathers and wings, of darkness and streaks of light. *You could fall right into it,* thinks Weiwei, *and never emerge.* But when she turns to Elena the stowaway has her hands pressed to the glass and a look on her face that could have been fear or yearning, as the roiling cloud of birds comes closer and closer until it is right above the train, and the mass of wings blocks out the light.

Now Weiwei and Alexei are in the crew mess, avoiding the passengers and eating dry crackers and cheese. Soup, the cook informs them, is off the menu for the time being, and drinking water is strictly rationed. Tots of stomach-churning liquor are passed around, however, even though it is barely past midday. Weiwei pours hers discreetly into the vase of wilting flowers in the middle of the table. The cloud of birds seems to have broken the uneasy balance in which the train had been held; now the trickle of grumblings and complaints about the rationing of water and the slowness of the journey has become a wave, and in both Third and First the sight of a crew uniform is likely to release a deluge of angry, raised voices.

"The Captain needs to come out," says Alexei, in a low voice. "The passengers aren't completely stupid, they know something's wrong, and they don't trust the Crows any more than we do."

Weiwei grunts. She is only half concentrating on what Alexei is saying, her mind on Elena. Since the appearance of the birds she has seemed unsure of herself, withdrawn, not even tempted by the promise of another trip to look at the furnace. Weiwei eyes the ceiling fans, balefully. The heat makes her mind feel sluggish. "Can't you get these to work better?"

"We are trying." He rubs his eyes. "We're not miracle workers. We just need to get to the well, it'll be better then."

But there are still many miles of crossing to go before the well.

She asks him, "Have you spoken to Marya Petrovna?"

"The widow? No, why would I?"

"I don't know, it's just . . . I heard she was in the tower when the birds came. And she's always asking questions. The Crows are noticing."

"The Crows think everyone is secretly working for the Society. She's probably lonely, bored. Just because you stick your nose into everyone's business doesn't mean that other people do."

She tries to look innocent. "I just thought that you might know what's going on in First, as you're such friends with Dr. Grey . . ."

Alexei chokes on the cracker he's eating. "I'm no friendlier with him than you are."

"I saw you talking with him, and thought you seemed—"

"You thought wrong." He holds her gaze. "For someone so concerned about everyone else, you don't seem to have visited the Professor yet."

"The doctor's not letting anyone see him."

"Really? I heard that Anya took him some soup this morning, and the doctor was more than happy to let her in."

She is about to give a sharp reply when a group of porters enter.

"Good to see the First Engineer working hard on our water problem." They drape themselves over the benches at the next table, and smirk.

"Don't let us rush you, we know the engineers need time to rest their brains."

Alexei fixes his eyes on the table, but Weiwei can see him gripping his mug.

"Just ignore them," she says.

"Or is he too busy making sweet talk?"

A roar of laughter, and Alexei stands up so quickly his plate clatters to the floor. The carriage goes silent as he strides out.

"Proud of yourselves?" says Weiwei, but not loudly, because she doesn't like the reddened faces of the porters, the smell of liquor on their breath. She doesn't like the tense, anxious feeling in the air.

For the rest of the afternoon and evening she is kept busy with chores and with answering the passengers' increasingly fractious demands. There is always something about this region that sets the passengers' teeth on edge—something to do with its dryness, Weiwei thinks; with the towering stacks of lichen, in queasy yellow and burned orange. So it is dark by the time she finally manages to return to the roof space.

Elena grimaces at the small cup of water Weiwei has brought. "It tastes wrong."

"It's gone around the pipes too many times," says Weiwei. She can taste it in her own mouth. Metallic, stagnant.

"There's something outside." Elena looks up, suddenly. "Can you feel it?" She takes Weiwei's hand and presses it to the wall. "There . . ."

Weiwei can't feel anything but the rhythm of the train. "Is it the birds again?" she asks, tensing as if they might suddenly hear the sound of thousands of beating wings.

"No." Elena seems puzzled. "Something else." She tilts her head, listening. Then she starts to scrabble at the roof, and Weiwei realizes she is reaching for the skylight.

"Elena, no!" She grabs her hand as it searches for the opening mechanism. "It's dangerous, you'll be seen."

There is power in the stowaway's hand, in the tension in her limbs. *She could fling me away,* thinks Weiwei, *and there is nothing I could do. She is far stronger.*

But Elena waits, watching her. "It won't hurt you," she says, softly.

"What?"

"Breathing the air outside. It won't hurt you."

"It did hurt us." More accusingly than she intended. "On the last crossing."

"But you are still here. Unchanged."

Nothing has changed. "Do you know what happened? If you were watching, if everything is connected, do you know why we can't remember?"

The stowaway purses her lips. Then, to Weiwei's surprise, she takes her face in her hands, as if she wants to look at her as closely as possible. "I don't know," she says. "But why do you want to? Why does it matter?"

Her eyes aren't just one color, thinks Weiwei, *but a swirl of blue and green and brown.*

"Why does it matter?" *Because everything* has *changed. Because she wants to understand why.*

"Has it not made you more curious?" says Elena. "Isn't that why you have helped me?"

And she lets go of Weiwei and pulls down the trapdoor and the Wastelands air floods in.

The noise fills Weiwei's ears. The rush of wind whips away the words at her lips and she gasps in panic, her lungs burning, she struggles backward, covering her face, knocking over the lamp she had set down on the floor.

"The air cannot hurt you." Elena is beside her. "Do you trust me? Look. Look up."

And Weiwei slowly unfurls herself, looking up into the square of sky revealed in the roof, into a kaleidoscope of stars. The stowaway's skin is almost translucent in the light from above.

"You have shown me the train, let me show you this." She is about to stand up when Weiwei pulls her back.

"Be careful. They might see us from the watchtowers."

They raise themselves slowly out of the skylight and Weiwei is amazed by the feeling of speed—so much faster, it feels, than from inside the train. The towers are dark but their windows glint, caught by lights from the carriages below. She imagines Oleg, the gunner, training his sights along the roof of the train, catching a glimpse of something moving that should not be there, holding them in the crosshairs.

It is dizzying, feeling the wind rush across her skin and tug at her hair; feeling such terror, freedom, speed. Her breath catches in her throat and her chest tightens at the thought of Wastelands air in her lungs, but as she feels her panic rising Elena places a hand on hers.

"Look."

She follows Elena's gaze and if the wind hadn't stolen her voice she would have cried out, because there on the horizon are huge pale shapes, moving slowly, ponderously, lifting their antlers into the air. Shapes that seem lit by moonlight from within. There are eight, nine of them, taller than the silhouettes of the trees. She has never seen them before, never known that there are creatures like this, going about their slow, secret lives as the train passes by, and above the roar of the rails they hear a sound, mournful and low, and Weiwei thinks—*they are singing*. And she realizes that she had never thought about what the Wastelands might sound like, and even if she had, she is sure that she would not have thought that it would sound like a song.

"Can you understand them?"

Elena doesn't reply, she is listening, her expression rapt. But Weiwei sees it—the tiny change, the slight drawing in of her brows. "No," says Elena, after a while.

They watch the creatures for a long time, until the train finally leaves them behind. Clouds have begun to cover the stars, and the landscape dims, but she doesn't want it to end, this feeling of flying. They lean their chins on their arms on the rooftop, and she could stay here all night, the two of them caught between the earth and the sky, carried weightless through the air.

Here and there she sees tiny flickers of light, as if a match has been lit, burning blue before being eaten up by the wind. But Elena is looking skywards. She holds her palms up then licks her fingers.

"Something is changing," she says.

Weiwei looks up. "Is rain coming? We've been praying for rain, to fill up the water tanks. Perhaps there will be a storm."

Elena doesn't answer, but keeps her face tilted upward.

Weiwei can feel it through her scalp and down to her fingers. A crackle in the air, as if it is charged with energy. As if the sky is waiting to burst into life around them.

6

VALENTIN'S FIRE

The turquoise sky of the past few days has turned a pale, churning gray. Empty of birds, it feels lower, heavier than it has done before, as though a thick veil is descending onto the trees below. How will she go back home after this? Marya thinks. How will she sit in upholstered parlors, speaking of the latest recitals or the fashions at the palace, when she knows that there are landscapes made of bone, that there are murmurations of birds that fill the sky? How will she bear it when tedious young men speak of their grand tours, of their churches and museums, when she has seen these cathedrals of birches?

Of course, she reminds herself, that life—for all that she did not want it—will not be possible for much longer, anyway. She will have to earn a living, and perhaps that too will be harder, after this.

"But my dear, it must have been positively spine-chilling. Were you very terrified?" A tap from the Countess's fan interrupts her thoughts. Following the incident with the birds, Marya has found herself at the center of attention, cast in the role of a gothic heroine by Guillaume and the Countess, who have been found to share a fondness for blood-curdling literature. Her position in the hierarchy of First Class, she realizes, has changed, marked at breakfast when the LaFontaines descend on the table where she and the Countess are seated. At the next table, the Leskovs and the merchant Wu Jinlu are listening carefully.

"You must tell us *everything*," says Guillaume.

"I imagine you must be having terrible nightmares." The Countess sips her coffee.

"No, I am sleeping quite well, thank you."

"But it is so hot, I cannot get a moment's rest. Vera has some wonderful tinctures, if you need them."

"I should never sleep again, if I had been there," says Galina Ivanovna, crossing herself. "You must be blessed with a stronger constitution than I."

Marya very much hopes so. "I assure you, it happened so fast that I cannot even really quite recall it in detail." This is a lie, of course. She wishes she could put her eye to the glass again, to feel that sense of attention. What had Rostov said? *A world always just out of reach. I grasped at it only to feel it slip through my fingers.*

Is this what the Cartographer feels each day? she wonders. *To be so close to a sky full of impossible birds. Is he there now, in his tower, watching?*

"And the Captain, where was she when this attack happened?" Galina Ivanovna clutches at her husband's hand. "I thought we had been assured that we are completely safe?"

"The gunner saw the birds in plenty of time. It was his shot that scared them away." Marya feels a sudden weariness, trapped in this same conversation which has gone round and round since the previous day.

"But what if they are not so easily scared, next time? What then?"

"Then, madam, we must hope that we all share Marya Petrovna's *sang-froid*." Guillaume wipes his lips delicately with his napkin, and Marya, not for the first time, admires the adherence to social niceties, despite their situation.

A steward sets down plates of cold meats and thinly sliced winter melon in front of them.

"Is there no congee, again?" demands Wu Jinlu. The steward gives his sincerest apologies, but begs a little more patience.

"There was no water for my bath this morning," says Galina Ivanovna. "I do think it's a shame that this train falls *quite* so short of what was promised."

"Well, it just makes it all the more exciting, does it not, my darling?" Leskov takes his wife's hand and she gives him an indulgent smile, and Marya can't stop herself from wondering what it might feel like for her own hand to be taken by Suzuki, to feel the touch of those long, slim fingers, in reassurance. She pushes the thought from her mind.

"My wife chides me for an over-indulgence in novelty and adventure," says Guillaume. "But in the face of such marvels, what other path should we take? Is it not complacent, *ungrateful*, even, to treat such things as commonplace?"

"You must excuse my husband," says Sophie. "He becomes poetic in the face of a captive audience."

"What I mean is that there is no need for fear." Guillaume tucks into the food with more enthusiasm than Marya feels is warranted. "Have we not seen how strong these walls and windows are?"

"I think a little fear is a healthy thing," Sophie says.

"A sentiment I share," says Marya. She notices the slight smile playing around Guillaume's lips as he regards her and his wife. *And in his mind all is well,* she thinks, *for it is right that the women should be fearful and the men should be brave.*

Before she can leave she is cornered by Henry Grey, who, like everyone else, wants to know about the birds. Can she describe them more clearly? How big, exactly, would she say their wingspan was? He had seen the murmuration from afar and, upon realizing what was happening, had raced up to the Cartographer's tower to see for himself, but was devastated to be too late. Now he has his little notebook with him and is staring at her eagerly.

She sees the looks the others pass between themselves. How deeply unfashionable his seriousness is; how amusing, to care so much.

"Mr. Suzuki said he has seen such murmurations before, but never one so large, and never so close to the train."

Grey nods and scribbles in his notebook then looks up, expectantly.

"They had yellow eyes, with large black pupils." *That stared right at her, through the scope. As if one had hovered there, waiting. Watching on behalf of the many.* "And their feathers looked brown, but there were other colors when they caught the light. Green and gold."

"And their behavior? Were there predators in the sky, causing them to murmurate? Or did you notice anything else?"

The carriage is listening, the clink of cutlery and conversation has stilled.

The feeling of intent. Of a mind, thinking.

"No," she says. "The sky was empty, otherwise. But it all happened quickly. I wish I could tell you more, I am a sorry excuse for a naturalist."

"No, no, under the circumstances it is quite understandable." Though he clearly agrees with her.

She is about to say more when the Countess exclaims, "Goodness, what is that?"

They follow her gaze through the window. Pale flames, bluish-white, flicker over the ground, tumbling and turning like blown leaves, before dancing up into the air and vanishing.

A clatter of crockery as the steward drops his tray rather hard onto the table.

"I have read about this. Valentin's Fire, it is called," says Grey. "It is very rare, I believe, only occurring under particular atmospheric conditions."

The flames seem to ripple around the train and over the tracks.

Marya has read about it too, in Rostov's guide. Named for the rage of a peasant boy whose village was burned by the Tsar. The boy wept at the loss of his home and fields, and his tears turned to fire when they fell on the ground. After this, when the Tsar harmed the land, the fire would return, presaging disaster.

"A warning, according to Rostov," she says.

Grey shakes his head, dismissively. "It is caused by gases from the ground and the conditions of the air. I assure you it contains no warning."

But the steward has gone very white, she notices, and his hands shake as he tidies up the table.

After breakfast she accompanies the Countess to the observation car. Vera refuses to enter, and no amount of entreaties can persuade her that the blue flames will not harm them.

"Yuri Petrovich, curse his eyes, told her that it was the fires of Hell, reaching up from below," says the Countess, once Vera has vanished, "and she insists that she'll not risk her soul by getting too close to them."

Anna Mikhailovna herself has no such worries about her soul, thinks Marya, as the Countess holds forth from her armchair on the annoyances of clerics filling servants' heads with nonsense, before her eyes close and her breathing slows. Marya, though, is wide awake. It is too much to hold in her head—the Cartographer, the birds. Did she really see that great eye? It is like trying to grasp at the remnants of a dream that is both vivid and vanishing rapidly. And what must Suzuki think of her, appearing unaccompanied at his door? *Too bold,* she chides herself.

"You know, my dear, there may be questions about what you were doing there, alone." The Countess, as if she has just been woken by Marya's thoughts, fixes her with a keen stare. "And while I have no desire to bow to trivial social mores, I do not wish to see you . . ." she pauses, thoughtfully, ". . . compromised." She closes her eyes again. "It is just a notion."

Marya sits very still. The Countess is right, of course. But how then is she to find out what she needs?

"Contrary, that's what your daughter is," her mother used to complain to her father. *"To do a thing simply because she's been told not to, it's just too provoking."* But she had never meant to provoke, she just couldn't help wanting to see what happened, so that later she could scribble it down in her diary, fix it in place and try to make sense of it in the privacy of her room.

No. Demureness will not get her the answers she wants.

She waits until the Countess has fallen asleep, and then, stopping first to choose a novel from the library carriage, she walks through Third Class, her head held high, until she reaches the infirmary carriage.

She knocks on the doctor's door, and is greeted by a small, neat man with an unnerving smile. He regards her with an intensity that makes her feel as though he would like to trap her under his microscope, peel away her skin layer by layer, exclaiming at what lies beneath.

"I can allow a short visit, but you must not tire my patient out," the doctor says. "And forgive me, but reading is not the best medicine for him . . . He must try to avoid over-exerting his mind, you understand." He takes the book she has brought and places it on the table, giving the cover a little pat.

He leads her to an adjoining door, unlocking it with a key he takes from his pocket. "Just a precaution," he says, seeing her frown.

The man—the Professor, as Weiwei called him—sits propped up on a narrow bed, a blanket pulled to his waist, though the cabin is very warm.

"Just a few minutes," says the doctor. "I will be right next door." She hears the key turn in the lock and feels a tightening in her chest. The cabin is windowless, the walls padded.

"I hope you don't mind me visiting," Marya begins, and introduces herself, awkward beneath the man's scrutiny. She wishes the doctor hadn't taken away the novel. At least that would have given her a more plausible reason for being here, a topic of conversation.

"Of course not, my dear. I am pleased to meet you again, after our previous conversation was brought to an unfortunate halt. And I feel quite well, I have been assured that I am not suffering from . . ." he hesitates, "from any sickness that would pose a danger to you. Despite appearances." He gestures to the padded walls. Those afflicted have been known to become violent, when they cannot reach the outside. She can't imagine that this man could hurt her, but she has read that victims can find uncommon strength in the throes of their mania.

"Just a precaution," she says, and the Professor nods. But he is wary, she thinks. He is wary, as well he should be, of her borrowed name and clothes, and she feels a stab of distaste for what she is doing. *No*—what the Company has forced her to do.

The silence stretches out, and she says, for want of anything better, "Have you enough food? Or is there anything I can fetch for you? I know when I have been ill that all I want is some familiar food, and I am happy to ask in the kitchens for—"

"Why are you really here?" the Professor interrupts her, and behind his frail, scholarly exterior she sees a flash of steel.

She begins to stutter a reply but he goes on: "Because if you have been sent by the Company, then they have wasted their time, I don't know anything." He folds his arms, a challenge in his eyes.

"What? No, nobody has sent me here, please believe me."

"But you are not simply here out of a concern for my health," he says.

If she is honest with him then perhaps he will do her the same favor in return. She takes a deep breath, and in a voice that she hopes is low enough for the doctor not to hear, if he happens to be listening on the other side of the door, says, "I am looking for answers, about what happened on the last crossing."

The Professor's face is carefully blank. "Go on," he says.

"I had hoped to find someone, anyone, who might remember. Who might know if it was really the glass that was at fault."

"The Company says it was."

"Yes," she says, holding his gaze. "That's what they say. But I believe that the glassmaker—" How honest should she be? "That he was planning to write to Artemis, that perhaps he *did* write, to reveal what he couldn't say elsewhere."

Again, that flicker across his face.

"The glassmaker's name is discredited—"

"And yet Artemis would listen, wouldn't he? If there was a truth to be uncovered—isn't this what the Society does? It *looks*, even when the Company doesn't want it to."

The Professor is silent. "*Verum per vitrum videmus,*" he says, eventually.

"Through glass we see the truth," echoes Marya. The motto of the St. Petersburg glassmakers' guild. In Latin—looking west, as the city so often did.

The Professor nods at her and she feels she has passed a test. "You knew him," he says.

"Only by reputation," replies Marya, in the words she has rehearsed. "I am from St. Petersburg, you see, and my family too has worked in the glass trade."

He pushes his glasses up his nose. "I see," he says. And then, "But it is not always possible to see, however hard we look. And sometimes, perhaps, it is best not to." He gives her a look that reminds her a little bit of the Countess, as if he is scrying out all her secrets. "Do you know how powerful the Company is?" he says.

"Of course. The world knows how powerful they are."

"But do you really understand it? I think most people don't." A flush is growing on his cheeks. "Do you know how many tons of tea are transported on the rail? How much cloth, how much porcelain? The value of all the ideas and information it carries? And while the train has sat idle in its yard all these months, do you know how much they lost, how unthinkable this is for a corporation so entangled with parliaments and ministers and courts? The train must run. That is the only truth that matters. Not who is destroyed along the way."

The only truth that matters.

He beckons her closer. "Go to the window where we first met. Look closely."

She opens her mouth to ask more but before she can speak there is the sound of a key in the lock. The Professor sits back and closes his eyes and Marya rises from her chair as the door to the cabin opens and black coats fill the threshold. As if they have appeared at the sound of the Company's name.

"Madam." They enter the cabin and bow to her, eerily twinned, making the cabin far too small, the walls too close.

"We have come to check on the patient, but find that he has a visitor already." The Russian speaks a clipped, perfect English, much better than her own. "Perhaps you were acquainted already?"

"No, I was simply concerned—"

"We have mutual friends in Petersburg," the Professor interrupts, not looking at her. "Please pass on my best wishes."

Marya hesitates. "Of course." She is aware of the appraising gaze of the Crows. "I was about to leave, the Professor is feeling tired."

"Your concern is laudable. We will not take up too much of his time." They usher her out of the door, and though she tries to look back at the Professor he is hidden from view by dark cloth.

Slowly, she walks back through the crew quarters and stops in the vestibule before Third Class. More boxes have been piled up in front of the window where she had first met the Professor. She heaves them away, praying that no crew members come past to demand what she is doing. Eventually, she makes a space big enough to squeeze into, where she can look closely at the window, as the Professor instructed. She can't see anything at first. Then there it is—tucked into the bottom right-hand corner of the window, so faint that it would escape the gaze of anyone not pressed right against the glass. It could easily be taken for nothing more than a scratch but to her it is unmistakable—a weather vane in the shape of a ship; a symbol of St. Petersburg—and the mark of her father's glassworks.

She freezes, then runs her fingers over the little ship. It is as if she is seeing his signature. After everything, after all they had said, after the blame and the scandal, they are using the same glass that they claimed had been flawed—that they claimed had let the Wastelands into the train.

Here, though, is proof that the Company lied about her father, or proof that they are dangerously careless—either way, surely it is enough to damage them, enough to help clear her father's name . . . But the Professor's words echo in her head: *Do you know how powerful the Company is? That is the only truth that matters.*

She stares at the ship. Outside, blue fire crackles along the ground and over the rocks. In the distance, the sky is darkening.

7

THE STORM

Weather in the Wastelands is unpredictable: in summer, snow clouds can gather in clear blue skies, rain can fall and hang suspended in midair, and if you look closely enough there are impossible patterns in the raindrops. Storms can whip themselves up into a frenzy and burst over the plains, only to vanish, as if the sky is suddenly wiped clean. Weiwei was born in a storm, the thunder drowning out her poor mother's cries, Anya Kasharina told her. "And you, it was as if you heard the thunder calling, and wanted to be out in this world though your mother was leaving it." The crew shakes their heads sadly when they speak of her mother. In their telling, she has become beautiful, brave, though no one has described her to Weiwei in a way that makes her seem real. She wonders if she should be sad too, but she can't seem to work up the proper feelings.

"That's because you've got oil in your veins, not blood," the Professor has always told her. "That's because you're the child of the train and the train doesn't weep or complain, it just gets on with it." She feels another stab of guilt. She has still not visited him, but she can't seem to force her feet to carry her to the infirmary. She can't bear to see him turn his back on his work, to face the possibility that this could be his last crossing. He has oil in his veins too. Oil and ink.

In the early hours she is woken up to go on watch duty; sent to the watchtower to provide support for the gunner. All night the storm has been at their back, a roiling mass of cloud, broken open by flashes of lightning.

No light burns in the tower, so Oleg is only a hunched figure in the silvery dimness. He nods to her briefly and hands her a pair of field glasses. Seen closer, the storm clouds look heavy with rain. *They need to burst,* she thinks, *so they can drench the ground with cool water.*

Thinking about water makes her aware of her dry throat, her unwashed skin. She touches her fingertips to her face. Is there Wastelands dust in her lungs? She tries to gauge whether she can feel a change beginning inside her, like the way she used to explore for a loose tooth as a child; feeling tentatively for a wrongness, for a part of her turning unfamiliar. Can she feel it? She's not sure anymore. Not sure she has felt normal since the last crossing, anyway; the lost memories as jarring as a missing limb.

She watches the clouds grow and twist, in an odd echo of the birds above the Cartographer's tower. They seem to scud closer, keeping up with the train.

"Not much a gun can do," says Oleg.

If only a gun could shoot them down so that rain would fall.

"Has the Captain been up?" she asks.

There's a fraction of a pause. "Briefly. An hour or so ago. Said she was going to the cab."

"How did she seem?"

The gunner grunts. "Like the captain of a train that's low on water and trying to outrun a storm."

In the morning the passengers are fretful with lack of sleep. The storm clouds are closer and the sky seems to flicker with bluish light, as if the flames of Valentin's Fire have been caught in the air. She thinks she feels the wind shake the train as well, as if testing its strength. If only it would rain. If it rains this terrible tension might ease. If it rains there would be water to help quench the train's thirst, to keep them going a bit longer, until they reach the well and one less fear will haunt them.

She avoids First, not wanting to explain yet again that there is nothing she can do, that she is sorry but the fans can't work any harder, that no, there is no iced water available. At least in Third they don't demand to speak to her superior, they just grumble and deliver some choice words of displeasure. Still, they are hot and tense and unhappy, curtains closed against the unnatural light outside. "It is normal," Weiwei tells them, again and again. "It's Wastelands weather, we are used to it."

But they know she is lying, she can see it in the way they turn away from her, angry at their helplessness.

A young boy runs up to her and her heart sinks. His hair is plastered to his forehead, his eyes wide and watery. "My mama is all wrong, please come, please." He tugs on her hand and she follows, reluctantly, to find his mother sitting on her bottom bunk, the detritus of the journey all around her.

"What is it wanting?" she moans. "How does it expect us to *know*?" Her back is to the window, her hands over her ears. When the boy puts a tentative hand on her shoulder she pushes him away, and though he tries to hide it, Weiwei sees the anguish on his face.

"Leave her be," she says to him. "It happens like this, sometimes. She'll be fine again when the storm passes." Though, she will be a case for the doctor, Weiwei fears, if it goes on much longer.

"But what if it doesn't pass?"

"It will, don't worry. We'll outrun it." She tries to make her voice reassuring, but the truth is that she feels it too. A deliberateness, as if the storm is *thinking*. Another angry gust rocks the train and she thinks about Elena, crouched beneath the skylight, thirsty. She brought her more water last night, but it has been getting harder, the more carefully rationed it is.

"The walls are strong," she continues. "The train is strong, stronger than any train ever made." It is like an incantation. If you say it enough, it will be true. It *is* true.

"And the rails?" The boy looks up at her. "How strong are the rails?"

"Stronger than any others, anywhere else in the world." And then, "What's your name?"

"Jing Tang," he whispers, wiping his wet nose on his sleeve, making her recoil a little. She is always amazed by how leaky children are, yet how their parents seem willing to hold them all the same.

"What about your father, is he here?"

The little boy points to a group of men huddled around a game of cards and Weiwei is about to suggest, though without much confidence, that his father might look after him, when her eye is caught by a glimpse of blue cloth. Elena. Moving slowly through the carriage, looking from the windows to the passengers, rubbing at her arms as if she is cold.

"I'll come back later to check on your mother." Weiwei crouches down to speak to Jing Tang, trying not to look directly at Elena. "Don't worry." But the boy twists round, looking down the carriage then back at Weiwei, wrinkling his brow. He is not the only one. There is a stir of unease among the passengers, who are moving out of Elena's way. Not looking at her, but leaving a space around her. It is not working anymore, whatever trick she had played. They know she is here.

"Stay with your mother," Weiwei says quickly to Jing Tang.

A crack of thunder sends a shudder passing through the train, as though the rails themselves are charged with lightning. Someone begins to wail.

"It's my fault," whispers Elena, when Weiwei approaches.

"It's just a storm," she says, trying to guide her out of the carriage. Elena's hair hangs lank and lusterless and there are patches of discolored skin on her arms, greenish-brown. "Let's go back to the storage car, you can rest."

"No—*look*." Elena yanks open the thick curtain. From low, roiling clouds in a yellowing sky, lightning flashes earthwards in great zigzags. Weiwei leans closer then snatches her fingers from the window frame as a shock courses across her skin.

Beside her, Elena is vibrating with tension. "Not at the sky, at the ground."

A dark shape catches her eye.

"What is it?" Others have seen it too, those who have been unable to resist pulling open the curtains, and alarm ripples through the carriage. She looks closer, squinting in disbelief. "Trains?" Yes—shadow trains growing from the earth. They heave themselves out from the ground, sinuous and glistening, smoke breathed out from orifices beneath the armor of their skin. They keep pace with the train, effortlessly, sometimes diving back down into the earth, sometimes winding around obstacles in their way. They move with a smooth, rolling ease that she finds sickening. They are wrong, all wrong.

"It's as if they mock us," Weiwei says. *Anything that moves with such purpose,* she thinks, *anything like that must have a mind of its own.*

"No," whispers Elena. "They mock me."

Another crack of thunder, another shake of the train, and the shadow trains shake too, as if the ground is charged with electricity. Someone is praying, someone is crying.

"Close the damn curtains!" The steward barrels through.

She turns to Elena. "Come, let's—" But the stowaway is nowhere in sight.

Thunder crashes.

Weiwei remembers Elena when the birds came, pressed to the window, fear and longing on her face. Had she felt them calling her? Or pushing her away?

8

VISIONS

Henry Grey has always felt the approach of a storm as a heaviness of the mind, a metallic taste in the mouth. His spaniel, Emily, would prowl the cottage, barking to be allowed out then freezing on the threshold, retreating back inside with a whimper. He would remain at the door, feeling the expectation in the air. They were days when earth and sky seemed closer together, when his bones felt the tug of the ground. The pressure in his head would only ease at the breaking of the storm, at the release that lightning brought, and with it would come an exhilaration; he would be unable to sit still, would stride out onto the moors, ignoring his housekeeper's tearful premonitions that he would surely be struck by lightning and burned to a crisp. In Germany they sometimes call the stag beetle *hausbrenner*, house-burner, believing that the beetles carry coals in their powerful jaws, and cause houses to be struck by lightning, an image he had always rather liked. The European plowman beetle was thought to cause thunder by the beating of its wings. As he walked out, there was a part of him that wanted to call the thunder and lightning down, dare it to strike him.

He feels the same now, while his fellow passengers cower in their cabins. A current across his skin, as if every follicle were charged, a breathless excitement that races through his veins at each crack of thunder, each flash of light.

Through his cabin wall he can hear the drone of a repeated

prayer. Yuri Petrovich, on his knees, no doubt. The sound is maddening, a discord just on the edge of hearing.

Finally he can bear it no longer. He needs to be moving. He picks up his notebook and pen and flings himself out of his cabin, without really thinking where he is going. A crash of thunder and it feels as though the train is being rocked by angry hands. *No,* he thinks, *no. We are safe in the hands of God.* He places his own on the windowsill then snatches them away as a shock runs through them. "Dear Lord." The words spring unbidden to his lips. "Dear Lord, have mercy upon us, keep us safe. Dear Lord, be near me."

Movement outside. Creatures rising from the earth, their carapaces sleek and brown. A class of giant centipede? No, they are not moving on legs, yet it is certainly chitinous, that casing, and from beneath it the creatures appear to be emitting a substance like smoke. He presses his hands to the window, willing the glass and the iron away. They are following the train, moving through the earth as though it were water, moving in a way he has never seen, and he thinks—*They are mimicking.* He must get it down. Sketches, notes. If they have been observed before, then he is sure they have never been described in print. He runs through classifications in his mind, trying to keep the creatures in sight, but the train is speeding up, as if they are trying to outrun the storm, and he can see them only in glimpses. Another violent shake of the carriage makes him stumble, and the lights flicker. *There, count their numbers, watch the way they move, keep your mind on the work. Have they been called up by the storm? Or are they the house-burners of the Wastelands, calling lightning down onto the train? Segmented bodies,* he says to himself. *Invertebrate.* The lights in the carriage go out the moment he enters, but in the lightning flash he sees it. A figure surrounded by light, like a marble angel in a churchyard, as grave and as calm and as still. Ghostly. *Just another passenger,* goes the rational part of his brain, *only elevated by the storm into something supernatural.* But this is no human figure, not even the storm can hide that, and he is compelled to reach out a hand to it, he fights against the urge to fall to his knees in reverence.

And then a distant crash, like earth opening and metal and wood splintering all at once, and a shudder goes through the train that sends him to his knees after all. He feels the train's brakes as though his bones are being squeezed, as though there is a pull on his own sinews. Slower and slower, and it will tear the train apart, this agonizing pressure, tear it apart and all of them inside it, and he thinks—*At the end we are granted a vision.* And he is grateful.

9

THE END OF THE LINE

By the time Weiwei reaches the First Class dining car the lights have
failed completely. She navigates by the flashes of lightning. Standing
in the doorway, breathless, she waits for the next flash, and when it
arrives there is Elena, in the center of the carriage, illuminated.

At the other end of the carriage, the door opens. It is Henry Grey,
dazed, dream-like. He stares at Elena in wonder.

Ahead of them the line explodes.

Part Four

Days 9–14

There are those who embrace what they see as the pure irrationality of Greater Siberia, who find that its chaotic profusion of forms chimes with their own ideas of anarchy, nihilism, freedom. But we must not dismiss this as the trifling indulgences of the young—there are many older and wiser whose heads have been as easily turned. Indeed, the Traveller may find their thoughts turning more and more toward those parts of the landscape out of reach of the train, and the promise of the new and unknown. There is danger in letting the mind wander. Should the urge to lose oneself in that landscape become too powerful, it is advised that a strong tincture of ginger can purge the body and mind quite effectively.

The Cautious Traveller's Guide to the Wastelands, page 48

1

THE GHOST RAILS

The train moves achingly slowly. Inch by inch, as tentative as a man balanced on a rope bridge high above a ravine, unsure at every moment whether the rope will snap, whether his balance will keep him impossibly aloft. Onto the minor rails, the ghost rails. Weiwei tries not to think of rotting wood or rusted metal. She tries to keep from flinching at every shudder or jolt. If she looks back she can still see the fire burning on the main line where the lightning struck, flames illuminating the night sky.

What luck, the passengers have been saying, that it happened so close to a junction with one of the abandoned lines. What luck, as if the old builders were there, watching over them, gifting them a lifeline. And the Captain, she has guided them safely, preparing them for this change of line, reassuring them that all will be well.

"Please remain in your cabins and bunks while the crew work." The speakers make the Captain sound tinny and distant, but there is not a tremor in her voice, thinks Weiwei, not a sign that being forced off the rail was an uncommon occurrence, and yet the crew know that it is nothing more than an imitation of a captain, a clever act. *How dare she?*

Weiwei is shocked by the depths of her own resentment.

———

Where is Elena? Weiwei has taken what water she can and left the flask in the roof space, though she is all too aware of how light it feels, how little water there is. All she can hope is that the stowaway is somewhere hidden and safe.

They have left the storm behind, that is all the passengers care about, huddled in their bunks or clutching drinks in the saloon car, and the crew leave them to their relief—the one kindness they can bestow. How lucky they have been, they agree.

But the crew know better. They have lost their accustomed swagger; with their legs no longer able to predict the swaying of the carriages, they walk like drunken men. The passengers are subdued, wary, grasping toward something but unable to see its full enormity, to truly understand what it means. Only the crew understand—the loss of the line, of the one certainty.

The main line itself is maintained by special trains and repair crews which fix any problems spotted by the Cartographer and engineers. These rails, though, have no such care lavished upon them, and the few maps Suzuki has of them are many years out of date. There is no way of knowing if the minor rails are undamaged, if they will hold. Long-abandoned, now they are nothing more than ghosts. The crew step carefully, as if they are afraid that their weight might crush the rails below them.

Early morning. A sky drained of color, as if exhausted by the exertions of the previous days; the train heaving itself, mile by painful mile, through a landscape that seems to be bearing down on them, contracted into this treeless valley, this sharp rockface, these shadows on the cusp of unfolding. Weiwei kneels on one of the couches beneath the windows in the saloon car. If she looks closely she can see colors in the rock, but when she tries to put a name to them she can't find the words. She lets her eyes become unfocused; sees faces form, bulging from the cliffs. The human mind sees what it wants to, the Professor always says. We see faces in the bark of trees, in wallpaper patterns, because we look for ourselves in everything. But the faces Weiwei sees in the stone are bulbous and contorted; terrified, trapped. She tears her gaze away.

"The question is," Vassily is saying, from behind the bar, "do you believe in heavenly visitors?"

"What?" Weiwei looks over, quickly.

Alexei snorts, but Weiwei can see his heart's not in it. He is twitchy, distracted. None of them have slept since they left the main line, but although Weiwei's eyes itch with tiredness she shares the general disinclination to retire to the solitude of her bunk.

"What do you mean, heavenly visitors?" she demands.

"That's what the rumor is—an angelic vision, just before the lightning struck, arriving to warn us. Sent by your preferred deity, I suppose."

"The Lord would do better to save us from overwrought imaginations," says Alexei.

"I'm only passing on what I've heard the passengers saying."

Weiwei tries not to let the worry show on her face.

"You shouldn't encourage them," says Alexei, "they're all worked up into a fever as it is."

Vassily straightens. "Crows approaching."

Even the Crows' feathers are ruffled, thinks Weiwei. Their habitually bland expressions look strained, and Mr. Petrov's tie is not quite straight. They have lost their symmetry.

"We trust you are well, despite the unexpected change in our circumstances." He allows himself a small, dry smile, as if he has made a joke. No one replies. Not even a matching smile from his partner. Another slip in the symmetry.

"Will we be paid for these extra days?" Alexei asks, and Vassily closes his eyes. "It is likely to add considerable time to our journey, after all."

The Crows turn their heads to him. Mr. Li says, "As you know, the Trans-Siberia Company is dedicated to compensating all its workers adequately. Now, has the water been diverted from Third?"

A pained look crosses Alexei's face. "Yes, from one of the carriages—"

"We asked that it be both. Did you not understand our orders?"

"Water is already rationed, there needs to be at least some available for washing, or—"

"Sacrifices need to be made for the good of the train, I'm sure we don't need to explain further." Mr. Li's tone is saccharine. "Passengers in First may have a jug of water in the morning. There are far too many in Third to allow for this. Better for none to have any, than only some. They will understand. Please see that it is done."

Alexei's face is white. "I take my orders from the Captain."

"The Captain is in agreement with us. Though you may of course ask her yourself."

They let the silence stretch out. *They know he won't,* thinks Weiwei. *They know that none of us will.* It would hurt too much to hear it from her lips.

"We thank you for your hard work." And the Crows stride away, their buckles clinking.

Weiwei watches their retreating backs, then turns to Alexei. "You're not going to do it, are you?"

He gives an exaggerated sigh and she has a sudden, vivid memory of the boy she knew when he first joined the train, strutting around in a uniform that was too big for him, exasperated by a small girl daring him to sneak into all the places he shouldn't go. "*It's me who gets into trouble for it, not you.*"

"What choice do I have? And anyway, they're right—the water needs to be saved from somewhere." His voice is dull, resigned.

"But Third is restless already. Any more rationing and they're going to be at our throats."

"Well, they're just going to have to put up with it. I need more time."

"But we'll be back on the main line before we reach the well, won't we?" She feels Vassily go very still. "Won't we?"

Alexei holds her gaze. "Suzuki says there's no way back to the main line until after the well."

"What does that mean? Won't we be—"

"Cutting it very close? Yes. But we have no other choice. If we ration the water even more strictly, we should be able to make it to the next well."

"They're going to be furious. There's going to be a revolt."

"We'll tell the passengers that it's because we've left the main line. There's no need for them to know anything else."

"And when we get off the ghost rails and the water's still rationed?"

"One thing at a time. We'll face that when we get to it."

"But isn't there—"

"For the love of iron, Zhang, we're all in the same position here, we're all going to have to suffer because of this, but it's me who has to take responsibility, something *you* couldn't possibly understand." He stops. "I didn't mean it to sound like that."

"I know what you meant." She tries to say it lightly, but it comes out as an accusation and she sees Alexei's lips tighten. With a curt nod he strides out of the carriage.

"Best to leave him be," says Vassily. "It's the Crows he's angry at, not you."

"Isn't it strange," she says, partly to distract him from noticing her red cheeks, but partly because it has been bothering her all morning, "that the rails are not more damaged and worn? I thought they would be more overgrown." Though repair teams kept the lines up after they'd been abandoned, just in case they were needed, they gave up eventually, years ago. But here, where everything grows, where moss can cover whole rock faces from one crossing to the next, where vines snake up tree trunks before your eyes, the ghost rails are bare. As if they've been waiting.

Vassily gives a bark of laughter. "Are you complaining now that we have too much luck?" He goes to the icon hanging on the wall beside the shelves of bottles, touches its iron frame and then the face of the saint. Despite herself, Weiwei touches the iron around the window. *Not too much luck,* she thinks. *Too little.* Everything is wrong—not just the ghost rails, the storm, the water. Everything. The Professor had been right when he said that some changes were too big to return from. He had been right all along.

Walking through the train seems to take longer, now, as it moves so slowly. In the kitchen carriages, there's a clattering of pans and knives. The smell of peppercorns and spices reaches her nose and she knows what they are doing, they are covering up leftovers with strong flavors, the better to eke out the food as long as possible. *How long?* How many days will the ghost rails add to their journey? She tries not to think about Elena's thirst, the dry skin around her lips, the way she pressed herself to the window to look out at the storm clouds. The way the passengers turned toward her, knowing that a stranger was in their midst. She reaches the infirmary carriage, and takes a deep breath.

He lies curled up on the bed, his glasses on the table beside him, his eyes closed. Asleep, he seems so frail, as if he might crumble to dust if she touches him.

"Professor?"

He doesn't stir.

She pulls the chair closer to the bed and takes his hand. "It's me," she whispers. "Can you hear me?"

The Professor slowly opens his eyes, unfocused, before a smile twitches at his lips. "You have come back. Did you see it, on the glass? I have been thinking . . . about what you said. Perhaps I have been too quick to give up. Perhaps it is time to write again."

"That is wonderful to hear," says Weiwei, squeezing his fingers, though she fears his mind is wandering. "When you are better, I will help you, like I used to."

His face folds into a frown. "I didn't tell them anything. They wanted to know . . . They fear that you are not who you say . . ." He blinks. "Weiwei?"

She smiles at him, trying not to show her concern at his drawn face, the confusion in his mind. "Has someone else visited you?"

"I forget her name . . . Dressed in black . . ." He yawns, and Weiwei smells a sweetness on him that she recognizes.

"Marya . . ." she says. "A passenger from First—was it her?"

"Tell her to be careful." His eyes are closing.

She waits, but his breathing is regular and deep. Gently, she rolls up his right sleeve. There, in the papery skin at the top of his arm, is a cluster of puncture marks.

Back outside the doctor's cabin, she presses her forehead against the window. She should have visited him sooner. Is he really ill enough to be drugged? She knows it can be the kindest thing, to stop sufferers from hurting themselves. Or is there another reason, to do with his visit from the widow? Weiwei scratches at her damp collar. The changed rhythm of the unfamiliar rails makes it difficult to think. Marya Petrovna, always asking questions, always where she shouldn't be. *They fear she is not who she says she is . . .* She could go to First right now, pass on the warning and demand to know what it is she wants. But perhaps she should not show her hand so soon. What if the widow was trying to get information out of the Professor . . . Could she know who he really is? Weiwei thinks of the Professor's unfocused eyes, the frailty of his hand in hers and she feels an irresistible urge to find a quiet space to curl up and screw her eyes shut. She is so tired, and she doesn't know what she should do. Without the Captain, without the Professor, she is just—what? A rail rat. A nobody.

A soft noise makes her look up. Dima is padding down the corridor in the direction of the service car, his nose to the floor, tail raised and alert.

"Dima, Dimochka . . ." She crouches down but he ignores her and walks straight past, with an air of determination. She sits back on her heels, feeling, absurdly, tears prickling at her eyes. But then she smells it—the damp, musty smell she associates with Elena, and she sees, if she looks closely, damp patches on the carpet, thin ribbons of weeds. She curses, rubbing at the carpet with her feet and stuffing the weeds into her pockets, hoping that they haven't been noticed yet. The passengers had known Elena was there, she remembers—during the storm, they had felt her presence. And Grey. Henry Grey had seen her. Would they believe what he saw? It doesn't matter—rumors and fear spread as fast as the train itself. Faster. They would all be watching, now, for Grey's visitor; *angel, ghost, monster.*

She follows Dima to the storage carriage, where he stops just outside the door and begins to wash himself, with an air of studied unconcern. "Thank you, Dimochka," she says, rubbing his head.

Elena is sitting on the floor of the carriage, open boxes and spilled goods all around her.

"No! We can't let anyone know we've been here." Weiwei starts to tidy up, but Elena tugs on her sleeve. There are marks now like greenish bruises on her skin, and her lips are dry and flaking.

"We are moving so *slowly*. When will there be speed again?"

"We've no choice, we don't know if these rails are safe. It won't be for long." Weiwei tries to keep the doubt from her voice.

"We must play! It is my turn—no, it is your turn—you must reach the cab. Look—I will hide here and watch—"

"Elena, no." Weiwei takes her hands, feeling their clamminess. "No." She holds on, as if she could root the stowaway in place. "Someone saw you. A passenger saw you. You have to stay hidden. Do you understand? No more walking the corridors."

But Elena has already darted out of the door. "There is no one here! I will play—you can watch."

There is a feverishness to her now, a restless energy that Weiwei associates with those afflicted by the sickness. She has seen it sometimes, before an attempt to wrest open the doors to the outside, to pull and pull at the lock until they collapse, out of exhaustion or the needle of a syringe.

"Come back," Weiwei whispers as gently as she can, then sees Elena's attention sliding away, to the window beyond. "What is it?"

"Nothing, nothing. Come. I will hide, you must find me."

"Wait—"

Outside, a black dog is slipping past, its yellow eyes turned toward the train. *No,* she thinks, *a fox*—its ears and tail pointed. As she watches, another emerges, like a shadow sliding free from its owner, then another, and another, one becoming two becoming four until there is a sea of lithe bodies beside them, keeping pace with the train, flashes of silver, of rust red in their coats. *They are beautiful,* she thinks. They are not like the foxes in the city; they are bigger, sleeker; they seem to slip in and out of time—you can't follow a single creature, your eyes won't let you, even though theirs are fixed on the train.

"You mustn't look," says Elena, tugging on her arm, an odd cadence in her voice. "You must pretend not to see."

"They can't harm us, we're safe in here." Their pupils are a dark, vertical line. Their eyelids close sideways, like a lizard's. *They are watching me,* she thinks. *No—they are watching Elena.*

"*Please.*" She pulls so hard that Weiwei falls backward, banging her head against the wall. Elena crouches down beside her, remorse on her face. "I'm sorry," she says. "I'm sorry."

"What's wrong? Please tell me." Weiwei rubs her head. "It's not just the water, is it?"

"I told you," whispers Elena. "I don't know what I am anymore. Since I followed the rail, since I started to watch, and learn . . . And *they* do not know what I am, either."

Weiwei half expects to see the foxes' snouts at the window, their eyes staring in.

Elena says, "I can't hear them anymore, I can't feel them. I don't know whether they are taunting me or calling me back."

2

SECRETS

Marya has retreated to the library carriage. She can't bear to be shut up in her cabin any longer, but she is grateful to escape the nervous chatter of her fellow passengers. Relief at outrunning the storm has turned to anxiety and to bitter complaints about the slowness of their journey and the stricter rationing of water. The crew are trying to present a picture of calm competency, but she can see cracks appearing. The elderly steward who is usually on duty in the library carriage is missing, perhaps because the fans in the library carriage seem even more sluggish than those elsewhere, simply pushing the hot air around. She sinks into a chair by the window. It is like breathing in an oven, but it is worth the discomfort for the blissful solitude.

The Crows have been watching her, she is sure of it.

Outside, the birches cluster close to the train and she thinks she sees glimpses of yellow-eyed foxes weaving their way between the trunks. Now that they have left the main line behind, and the comfort of Rostov's guide, she cannot help but feel as though a chain has been broken, a safety line cut. She taps at the glass with her fingernail. She has found no other windows that contain the signature of her father's glassworks, but still—that one is enough. She wishes she could go back to talk again to the Professor. What else does he know? There is more, she is sure of it. In fact, she feels a growing conviction that she knows exactly who he is. *"The only truth that matters."* Hadn't Artemis written those same words? What better place to hide than on the train itself, behind the scholarly persona of the Professor, so obvious that it was impossible to see? But she hasn't dared go back to visit him. She hadn't liked how the Crows had appeared; she hadn't liked the thoughtful way they had regarded them both. What if she had led them to Artemis? Hidden right before their eyes this whole time, what if she had uncovered him at last for them? It makes her sick to think of it. And yet, with the sense that their eyes are upon her, she hasn't been able to search the train any further.

It is a moment before she realizes that someone is saying her name, and she turns around with a start.

Suzuki looks apologetic. "I'm sorry. You were looking out so intently."

Recovering herself, she says, "I wasn't disappearing, don't worry. I am armed against it." She opens her palm to show him the glass marble with its swirl of blue. It is warm to the touch, as if she had been gripping it tightly, though she had hardly been aware that she had taken it out.

"Ah." He looks closely. "You must be honored—there are not many people with whom Weiwei would share one of these."

"Really? I had the impression that she found me quite tiresome."

Suzuki laughs. "An impression she has cultivated carefully. They were made for her when she was very small," he goes on. "By our glassmaker. Of course, the crew all cursed him, when they found them under their feet at the most inconvenient of times."

She curls her fingers around the marble. Is there something there, behind his words? She is afraid to raise her eyes—because of what he might see on her face, or what she might see on his?

"Forgive me, I hope I haven't—"

"No, no." She looks up and smiles. And all she sees in his face is concern; worry that he has said the wrong thing. He holds her gaze, and she feels as if a thread between them is being pulled taut.

"There must be interesting research to be done, on these old rails," she begins, at the same time as Suzuki says, "I had hoped to see you—"

They both stop.

"The Company men, Petrov and Li, have been asking questions about you," says Suzuki. "I thought you should know."

"I see" is all she can think of to say.

"They have been preoccupied, these past months, with protecting the good name of the Company. It has perhaps made them rather quick to judge. Although," he adds, "they have always had an untrusting turn of mind."

He takes a step closer to her, and there is worry in his dark eyes. "What I mean is that you should be careful. Whatever it is you want, you should be careful how you go about getting it." She thinks he is going to reach out and take her hand but he draws back.

"I—"

She stops, as the door is flung open and the elderly steward hurries into the carriage, heaving himself into a seat at the far end.

"I fear I am neglecting my duties," says Suzuki, his posture stiffening.

"Of course, you must be busier than ever," she says, quickly.

He bows, and turns to leave, then hesitates.

"I have asked Mr. Petrov and Mr. Li to come to the tower," he says, without turning around. "It seems right that the Company observes the state of the maps for themselves. I imagine that it will take at least half an hour to fully explain the situation."

She looks at his back. It gives nothing away.

"I see," she says, again.

Marya stops at her own cabin, rummaging in her jewelry box and wondering what on earth she is thinking. Had she understood Suzuki's meaning? Yes, she is sure. He is giving her time—an opportunity to act unnoticed, unseen. But his motivation—that she does not understand.

No time to worry now—here it is, a special hairpin, bent just so, the fruits of a childhood spent rebelling against the locked doors and silences of her family home. She has kept it with her ever since, waiting for the time when she would have as much bravery as she had when she was younger. *Now,* she tells herself, to calm her shaking hands. *Now it is time.*

She walks to the farthest end of the carriage, to the cabin with a silver 12 inlaid on the door. Marya puts her ear close to the polished wood and hears no sound from within. She takes a last look down the corridor, then takes the hairpin and fits it into the lock. It is the work of moments to hear a click and slip into the cabin, closing the door behind her.

She is in a cabin suite, bigger than her own, with two doors off to one side. There is a large desk in the center of the main room, with a chair on either side, and rows of shelves around the walls. She wants to sit down at the tidy walnut desk and score deep black lines of ink through all of their papers, to say *I was here.*

"Concentrate," she whispers to herself. There is no telling how long Suzuki will be able to keep the Crows away. But while she flinches at every creak, freezes as her skirts brush against the table and set it rattling, there is also a part of her that is thrilled. The secrecy, the risk. She shuffles through the papers on the desk but finds nothing incriminating. Though how would she understand it, even if she did? All these names and figures in tidy copperplate mean nothing to her. The ledgers on the bookshelves are equally opaque but she recognizes some of the names—ministers for the treasury, for the Department of Ways and Communications. *All in the deep pockets of the Company,* she thinks.

She crouches down to open a cupboard. Inside are at least six large flasks—each of them filled with water. Her lip curls. The Crows have not been going thirsty, of course they haven't—the Company takes what it wants.

There is a framed map on the wall. At its center, picked out in gold, is the line of the rail, joining the continents. And from the rail countless other lines of different colors stretch out, threads linking the cities of the world. The lines of the rail and the sea. Here you can trace the routes of the goods the train carries, taking porcelain and tea from the west of China to Beijing to Moscow then Paris, Rome, New York. Taking wool from England to Beijing. Threads of power and plenty. No wonder the Company has been so desperate for the train to run again.

She has been trying not to look outside, afraid of disappearing into that dangerous, dream-like state, but a flash of sunlight catches her eye and she sees something shimmering up ahead, through the trees. Water. This must be why the train is slowing. She must move faster.

She hurries over to the ledgers on the shelves. All contain columns of goods and figures. She screws up her nose and wishes she had paid more attention to Artemis's columns. There have been accusations of corruption, of silks and ceramics vanishing before reaching Moscow, of funds diverted, lost between one ledger and another, though nothing is ever proved. She glances at the clock on the wall. She has been in here for a quarter of an hour already.

She opens a box file, one that had been tucked away in a corner. Page after page of reports, all meaningless, then at the very bottom—

—her father's handwriting.

She takes out the flimsy sheets, trying to keep her hands steady. They are clipped behind a letter written on much better quality paper and bearing the logo of the Trans-Siberia Company. The letter is written in English and addressed to *Messrs Li and Petrov*. It is one line long and signed by the Chairman of the Board. *Dear Sirs,* it says. *The following has come to our attention. We trust it to your experience and discretion.*

She turns to the attached pages. She makes out the date—just before the final crossing—and that the letter is addressed from her father to the Board of the Trans-Siberia Company, but the words and phrases dance in front of her eyes: *The new lenses, along with the photographic records, have provided irrefutable proof of the increasing rate of change, which correlates with the increase in crossings. There can no longer be any doubt that the train itself is causing specific and localized changes. We have advised a reduction in the number of crossings but to no avail.*

A warning to the Company. Her father had seen that there was danger already—even before the last crossing.

A jolt of the train makes her lose her balance. Are they slowing down further? She forces herself to take in more of the words. *I cannot in all good faith keep silent, when the safety of hundreds of lives is at stake.*

Not just a warning—a threat.

She hears knocking on cabin doors down the corridor, the sound of footsteps hurrying past, and she quickly folds the papers and hides them in her bodice, returning the file to its corner. She slips out of the cabin, locking the door carefully behind her.

We trust it to your experience and discretion.

3
PRAYERS

Here is Henry Grey, on his knees. Surrounding him on the floor of his cabin, a carpet of sketches. The train-like creatures wind between sheets of paper, sometimes disappearing beneath skeletal trees, profusions of flowers. And among them, a small figure emerges, again and again. Henry Grey is prayerful, his mind is clear. He had asked for a sign and a sign was given. Patience, this is all he needs. An answer will appear, he knows it now. He heaves himself to his feet, the pain in his stomach burning. Outside, the air ripples in the heat. The sun catches a brightness in the distance, through the trees, as if the land is turning to glass, earth melting into water. As in John Morland's poem: *in water the mirror of the Heavens*.

A knock on the door. "Who's there?" he says impatiently.

"Let me in." It is the low voice of the engineer, Alexei.

When he opens the door, the engineer shuts it behind him, quickly. In one hand he holds a set of keys. In the other, a small dart gun, the kind that Grey has seen in locked glass cases on the walls of the train.

"The train is going to stop," he says, without waiting for Grey to speak. "There's a lake up ahead and we're going to gauge its depth. I can give you an hour."

Grey feels a light suffusing him. A glorious certainty. He puts his hands on the engineer's shoulders. "You have made the right choice," he says. "Your part in this will not be forgotten." He feels a fraternal bond so strong that it brings tears to his eyes.

"You'll use the last door in this carriage, just before the dining car," says Alexei, brusquely. "I'll make sure everyone is looking in another direction. You have to make sure the suit and helmet are fitted tightly. You know the dangers."

"I understand."

He holds up the keys. "Each of the double doors has a key, and each key requires a different combination, so you have to listen carefully. The silver key unlocks the inner door—two clicks to the left and five to the right. The gold key unlocks the outer door—four clicks to the right and six to the left."

Grey writes it down.

"And this." Alexei holds out the dart gun. "It will tranquilize, only—it's what's used on board when there's bad cases of the sickness, passengers harming themselves or the train. You load it like this." He takes out a small vial and syringe and locks it into the gun. "It's no use on anything big and fast, but it'll give you some measure of protection. And here are all the vials I could take without attracting notice." He hands them over, and Grey sets them down carefully on the table. "I can give you an hour only. And I can't guarantee the consequences, if the Company finds out. But there'll be no mention of my name, is that clear?"

"Quite clear, there is no need to worry."

The engineer puts the keys down. Then he's gone, the expression on his face far different than that of the uncertain young man Grey had first met.

Grey clasps his hands around the keys and the gun as if they are holy relics. He gives thanks. The train begins to slow and he goes to stand at the window. Ahead, he sees sunlight on water. *Signs and blessings in abundance.*

4

WRAITHS

Water. Shimmering through the trees. Weiwei can feel the crew holding their breath as it gets closer. Water for the engine, water to tide them over until they get back onto the main line. Yet the risks of using it, even if only for the furnace, are so great . . . Wastelands water, untested, unknown. Who knows what changes it may bring? Pressing her face to the window, she can see that the ground is soft and damp, grass and soil glistening. Ahead, a birch tree forest seems to emerge from a shallow lake. She realizes she is holding the handrail so tight her fingers ache.

The train is going to stop. For the first time that any of them can remember, it is going to stop. The air in every carriage is thick with tension. *The train is going to stop.*

When the water was sighted her first thought had been to rush to the stowaway and tell her the news—*It is almost over, soon you will be well again*—but she had held back. What if the water was deemed too badly tainted, the risk too great? She couldn't bear to think of the look on Elena's face. But there is another sneaking, selfish thought—*"I don't know whether they are taunting me or calling me back,"* Elena had said. If she saw the water, if she felt its pull . . . Weiwei tries to put it from her mind.

"Who's going out?" she demands, when she sees Alexei in the crew mess. Someone will go to gauge the depth, to bring back a sample for Suzuki to test. "One of the Repairmen?"

"The Captain," he says, a strained look on his face.

"What? But surely, she wouldn't—" It's protocol for the Captain always to stay on the train. She is too important to risk.

"She's insisting on it. Now, of all times, to finally decide to show herself." He shakes his head.

"But . . ." She feels sick. The train stopping, here on the ghost rails, here where they do not even have Suzuki's maps to guide them. "How can she leave? She's needed here, the passengers are already terrified."

"Hasn't she left already? Did she ever arrive?"

She is taken aback by the venom in his voice.

In Third, as expected, the passengers are frightened and demanding, but the promise of water helps to calm them down. She hopes it is a promise they can keep. She leaves the steward to deal with the passengers and slips away toward First, intending to finally find Marya.

The First Class passengers are being gathered together in the saloon car, the Countess demanding loudly why they are to be treated like children, the stewards wearing expressions of strained patience.

"Have you seen Marya Petrovna?" Weiwei asks.

"I have not seen her since breakfast," says the Countess. "I'm afraid she was suffering from a headache and retired to her cabin."

But Weiwei has already knocked, and the young widow was not there. "Ah," she says, "I will check on her," dropping her eyes under the Countess's scrutiny.

The stewards nod at her. They are closing the curtains. "For your safety, ma'am," they say, before the Countess has time to object. "It is best not to look." *Or be looked at.*

Weiwei sets off back toward the crew carriages, closing curtains on her way, even though there are no passengers now in the corridors. She doesn't want to see, either. All around them is water, dripping from branches and leaves, pooling on the ground, catching the colors of the sky and the trees but other colors as well, ones which aren't there and which her eyes don't understand.

She is about to close the final set of curtains in the Third Class dining car when she smells it. "Elena . . ." Weiwei spins around, not sure whether to be worried or relieved.

"Have you seen them?" There is a spiderweb of dark veins blooming on Elena's skin, the whites of her eyes have turned watery green, her pupils huge and black.

Decaying, thinks Weiwei, forcing herself not to recoil. "You're not well," she begins, but Elena interrupts her.

"Look," she says, pointing outside. "They are waiting."

Weiwei looks. There between the trees is just a flicker, at first, something that could have been dust kicked up by the train, before resolving into something more; the outline of a figure—no, not even that; more like the memory of a figure, as though a thousand specks of dust had gathered together into the idea, the echo, of a human, right down to its hair ruffled by an absent wind, its clothes flapping around it. It looks straight at the train. And then—impossibly—it raises its arm. As if in an echo of Elena's.

Weiwei steps backward, she can't help herself. The train is moving so slowly now that she can see other wraiths appearing, like figures emerging from a painting, solid from a distance but close up just a collection of brushstrokes and dots.

She thinks they are beckoning.

"You mustn't look, you told me that yourself." Weiwei takes Elena by the shoulders, feeling bone jutting beneath the skin, feeling flakes of skin dry beneath her touch. "They are just a Wastelands trick. If you don't look they can't hurt you."

But Elena is looking and there is a terrible hunger on her face and Weiwei remembers her words when they saw the foxes—*"I can't hear them anymore, I can't feel them"*—and she opens her mouth to say, *No, it doesn't matter, this is where you belong now,* but it is too late, Elena is retreating, closing in on herself.

"Wait—" But the stowaway is fleeing the carriage in a tangle of hair and limbs. "Elena, stop!" But she is gone, and Weiwei stumbles into the doorframe as the carriage jolts and wheezes, as the brakes shriek, as the train heaves itself to a halt.

5

STOPPED

The great train has stopped. All the power they thought they had seems to dissolve in the air with the last of the steam. The passengers hold themselves still, as if afraid that their movement will draw the attention of all the curious, watchful, hungry things outside. The crew keep the curtains closed. Best not to see or be seen. Best not to think of how small they are; how the train, stopped out here in the vastness, is not as great as they tell themselves, as they boast to the passengers. All boasts are meaningless here. All promises waiting to be broken.

Marya, at the window of her cabin, holds her father's letter in her hands, and although the train no longer moves she has to force the words to be still. She cannot understand all the details, but there is enough here to clear his name—to show that he had desperately tried to get the Company to understand the danger the train was in—that it was *causing*. This, together with the signature on the glass, must surely be enough. When they reach Moscow, she will follow her father's lead and go straight to the newspapers. Or perhaps, if the Professor really is Artemis, she could persuade him to take up his pen once more.

If they reach Moscow, she thinks.

Her father had tried to stop the train from running. He had known it wasn't safe.

I cannot in all good faith keep silent, he wrote. *What I have seen weighs on my mind more heavily day by day.*

She leans her forehead on the glass.

Henry Grey, his movements clumsy in his borrowed suit and helmet, fits the key into the first door. What if the engineer had never set the combination at all? What if all this was for nothing? He closes his eyes. To be so close, only to let it slip away . . . *"Two clicks to the left and five to the right"*—and the door opens. He steps into a small space, shuts the door behind him. Now, the outside door. *"Four clicks to the right and six to the left."* A thud of machinery, and it is done, the door is opening, he is stepping down, his feet, in their thick boots, touching untouched ground.

An explorer into Eden.

Weiwei, rushing headlong through the carriages toward the storage car, toward the skylight, toward where she knows, instinctively, the stowaway is fleeing. How fast can Elena run? Fast. Much faster than Weiwei can, and here, blocking her path, a crowd around a window in the crew mess.

"There—there she is."

They are watching a slow-moving figure in a suit and helmet, a long cord attaching her to the train. The Captain, carrying glass vials and a measuring stick.

"It shouldn't have been her," mutters one of the engineers.

"She insisted. Wouldn't ask anyone else to take the risk, she said."

No one asks—*What if the water is too deep for the train? What if it is tested and found to be unsafe?* Better to keep silent and pray to the gods of the rail. And Weiwei thinks, as she tries to wriggle past, unseen—*there is still pride in their voices.* They still revere their Captain, still want to believe that she will make everything right.

"Miss Zhang." A voice stops her in her tracks. She closes her eyes, and considers just keeping on running, but the Crows are in her way. "Where are you running to so fast?"

"There is no need to worry." They look down on her. "The Captain is protected by the gunner, she will be quite safe."

But the Crows are not quite managing to hide the worry from their own faces. *They are losing control,* she thinks.

"Urgent errand for a passenger," she says. "Need to get through to the storage car. A passenger from First Class."

They look at her for a moment longer than necessary, then part to let her through, but then Alexei is calling her urgently, and she has to stop herself from sobbing in frustration. "This way, look," he is saying, but she doesn't, she looks back at the opposite side, and so she is the only one who sees another figure leap awkwardly from the train, weighed down by jars and nets and boxes.

Henry Grey.

She hesitates. Then she sees a sudden movement closer to the train. A flash of blue, of matted hair and pale skin, and then it is gone, and she knows she has failed and she feels her legs threatening to give way beneath her. Elena is thirsty and panicked—if Grey sees her before she reaches water she will not be able to hide herself. He will catch her in his nets like one of his specimens. He will trap her and keep her behind glass.

Marya isn't sure where she is going, only that there are no safe hiding places in her own cabin. Her father had warned the Company and been ignored. Not just ignored—scapegoated, ruined. They will know the letter is missing. They already suspect her. She must make it difficult for them to catch up.

I cannot in all good faith keep silent.

And Suzuki, she thinks. *Suzuki must have known it too, but he didn't speak up.* She feels her chest tighten. Why hadn't he defended her father? And had he known that she would come here, that she would find this letter? Did he know who she really was?

Her feet carry her into the saloon car.

"There you are! You must come and join us, we have taken to

gambling to distract ourselves, it is the only way." The Countess beckons her over, and she goes to sit by her side, picks up the cards she is given, looks at them without seeing.

When no one is looking, she takes the letter from her bodice and slips it as far down the side of her chair as it will go.

After a while, Sophie LaFontaine looks up from her cards and says, "But where is Dr. Grey?"

Weiwei has banged on the window, shouted the alarm, there is confusion all around her.

"Who is that—"

"How did they get out?"

"How did they get a suit?"

"Henry Grey," she says, her voice sounding as if it is coming from very far away. "The naturalist. I've seen those jars in his cabin."

She sees the color drain from Alexei's face.

"He's going to get the Captain killed."

"He'll be killed himself . . ."

How long has it been, now? How far could Elena have got? The walls of the train seem to be softening like treacle and she feels hollow inside. When did she last eat? She can't remember.

"Let me go out. I will fetch him back." She will catch him and keep him away from Elena, that is all she can do now. She tries to ignore the little voice that says, *Or you can leave him to take his chances. You can find Elena. You can beg her to come back.*

A moment of silence, then uproar again as they all start arguing.

"Don't be ridiculous, Zhang, I'll go." Alexei is looking at her as if he's seen a ghost. "We don't have another cord, it's far too dangerous."

"No. She is right." Petrov and Li, silencing the arguments. "We cannot allow our chief engineer to leave the train at this delicate time, but Miss Zhang has proved herself to be quick and resourceful. Her size and speed will give her an advantage." They turn calculating eyes upon her, their thoughts so easy to read it is almost laughable, and she would be angry at how little they value her safety, but for it being the only thing that will let her out.

"Though we would not, of course, ask her to take such a risk unless she is sure—"

"Of course she's not sure, she doesn't know what she's talking about." Alexei's voice rises.

"Please," she says. "We are wasting time."

It takes three of them to help her into the suit. It is far too big, it weighs her down, makes it difficult to breathe. Through the smeared glass of the helmet she sees Alexei—silent, retreating; miserable.

"You don't have to do this," he says. "They can't ask you to, they have no right." His voice is muffled. The helmet makes everything seem far away and not quite real.

She wants to say something to reassure him but the panicked hammering of her heart makes it hard to think. *How long has it been now? Has he seen her? Or has she vanished into the water, into the woods?* The Crows are watching her, their hands clasped in front of them.

"If the Professor knew . . ." says Alexei, his voice cracking.

"We'll tell him about it afterward," she says. "It will make a good story."

"Don't lose sight of the rail," he says. "Without the cord you're on your own. You can't trust the landscape. Only the rail. Do you understand? Just keep the rail in sight. And if you haven't found him by the time the sun gets to the top of those trees"—he points out of the window at the highest birches—"you come back, is that clear?"

She nods, clumsily, and he steps toward her, then seems to think better of it. "Just come back."

The others help her to the first of the locked doors, open it for her with a gallantry that makes her want to laugh. She is handed the key, she hasn't put her gloves on yet. And then the door is closing and they are watching her as it shuts with a heavy thump. She puts the key in the outer door and with a prayer to the god of the rail she steps down into the Wastelands.

6

OUTSIDE

Henry Grey is hunched up under the sun, running awkwardly through the grass, his knees complaining. Days of stillness have left him aching and stiff, and the dart gun tucked in his belt is digging into his side. It is a physical shock, the sound of it all, even muffled by his helmet; the harsh cries and melodic song of birds he does not recognize, the whirring and buzzing of insects around him and he wants to capture it all, to keep it and study it and learn, but there is far too much, he cannot possibly hold it in his hands.

He has no need now for spoken prayers, for what is this but an act of praise? Sunlight through the leaves dapples the ground. He looks up at the trees—silver birches, their pale bark shedding like delicate paper. How apt, a symbol of purity. But no. What he'd taken as the fissures of aging bark are streaks of deep red, thick and oozing. It is sap, he realizes, red sap, as though the trees are bleeding. That a landscape may be so imbued with meaning—how can one not see symbolism here? He reaches into his knapsack for a glass vial and pipette, hands shaking in excitement. But the red sap seems to withdraw from his touch—the moment he places the pipette close it coils back on itself. He stares. Perhaps it is the brightness of the sun, an optical illusion. But no matter how hard he tries, he collects no sap. Extraordinary . . . Is it protecting itself? Protecting the tree? Frustrating, but nonetheless fascinating. Yet time is too precious, he cannot afford to linger when there are other wonders to discover.

He veers away from the track, but not too far. He has thought little of his return. That will come later. For now, he takes out his traps and his nets. The edge of a body of water, that is always a rich place to be, and if he stays very still, yes, just like this, they come to perch on his arms, to investigate his boots—species of dragonflies, beetles, hoverflies, all unknown, unknown to *anyone*. Translucent wings flicker near his cheek; delicate legs brush across his jacket. Any of them could bring death; instantaneous or drawn-out, agonizing. He thinks about the maps he has pored over. Before the changes, this region was arable land, forest, lakes. You could have found death, perhaps, in the malarial swamps, but no other small creature could kill you. Now, though, who knows what poison the miniscule bodies of these flies contain, what toxins these delicate feet might leave on your skin?

He should be afraid. But he knows how to be still, he knows about mimicry—borrow the appearance of a predator to keep enemies away. Or borrow the appearance of something benign; make yourself into a rock or a tree, this is what he learned to do over many years on the moors back home; to slow his breathing, slow his movements, so these creatures who live so quickly do not perceive him as living at all.

Something brushes across his helmet. He swipes at it, suddenly panicked. Just a vine. He feels a stab of embarrassment, then allows himself a smile at its absurdity—the social burden of an Englishman. The vines drip from branches all around, glistening red. They look like giant spiderwebs, hanging in complex patterns between the trees, shining in what thin sunlight pierces through the branches. No, spiderwebs are the wrong analogy, there is no careful symmetry here, no patient repetitions; they are terrifying in their irregularity, their arbitrariness. Nature is deliberate, he understands this; it is *mathematical*. But not here.

A rustling from above. He looks up in time to see a huge bird, pale and ghostly, fly through the top-most level of the trees, wings tipping and turning to navigate the branches. He wipes at the glass of the helmet, frustrated by the way it deadens all sound. He wants to feel the air on his face; he wants to smell and touch it all, and he cannot help himself—he takes off his helmet. Instantly, he is overwhelmed by a myriad of scents, dazzled by the cacophony of birdsong. He gazes upward. The bird's beak is sharp and curved and dripping red, and he watches in fascination as it coughs up a thick liquid. When a long thread hangs from its beak it perches on a branch and dips it in the red sap then takes off again, flying between two trees, weaving a web of dripping silk. He scrabbles for his notebook, wishing desperately for more time. If only he could stay longer, there is so much more he could discover, so much to drink in, to smell, to touch, to pin down. But how long would be long enough? It would take a lifetime to understand it all.

Something pushes past him, hard, and he falls. The ground is full of sharp stones and twigs, and the pain brings him back to himself, tears smarting at his eyes. He looks up, his vision blurred, then falls backward. Somehow, he is right in front of the bird's web, though he can't remember walking toward it. But now there is something caught in the web, something between an insect and a bird but as big as a horse, its wings black-feathered and its body furred, though it is struggling so much that he can't fit the pieces together in his mind. Already wet and dripping in the red sap, already beginning to move more sluggishly when the pale bird swoops down headfirst from its perch, wings outstretched, glassy eyes fixed on the struggling creature in the web. There is a desperate moment of thrashing wings and stabbing red beak, of hideous cries that echo around the wood before being cut off, abruptly. Then the pale bird settles itself on the web and falls on its meal. He looks away. Whatever it was, the creature had saved him with its headlong rush into the trap.

What do the webs do? Is it a kind of hypnosis? He has heard of insects tricking their prey in this way, but never birds. The weaving of webs is itself astounding, but for them to have this effect on the mind—on the *human* mind, not only the animal . . . If he could only take back some proof. If he could show it at the Exhibition . . . Shakily, he climbs back onto his feet, ignoring the pain. An entirely new species, a previously unobserved behavior. What better illustration of New Edenic Thought?

He edges toward the web. If he can just take a sample, that's all he needs . . . He stretches out his hand—

And the trees grow wings and come to life.

Birds launch themselves upward from branch after branch with discordant shrieks until the air is full of pale wings and bright-red beaks. They soar and dive and they cough up the thick, sticky silk and Henry Grey begins to run, but glistening red threads appear across his path and settle on his hair and stick to his skin. He can't get the gun out of his belt, though he tugs and tugs, and what good would a tranquilizer dart do, anyway, against these numbers? Blinded, he plunges on, the shrieks mocking him, the sound of wings ever closer, beaks snapping as the ground beneath him gives way and he stumbles into water, gasping in shock at the cold. The threads weigh him down and the birds tear at his arms as he raises them up to protect his head. He slides farther down. He has always hated water, the dark reservoirs on the moors dead and inert, dragging the sky down into their depths. They made him feel the pull of oblivion. He is a boy again, thrashing in the shallows of a river while his schoolfellows dive and splash, taunting him, grabbing hold of his legs, trying to pull him under. He is sinking; strong arms have wrapped themselves around him, pulling him further and further down, away from the beaks and claws of the birds but toward another kind of darkness. He struggles, scrabbling at whatever is holding him but the arms grip tight. *No. Not like this, knowing I have failed . . .* He tries to open his eyes in the murky water, but it is hard to see anything at all and blackness is gathering at the edges of his vision. Weeds float before him, hair-like, a flash of iridescence.

Then—firm arms around him, lifting him up, lifting him out of the pool and setting him down on the ground. Weeds and water becoming human-like. Woman-like. No, a fragment of a dream. His lungs ache. A hand on his face, at his lips. He gasps for breath, coughing up water. How is it possible he is saved? He grasps for the hand, feels a slim wrist, catches a glimpse of skin and eyes. Human but not human. Familiar. He knows this figure, he saw it in the storm. A vision, he had thought, but now he sees that he was wrong. A Wastelands creature.

7

IN THE WILDERNESS

The child of the train, stumbling toward the trees, her suit weighing her down, her steps clumsy. She looks backward at the train. She has never seen it from this distance before, never seen it out of the station, and it has always seemed impossibly huge, dwarfing everything around it. Yet now she sees it diminished beneath the Wastelands sky. Glints of light from the watchtowers—they watch her through their lenses, through their sights. They watch for movement around her.

She turns, keeps walking, trying to ignore the pull of it, the wrongness of walking away. But once it is out of sight, she pulls off her helmet, gasping in relief then recoiling at the assault of sounds and smells. She should be afraid. She *is* afraid. But in spite of it all she can't help but feel a burst of sheer exhilaration. The freedom, the space. And the colors—brighter than they seemed from behind glass, more vivid, more *here*. She could drink them up with her eyes; the clear blue, the extravagant green, the flitting, buzzing, darting life; flying creatures like delicate jewels, their wings like the glass in Moscow churches.

Elena would go straight toward the water. What about Grey? Surely he would be trying to avoid the Captain, keeping away from where the rails meet the water, where the Captain would be gauging the depth, collecting samples for Suzuki to test. No, they would both be leaving the rails behind, keeping themselves hidden within the trees, where other pools glisten. Weiwei looks around, helplessly. In the heat and the noise her clarity of purpose is leaking away. It had seemed simple, when she was watching from the windows. Find Grey. Keep him away from Elena, to give her time to find water; to regain her strength. *But that isn't all, is it?* Now, outside, that other, selfish desire asserts itself. *You just don't want her to leave you.* She feels a sudden dizziness and puts her hand out to the tree, then recoils at the sight of its red sap.

She feels as if the landscape is watching her, reaching out to touch her skin, curious, *hungry*. She feels each blade of grass as if it is humming.

Further into the trees, her feet sinking into the ground as it dips down toward the water. Branches arch overhead like a high, vaulted ceiling, light filtering through the leaves to become green and gold, and the water turns it all into motion, the world wavering, never still.

She can already feel herself losing track of the minutes that have passed. It seems that her life has always been driven by chimes and clocks and timetables but not now, not out here. Here she has lost the certainty of time.

She tucks her helmet under her arm and looks more closely at the boggy ground. What she had taken to be white twigs scattered all around beneath the trees are not twigs at all but bones. Big bones and small bones and things that could only be teeth. Her first instinct is to run but she forces herself to steady her breathing, to stay rooted to the ground. Insects drone around her, bumping into her face. There is a sweet, sickly smell mixing with her own sweat. She has always liked being small. Being small lets you slip through the world unnoticed, lets you hide and sneak and stay safe. But here in the trees she feels far too small to be safe. She has never been alone and here she is very alone, surrounded by so *much* of everything else. So many insects and bones and buzzings, so many trees, rising above her too high, and she is too small and too human, too out of place.

Howls from somewhere close by. She hears them and thinks, *Something is being consumed*—and it fills her with the mindless, primitive urge to flee. The howls come from further into the trees and she runs in the opposite direction because whatever Alexei says of her, she has not completely taken leave of her senses. She runs until she is forced to stop, her lungs burning. Around her, the trees have changed. They are misshapen, strangely colored, covered in growths that seem to glisten and drip, turquoise and yellow and orange. They are hard to look at, like something from a fever dream. She edges closer and sees that the growths are not the trees themselves, but lichen, bigger and brighter than anything she has seen before. Lichen that seems to be growing before her eyes, pulsing and multiplying, growth upon growth. She blinks, rapidly. It reminds her of the colored glass on the train, but as hard and bright as if the glass had suddenly come to life, begun to move of its own accord. Watching it makes her head swim. She tears her gaze away but realizes that she has lost sight of the rail. She's not sure how it happened. It had been there, on her right, but she had got turned around somehow and now it is gone. Where had the howls come from? Her legs are aching and her breath is ragged in her chest. How did she ever think she could simply walk into the unknown? What right did she have?

But then she glimpses familiar shapes through the trees; human shapes, and though she knows she can't trust her own eyes, she starts to run toward them and as she draws nearer and their forms shift into meaning she stumbles, stops.

Elena is leaning over the prone form of Henry Grey. Her hair hangs down around his face, obscuring her own, and her posture makes Weiwei think about predators, and prey, about that first meeting in the dark of the storage car. She had felt it then, the presence of something watchful, hungry, strong. Inhuman. She had felt it in the hand pulling her down toward the bath water, seen it in the reflection of the not-quite-girl in the glass.

Weiwei takes a step back. She looks at Grey, his skin very pale, his eyes closed. Around him, thin white stalks are emerging out of the soil, questing toward him, and Elena is leaning closer and Weiwei can't stop herself from saying, "Don't—"

Elena jerks her head up, her eyes wide, her pupils dilated. Weiwei takes another step backward, opening her mouth to say Elena's name but the word dies on her lips. The stowaway's gaze has not left her face.

The birds have gone silent. Insects hover in the air, noiseless. There is no wind to move the branches of the trees. Even the white threads around Henry Grey seem to have slowed their movement. Everything here is waiting.

"Don't?" Elena rises slowly to her feet, her eyes fixed on Weiwei's face.

And Weiwei can read it in Elena's expression—realization; betrayal.

"I didn't mean—"

"He will be quite well, shortly. You can take him back to the train."

"Elena, please—"

"He was attacked by birds," Elena goes on, her voice hard. "They saw that he was neither prey nor predator. They saw he was a thief."

A thief. With his nets and collecting jars.

"I thought that he would see you, that he would try and catch you. That's why I followed him. I thought he would catch you in his nets." Weiwei's voice breaks.

Elena gives a sad smile. "He couldn't catch me. The weeds would hold him fast, the birds would peck out his eyes, the water would drown him." She stops, and twists her head to one side like Weiwei has seen owls do. Listening. In the distance, another scream, inhuman.

Where is the Captain? She must be back on the train by now, Weiwei tells herself. *She is protected by the gunner, she has not ventured far from the rails. She is safe.*

"You shouldn't be here," says Elena, "neither of you should be here."

"But . . ." Now that she is in front of her again, she has forgotten all the things she wanted to say. It is different here, seeing the way that Elena is part of the landscape, how she walks confidently, barefoot across the ground. She had wanted to save her. *She does not need saving.*

"Come back with me." She can't bear it, the thought of losing her, but even as she says the words they sound weak. "Please. There is so much you wanted to see."

Elena looks her in the eye. "I don't belong there," she says. "You were scared. You thought I was harming him."

"No—"

"Yes." Then, gently, "And I understand it. I do."

"Then I could stay." The words are out of her mouth before she has had time to consider them. "I could stay here. You could teach me how to live here. I could learn."

Elena doesn't reply. She crouches down and puts her hands flat on the wet grass. Then she says, without looking up, "We killed him, your Rostov."

Weiwei can hear the wind in the branches of the trees, the hum of insects. The blood pounding in her ears.

"He came back," Elena goes on. "He was older. He came past the Wall and the guards. He wanted the wide-open spaces, he wanted the soil and the grass and the stone. He couldn't sleep, you see. He said that we called to him in his dreams, that we would not let him rest. He knelt in the grass and wept."

"I don't understand—"

"We killed him. His bones lie in the earth. He didn't belong here."

"No, no, he lost his reason, he fell into the river, he . . . No one can get past the Wall."

"There are ways, if a person is determined. But no ways to survive. Not here." She looks up. "So you see, you cannot stay."

"I don't believe you."

Grey stirs. "Come back," he mumbles, and coughs, wetly. "Please . . ."

Elena backs away. "You must help him return. There is something else out here."

"It's the Captain, she's checking the depth of the water . . ."

"No, another." Elena is utterly still. That familiar stance, poised, alert, every part of her listening. "It knows you are here."

Weiwei follows her gaze. Is that movement in the trees? A rotting smell on the air? *Is this what Rostov sensed, when he knelt in the grass and wept? Did he wait for the earth to embrace him? Was he afraid?*

"I will lead it away," says Elena. "You must get him back to the train." She looks at Grey. "He must not take anything. It is not his to take."

"Wait—"

"There is something coming, Weiwei." There is fear on her face, and she begins to run. "*Go!*"

Weiwei is rooted to the ground. Now that Elena has gone, the noises around her are growing more urgent, but she can't make herself move. The trees seem to be growing around her, their branches lengthening, reaching out, there is water bubbling up from the soil; a ring of tiny mushrooms, bone white, have fruited on the toe of her boot—

Grey's retching brings her back.

She shakes her foot with a yelp and jumps away from the marshy ground.

"She was here . . ." He is on his hands and knees. He tries to look around but slumps back down. He doesn't seem to question what Weiwei is doing out here, as if he were taking it for granted that a crew member would be waiting to serve him, even after he has broken every rule of the train. "Did you see her? You have to help me find her . . . She is the proof I have needed . . ."

She feels a wave of revulsion for him. How dare he speak of Elena as *proof*? How dare he speak of her at all? As if she is something he could possess, as if he had any right to her. She pictures herself leaving him here—"*He ran into the forest alone, there was nothing I could do*"—and letting the Wastelands creatures have him. She feels the pull of it, how easy it would be. His vanishing would let Elena vanish too. It would keep her safe from all the other curious men who might come later.

"Please," he begs. Curled on the ground, mud on his face.

She grabs his arm and pulls. "We have to go. There was no one here. You fell in the water."

"No, she saved me, a creature like . . . Some kind of . . . She was extraordinary." He heaves himself up.

"They say the Wastelands make you imagine strange things, sir," she says. "Don't they? It makes your mind play tricks on you." She looks around for her helmet, puts it back on.

"You don't understand," says Grey, "I was drowning—no, they were attacking me, the birds, I was in the water—"

"Sir," she says, crouching down beside him. "You've had a bad shock but we have to get back to the train, it's not safe."

He scrabbles around on the ground, his fingers pulling at the fruiting bodies.

"We need to go," she says, more loudly, but he clutches at her arm.

"There are things here, wonderful things. Don't you want them to be saved?" She tries to pull away but he holds her tight. "You understand, don't you? Don't you want to hold it in your hands? We have a duty to study it . . . to make sense of it."

She wants to get away from him, from his desperate need; from the kinship he seems to feel with her.

"It's already tried to kill you," she whispers. "Everything here is hungry."

But he is hungry himself, starving. She can see it in his eyes, the same light that Elena had when she stared at the water from the train, and despite herself, she understands it.

He heaves himself to his feet, patting his pockets and bringing out a bunch of little muslin bags. "I won't collect anything large, there won't be anything that can bring harm to the train."

"It is not his to take."

She hesitates. Her eyes rest on the lichen on the trees. There is a piece that looks just like a lady's fan, in colors that remind her of Elena; the blues and the greens, the way your eyes can't quite decide what they're seeing. An ornament so beautiful you can't tear your eyes away. And she is overwhelmed by a feeling of need, a conviction that if she could only possess it, only keep it with her always, then she will have a way of filling the emptiness of Elena's absence.

Grey is breaking off pieces of the lichen and wrapping them in the bags. He takes out a box that she realizes must be a kind of trap. He waits on all fours on the ground, crouching above it. Despite his wet clothes, his mud-streaked face, despite the danger all around him, he has the air of a man who has all the time in the world.

She should stop him, but she stands back instead. And while his back is turned, she breaks off the piece of blue-green lichen, and she slips it into her pocket.

There is a roar in the distance. Something large and inhuman, in the trees. She spins to look at Grey but he is already crouching, staring up at the sky, and she realizes that she has no idea how to return to the train. She lost the path long ago, and the ground seems to have eaten up their footprints.

"Which way?" There is fear in Grey's voice.

She doesn't know. Nothing is familiar. Every time she looks in a different direction it appears new again, as if it is changing in front of their eyes. Another shriek, hoarse and high-pitched, and then they hear it—the long whistle of the train, as if in answer.

They follow the sound of the train, though it seems a long way back, their feet sinking into the boggy earth, each step like the kind of dream where the ground is too soft, where it sucks you down to stop you ever getting where you want to go.

Finally, they emerge from the trees onto firmer ground, and there is the train, so utterly out of place that it brings them to a stop.

An insect lands on the glass of Weiwei's helmet and she flicks it off, catching only a glimpse of a long greenish body and delicate wings. A dragonfly. Another arrives, and she flicks it away, and then another, and despite the helmet she can hear a chime in the air, many, many chimes, as if someone had struck the rim of one glass after another, each filled with different amounts of water, until the air is full of ringing. Beside her she feels Grey doubling up, trying to protect his head with his arms, and she sees, to one side of the train, that the dragonflies are gathering together—hundreds of them, thousands, and the sound is like a separate being, relentless.

"Quickly," she shouts at Grey, though her voice is lost in the din. They try to hurry their steps, though not before she has glimpsed patches of red on the ground beneath the dragonflies, and seen them darting down, landing for a moment in the red then taking off again. More sap from the trees? No. They are out in the open now, away from the trees. This is blood, spilled blood, and as the dragonflies rise up they seem to shiver and vanish in and out of sight, as if the beating of their wings lets them hover not just in *this* air, but somewhere else as well. *Whose blood?* The chiming hurts her head, the ground is not where she expects it to be; at each step it comes toward her faster than she expects, or is further away, jarring the bones in her legs.

Another roar, much closer this time. "You have to run faster," she yells, but Grey is slowing, stumbling every few steps, and it is harder and harder to pull him along with her and she is beginning to wish she could just leave him here to fend for himself, when a suited figure bursts from the train and runs toward them, grabbing Grey's other arm and putting it over their shoulder. The Captain. Weiwei feels her own legs turn weak with relief. They start to move faster, and despite their clumsy, six-legged pace, they begin to cover the ground toward the train.

Weiwei can see faces at the windows now, eyes moving between them and the growing spiral of insects. She can see Alexei gesturing at them to run faster, and others beside him, increasingly frantic, and then the door is opening and the Captain is pushing them onboard, before pulling herself up and slamming the door closed behind them.

It is too much to take in. Everyone is talking at once, and Weiwei struggles out of her helmet and stares at the Captain. As contained and unreadable as ever but finally, miraculously present. She puts her hand on Weiwei's arm and gives her an inquiring look.

"All fine," says Weiwei, her voice cracking, though there is so much more she wants to say, and she is afraid to look away in case the Captain vanishes again. But shouts of alarm make her turn back to the window, though she can't at first understand what she's seeing. It is made up of too many disparate parts to make sense, to exist at all. It is too big, too *much*. Skin like a lizard, tongue flicking out from a mouth with too many teeth. A mouth opening and swallowing dragonflies by the hundreds, rearing up on its hind legs to catch the very highest ones. White shells glint on its back, like the barnacles she has seen in the seafood markets in Beijing. Tears roll down her cheeks. She can't understand it, this physical reaction. She is furious at her weakness.

Grey presses his face to the glass. No tears for Henry Grey, only wonder, fascination. She is suddenly, incandescently jealous. She wants it—this wonder. She wants it bestowed on her, like a gift, like the gift Henry Grey received so lightly, but all she can feel is a terrible, rushing incomprehension. She could drown in it, as the eyes of the creature turn toward the train then turn back to the insects, dismissing the train as trivial, unimportant to its own business of feeding, surviving. She wraps her arms around herself and feels the sharp angles of the lichen fan in her suit pocket, its odd, smooth surface. It is deep blue and emerald green. It is the colors Elena would be, if she were here.

"It just appeared from the forest," says Alexei, and she sees that his face is pale, with a sickly sheen. "Just as you were getting closer." The Captain moves over to the speaking apparatus and speaks into the brass mouthpiece and seconds later Weiwei feels the rumble of the engine. The stokers must have been ready, waiting, keeping the train on the edge of waking. The creature turns its head toward the front of the train, where smoke is rising. It opens its jaws wider as if to taste the unfamiliar flavors on the air.

"More," says the Captain, into the speaking apparatus, and they feel the creak and strain of the acceleration, and the creature roars as they pass it, raising its head high so that she is sure it will crash down upon them. Water splashes up at the windows and the birches press in closer, obscuring their view of its claws and scales.

"Is it following?"

They are tense, all of them. Waiting for the crash, for the weight of that enormous jaw, for a devastating blow from that thick, armored tail. But the train plunges on through the water, unimpeded, and Weiwei can't tear her eyes away, watching for a flash of dark hair, of muddy blue cloth.

8
CONSEQUENCES

"I have heard it is the end for the Captain, you know." Guillaume speaks in the hushed, delighted tones of one starved of gossip.

"Well, she let it happen, didn't she?" says Wu Jinlu. "With all their boasts about the strongest train in the world, et cetera et cetera, he still managed to get out. Not so secure after all."

"Such hubris always comes before the fall," murmurs Galina Ivanovna, piously.

It is early evening. The rhythm of the train has resumed—dinner served on fine porcelain, wine poured by stewards wearing pristine white gloves. The atmosphere has lightened with the news that the water rationing is over, though Marya notices that the soup has largely gone uneaten. She dips her spoon into her bowl and for a moment she sees an oily sheen on the surface, a ripple of a color she cannot name.

The Countess inquires, "Has anyone seen our intrepid escapee?"

"Under observation by the doctor, I heard," says Wu. "Quarantined. He took his helmet off, it seems, and somehow ended up half-drowned in a swamp."

Galina Ivanovna shudders. "But how will they know if he is . . . if he has become, well, *infected*?"

"I presume it will become clear soon enough, and that the necessary measures will be taken," says Wu.

"These English fellows," says Guillaume, "I'm sure he'll not have picked anything up, they never do. Their miserable climate makes them immune."

"The girl went out as well, after him, you know," remarks Wu Jinlu. "The little train orphan. Not a thought for her own safety, I hear, really quite heroic."

"They're saying that Grey had some kind of breakdown, didn't know where he was or what he was doing," says the Countess, with relish.

"Poor man," says Guillaume. "They do say that some minds simply cannot cope with it." He looks satisfied that his mind is made of stronger stuff.

"And the creature," says the Countess. "Did you get a look at it? I can't help expecting to see it every time I glance outside." But her question is met with an uncomfortable silence. *They don't want to remember,* thinks Marya. They don't want to think about the sharp teeth, the mighty jaw. Easier to speak of Henry Grey and his human frailty.

"If the Captain is being punished for this lapse," Galina Ivanovna says, "what about Dr. Grey, then? Will he just come back after his quarantine? Are we to treat him as if nothing has happened?"

"I imagine that that is exactly what our two Company gentlemen would like," says the Countess. "The Trans-Siberia Company seems to put a high value on the virtue of forgetting."

The Company gentlemen have not appeared for dinner. Marya pictures them standing in their cabin, puzzlement changing into anger as they see the signs left behind by an uninvited guest; by a curious, incautious thief. She imagines them counting, calculating, trying to enumerate what is missing. Did she leave anything behind? Her appetite has deserted her, the wine tastes bitter on her tongue.

"Forgive me, I think I will return to my cabin a little early this evening," she says, setting aside her napkin and rising from the table. She needs to be away from the brittle chatter of First.

The gentlemen stand up with her.

"But you will be joining us later, won't you?" Anna Mikhailovna's tone suggests that this is less of a question than a command. "We need a fourth at bridge."

As Marya is searching for a suitably non-committal reply, the carriage door opens, and the Crows enter, in their habitual black suits, with their habitual blank expressions. "Yes, of course," she says. The Company men are watching her, their eyes shrewd. "I look forward to joining you." She begins to move away but the Crows block her path to the door.

"We hope you have not been too alarmed by today's events," says the Russian. "The safety and well-being of our passengers is of the utmost importance to us, as you know."

They both glance around to make sure the other passengers are listening. "And we can assure you that today's scientific expedition was carried out under the strictest of conditions, and that Dr. Grey's findings will be used to help our understanding of the Wastelands, thus making our journeys even safer for our passengers."

Marya realizes she is staring at them with her mouth open, and clamps her lips shut. She glances back at her table, and sees the Countess frowning.

Light is dawning on Guillaume's face. "Oh, so it was *planned*, was it? Well, I do think he might have told us in advance, to save us all worrying about him so much."

Marya imagines there had been very little worrying for Grey's safety, but the Crows are contorting their faces into expressions of contrition.

"Dr. Grey was insistent that nobody should know of his intended excursion. I am sure you know that he is a modest man, and he wanted neither an audience nor to give undue anxiety."

The Countess is raising her eyebrows, and there are other dubious looks among the passengers, but no one speaks until Galina Ivanovna announces, brightly, "Well, we have all said how much we admire his dedication to his work." There are a few slow nods of agreement.

It is like a spell, thinks Marya. Words transmuted into being. *I say, therefore it is.* Even so weak a story. Has no one thought to ask why Weiwei needed to bring him back, if it was really all planned? Have the Company gentlemen come to believe it themselves, convinced that whatever lie they tell is the truth? This is the power the Company has. How dare they? She can feel the words clawing at her throat. *Liars!* How they hide behind their neat black suits, their smooth, reassuring words. She wants to scratch off the veneer, to expose the rot within. Her head swims and she can see the Countess looking at her in concern but there is nothing she can do; she will be sick if she does not speak—

"May I accompany you back? Perhaps I can show you the book you were asking about?"

Marya spins around to see Suzuki, a hand hovering at her elbow, and she tenses. She hasn't wanted to face him; hasn't wanted to ask him all the questions she has.

"The history of the train, that I had mentioned? I have found it in the library and asked the steward to set it aside for you." He is guiding her gently but firmly to the door. "I believe you will find it a fascinating read."

They are halfway down the sleeping carriage before she trusts herself to speak. "There was no need—" she begins.

"In that case, I offer my apologies for my misreading, for I thought you were about to reveal to our Company friends and the whole of First Class just who you really are."

There is a long moment of silence between them.

"I am right, am I not, Marya Antonovna Fyodorova?"

A ringing begins in her ears. It has been so long since she has heard her real name. She had thought, after their last meeting, that he must know, but she had not wanted to examine the thought too closely. She had not wanted to think about him at all. "How did you know?" she asks, eventually.

The look he gives her is half-amused, half-disbelieving. "All those questions you asked, the telescope that you knew how to use . . . You may not have a high opinion of me, but I am not stupid." She flushes, but he goes on. "And I thought, of course . . . Of course Anton Ivan-ovich's daughter would come to find out the truth."

"The truth," she says, trying to keep her voice steady. "And what truth is this?"

Suzuki glances back down the corridor. "Come," he says. "It will be better if we maintain our fiction." He leads her into the library car, where a steward is dozing in a corner, though he sits up to attention when they enter. Suzuki whispers something in the man's ear, who gives a grin and hurries out of the carriage, casting a look at Marya on his way.

"Better to be the subject of crew gossip than to raise the suspicions of the Crows any further," says Suzuki, though he doesn't meet her eye. He goes to one of the bookcases and takes out a heavy volume, which he opens on a table, turning on the reading light above it. "Perhaps you would like a seat?" he says. She notices that there are dark smudges beneath his eyes and although his expression is calm, his long fingers fidget at his shirtsleeves, pulling them further down over his hands. His awkwardness makes her feel self-conscious. "I am fine to stand, thank you," she says, and she will not help him more than this, she will harden her heart to the pain she sees on his face.

"Ask me," he says. "Ask me your questions and I will give you what truths I can."

"Truths that I shouldn't have to find for myself," she says, and he flinches as if she has slapped him. She says, "Is it true that the glass was flawed?"

"No," he says, "it is not true," and reaches out to touch the window, as if touching the icon of a saint. The reverence of the gesture makes Marya's breath catch in her throat. Then he goes on, his fingertips still on the window, "It cracked, of course."

The lightness that Marya had begun to feel comes crashing down. "But—"

"It cracked and there was the answer the Company wanted to that impossible question, *What went wrong?* An easy answer, it must have made them breathe a sigh of relief—the glass cracked, everyone could see it—a window in Third. That was what caused it all, the hysteria, the memory loss. Never mind that your father had warned the Company that we were making too many crossings; never mind that the glass needed to be replaced more often if we were going to push the train to such speeds, with such frequency—here was their answer and their solution; the fault was with the glass and the glassmaker, they let the outside in."

He is angry, she realizes. Angry at the Company, angry at himself, and somehow his anger helps to ease some of her own rage. "Then why do you say that the glass was not to blame?"

He takes his hand from the window, as if only just realizing what he is doing. "Because the changes had already begun."

She stares at him. "What do you mean?"

She lets the silence between them spool out. She listens to the sounds of the rail and the ticking of the clock on the wall.

And Suzuki begins to speak.

"Your father and I shared an interest," he says, "in mapping the Wastelands, in observing as closely as we could every change, however small. We wanted to see closer and closer. Your father developed lenses that built on the work being done in astronomy, but instead of looking into the night sky he let us look into the world around us."

"I know all this. The telescope in your tower, the prototype . . . It consumed him, the idea that he could get close enough to see how the petals of a flower were made, the building blocks of life, he said. And they took that away from him, your Company. All of you. If he had had more time, he could have made it work, there was so much else he could have done."

But Suzuki is shaking his head, and before she can ask him how *dare* he try to contradict her, he says, "But he did do it. The prototype worked."

She tries to grasp what he is saying, how it all fits together. "But you said it was faulty . . ." Though there had been something in his voice, up there in the tower. *Fear,* she thinks.

"It worked better than we could possibly have imagined but in ways we couldn't understand. That we didn't understand, until—" He stops, and she can see him putting his thoughts in order, as carefully as he orders his maps. "When we tested the lenses in Beijing, we saw the most extraordinary detail. Through a scope small enough to carry up a flight of stairs, we could count the tiles on a rooftop a mile away. But when we used it in the Wastelands, we saw—" He shakes his head. "We saw veins running through every living thing, connecting one to another, like threads . . . it is hard to explain . . . but it was as if we were seeing a tapestry and the reverse of the tapestry at the same time—the pattern and how the pattern is made. Does it make sense? No, I am sure it does not . . ."

What I have seen weighs on my mind more heavily day by day, her father's letter had said. What he saw had convinced him the train must stop.

"Go on," Marya says.

"It was the most astonishing breakthrough. Crossing from Beijing to Moscow, we could hardly bear to take our eyes from the scope. We hypothesized at first that it could be a localized effect, a particular regional change that we had simply never been able to observe before, but we soon realized that the threads, the veins—we each had our preferred term—stretched through the whole of the Wastelands, connecting everything. And we realized too that we could follow the pattern of changes as they were made—we could watch as a spiral in the heart of a flower was drawn in the air by a flock of birds; how the order of markings on an insect's wing was mimicked in the fruiting body of a mushroom."

She can imagine her father's joy. *"They are windows, all of them,"* he had said, holding up the lenses of a telescope for her to see. How proud he must have been.

"And we saw the train too," Suzuki goes on. "We saw the train in the patterns—its shape repeated in the leaves, the rail running through the bark of trees. We saw wheels in the lichen that covered the rocks."

"Those creatures," says Marya, slowly. "The worms, or whatever they were, they seemed to be mimicking the train."

Suzuki nods. "As we are observing, we are being observed in turn."

"It made my father afraid. I found the letter that he wrote to the Company . . . You knew I would, didn't you? You knew it was in the Crows' cabin."

"As soon as we reached Moscow, he insisted on sharing our findings with the Company Board. We had proof, he said, that the land is learning, that what we have always feared—the unpredictability of the changes, their random nature—is not the true danger at all. What is dangerous is that there *is* meaning, intent behind them, and we can see it now with our own eyes."

"The pattern and how the pattern is made," Marya whispers.

"I tried to dissuade him," Suzuki goes on. "To my shame, I refused to put my name to his letter. I argued that we needed more time to understand what we were seeing, and when we received no response from the Company in Moscow, I was relieved." He closes his eyes. "And then, on the crossing back to Beijing—that last crossing—as soon as we passed through the Wall we saw again the patterns outside, but this time we saw them *inside* as well. In the train itself. We saw the outline of ferns in the wood paneling, the patterns of water in the cloth of the curtains. We started to doubt our own sanity, the evidence of our own eyes, and then . . ." He stops. "And then it goes dark. Whatever had happened, it vanished from our memory. When we came back to ourselves, we had reached the Beijing Wall and the glass had cracked. There was no sign of any of the things we had seen. And your father . . ." His voice breaks. "Your father blamed himself. He was too ready to take responsibility for the glass, to dismiss what we had seen in favor of what the Company called *the most obvious explanation.*"

"Then why did you stay silent? It ruined him, the loss of his reputation, his livelihood. It killed him."

Grief suffuses his face and he holds on to the back of the chair as if he cannot keep himself from falling. "Because I am a coward. Because the train is all I have and if the doors to the Wastelands close for good, then I am left with nothing. The moment I left Japan I became a man of no country and became a Company man instead, a man of the train. Without it I belong nowhere. I was not strong enough . . . Not selfless enough to bear the thought that what we had discovered could lead to the destruction of the Company."

"It *should* be destroyed. It has put us all in danger—*you* have put us in danger."

He looks utterly defeated. "I have tried to convince myself that we were wrong, that what we saw was a Wastelands trick; that the walls of the train are as strong as the Company boasts. I have locked away the new telescope. I have forced myself *not* to see, though it has been seeing, observing, that has given my life meaning."

She tries to steady the shaking in her legs. She doesn't know if it is sadness or anger or something else, something too complicated to put a name to, too big to try and grasp while standing here, in this dimly lit carriage, on these unfamiliar rails.

"And you are trying to atone," she says, quietly.

9

CAPTIVITY

Henry Grey's clothes and shoes have been taken from him and burned. He has been scrubbed until his skin is pink and prickling. And now he has been confined to a cabin in the infirmary. The bed is narrow and hard and the padded walls deaden sounds and make his own breathing seem maddeningly loud, but it is the lack of a window that scratches at him. He had begged to be allowed to remain in his own cabin, promising not to leave under any circumstances until the period of his quarantine is over, but the Captain and the doctor had been adamant.

"It is for your own safety," the doctor had said. "Since you were exposed to the air, without your helmet, and to water."

"I assure you, I feel completely well."

But the doctor had been too busy measuring the size of his forehead and bleeding him and shining a tiny torch into his eyes. "Merely as a precaution," he had said. He had worn a mask over his mouth, and he smelled of disinfecting lotion.

Later the two Company men had come to see him, although they had stood outside the door, which had a little sliding hatch at head height, and they had spoken to him through the gap. They had expressed, in tortuously bureaucratic terms, the Company's apologies for any current discomfort, and reminded him of the forms he had completed before boarding, waiving the Company of responsibility for effects arising from his exposure to the outside. And then they had asked question after question about how he had managed to get out of the train and who had helped him and what he had hoped to do, and he had drawn himself up and declared that an Englishman would not be intimidated.

And now he is alone. The only thing he can cling to is that the girl had had the presence of mind to demand his suit almost as soon as they had thrown themselves onto the train, while everyone was watching the great creature from the forest. He had handed it to her dumbly, its pockets heavy with the precious few specimens he had had time to collect, and he had watched her vanish and return, empty-handed, moments later. Remarkable, for his saviors to come in such unexpected shapes. A scrawny train-girl, a Wastelands creature.

He stretches out on the hard bed and after a while he feels the cool water around him again. Birds scream above him, searching. Perhaps they are blinded by the shifting patterns of sun on the water, because they don't seem to know where he is. Their sharp beaks plunge wildly around him but he is vanishing, drowning; weeds are reaching up to wrap around his wrists and ankles, to drag him down into darkness the sun cannot pierce. And then—strong arms around him; the weeds have turned into hair, dark and shining beneath the water, then curling around him in slick tendrils as he is hauled back into the air and onto firmer ground, returned to life. In his memory he opens his eyes but sun and shade fragment her face into disparate pieces he cannot put together. He calls out in frustration and moments later hears a click as another hatch slides open, this one in the wall adjoining the doctor's cabin.

"Dr. Grey? Are you well?"

He opens his eyes and sees the doctor's face peering at him through a grill. "Just a bad dream," he says, shortly.

"Can you describe your dream, Dr. Grey?" He hears a rustling of papers, the doctor turning the pages of a notebook. "Anything at all, any detail." The doctor makes no attempt to keep the eagerness from his voice. His little eyes watch Grey, greedily. It makes his stomach turn.

"Well, I do remember certain details, although they are very indistinct . . ."

"Anything, Dr. Grey, anything. Before you forget . . ."

"A woman—"

"Yes?"

"She was dressed just like my mother used to, but as I approached her she turned into the very image of Her Majesty the Queen . . ." He is pleased to see the flash of disappointment in the doctor's expression, and hears the notebook being put away.

"Could it be the effects of the Wastelands? My dear mother has been in her grave these past twenty years."

"It certainly could, indeed," says the doctor, in the tone of one praising a slow but well-intentioned child. "Good, good. Well, I am here if you need me, don't hesitate to call if you start to feel not quite yourself."

The hatch closes, and Grey folds his arms over his chest, warmed by a glow of petty satisfaction. But the doctor's words echo in his head. *Does* he feel quite himself? He's not sure anymore, not sure if he remembers how he is meant to feel. The pain in his stomach is a constant companion. But there is something else, a tug at his ribs, a pull that he has been feeling since the night of the storm and the apparition he had seen.

He sits upright so quickly that blackness hovers at the edges of his vision. He had seen her, she was real, however much the rail girl tried to convince him otherwise. She had been on the train and in the water. She had followed him—she had made sure he was safe. He stands up from the bed, unable to bear his own stillness any longer. The tug at his ribs grows stronger, as if something is pulling at him on a line so thin as to be invisible, yet strong as knotted rope. The energy in his legs makes them ache. He has read accounts of this—an elation that comes with unexpected salvation, of a life returned. He has always put them down to weak sentimentality, but what he feels now is not simply gratitude or joy but a fiercer burning. A life returned is a life borrowed; more fragile and brighter than he ever could have imagined. A life no longer his own. He can feel it burning away all doubt, all hesitation. "A new Eden," he whispers. "A new Eden."

He will have his specimens for the Exhibition. There will be time to study them, to consider how best to display them. But they will be only the beginning—a gateway to the knowledge he will bring.

The doctor brings him his evening meal and with it more questions, more tests. The answers trip off his tongue in easy, fluent lies. Enough to keep the doctor convinced of his eagerness to help, yet nothing so interesting as to keep him here any longer than necessary. Afterward, the Company men, again, and this time he gathers that they have been saying that his excursion outside was planned, permitted. That it was the Company, indeed, in their eagerness for scientific knowledge, who provided the brains behind it. He was only the tool.

"And what am I . . . Excuse me, what are *we* supposed to have achieved in this endeavor? Will they not ask to see the fruits of my labors? Or ask what I have learned? All I have to show are torn clothes and scratches, and I remember nothing of the outside." *Only the hum of bluebottles and the iridescent wing cases of beetles; webs dripping with red sap; the white feathers of the huge birds; the peaty smell of his rescuer, her hair brushing against his skin.*

The Company men smile thinly and say they are sure that a man of his learning can extemporize if necessary.

"And may I ask the reason for this pretense?" He is fairly sure that he understands why they are doing it, but he wants to hear them say it. He dislikes this obfuscation, this hiding beneath layers of words and meanings, but he cannot help feeling a certain glee—the Company's own greed led to their hoarding of knowledge, their determination that no one else would learn of the Wastelands' riches. Well now, let them watch what he can do.

"We do what is best for the train, Dr. Grey," says Petrov.

"Best that our passengers believe that everything happens for a reason," says Li. "Of course, should they find out anything to the contrary, it would be within our means to take further punitive action, on a legal basis, of course."

The Company men regard him sternly and Grey replies, "Yes, yes, of course." But he is thinking—*Yes, perhaps everything does happen for a reason,* and a flush of elation suffuses him again. *Perhaps it does.*

10
MUTATIONS

Weiwei's face aches with the effort of keeping a mask of innocence in place. She desperately wants to be left alone, but the doctor insists on asking her interminable questions about how she feels and if she took her helmet or protective suit off at any point (she says that of course she did not), and if she is experiencing any nausea or headaches. He seems rather disappointed when she assures him that she feels completely normal and tells her to come back later for another examination. The kitchen boys follow her around, demanding to know what it's like, *out there*. She keeps the mask on, gives them just enough hair-raising details to send them away happy. She tries to find Alexei but he is nowhere to be seen.

In the confusion of their return to the train she had rushed to the crew quarters and stowed the jars and bags in her own bunk, covering them with her blankets. She can only hope that, with all the excitement, any thought of spot inspections will have vanished, at least for the time being. Now, she has retreated back here, to escape the questions and stares, and to make the most of the fact that her decision to go after Grey is being seen as heroic, and as such she is being allowed, for the time being, to leave her chores undone. But she wishes she could enjoy such unexpected freedom. Instead, a wave of loneliness washes over her. How quickly she had become accustomed to Elena's presence. To racing through her chores so that she could join her in her explorations; to sitting in the dark, reading out chapters from Rostov's guide, Elena interrupting with questions she usually couldn't answer. She runs her fingers across the silvery-blue scales of the lichen, half expecting them to dissolve into water. This she will not return to Grey. It is for her alone, her piece of the Wastelands, of Elena.

But the guilt of her theft weighs on her. Was this what Rostov wanted? Something he could not have? She wonders if the forest creature will find what is missing, if it will open its huge jaws in fury. She wonders if Elena feels the theft like a wound.

Her reverie is broken by the crackle of the speakers and she is about to bury her head in her pillow when she hears her own name. *"Zhang Weiwei . . . Report to the Captain's quarters . . . immediately."* She sits bolt upright, while the message comes through again. *The Captain knows,* she thinks, wildly. She knows about Elena, she knows about the stolen specimens. What punishment would possibly be enough?

"Zhang, are you really going to keep her waiting?" a steward yells up to her, and when she climbs down from her bunk it is to a gaggle of expectant faces, staring at her with a mixture of apprehension and envy.

Her legs feel unsteady. The water the train has taken on means they can increase speed, though they still proceed carefully, on the unfamiliar line. Yet the sound of the rail seems louder than usual, the rhythm of the train distracting, as if the boundary between her body and the rails is thinning, as if the pistons and cogs, the intricate puzzle of moving pieces that Alexei understands so well, are mirroring the beating of her own heart, the pumping of her blood.

When she knocks on the door she does not quite believe it will be opened, despite the summons, yet the Captain opens the door herself. She looks Weiwei up and down, then goes over to the table, pours something out of a brown bottle and hands her the glass, nodding to an armchair. "You're looking peaky, drink this."

Weiwei sits and sips the fiery liquid, coughing as it burns.

The Captain raises her eyebrows. "Better?"

"Better," she splutters, though if anything it has only made the sensation of thinness worse. Her bones are humming still. Is the Wastelands air working its changes after all?

The Captain doesn't pour herself a glass. She stands at the window and Weiwei thinks how rarely she has seen her sit, as though she cannot bear to let herself soften enough to sink into a chair.

Go on. Get it over with. It will come as a relief, after all these secrets. It will be a deserved punishment, whatever it is, for a traitor to the train, for a thief.

Finally, the Captain turns; abruptly, as if she has just come to a decision. "I trust you are undamaged by your earlier adventure?"

Weiwei tries to nod and shrug at the same time and spills her drink onto her uniform.

"If I were to ask you who helped Grey leave the train, I assume you would say you do not know, so I won't insult your loyalty." *The lines across her forehead have deepened during this crossing,* thinks Weiwei. Her cheekbones have sharpened, her skin thin and papery. Yet Weiwei had felt her strength, when she had hauled her and Grey back onto the train.

Weiwei opens her mouth, then closes it again. Trying to read the Captain's thoughts is an impossible task, but she feels that there is something hiding behind her words that she should understand, currents of meaning that she should be able to grasp, but can't. Even when she was very young she was aware that the Captain never treated her like a child, but sometimes she wishes she would. She wishes that she would tell her that everything will be well.

The Captain goes over to the table and picks up the brown bottle then puts it down again. "The Company has requested that I stand down," she says.

Weiwei sits very still. She doesn't trust herself to move.

"I will take us to the Moscow Exhibition, of course, after which a new Captain will step up. This is not how I wish my time on this train to end, but . . . I have not guided us well of late. It will be in the best interest of the train."

The blood pounds in her ears. "Why are you telling me this?"

"I will share it with the rest of the crew when the time is right, but I am telling you now because you have a right to know. Because you and this train are connected in a way that . . ." She hesitates. "In a way that I think none of us quite understand."

"Then why won't you just be our Captain?" Her voice shakes but she no longer cares. "*You* are connected to this train too, but where have you been? Why have you let them push you out, why haven't you fought them?" She wants to stamp her feet, to cry angry tears, to make the ground burst into flame like the fury of Valentin's Fire.

The Captain turns back to the window. "That is all," she says.

She is barely aware of leaving the Captain's quarters, walking numbly down the corridor back toward the safety of her bunk. She cannot force her thoughts into order, it is impossible to imagine the train without the Captain, it makes no sense. She must tell the crew—if they band together they could force the Company not to accept her resignation; they could refuse to work, they could go to the newspapers . . .

But here, before she can think any further, is the clink of buckles, and the Crows are descending as if drawn by the stench of disloyalty. They sit her down on a lower bunk while they stand, eyeing her hungrily, and though she knows it is simply an effect of her tiredness and worry, their suits seem to hang more loosely from their arms, their shoulder blades jutting more sharply from their backs; not crows anymore, nor men, but a poor mimicry of both.

"We see that the Captain has spoken to you, Miss Zhang. It is unfortunate that she did not consult with us first."

"We would have asked her not to upset you needlessly."

She can't read their faces. Looking up at them, she struggles even to tell them apart, to make out who is speaking. "I'm not upset," she mutters.

"We are sure you understand that what she said must remain between us."

"Our secret."

"We would not like to complicate matters by revealing more detail than is absolutely necessary. We of course value Alexei Stepanovich and his role on the train. One foolish action should not imperil a career, we are sure you would agree, but if word of the Captain's decision were to get out—"

"If the crew felt that she was treated unfairly—"

"Then the truth must of course be told."

Weiwei tries to keep control of her expression. *How do they know it was Alexei?* But of course they know—his guilt had been written all over him, he had never been as good as she is at deception and pretense. She feels a rising nausea. There is no one she can talk to. Nothing she can do.

That night, curled in her bunk, she wants to close her eyes and fall into blissful forgetfulness. She wants to wake up and find that everything that hurt her has melted away; that there is no more talk of leaving; that they are back on the right rails, that all this time on the ghost rails has been nothing more than a bad dream, a Wastelands trick. At some point in the night she feels the warm weight of Dima flexing his paws on the mattress, but even he seems unable to find rest beside her and springs away.

She has taken the specimens from where they were hidden, beneath the blankets, and lined them up on the little shelf that runs along the wall. That's what she has taken to calling them already, specimens, like Dr. Grey does. Her own, though, the lichen fan, is different. Not a specimen of anything but all its own, all *her* own, that nothing and no one can take away. She has placed it closest to her, so that when she lies on her side with her head on her pillow it is closest to her line of sight. The insects that he collected she has placed furthest away and covered with cloth. She doesn't like the way they tap at the glass with their forelegs, or the way the thin stalks on their heads wave as if they are tasting the air, tasting her. In one of the muslin bags is a roll of moss, a deep, shadowy green. This she likes. She imagines lying down on it, sinking into its earthy coolness. Sleeping.

When she wakes again she can hear unfamiliar sounds in the darkness, as if something is tapping against glass. As if something is growing.

Part Five

Days 15–17

Some of the phenomena in the Wastelands have been studied and understood; the effects of the weather and atmospheric pressure causing mirages—the sudden appearance of what seems to be an encampment, for example, flags flying from the tops of tents—or the spectral light of Valentin's Fire. Other sightings challenge everything we know about nature. They force us to read the Wastelands as we would read a book in a lost language; a series of signs which we cannot hope to decipher.

The Cautious Traveller's Guide to the Wastelands, page 55

1

HAUNTINGS

Marya is dreaming of veins growing from the earth. Of her skin turning to birch bark; of everything changing around her, leaves growing and dying and falling and growing again. She wakes with her sheets twisted around her limbs. She touches her hair, sure that there will be dried leaves tangled in it, certain that there will be soil beneath her fingernails.

The clock on the wall says it is three o'clock in the morning. She opens the curtains, against all advice, to a clear night sky. They are travelling still through a region of marshes and pools, turned bright silver by the moon. They stretch away into the distance, scattered across the landscape. The night changes your sense of perspective. They look close enough that she could leap from one to another, as she had done as a child, splashing from puddle to puddle in the lane outside their dacha, watching the sky and the trees shatter beneath her. In St. Petersburg she had always had an adult clutching her hand, forcing her to walk beside them. It was only in the countryside that she had had the freedom to leap and splash, away from watchful eyes.

She glances at the neat package on the table, then looks away. The parcel had been brought to her cabin earlier in the evening, and with it a note from the Cartographer. *These were your father's* was all it said. She had hesitated, inexplicably afraid of what she might find.

When she had finally torn open the brown paper, it had revealed five sketchpads. She had opened the first one, her hand unsteady. A swirl of dark lines coalescing into a rose. Vines weaving their way between the branches of spindly trees. Thin white roots spreading through soil; purple fruit heavy and ripe on green stalks. A moth, its wings spread, revealing two spots like the eyes of an owl. They are different, these drawings, from anything else she has seen of her father's ornamental work. The stained-glass panels which decorate the train are simple and austere, the natural forms they depict reduced to their essence, held solid and immobile in glass. But in these sketchbooks, everything is blooming, growing; so full of life, of ripeness, that it makes her queasy.

So full of life that her father had come to think it was putting them in danger.

On a sudden impulse, she puts her dressing gown on over her nightclothes and pads out into the corridor. She wants more of the sky than her cabin window can give her. All other cabin doors are shut, and a steward sleeps, folded over on his arms, at the end of the corridor. Through the saloon car and the library car, empty and lit by single lamps, into the passage alongside Suzuki's laboratory. She notices that the door to the observation tower is ajar, light spilling out onto the floor, and she speeds her footsteps past it.

No lights in the observation car. Only glass and water and moonlight. She hesitates at the doorway then forces herself to step inside, feeling faintly ridiculous to be standing there in her nightclothes. It is beautiful, the landscape; the pools as still as mirrors, the horizon vanishing in the darkness. She walks further inside, clenching her fists against the feeling of walking under the open sky, all the way to the very end of the carriage, where it feels more like a ship than a train, the rails like a wake they leave behind them in the water. She can almost feel the night air on her face, taste the wetness and salt. Clouds passing across the moon throw the landscape in and out of darkness. *There is no one here,* she thinks. *No one human between me and the Wall, a thousand miles back in the distance.*

A sound, just on the edge of her hearing, makes her turn. A smell, earthy and damp. A clammy feeling on her neck.

The carriage is empty. Low tables and armchairs illuminated by pale light. But at the very end, nearest the door, shadows obscure the furthest seats and she thinks, with a prickle of horror, *Someone is there.* The feeling of exposure—to the sky, the outside, to anyone looking out or in, returns. She can't move. "Who's there?" she tries to say, but no sound comes out, and who would be there, in the darkness, in the middle of the night, hiding in the shadows? No, she has succumbed to the sickness they all talk about, the Professor and the passengers in Third, though those in First choose to ignore it, as if their wealth and their luxurious cabins can protect them.

"Who's there?" Her voice stronger this time. She lets go of the glass and walks toward the door. Surely the shadows will turn out to be cushions; the sound nothing more than the creaks of the train; the smell nothing more than a memory of an old dacha and a country lane. But as she approaches she is sure she sees something move, she is sure that someone is there, hiding, watching.

Marya Antonovna, in her sheltered life, would have run away. She would have run and curled up in a ball and waited for someone to come and tell her that it was alright, because somebody *always* told her that it was alright. Somebody always looked after her. Her family; a succession of governesses. But Marya Petrovna is different. Marya Petrovna stands her ground. She has nothing to be afraid of because she doesn't really exist. Or does she exist more fully than that other Marya ever had? She isn't sure anymore. Perhaps this really is Wastelands sickness. Or perhaps her mother was right—moonlight is dangerous for young ladies.

"I know you're there," she says. Steps closer.

And a cloud obscures the moon, throwing the carriage into a momentary darkness that carries the stranger away. She hears footsteps and a rustle of cloth, then only silence remains. When the cloud passes away the carriage is empty. She pokes at the cushions a few times, just to be sure, but it leaves her feeling foolish.

Only the smell lingers.

She waits until her heartbeat has slowed, then walks carefully out of the carriage. *A child from Third,* she thinks; *escaping from their parents for a nighttime adventure, keeping a guilty silence. Yes, that is all it was.* Now she is out in the well-lit corridor, the solid bulk of the scientific equipment behind the glass beside her, rationality returns.

But surely a child would giggle, or cry. They would give themselves away. Her legs feel suddenly unsteady and she grasps the brass hand-rail, and just as she is feeling irritated at her own behavior, the light from the door to the Cartographer's tower grows brighter, and Suzuki himself appears at the bottom of the stairs, still buttoning up his shirt.

Their gazes meet through the glass and she feels her cheeks burn. How ridiculous, to be found wandering in the middle of the night in her dressing gown; to be right outside his carriage like an incompetent spy.

He opens the door to the corridor. "Are you quite well? You look—" He stops, as if he is just becoming aware of his own state of undress, his shirt untucked, his sleeves loose at the cuffs.

"I thought I heard a noise," she says, stiffly, "but it was just my imagination playing tricks. I didn't mean to disturb you." Is that true? Hadn't she hoped that he might be as restless as she was, that even as he stared out at the line, part of him was thinking of her?

"Your hands," she says, suddenly. "Those lines . . ." She had thought at first they were ink stains, but she is sure she sees a pattern in them.

Suzuki steps back, pulling his cuffs further over his hands just as she reaches for his wrist then freezes, shocked at her own boldness. "Let me see," she whispers.

He tenses, but pushes up his sleeve and there, winding around his arm, are lines of ink. Tattoos? She has seen them only at a fair, a tattooed man with fairy tales inked all over his body, twitching his muscles to make tigers move and trees grow. But no, Suzuki is quite still, hardly seeming to breathe, and yet the lines are moving, and they are not simply lines but rivers, contours, thin winding paths. And the railway, a black line like a vein from his wrist, a line mapping their journey onto his skin.

She stares, unable to understand what she is seeing. "You have it, the sickness . . ."

"No, it is not—"

"Another thing you have hidden."

"Please, you have to understand." At a sound coming from the tower he looks back. "We will be returning to the main line, I must go, but I would speak further of this—"

But she backs away. She needs to be away from him, from the way his body is an etching of the hungry lands outside; from his restless, changing skin.

2

CROSSING THE LINE

"Nearly there," says Vassily.

"I can see it!" shouts Luca, one of the kitchen boys.

"Liar, no one has eyesight that good." One of the porters gives him a shove and sends him toppling from his perch on the table.

"I *can*, it's up ahead." Luca rights himself.

They're in the Third Class dining car, where the tables have all been pushed to the walls. Since their return to the main line the atmosphere has lifted; there is a sense of almost giddy relief, as the train has picked up speed once more. And now the crossing of the line is in sight.

Weiwei cranes her neck to see, and there it is—a white stone, about the height of a man, nondescript, half-covered by grasses and creeping vines. Another stands on the other side of the rail, two austere markers, all that signifies the crossing of continents.

She remembers being told the story when she was very young. She remembers the Professor holding her up to the window as they passed between the stones and telling her about the builders.

When the line was built, the Company, in their offices in Beijing and Moscow, had wanted black stones from the quarries of Arkhangelsk, and poems inscribed upon them—verses to glorify their great empires. The builders of the rail, however, had wanted them to hold the names of those who had given their lives to lay down the tracks.

Neither side could agree, so the stones were left plain, although the builders got the last laugh. They ordered pure white stone, the Chinese color of mourning, and by the time word reached the men who sat snug in their offices, it was too late. And in this way those lost on the rail gained their tomb.

She never fails to feel a shivery sense of time stretched thin as the train passes between the markers. As though the shades of those first builders are lined up to watch them pass, leaning on their shovels, narrowing their eyes as the train thunders over their bones. The crew take off their hats or reach out to touch iron. She glances at the passengers, sees apprehension at the gaining of a new continent, relief at a familiar one. The violin player begins a song both urgent and sad, an insistent, repeating melody that the kitchen boys take up with their spoons and pans, and the crew with unmelodious whistles or hums, and the passengers join in, uncertain at first, then growing in confidence as the sound fills the carriage and the song rises and falls through the octaves, looping and changing and playing them into Europe.

She looks around, at the Portuguese priest closing his eyes and nodding his head in time to the music; at the three brothers from the South, tipping tiny glasses of liquor down their throats; at the couples and families and the lone travellers who have formed friendships because it isn't possible to be alone in Third Class, and the musician's song is weaving them together ever more closely. Her ears pick up an oddness in the melody and she realizes that the violin player is twining together a Chinese folk song with a Russian one, their keys clashing then smoothing out then clashing again. His eyes are closed as he plays, and she wonders what it feels like, to be so lost within the sound. She feels her own feet start to move as the kitchen boys begin their chant, like another line of percussion beneath the music, *"We're crossing, we're crossing, we're crossing,"* and the porters take it up too, and the stewards, and the passengers, they take up the years of superstition, the ritual—boundaries have to be marked, after all, and what is it about a line that brings on the urge to leap over it? The carriage floor is shaking beneath her as they stamp over the line, *"We're crossing, we're crossing, we're crossing."* Because boundaries are guarded, and boundary guardians always need to be told that those who cross are not afraid.

She takes a deep breath. There is a kind of ecstasy in the faces of the people in the carriage. *This is why we have our rituals,* she thinks. *This is why they are needed—so that we can lose ourselves for a while.*

She wishes she could lose herself. Lose the stinging absence where Elena had been; where the Captain, the Professor had once been to keep her safe. Lose the fear of what she has helped bring to the train.

Thief. Traitor. What would they say, these swaying, dancing passengers, if they knew what she had done? If they knew she had let the outside in? She thinks about the scales of lichen, growing in the darkness; the insects waiting in their little cocoons, and she is sure that they are moving, as though they feel the music too. She is sure she can feel them all growing.

The sensation makes her dizzy.

"They're drinking themselves into oblivion in First," says Alexei, appearing beside her. His own skin is flushed, and there is liquor on his breath. He has barely spoken to her since her trip outside. Perhaps he is jealous, she thinks, that she went in his place.

"And there have been rumors of a ghost walking the corridors."

"What?"

"Haunting the First Class bathroom. I'd forgotten how much I hate crossing the line."

"Hey!" She has reached the first of the sleeping cars when a small figure hurtles toward her and she grabs him as he tries to dodge past, holding him fast as he squirms in her grip. She has played this game herself more times than she can count, and is faster than any Beijing ruffian, and has no intention of flattening herself against the wall, which is the aim of the dedicated contestants.

"Tell me about the ghost."

"What?" Jing Tang falls still at this unexpected question.

"I hear you've been telling stories about ghosts in bathrooms." She yanks him closer. "Don't you know it's bad luck to talk about ghosts? They will hear you and think that they're welcome."

The boy tries to pull away. "But it's *true*. I saw her in the mirror, in there." He points to one of the First Class bathrooms then cries, "You're hurting me!"

She releases the grip on his arm that she had tightened suddenly. "In there?"

He nods, guiltily.

A moment's hesitation, then, before she can think too much, she grabs his shoulder and marches him to the door, pushes it open, her stomach churning in—what? Anticipation? Fear?

A dripping tap can be heard even over the noise of the rails. The room is clear of steam. No one has been bathing at this hour, even now that there is water again for these purposes. The bath is empty, there is no water flowing over its edges, no drowned girl rising. She feels a disappointment so vast, it threatens to drown her too.

"Nothing," she says, her voice too loud. "No ghost."

Jing Tang looks sullen. "She was here. I saw her in the mirror."

"You saw a passenger, that's all."

"No. A ghost."

She appreciates his stubbornness—it is a trait that has served her well—so she merely ruffles his hair in a way she knows he will hate, and steers him out of the bathroom. "You know you're not allowed in this part of the train. Won't your parents be wondering where you are?"

"They won't have noticed I'm gone."

She imagines he's correct, but refrains from comment. "Well, the stewards have noticed, and they'll be press-ganging you to work as a rail rat if you keep scurrying around where you don't belong."

"Really? I could work on the train? Like you?"

"Well—"

But she can see the boy imagining himself in uniform, striding down the corridors of the train. He has begun to hold himself a little straighter.

They reach the Third Class dining carriage, where music and dancers envelop them.

"Come on, we're going through to your sleeping carriage," she says, but Jing Tang exclaims "Look!" and she sees his mother, back to herself again, sitting squashed around one of the tables with his father, in the midst of a lively game of cards and dice. His father looks up and stretches out an arm.

"Come, little gambler, perhaps you will bring us luck!" cries one of the other players, and the boy is enfolded into the group, squeezing onto his father's lap as his mother puts her arm around both of them.

Weiwei turns away. Don't they know the Vigil approaches? The incessant beating of the makeshift drums makes her bones ache. The air feels sticky and cloying. A shriek of high-pitched laughter, a shattering of glass. She sees the Third Class steward arguing with a belligerent farmer, Alexei with a drink in his hand. The lights in Third are fewer and not as bright as in First, and in the dimness she feels the scene dissolving; passengers melting into shadows, the violin player in silhouette, like a faded outline on a temple wall, a point of stillness in the roiling, swaying mass. She slips behind the heavy window curtain and rests her forehead against the glass, glad of its relative coolness. Closes her eyes. Just as it had when she was a child, the world on the other side of the curtain falls away, the sound muffled even by so flimsy a barrier.

She opens her eyes onto the darkness. The stewards used to scold her for staring outside for so long at night. *It's not safe,* they would say; *don't stare so, you don't want to see what's staring back.* But she did want to see. She always has. She opens her eyes as wide as she used to, until the indistinct shapes outside resolve themselves into a landscape she can read. There. Movement in the distance. Wings rising from the shadows of the trees. *Owls,* she thinks; *hunting.*

And then her eye is caught, not by the landscape outside but by something much closer. There are pale shapes blooming on the other side of the glass; veins of mold, like the lines left behind by saltwater, growing before her eyes. She takes a step backward, and hears a muffled cry of surprise as she collides with someone.

"Just cleaning," she says, reappearing to tipsy applause, as if she has just performed a magic trick—*Produce a girl from behind a curtain*—and cries of, "Who else is behind there?"

She twitches the other curtains aside, careful not to let the passengers see, and on each of the other windows the same patterns are forming. She touches the glass. It is definitely on the outside, and yet . . . She pictures the stolen specimens, proliferating; pictures scales on the walls, spores on the air, everything growing. Her fingertips feel it through the glass, the deep hum of life expanding, and she snatches her hand away.

She elbows her way out of Third, through the crew mess, where there is still food being eaten and dice being thrown, and into the crew sleeping car.

The carriage is dark and noiseless but for the ever-present rattle of the rails. She stands in the doorway, revelling in the emptiness, in the relief that comes with being unobserved. But as she enters she thinks—*No.* Something else is here. She can feel it when she puts her hand to the wall; there, behind the sound of the train and the rails, she feels it again—*something growing.*

She doesn't stop to look behind the curtains, she makes straight for her own bunk, needing no light to guide her steps, not even to climb the ladder, and when she reaches the top she stretches out her hand to find her lichen fan, but it is not there—

She freezes. As her eyes grow used to the darkness she sees patterns on the wall; not on the outside of the windows anymore, but *inside*, the lichen spreading scales of silver and blue toward the ceiling. There is movement at the other end of her bunk, a crouched shape—

"*Thief,*" hisses Elena.

3

EDEN

"A new Eden," says Dr. Henry Grey. He has just been released from
quarantine. Sweat stains his collar and he looks not to have shaved
for days. There is a tremor in his voice which Marya has not noticed
before, that puts her in mind of the fire-and-brimstone preachers on
the Petersburg docks, proclaiming the world to come. "This is what
we are making, a new Eden, more perfect and marvelous, more full
of life, more—"

"More furnished with serpents?" Guillaume raises his glass, to
appreciative laughter, then gestures at the steward to refill it. Henry
Grey appears unperturbed. He has been holding forth all evening to
whoever will listen and he returns, again and again, with evangelical
fervor, to his great glass palace.

Beside Marya, Sophie LaFontaine is sketching.

"It's beautiful," says Marya, looking at the quick gray lines of the
birches beneath her fingers. "It makes me want to reach in and touch
the bark of the trees."

Sophie smiles at her. "Perhaps it will be a gift for Dr. Grey," she
says. "Though I fear it is only a pale imitation of his Eden." She tilts the
paper away, slightly, but as she does so the sheet below it is revealed,
and a sketched figure catches Marya's eye. It is just a few pencil lines,
a young woman in a doorway, but Sophie has given her a sense of
movement, of lifelikeness. Marya can't say why, but it makes her un-

easy. Perhaps it is the fact that the figure's face is blurred, and yet there is the distinct feeling that she is *watching*.

Sophie covers up the picture, hurriedly.

"Is she a passenger?" Marya asks.

"From Third Class, perhaps," says Sophie. Then she goes on, in a low voice, "You will think me foolish, and I know that it is just a lack of skill on my part, nothing else, but although I have seen her, at different times on our journey, I have never been able to capture her face." She flicks through other pages in her sketchbook and Marya sees the same figure, always in a doorway or beside a wall, always with her features indistinct, as if she has been caught by a camera in the act of moving.

"No," says Marya, "I don't think you're foolish at all, nor lacking in skill." She remembers the conviction she had felt in the observation car, how sure she had been that there was someone there. She remembers Henry Grey's angel.

"We are being observed in turn," Suzuki had said. She pushes the thought of him away, of his changing skin.

"Now, my dear, you are not boring our friend, are you? I am sure modern ladies have more to speak about than pretty drawings, is that not right?" Guillaume leans over to his wife and takes the sketchbook out of her hands, tossing it carelessly onto the seat beside them.

Marya can smell the liquor on his breath. "We were having a perfectly pleasant conversation, thank you," she says, not attempting any pretense at warmth.

"But don't you see," Henry Grey has raised his voice, "we *understand* the garden now. We are a new people, *homo scientificus*, we have been granted a new opportunity, a second chance. We must not throw it away, not let ourselves be distracted, this is what I shall present at the Exhibition . . ."

"I would pity him," the Countess remarks, "but I fear he would mistake it for encouragement."

Marya tries to respond but she is finding it hard to concentrate. It is late. She has not heard the chimes of the clock all evening over the rising noise and the merry songs of the musician, who remains nonetheless as morose as if he were playing a funeral dirge. At the passing of the boundary line they had drunk a toast to entering Europe, then another, and another, and now the night is slipping away and the music has ended but there is a general reluctance to go to bed.

"The poor man has nothing, of course. Just a few cases of dead butterflies and an inflated belief in his own brilliance." Anna Mikhailovna delicately sips her *sirop de cassis*.

Marya pictures the lines on Suzuki's skin, their slow, deliberate movement. What would Grey do if he saw them? What part would they play in his so-called Eden?

"I wish he would stop," she says, suddenly, more fiercely than she intended. "Why is everyone just letting him talk like this?"

"Oh, he will talk himself out, they always do, these men." The Countess waves a dismissive hand, but Marya sees the cleric, Yuri Petrovich, twitching in his chair, his slow, volcanic energy threatening to erupt. Beside him, the Countess sits back, with the look of one settling in to enjoy a spectacle.

"Blasphemy!" He hits the arm of his chair with his fist. The Countess doesn't react. "A new Eden? Such dangerous, blinkered nonsense I have never in my life heard. You think you found God in this wilderness? You found the Deceiver! You were taken in, as all weak fools are!"

This outburst silences the carriage but Yuri Petrovich's moment center stage is spoiled by the sudden arrival of a small boy, who crashes through the carriage door, stares at the faces turned toward him, and dashes back out again.

"Yuri Petrovich, you are scaring the infants," calls Guillaume, but the cleric is not to be distracted from the target of his ire.

"Don't you see? Don't you see they are laughing at you? All your talk of paradise when we are in Hell. And these pampered travellers, these tourists in the infernal regions, they take you for a fool!"

"Steady on," says Guillaume. Sophie and other passengers look away, embarrassed, though whether for themselves or for Yuri Petrovich or even Grey, Marya does not know. Grey is too far lost in his zealotry to care.

"There will always be doubters," he says, almost to himself. "There will also be those who do not see. They look but they do not see, because they themselves have been out in the wilderness for too long. They have not yet felt the touch of true understanding. The gift . . ." He raises his hands as if in prayer and she thinks she sees tears glistening on his cheeks.

"Who are you calling—" Yuri Petrovich rises to his feet.

"Gentlemen." Wu Jinlu reacts impressively quickly, appearing beside the cleric in such a way as to suggest that he merely happened to find himself there, and placing a hand on his arm.

"He slanders me," growls the cleric.

"I believe it was you, sir, who accused me of blasphemy—"

"You dare to call yourself a man of God! All of you here, you should be ashamed, drinking and making merry. You have given in to the temptations outside. I will pray for your souls." Yuri Petrovich shakes off Wu Jinlu's hand and strides out of the carriage.

"Well, that has certainly put us in our place," remarks the Countess, who, Marya notices, can barely keep the gleeful expression off her face.

But Grey is on his feet, shaken. "I must make him understand," he says. "It is too important—"

"Perhaps a task for tomorrow," says Wu Jinlu. "You look as if you need some sleep." And it is true, the Englishman is swaying. Marya rises to help steady him and Wu looks at her gratefully. "Let us help you to your cabin."

They maneuver him out of the saloon car and down the corridor of the sleeping carriage.

"I saw her," he mumbles, like one of the drunkards Marya used to see down by the water in Petersburg, stumbling from the riverside inns. "She saved my life."

"The woman outside, in the forest," explains Wu, with a raise of his eyebrows.

"No." Grey stops, forcing the three of them to come to an undignified halt, squashed together in the narrow corridor. "She was here. I saw her here first, on the train."

Marya thinks about the figure in Sophie's drawings. Hovering in doorways. Watching.

"It was just the storm," says Wu Jinlu, calmly. "It set us all on edge. Come, we are nearly at your cabin."

They enter awkwardly, depositing Grey onto one of the armchairs before they're able to turn on the lights. As Marya reaches out to the lamp on the table she gasps, and recoils.

Grey had left the curtains open, or the steward had forgotten to come in and close them, so the window and the night outside are exposed. But it isn't the landscape that makes them stare but the patterns on the glass. The window is covered in them, as if it were frosted over, despite the summer heat, or as if the ghosts of flowers had been imprinted into the glass, in patterns more delicate than even her father had made.

"I told you," says Grey. "We are blessed."

"Mold," says the merchant, stepping backwards. "But growing so fast."

He's right, it is growing before their eyes. "We should close the curtains," she says. She is afraid. Suddenly, horribly afraid.

"No, don't—" begins Grey, but she flicks the lamps on and tugs the curtains closed.

She and Wu exchange a glance. She can see her own fear reflected on his face. He wipes his forehead with a handkerchief.

"Nothing that this train hasn't seen before, I am sure," he says, though he has lost his habitual air of confidence.

A sound behind them makes her turn. Shadows fill the doorway. "Good evening to all of you. Is Dr. Grey feeling more himself?"

The Crows.

"I have never felt better, but I have work to do, I must make a record . . ." His hand twitches toward the curtain and she tries to stand in his way.

"Dr. Grey is simply overtired." *They will lock him away,* she thinks. *They will say it's for his own protection.* She looks at his trembling hands and is sure that he will not survive it.

"A good night's sleep is all he needs," adds Wu Jinlu.

The Company men both nod, and smile, though their smiles don't reach their eyes. They have started to lose their composure; to cast off some of their polish and shine. The journey is taking its toll.

"Of course," says Mr. Li. "We would not want to keep Dr. Grey from his work." Perhaps seeing her expression, he goes on: "We have invited him to speak at our own Exhibition stand. He will show the great contribution the Company makes to the scientific understanding of the Wastelands. It will be a great opportunity for us all." Is it her imagination or is there an odd emphasis in his words?

"Ah, I see," says Wu Jinlu, though a puzzled expression flits across his face. Marya says nothing. The Crows are looking at her with appraising gazes and she feels the first stirrings of fear. She wants to laugh at her own naivety. Grey is a blasphemer to clerics like Yuri Petrovich, yet an evangelist to the Company. Why would they wish to silence such fervor? He is useful to them. *Come and see our wonders, they are blessed by God.*

"How are you feeling, Marya Petrovna?" *They know,* she thinks. *They know exactly who I am. They see me as clearly as if I had my own truths tattooed on my skin.* How had they found out? Had she given herself away? *Had Suzuki?* No—that she cannot believe. She will not.

She tries to calm herself, but there is a ringing in her ears and the cabin is far too small; it is hard to breathe. She needs to get out but the Company men are blocking the door, as though they are spreading their wings and filling more and more of the space around them.

"Marya Petrovna? Could you accompany us, madam?"

"What do you mean by this?" demands Wu Jinlu.

"Please, this is for your own good." Mr. Petrov steps forward to take her arm, and she recoils, crashing into the table. Grey gives an exclamation of annoyance.

"We're afraid Marya Petrovna is unwell. We simply need her to come with us for her own safety, and that of others."

She sees the meaningful glance pass between Petrov and Wu. Sees Wu step away from her, stare down at his feet.

"I am quite well, I assure you." She tries to make her voice hard and steady but she can feel the shake in her throat.

"There is nothing to be worried about, it is just for observation."

"Don't cause a scene," her mother says, in her head. Her mother was afraid above all things of causing a scene, but this is exactly what she should do. She should shout and scream and bring the other passengers running; tell them that these men are liars, that *they* are the dangerous ones, that they will protect themselves, protect the Company, no matter what the cost.

But the look on Wu Jinlu's face weakens her resolve. He's afraid of her, of what she might do in the throes of a sickness that takes hold of the mind. She can stamp her foot and scream and plead that there is nothing wrong, she is perfectly fine, but that will only convince them more—they will all shake their heads and murmur politely that it is for the best. She can accuse the Company of anything she likes—no one will listen if they believe she is tainted.

There is movement behind the Crows and she sees the neat little Company doctor hovering in the doorway, one hand in a pocket to clumsily hide the bulge of a syringe. Petrov takes her by the arm. As they leave the cabin she looks back to see Grey leaning over his books, scribbling furiously, Wu Jinlu looking down, unable to lift his eyes to meet hers.

4

A BREACH

She is different this time, the stowaway. Weiwei can't say exactly
what it is, but Elena's presence seems more solid, as if she is taking
up more space. They crouch on opposite ends of the bunk.

"*Thief.*"

She makes the cramped space between the bunk and the ceiling
seem even smaller.

"I didn't know," says Weiwei. "I didn't know what it would do."
Didn't you? The patterns on the wall are moving, the lichen growing
before her eyes.

"Why did you take it? It wasn't yours."

Because I wanted it, she wants to say. *I wanted to hold it and keep it.
I wanted something that couldn't leave, that couldn't be lost.* But instead
all she says is, "I'm sorry. I'm so sorry." The train thunders in her
head, the rails rattle in her bones, and it is not Elena's fault, it is hers,
all hers. She has brought the outside into the train, and the Vigil is
approaching and there is nothing she can do. She sees again the fear in
Alexei's face, the guilt he has wrapped around himself, and her guilt
grows stronger still. "Why did you come back?" She doesn't mean it
to sound so abrupt. "Henry Grey's looking for you." *He will see her,*
she thinks. He is like Rostov, like *her.* All looking for something, all
unsatisfied with what they have. "He believes you're a messenger, an
angel . . ."

"Not a monster?" Elena touches the wall, and the lichen moves like ripples in the water, flowing outward then turning inward, exploring, lapping at her fingers.

"No, that's not—"

"Not what you think? Isn't it? Out there, you thought I had hurt him. That it's what monsters do. That it's where we belong."

"No . . ." But she sees it again in her mind's eye, Henry Grey sprawled on the ground, Elena crouching over him. "*Don't!*" Elena looking up. Betrayed.

"That's not true." Weiwei reaches out to take her hand, but she knows that the words are hollow and dry. Elena will always be a stowaway, an uninvited guest; she will always be a monster—to be feared, hunted, caught. "We will find somewhere for you to belong," Weiwei says. "We will reach Russia and you will see all the world that you wanted, all the things you imagined—"

But Elena is pulling away, twisting her hair between her fingers.

"What?"

"That's not why I came back, you don't understand."

"But I *want* to, because otherwise how can I understand all this? All these changes . . ." She needs to get rid of it. She turns to the wall, starts trying to break off the lichen that has grown now all the way to the ceiling; starts trying to scratch it with her fingernails—

"Weiwei, no—"

—and it is as if a sudden spill of ink floods over her mind, and all is dark and empty until the ink is washed away and she is—

—Somewhere she should not be. In the thunderous inferno of the engine room, watching the stokers feed the mouth of the train, flames reflected in their protective goggles, scorch marks on their gloves. Through the grime of the windows she sees that they are not far from the Russian Wall, near the beginning of their crossing. *The last crossing.* A memory? No, something else. Bright-orange sparks hang in the air but when they fall onto her skin they do not burn her—not sparks but spores, dancing toward the firebox, searching for the heat that powers the train. She sees other spores emerge again from the fire, follows one to where it settles on the wall; she crouches down to see a metallic sheen forming, iridescent greens and silvers, as if part of the metal of the wall, but growing, pulsing in time with the roar of the engine, with the rhythm of the rails—

—and fights have broken out in First. The passengers complain of disturbed sleep, they say that when they catch sight of their reflections in the window they are not their own; they have smashed the mirrors in the Third Class bathroom. Weiwei looks down at the angry red cut on the palm of her right hand, from a shard of glass. She has seen herself in it, distorted into a sly, creeping creature, a starved look on her face. She stands, dripping blood onto the black-and-white tiles of the bathroom, unable to tear her eyes away from the glass.

"I had to do it." A woman with her back to the wall, staring at the remains of the mirror, her own hands bloodied. "It was lying, it was lying."

But Weiwei thinks, *Perhaps it was telling the truth—*

—and the Captain is raging at the landscape. They are in the lookout tower and the great lake is beside them, almost white beneath the late summer sun, the horizon disappearing into a bleached-out sky. The Captain is shouting for her to close the shutters, to hide the outside away.

"Shall I fetch the doctor?"

"No."

"Some water, then . . ." Weiwei wants to be out of the tower, to be away from this unfamiliar version of the Captain. She makes for the door.

"How are we to bear it?"

Weiwei stops.

The Captain looks up, her skin pale and clammy. "Don't you feel it? As if it is trying to get in . . . Always there, growing, whatever we do, however strong we are . . . How do you bear it?"

Weiwei stares, pinned down by the intensity of her gaze and she sees the Captain revealed, unmasked—*afraid*. Afraid of the landscape outside. She had never imagined that beneath it all the Captain would be scared. The walls of the train suddenly seem a little less strong, the floor a little less solid.

"You're unwell," she whispers. "Let me take you down to your quarters." But the Captain gives a wave of dismissal.

"Leave me be."

"But you're not—"

"Leave me!" She turns with a ferocity that sends Weiwei scuttling away, down the stairs and into the dark—

—and into the Third Class sleeping carriage, the stillness more shocking than anything she has seen. They are sleeping, the passengers, but in such silence that she has to check for signs of life. Yes, the slow rise and fall of chests, the parting of lips. There are lamps burning but the curtains are open to the night outside. On the edge of her hearing, a small sound. A splintering. Around the nearest window, there is the same metallic sheen she had seen on the engine wall, pulsing with life. She puts her hand to the glass and feels the same, slow pulse. There are veins appearing, silvering beneath her fingers, veins stretching from one window to the other and here is the splintering noise again and the window cracks—

"Come back!"

She snatches her hand away from the lichen on the wall. Elena is leaning toward her. "How do you feel? What did you see?"

Weiwei tries to form the words but she can still feel the glass, *alive*, then gone. She can still see the spores, floating in the dark, luminescent. The lost days of the last crossing. The train changed, *invaded*.

"It wasn't the glass," she whispers. "The Company was wrong, the walls of the train had already been breached, the outside had already come in." She remembers the spores, dancing toward the furnace. The sense of purpose.

"What happened?" There is a look on Elena's face that Weiwei recognizes, the same hunger as when she had looked outside at the birds, the foxes—at all the things that were calling her yet keeping her away.

"We were part of it all. Connected." She can barely raise her voice above a whisper. Under her fingers, she feels the raised scar on the palm of her hand. She remembers picking the shard of glass from her skin. Remembers her reflection in the shattered mirror, small and mean and hungry, as if she had seen a part of herself that she kept hidden from view. "We were shown the different parts of ourselves. And then . . ." The glass cracked. The connection was lost. She can feel its absence, like the ache she gets when the train has stopped. "Is this how you feel?" she manages. "Empty?"

"Empty," Elena repeats, as if tasting the word. Then she says, "Outside, in the grass and the trees and the water, I felt strong again. I thought that I was home."

Weiwei waits.

"But I had betrayed my home. I left it and it would not welcome me back. It has learned too; it has changed."

From us, thinks Weiwei. *It has learned from us—from all parts of us, our best parts and our worst.* She feels the blood pounding in her temples. "But what does that mean?"

Elena sits back against the wall. She says, "It means that they will not stop now. It does not matter how strong the train might be, there is nothing that can hold them back anymore."

5

THREADS

The morning sun illuminates the patterns on the window, imbuing them with vibrant, vivid life. Henry Grey stretches his cramping fingers and reaches toward the glass. He is sure he can feel the blooms growing, pulsing with impatient energy, pulling every pore of his skin toward them. He wishes he could touch them, trap them, press them between the pages of a book like the albums of wildflowers stacked on his shelves at home.

He doesn't eat; the pain in his stomach makes the thought of food unbearable, and besides, he is too rich in visions to rest, too full of knowledge. He burns with it. The notebooks on his table are growing thick with his remembrances, with everything he had seen outside, with ideas that proliferate; he has to run after each thought before it bounds away from him, leaving bright trails that he must follow or lose forever.

He crouches down to unlock the doors of the little cabinet where he is keeping his specimens. The train girl had brought them to him, afraid. *"They are changing, Dr. Grey,"* she had said. Here, this jar had held a beetle-like creature, iridescent wings and strong black pincers that had tapped and tapped against the glass. But now there is no movement within, only a dry, brown thing, slightly furred. Breathing. In the dark, they are growing. His pieces of the Wastelands, waiting to emerge, to be brought out onto the stage of the Great Exhibition. A shiver of anticipation runs down his spine. *Not yet, not quite yet.* He shuts the door and locks it carefully, placing the key in his jacket pocket and brushing away a long white thread. He frowns, wiping at his suit with his hands. Has he changed his clothes already this morning? He is finding it harder to remember these things. Even the image of his cottage and garden is hard to bring to mind—England fading into dull obscurity against the vividness of the Wastelands. Anyway, the thread—has someone been in his cabin, snooping? But he looks closer and realizes it isn't a thread at all, but something more like a root, extraordinarily thin, caught in the air where he has brushed it away. *A hypha,* he thinks, *from a fungus.* And look, there are more, branching out from the walls to the floor. He kneels down and watches their filament-thin tips moving, as if they are searching out new ground. *A desert like the garden of the Lord,* he thinks, and he scrabbles with his fingernails at the cabin wall, scrabbling to reach the growth within it, the mycelial life. He breaks a piece of the wooden board off, and more of the thin white hyphae are revealed. "Extraordinary," he says, ignoring the pain in his bloodied fingers.

A knock on the door sends him to his feet. He grabs a couple of cushions from the bed and stacks them against the wall to disguise the damage.

"Who's there?" No answer, so he opens the door a crack. "I do not wish to be disturbed—" but Alexei pushes his way into the cabin, shutting the door quickly.

"You promised you would be careful," he hisses. He is unshaven, his eyes bloodshot.

"My dear boy—"

"You've poisoned us all."

"I have done nothing of the sort!" Grey feels a flush on his cheeks.

The engineer wipes his forehead and looks around the cabin. "You've got to get rid of it . . . whatever it is . . . before it does any more damage."

"There is really no need for this . . . this overreaction. I have not *poisoned* anything. Look." He guides the engineer over to the table, where the insects are safe in their little cocoons, inside their glass jars. "This is all I took, there is nothing here that you need to worry about. Nothing that is still alive." He watches the engineer, certain—almost certain—that he will not recognize a chrysalis.

Alexei stares at the jars, then up at the window, where the mold on the outside of the glass is shifting, pulsing with light. His shoulders sag.

"Can this really be my doing?" asks Grey, speaking as he might to a small child. "It is on the outside of the train, surely nothing to do with us. And is this not what we wanted? To discover for ourselves what these changes mean, how they can be understood? Did we not speak of what the Company is hiding from us? When we reach the Exhibition it will be *our* names that will be spoken. We will be remembered, my dear boy, as the men who unlocked the mysteries of the Wastelands, hidden for too long by a Company grown fat from its secrets."

But the engineer shakes his head and backs away. "I shouldn't have listened, it's my fault."

"Come now, it is natural to feel overwhelmed. Every great man who finds his purpose amidst a great undertaking must tremble in the face of his task. But the truly great are steadfast."

"But for this, we must actually reach Moscow, Dr. Grey. You understand that, don't you? We must pass the Vigil." The young man flings himself out of the cabin as abruptly as he came. *The pressure of the journey is weighing on him,* thinks Grey. *Poor boy.*

After the engineer leaves, Grey crouches down again by the wall, where the hyphae are bursting out, uncontainable. He glances around, imagining that every set of footsteps along the corridor signals an imminent crashing open of the door, but though he tries to stuff the thin tendrils back into the wall, there are too many of them, and they are growing too quickly. He feels a stab of panic. It will be impossible to hide them, impossible to explain that this is not his doing, but then he sits back on his heels and watches as they shift, as they reach tentatively out of the wall and onto the carpet, and he wants to laugh with astonishment, with joy. There is life all around him, new Eden breaking into the train itself.

6

LOST TIME

She looks at Elena and the silence between them stretches taut.

"Zhang!" A yell from the other end of the carriage makes her jump. Weiwei scrambles down the ladder before the voice can get any closer.

"There's unrest in First, you're needed," says a steward.

"I'll be along in a moment," she says. *Don't look up,* she tells herself. *Don't look up or he'll look up too.*

"Now," he says.

Mutely, she follows him. At her back, she is sure she can feel slivers of lichen, reaching out to follow her. She wishes her head would stop aching, but the roar of the train will not be stilled, nor will Elena's voice in her head. *"There is nothing that can hold them back anymore."* She trails after the steward into the saloon car, where the second steward is helpless in the face of the Countess's onslaught.

"I demand to see her immediately," she is saying.

"But madam, the doctor says—"

"What does he know? She was perfectly well yesterday, and I see no reason why she should be denied visitors."

With a sharp stab of foreboding, Weiwei looks around to see who is missing. Marya Petrovna. Guilt floods over her. The Professor had warned her—*"Tell her to be careful."* But she had ignored him. She had ignored Marya Petrovna, and now she has been taken away. Was

she really ill? She had been worried that the widow would discover
Elena, with her questions and curiosity, but now she suspects that
there is something else that she has been looking for.

The saloon car is loud with speculation.

"But are we not in danger ourselves, if we have been dining with
her all this time?" someone is saying. "Can we really be sure it is not
contagious?"

"I feel quite well, but for a slight headache that I'm sure is simply
worry on her behalf . . ."

"I for one would like to know why those gentlemen thought it
right to spirit her away like that . . ."

"It is the safest place for her, if she is ill . . ."

"Will you do something, my dear?" The Countess turns her attention to Weiwei, ignoring the steward. "She was taken away late
at night, it is really most odd."

"I'm sure it's just a precaution, for her health. The doctor is used
to treating the sickness," says Weiwei, without much conviction.

The Countess looks at her shrewdly. "It is not the sickness I am
worried about," she says, in a voice low enough for only Weiwei to hear.

Weiwei hurries back through the sleeping carriages toward the infirmary, resolving to put right her failure to speak to Marya, but
halfway along she sees Alexei leaving Henry Grey's cabin. *Sneaking,*
she thinks, but then she sees his expression, and freezes. His eyes are
red and there is such despair on his face that she is too shocked to try
to hide or turn in the opposite direction, pretending she hasn't seen
him. He looks at her and wipes his eyes, angrily. "What is it now?"
His uniform is creased and untidy, and there is stubble on his chin.
"For the love of iron, Zhang, what are you staring at?"

The roughness in his voice stings her. "What were you doing in
there?" she demands.

"He—" He stops, then puts his face in his hands and leans back
against the wall. "It's my fault," he says, his voice muffled.

"What do you mean?"

He takes his hands away and gestures to the mold on the windows.
"All of this, it's my fault—the danger I put you in."

"It's nothing to do with you," she says, touching his arm.

He looks at her, the lines on his forehead deepening, then says, in a rush of words, "I gave Grey the keys to get out. It's because of me that you nearly died, that the Captain risked her life to bring you back, that everything is changing. It was me who let the Wastelands in." He kneels to scrabble at the carpet with his fingernails.

"Stop! What are you doing? You'll hurt yourself." She tries to pull him away but he is much stronger.

"*Look!*"

His scrabbling has revealed thin white threads, snaking up from the floor. She stumbles backward as they move toward her, rising up as if tasting the air. She wishes she could talk to him like she always used to. Thoughtlessly, endlessly, like the little sister he complained that she resembled. But it's hard to tear her eyes from the white threads, from their undulating motion, their sense of purpose.

"Nothing that is happening is your fault," she says, urgently.

"You can't know that."

But I can, she wants to say. *I do know.*

They stare at each other, and in the silence an alarm starts to scream.

The Breach alarm. They have heard it only in drills, but still, on bad nights she has woken up, convinced she has heard it ringing through the train. An insistent, discordant jangling, telling the crew to get the First Class passengers to their cabins, Third Class to their bunks. Telling them to muster in the crew mess. *What will Elena do? Will she be afraid?*

Most are pale, and scared, and trying to pretend not to be, though Alexei looks worse than all of them; she sees heads turning toward him, feels him hunch into himself. She wants to squeeze his arm in reassurance but can't seem to make herself move, not when there are so many terrors piling one upon the other that it takes all her willpower to simply stay standing.

The Cartographer slips through the door. She has seen him so little on this crossing that his appearance is a shock. There is exhaustion on his face, as if it has been days since he has slept.

The alarm falls silent, and the Captain enters.

There is an audible stir among the crew. This must be the first time some of them have seen her face to face since the crossing began, realizes Weiwei. But the anger and confusion felt earlier in the crossing have turned into something else—even amidst the rumors of illness and incapacity, new stories of what happened outside have spread through the train like the flickers of Valentin's Fire. As they were crossing the line Weiwei had heard the kitchen boys describe how the Captain had rescued Henry Grey from the jaws of a Wastelands giant, fighting it off with her bare hands. And so her mythology grows.

But here she is, stern and austere, and the crew stand to attention, buttoning up undone collars and pulling down shirtsleeves. Weiwei tries to set her face in a neutral expression but when the Captain's gaze meets hers she drops her eyes. She feels Alexei clench and unclench his hands.

The Captain waits until a few last stragglers have entered. "Please sit," she says. Then she begins, without preamble, to explain that growths have been found inside the train, origin and classification unknown. Her voice is calm. She is as strong and unmoving as ever. It could feel, almost, as if nothing has changed, that order has been restored at last.

Weiwei remembers what she saw when she touched the lichen—*that the Captain was afraid*—though she knows that all the crew would swear that there was nothing in the world that the woman standing in front of them feared.

Disquiet ripples through the carriage as the meaning of the Captain's words sinks in, but she holds up her hand for silence. "It goes without saying that you must avoid touching anything. Our Repair team is already at work. But we must remain vigilant. Anything out of place must be reported directly to me. From now on, crew members will be assigned carriages to patrol, so that we have eyes on all parts of the train at all times. Breach protocol will apply."

The silence thickens. Breach protocol, allowing for the use of "extraordinary measures," of whatever means necessary to protect the train.

The Captain glances into the corner of the carriage and Weiwei turns to see the Crows, melting into the shadows. A small but discernible space has been left around them. They will be preparing for the worst, she realizes. The possibility that no one wants to think about. *The sealing of the doors, the moving of the train to a special yard, out of sight of the Company and any well-bred visitors to the Wall. The slow falling of silence.* The older crew members say that the doctor keeps a special medicine in his cabin—a draft that will ease your passing, like closing your eyes in a snowfall. But there is not enough for everyone, they say, only for the lucky ones, the ones able to hasten the end. Everyone else must wait, as the air grows stale, as it runs out completely.

She shakes the thought from her head.

When the Captain dismisses them Weiwei elbows Alexei. "Come with me," she says, and drags him behind her as she runs after the Cartographer, who is already striding away down the corridor. "Marya Petrovna has been taken to the infirmary," she calls.

Suzuki turns, what little color he had in his cheeks vanishing. "What?"

"They say it's Wastelands sickness, though the Countess seems to think this is dubious. I thought you might want to—"

"When?"

"Last night. Very suddenly, apparently." She thinks he's about to rush there immediately—*Why? What is she to you?*—but she sees him hesitate and follows his gaze. The Crows are standing in the doorway, watching them. Suzuki draws in a breath.

"Why is she important?" Weiwei demands, in a low voice. "Tell me or I will tell them that I believe she's a spy. That I've seen her sneaking around, that she asks too many questions."

Suzuki holds her gaze. Then he says, "Follow me."

They follow him into the crew sleeping carriage, which he checks is empty, then turns to them, pulling down the sleeves of his shirt, even though most of the crew have rolled up their sleeves in the heat, against all rules. *Even now,* she thinks, *even though he looks about ready to fall apart, the Cartographer follows the rules.*

"I don't understand," says Alexei, looking from one of them to the other. "What's this passenger got to do with you?"

"She has to do with all of us," says Suzuki.

Weiwei thinks about the young widow and the questions she has asked, all the places she has found her. "She wanted to know about the last crossing. She wanted . . ." She stops, realization dawning. Marya Petrovna, stumbling into Third Class, sneaking off to see the Cartographer, always asking questions. "She is something to do with Anton Ivanovich, isn't she?"

Suzuki's shoulders slump. She sees him making a decision, letting go. "His daughter," he says.

Alexei leans back against the wall, letting out a long whistle.

"The Professor knows; he wanted to warn her," says Weiwei. "But I didn't . . ." She has been too selfish. Too selfish and cowardly to try to help anyone else; not Marya, not Alexei. She has thought only of herself, this whole time. Always herself, before the crew or the passengers. Before the train.

The humming in her head, in her bones, grows louder. She thinks she can feel the pulsing of the lichen in the far corner of the carriage. Had any of them tried hard enough to defend the glassmaker, when the time had come to apportion blame? Or had they just been relieved that the burden on the rest of them had been lifted?

"We are all complicit," says Suzuki. "But I most of all. Anton Ivanovich tried to save us from this." He gestures to the white threads that have crept across the wall while they have been speaking. "He was afraid that we had pushed the train too far. Even before the last crossing. He was right." And they listen as he tells them what the glassmaker's new telescope had revealed, and what they had seen on the last crossing, and it all fits in with Elena's words: "*There is nothing that can hold them back anymore.*" Anton Ivanovich had seen what she had not. And now it is too late.

"And Marya?" demands Alexei.

"She has proof that her father tried to warn the Company," says Suzuki. "They have searched her cabin but I don't believe they have found anything." He starts to walk away, toward the opposite end of the carriage.

"Where are you going?"

"To find Marya Antonovna. To start atoning."

"She will think it's too late," says Alexei, his voice cold.

Suzuki stops. He says, "And she will be right."

He carries on, and Weiwei grabs Alexei's wrist. "Come on," she says, and as they reach the end of the carriage she looks up at her bunk, praying to the gods of the rail that Elena is hidden there, quiet and safe. She can see no sign of the stowaway, but the lichen has spread further across the wall, even in so short a time. It will be impossible to miss it, soon, but Alexei is looking instead at the clock beside the door.

"It's stopped," he says. "The one in the mess has stopped too."

They have fallen out of time.

7

WINGS

Marya's mind wanders. Without a window she feels unmoored. What did Rostov say about this region? Trees that vanish into the folds in the air. Purple flowers on the ground. She wishes she had a book, some paper, anything to keep her thoughts from festering. She must be in the cabin next door to the one the Professor had been in. Was he still there? She can hear nothing through the padded walls.

Eventually, a nervous kitchen boy brings her breakfast on a silver tray; steaming porridge and warm rolls and hot coffee, but the smells, which would have normally made her mouth water, turn her stomach, and besides, she is determined not to eat, out of principle. Eating from the neat silver tray would be accepting her situation, would be saying, *I understand why I am here.* She does not accept it. She has hammered on the wall and brought the doctor to the adjoining door, she has demanded to know upon what evidence they are keeping her here, but the doctor only stammered that it was for her own good.

Her mind keeps wandering to Suzuki and the map on his skin. Changing. *Like her father.* Skin turned into cartography, eyes turned into glass. What did it feel like? Did it hurt? She tries to push away the image of her father, his empty eyes. He had deteriorated, in those last months, he had suffered and there had been no one to speak to, no one who would understand, and she has pushed Suzuki away too, and she cannot bear to see it happen again, to see it happen to this man, who is kind and unhappy and alone; who is burning up with guilt. She needs to get out, to tell him what happened to her father. To stop it happening again.

She hammers on the door and shouts until she is hoarse but in the end it is an alarm that answers her. An ugly, incongruous sound, a warning of danger. She hears feet hurrying past, but no one stops, the doctor doesn't appear with reassurances. She feels the walls closing in further, her lungs struggling to take in enough air. It is too hot, too close in the little cabin, she can't breathe.

She rests her forehead against the wall, fighting the urge to panic. And it is then that she notices a discolored patch in the cream-colored padding and frowns, looking closer. A shape is emerging—a moth, trapped beneath the material. She can see the beating of its wings. Something bumps against her head and she brushes it away quickly. Another moth—how are they getting in? She has never liked their mindless, meaningless motion, the way they tangle in her hair. There are more and more now; the walls are moving, and she has to fight down the panic, the horror at being trapped with all these beating wings.

One of the insects lands on the back of her hand and she is about to shake it off when it spreads its wings and reveals two spots like the eyes of an owl, a deep black ringed with gold. She raises her hand and the moth remains, poised, its delicate proboscis testing the air. It is just like the ones her father drew, future ideas that never became glass. It could have flown right off the page. And she is suddenly unafraid.

The alarm falls silent. She hears noises from the doctor's cabin, the sound of something crashing to the floor. The doctor is weeping, but she doesn't care. The moth is so delicate, so perfect, she understands why her father wanted to immortalize it in glass. She stands in the middle of the cabin, her arms outstretched, as the moths soar and spiral around her, their wings beating at her skin, a hundred pairs of owls' eyes opening and closing.

They collect on the door to the corridor, more and more of them, as if they are trying to burrow through.

And then the door opens, to reveal a young woman in a dirty blue dress looking in, curiously. "Hello," she says, in Russian. Some of the moths settle on her hair and her shoulders, like a soft, gray cape. She has wide, dark eyes, like the patterns on the moths' wings, and the bare skin on her arms is slightly mottled.

Marya stares at her. She has seen her before—a figure always on the point of vanishing. Is this her? Henry Grey's angel, Sophie's faceless girl.

"I heard the moths," she says, to Marya's unasked question. "I wanted to come and find them."

This seems, thinks Marya, *a reasonable explanation.* "There is someone in the next-door cabin," she says, stepping out into the corridor and trying to force herself to stay calm. "Can you let him out as well?"

"Certainly," says the girl, with a formality that Marya might have found amusing, in another situation. The girl raises her hand, palm upward, and a dozen moths land, crawling over her fingers and each other. Then she blows them gently toward the door and they spread their wings as they land, patterning the wood and encircling the door handle until it opens. She looks back at Marya with something of the appearance of a child who wishes to be praised for their cleverness, and Marya gasps, obligingly.

The Professor emerges, his eyes wide, his hair and beard uncombed. *As wild as this girl,* thinks Marya, *as if he has just stepped out of the wilderness. As if he has just stepped out of one dream and into another.* She takes his arm. "We are in the company of Artemis, I believe," she says.

He smiles. "I had thought to have left that name behind me. But now . . . Now I am thinking again."

The girl is looking at him intently. "I know you," she says, her head to one side, scrutinizing him as one might a painting in a gallery. "I have seen you watching from the windows. For many years."

The Professor gives a low bow. "Grigori Danilovich. Otherwise known—" and he nods at Marya, "as Artemis. It is my pleasure, madam. But I am afraid you have me at a disadvantage . . ."

The girl looks at him, then at Marya.

"He means, may we ask your name?" Marya says.

8

TO THE SOURCE

A wilderness like Eden. He is chasing the hyphae, filament thin, down corridors, losing sight of them then finding them again, bursting from a window frame or weaving themselves through carpet like ghostly threads. An alarm is ringing, but he is doing his best to ignore it. He is sure that the creature—his Eve—and the threads are connected. He saw her on the train, in the storm, and then again on the outside, and now all these signs, this life bursting from the train . . . She was the harbinger, pointing out the truth to whoever would read it.

"Sir, you must return to your cabin." A young steward has the gall to take him by the arm, and he shakes him off.

"Can't you see that I am at work? I asked not to be disturbed!" he roars, and the boy cowers backward, almost tripping over his own feet in his haste to be away.

Grey rubs his face. Where was he? Yes, following the growth to its source. He has done it many times before, striding over moors, his head down, in search of the signs that will lead him to its budding, its birth. *To her.* He is prepared. He pats his jacket, feels the weight of the tranquilizer gun, the syringes. He has done well to keep them hidden and safe. He has lost her twice already, he will not do so again.

The dining car is empty. He has a feeling it should be lunchtime but the clock on the wall is stopped, and he cannot remember when he last ate. He feels rather light-headed and has to stop for a moment to lean on one of the tables while the darkness at the edges of his eyes recedes.

Third Class. Here, all is chaos and noise. There are stewards at the carriage doors, but they are trying to stop people from moving into First, not the other way around, so he slips through before anyone notices.

He pushes on, into the part of the train where passengers are not meant to go. He is struck by a thought: *Are they hiding her here? Have they known, all along? Impossible.* He dismisses it from his mind, but he is finding it hard to keep his thoughts in order. *Think of the great glass palace,* he tells himself. *Think of the exhibits, safe and labeled, held behind glass. Think of the name Henry Grey in the history books.*

Into the Captain's carriage. He has been here before, he is sure, but it feels like a long time ago now. The hyphae are easier to see, here, without the thick carpet or polished wood to obscure them. There are crew members trying to pull them out and he shouts at them to cease but they just stare at him blankly, and they try to manhandle him when he demands to see the Captain, and he has never experienced such rudeness. Up ahead he sees the train girl, together with the engineer (he will ignore him, of course—how dare he call him a liar, question his integrity?) and the Cartographer. "My dear!" he calls to her. How young she is, can she possibly understand the importance of his mission? And Chinese after all, what can she know of Eden? But isn't this what he will achieve—to spread the word to all people?

"Dr. Grey?" She is saying something to him, but he doesn't listen, because this is when he sees her, at the other end of the corridor, framed by the carriage door. Behind her, for some reason, are the young widow and an old man he doesn't recognize. Her dress is torn and her hair tangled, but it is her—the Wastelands creature, the white threads have brought him to her, just as he had theorized.

Something moves in her hair, as if she has brought a Wastelands wind with her, then he realizes that they are insects—moths. The kind that mimic the face of a predator, two wide eyes on their wings, ringed with gold.

And he realizes that it is not just the moths; *she* is mimicking.

He doesn't see a ragged girl in a dirty dress, with moths in her hair, he sees a young woman, a lace shawl over her head, in the style of pious women in his village church. Then he sees nothing at all, she has vanished, she has made herself part of the background, like a predator by a lake, waiting for its chance to pounce. *She is still here,* he tells himself. He just needs to *look*, in the same way that she does. He is not easy prey. He sees beneath the surface. Yes, there . . .

People are shouting, the engineer is tugging him backward, the stewards are grabbing the widow and the old man, pulling them away, as if they should be afraid of her, as if she will taint them, but look—she is perfect, she is emerging into the light . . .

He raises the gun.

9

DOORWAYS AND WEBS

Weiwei doesn't think about what she is doing, only moves toward Grey and the sleek silver gun in his hands. She knows what is inside the syringe—a strong concoction distilled from poppy seed. "*Harmless,*" the doctor says, but she has seen its effects and she knows this is not true. She cannot let such poison run in Elena's veins. Alexei is shouting her name, but she has eyes only for the gun, she is pushing it away; away from Elena, toward the lichen that is creeping across the ceiling in waves of silver and blue.

The dart flies out, pinning itself into the scales of the lichen—

—and pain floods over her, as if something is tearing at her sinews. She falls into darkness.

—When she opens her eyes, what must be only seconds later, she sees Suzuki crouched on the floor, Marya hurrying toward him; sees the scales of lichen on the ceiling and the pale threads across the floor; feels the train and the earth, and the earth and the train, woven together, and she is part of it too, she feels the point of the dart where it is embedded in the lichen; where the drug is spilling out.

"Are you hurt?" Alexei is leaning over her, patting her shoulders as if expecting to find a wound, and Weiwei tries to say *Yes* but she doesn't understand how she is hurt, only that there is a dull, thudding ache in all of her limbs, she doesn't know how to frame the words; she doesn't know how to separate the different parts of the scene before her.

Here is Elena, unmoving. Watching Weiwei with such intensity that she seems unaware of anyone else in the carriage.

Here is Henry Grey, grappling with the mechanics of the gun, his hands slipping on its bolt. She could tear it from him, if she could just make her legs work properly, but he seems to be getting further away, the closer she moves. She tries to form the words to tell Elena—*Run!*—but her mouth is too dry.

And behind her, a new set of footsteps, fast and light and determined. The Captain. *Breach protocol,* thinks Weiwei. The Captain could order not just a tranquilizer dart but any means necessary, she could call the gunner down from the watchtower to train his sights on Elena. She tries again to call out, to tell her to run, there is too much danger here, but no sound emerges. The Professor is approaching Elena, his arms held out as if to reassure a child. But the stowaway pays him no attention. She is looking up at where the dart is pinned to the scales of lichen in the ceiling, where darker veins are zigzagging out from beneath its point, as if they have drunk its poison, and Weiwei can feel the pulsing of the drug through her own veins, dulling her mind, making her thoughts sluggish and confused. Why is Alexei shaking her? She can't read the expression on his face, is he angry? Weiwei is not doing her job, there is somewhere she should be, she mustn't slack—

A clatter on the floor sends a wave of pain through her. Grey has dropped the gun, he is moving toward Elena, his hands together as if in supplication, but no, there is something in his hands, light glints off a silvery needle. He is holding one of the syringes for the dart gun; she is just another specimen, something to be trapped and held behind glass.

Elena leaps. It is not a movement any human could make. It leaves Grey falling forward, jabbing his syringe into empty space. It is an impossible leap onto the wall, clinging on in a tangle of limbs before springing onto the ceiling, spider-like, where she grabs hold of the dart and wrenches it from where it is embedded.

Weiwei feels the release, the waves of deeper blue racing through the lichen like water cooling a fever.

But she also feels the Captain go rigid beside her. She sees Alexei freeze, horror on his face. Realization. *A Wastelands creature on the train.* There is no disguising what Elena is, now. She crouches in the corner of the ceiling as if poised to pounce, looking down on them all.

Weiwei sees Alexei reach for the dart gun that Grey has dropped.

"No—" She manages only a whisper, but when he turns toward her Elena leaps again, landing lightly on all fours, keeping her eyes on Weiwei alone. *Now run, go!* she wants to shout. *Hide away and don't show yourself again—they will keep coming after you, with their needles and guns—you are not welcome here.* And she thinks that Elena understands, because with a final look the stowaway turns and plunges into the next carriage.

Henry Grey follows, with an inarticulate cry, pushing the Professor roughly aside.

Weiwei tries to get up. She has to stop him, she has to warn Elena that he is dangerous, this man, that though he may seem clumsy and foolish to her, there is a fanatical light in his eyes, but her legs buckle, and then Alexei and the Captain are on either side of her, holding her up.

"Steady now," says the Captain, and the thought flashes through Weiwei's mind that she has chosen to stay here, with her, rather than to follow in pursuit, and it is a thought that needs looking at, carefully, but Alexei is speaking, and there is barely contained anger in his voice.

"You knew it was here," he says.

"*She,*" Weiwei says. Her mouth is still dry but the words are returning. "Her name is Elena and she won't hurt us, she—"

"Won't hurt us?" Alexei interrupts her. "Her presence is enough to hurt us. Did you think there would be consequences? Did you not even think about the Vigil, about what will happen to all of us?"

"You're hardly one to speak," she snaps, and she is transported instantly back to their younger squabbles, to each of them accusing the other of their own misdeeds, to the outrage of perceived slights or injustices.

"Enough!" says the Captain.

Further down the carriage, Weiwei is aware of Suzuki protesting to Marya and the Professor that he is quite well. Above them, lichen creeps across the ceiling.

"No," says Weiwei. "No, let me speak. She won't hurt us—it isn't her fault, what's happening. And it isn't yours, either." She holds Alexei's eyes, long enough, she is sure, to convince him. He has gone so still, he hardly seems to be breathing. The Captain's expression, if you didn't know her well, has hardly changed. But Weiwei can read the smallest thinning of her lips, the movement of muscle beneath her eye. The Captain believes what has happened is her fault. The guilt has been eating her up.

Weiwei thinks—and it is a cruel, selfish thought—*Let her feel guilty a little longer.*

"I have to find Elena," she says to the Captain. "Grey doesn't understand her, he will try to catch her, they will hurt each other. Please, let me go." But it is not just Grey who doesn't understand, it is Elena. Elena who watches and mimics and believes that this means that she understands how people work, but there are cruelties she doesn't grasp, like the urge to trap and display, to possess for the sake of possessing.

The Captain is silent. She is weighing up the possibilities, as she always has done. *This is still her train,* thinks Weiwei, with a flicker of hope; she is still their Captain.

"Go," she says. "I will deal with what is happening elsewhere."

"But how will she follow them?" Alexei is looking toward the other end of the carriage, where criss-crossing the door to the infirmary are countless white threads, and as Weiwei moves closer she sees that they are woven into a web that is still moving, growing, blocking the path to Elena and Henry Grey.

"Don't touch them," says the Captain, and Weiwei can hear the fear in her voice, but she disobeys—she puts out her hand to them, and watches as they move and overlap, as if they are opening a door for her.

"Grey still has two syringes," says Alexei, abruptly. "Be careful."

The Captain gives the barest of nods.

Weiwei looks out of the window, through the gaps left by the blooms of mold. In the distance, a dark line appears. A first glimpse of the Russian Wall.

She pushes aside the threads and steps through the door.

Part Six

Days 18–20

The Vigil gives us the chance to do what is often impossible on the long journey of our lives: to pause and take stock, to contemplate not only where we have been and where we are going, but where we are. The night of the Vigil I dreamed that the river rose up and the waters engulfed us all. I watched from my cabin window as aquatic creatures pressed their faces against the glass. I heard the thunder of the falling Wall, powerless against the Flood, and I fell to my knees and prayed to an absent God.

The Cautious Traveller's Guide to the Wastelands, page 210

1

CHANGES

The train is changing. Inside the infirmary carriage, moths are gathering around the lamps; the thin white threads are winding around the doors to the medical cabins. There are unfamiliar noises—if she puts her ear to the cabin walls she can hear a ticking and scratching, as if the wood itself is growing. She has a flash of memory from her time outside—the sense of freedom, of boundaries expanding, despite the walls of the train around her. Even the habitual smell of the infirmary carriage, disinfectant mixed with oil, is fading beside an earthy, fragrant scent.

She follows the white threads, tangled now, with colors spreading within them, yellows and greens and the odd flash of red, as if mouths are opening up and closing. Some are creeping up the wall, some burrowing down through the floor like roots. She can't take her eyes off them. Is this what Rostov had felt? When he was drawn back to the Wastelands, did he feel this same mixture of repulsion and wonder? Did he take each step unsure if the ground beneath would hold?

The speaker beside her splutters into life. The Captain's voice. *"We are approaching the Russian Wall . . ."* A crackle of static. *". . . Please remain calm . . ."*

2

THE WALL

"It's ugly," says Marya. Grey stone that seems to swallow up all the light left in the already dull sky; that makes even the river seem dead before it.

"It was built to be strong, not to be beautiful," says Suzuki.

The implacable face of the Russian Empire, grimly defending its territory. Keeping the terrors out. For those entering the Wastelands, a final, fearsome warning that you are leaving the strong paternal embrace of the Tsar, that all order and safety from here on is lost. And for those approaching from the other side, a challenge: *You are not welcome here.*

We are the terrors now, she thinks.

They are in the Cartographer's tower, she and Suzuki and the Professor. Suzuki is still pale, and there is a sheen of sweat on his forehead, but he bats away her attempts to ease him into a chair.

"I am not about to keel over," he says.

"You just did," she snaps, more angrily than she intends. The Professor makes a little hum and turns away to examine something intently on one of the telescopes.

"It hurt you," she goes on. "When the dart pierced the lichen, it hurt you and Weiwei both."

"I am fine, it is not a sickness—"

"But it is weighing you down, can't you see it? You have to go to the infirmary, before we reach the Vigil, before it hurts you any-more." She sees her father, sand and water bleeding from empty eyes, and she cannot bear it—she cannot bear to see it happen again.

"There is nothing a doctor can do."

And he is right. What good will a physician do? No, her father could not save himself, but Suzuki can.

"Let me see through the telescope," she says, her eyes not leaving the Cartographer's face. "The prototype. If what you say is true then this is the last chance for me to see for myself, before we reach the Wall. Unlock it and let me see."

The Professor looks from her to Suzuki, a puzzled expression on his face.

Suzuki shakes his head. "No. No, you can't."

"Why not? Is it broken? You have said that you no longer want to see, but I do. I want to see what my father's skill has revealed. These threads, these veins. It is the least you can do for me." She goes to the scope and throws off its cover. She hardens her voice. "Let me see or tell me why I can't."

After a long moment, he says, quietly, "I think you know."

She knows. For all this time, she has thought only of the end of her father, but now she sees those final weeks; sees him always turning away, closing doors. She sees what he had kept so closely hidden. She begins, "When I found my father . . ." The words threaten to dry in her mouth but she forces herself to go on. "When I found him . . . that morning . . . there was water on the desk, sand on his cheeks. And his eyes were open, colorless. As if they had turned to glass and the glass had turned back into water and sand. As if he had wept away all that was left of his work." She had feared that saying the words out loud would make these fragile memories dissolve into the air, taking her father with them. But as she tells Suzuki and the Professor about how she had cleaned away the water and the sand, how she had closed her father's eyes so that no one would see what she had seen—she feels a burden lifting. "I thought it was the taint of the Wastelands, of sickness."

"And now?" Suzuki is standing up from his chair. "Now what do you think?"

She walks up to him. "I think that looking through his new

lenses didn't just let you see the patterns, the changes. I think that it changed you both as well." Slowly, she pushes up his sleeve, careful not to touch his skin but shocked nonetheless at her own boldness, at the intimacy of the action. He stays very still and she hears the Professor's intake of breath when the markings on his arm are revealed. "I am right, aren't I?" she says, stepping back.

He holds her gaze. "It was on the second crossing after we had begun to use the new scope," he says. "We realized then that we were both changing, as if the landscape was imprinting itself onto our bodies. I tried to hide it at first, but then your father came to me and told me that he had begun to see differently—*prismatically*, he called it. He said he could see too much, even without the scope. It was wonderful, he said. And unbearable." He stops, then begins again. "Your father thought that it was a warning, a sign of our hubris—that we had over-reached ourselves. We weren't meant to look too closely, he said. Another sign that we had to stop, to close the railway down for good. We argued. The last words that I remember speaking to him were words of anger."

Grief is etched into his face and it takes all her willpower to gesture to the scope and say, "I want to see. I want to see what you both saw."

"No, it's too dangerous. How you can ask this after—"

"And how can you still not *see*?" She raises her voice. "Did it not hurt you, just now, the needle in the lichen? As if the poison was in *your* veins. What you saw, the changes it caused in you . . . What if my father was wrong—it was not a warning, not a sickness but a *connection*? It hurt him, leaving the Wastelands behind. We thought it was the loss of his reputation, his livelihood, that broke him but it was more than that, it was the loss of all this that killed him." She sweeps her arm around the tower, the windows, the mold creeping inward from the edges of the glass, the patches of turquoise lichen appearing on the floor. "You mustn't try to stop it, to break the connection; you must keep looking."

Suzuki says nothing, but she feels the release of tension in his posture.

"You are not a man of the Company," she whispers. "You are a man of the train. And of the Wastelands. Of both, together."

He knows it. He knows it just as she knew what had happened to her father, though she couldn't admit it to herself. "I want to see what my father saw," she says, again. "What harm can it do now?"

Wordlessly, Suzuki takes a key from a drawer and unlocks the cover on the telescope's eyepiece. Marya puts her eye to the glass and adjusts the sights and it takes her a moment to understand what she is seeing—gleaming threads, like filaments caught in sunlight, stretching across the grasslands. She understands now what Suzuki had meant—like seeing a tapestry and its reverse at the same time. The pattern and how the pattern is made.

She steps aside to let the Professor look, and when he straightens up she sees him brushing tears from his eyes.

"All these years of watching," he says, "and now, to see this." But his voice is stronger; there is a new sense of purpose in his posture.

"Perhaps there is more work for Artemis after all," she says.

A little while later, Artemis—reborn—announces that he will return to his carriage and set to his work. "I will leave you to your"—he waves vaguely at the air—"talking."

"To think that I pride myself on my observation," says Suzuki, after he has gone. "I am tempted to hand back all my qualifications."

"He hid himself well," says Marya. "Only Weiwei knew."

"Weiwei! Of course she would know."

"What do we do now?" she says. "Let me get you some water, at least."

But Suzuki's eyes have drifted to her hair. "You have a passenger," he says, and she reaches up to feel the wings of a moth still tangled there. When she frees it, it rests on her hand.

"It's beautiful, isn't it?" she says. But he is only looking at her. He catches hold of her other hand, his fingers closing over hers. And when she looks down she sees the lines on his skin unfurling, spreading onto her own hand, winding up her bare arm. She jerks her hand away and the lines vanish. She had felt it, in those few seconds—the expanse of it, the immensity. The possibilities. All those lines, reaching out—all those contours and paths. All waiting.

Suzuki holds his arm to his chest. "I didn't mean—"

She breathes in to calm her skittering heart. Then she reaches out to take his hand again. The rail and the river and the Wall, imprinted on their skin.

They are slowing down as they approach the bridge, and the rhythm of the train changes as they leave the solidity of the ground. The river and the Wall stretch away into the distance on either side of them and she feels a sense of vertigo, caught between the heights and the depths.

A shadow under the water. The body of some great beast, following its own path down the river, oblivious to the train above it. And now the Wall is nearly upon them and it reaches up, impossibly high, and ahead there is an iron door, heavy and implacable, and even the great train must yield before it.

Suzuki rubs his fingers over her knuckles and touches his forehead to hers. She feels the pull of the brakes, the creaking of the train coming to a halt. Steam obscures the view from the windows.

The lines on their skin stop moving.

3

THE FOREST

The stillness of the train makes Grey stumble. He feels hot and shivery, his clothes heavy on his skin, a buzzing on the edge of his hearing. When he rights himself he understands that although its wheels have stopped turning, inside the movement remains. Vines creep down from the windows, thin branches splinter the doorframes and burst into leaf. "*Jasminum polyanthum,*" he murmurs, taking the pink, star-like flowers between his fingers. Some familiar plants, yet others he doesn't recognize—sharp-toothed snapping pods and spiky petals; ghostly white orchids and leaves that shiver open and shut with the touch of his breath. Insects whirr in the hot air, wing cases clicking in his ears, and he has to resist the urge to try to collect it all, to sink to the ground and feel the new life beneath his fingers. But there is not enough time—they may be right behind him, the Captain or the Company men, but she will not be safe with them, they will not understand her like he does. He turns, half expecting to see a flash of black suit. What do the crew call them? *Crows.* Yes, an apt name, though the crow is a much maligned bird—a creature cannot be good or evil, not like man, who is born good and pure, who must *learn* evil. Names matter. But he has seen an avidity in their eyes. What if they want her too? They will catch her in their claws, keep her all for themselves.

He forces his feet onward. How marvelous it will be, their

Exhibition—together they will turn the great glass palace into a forest all its own. Not display cases and velvet-lined trays—no, the public will push through the undergrowth and at every turn there will be new discoveries, the modern world setting out its ingenuity. Yet nothing will be as astonishing as Henry Grey's new Eden—or his new Eve. He has never felt so close to the divine. To be walking here, in the foothills of a new world.

He stumbles over a root and finds himself pressed against a window, mesmerized by the proliferating flowers on the glass. He puts his eye closer and closer, and through the flowers he can see wire fences and tall towers; men standing like statues, rifles resting on their shoulders. And a shadow falling across them all, a great wall, rising before them. He frowns, puzzled as to what it means, but then he pulls himself upright and finds that the men and the wire and the wall have all vanished, and when he sees a glimpse of blue ahead, he forgets them entirely.

"Wait!" he calls out, but she is always on the edge of vanishing. The corridor narrows. There she is, beckoning, or has she just brushed past him, gone back the way they came? Has she turned herself into a light-winged moth, to slip from his grasp?

A pain like a knife twisting in his abdomen makes him stop, bend over in agony. There—growing inside him too; bursting out of the ulcer, he can feel leaves, tendrils, the agony of sharp thorns.

4

THE GAME, AGAIN

Weiwei forces her feet to carry her forward, into the storage carriage, though it is changing around her—the flowers of mold on the window have come inside, they are patterning the walls, etching themselves onto the branches that are growing before her eyes. "Elena!" she calls, but she hears only the rustling of leaves. Now that the train has stopped, there is only an empty, echoing space where its heartbeat had been. Every step is an effort, and the corridors seem to be lengthening, the greener they grow, and she feels a terrible tiredness weighing her down, and her confidence ebbing away. She tries not to think of the water clock in the Vigil yard, already dripping away the minutes.

But then a figure emerges, stumbling toward her—Henry Grey, leaves caught in his hair and soil on his jacket, as if he has just risen up from the land itself. Weiwei feels a hot burst of fury. How dare he think that he could possibly trap Elena and take her for himself? How dare he hurt the train, *her* train? She feels her hands twitch with the urge to hurt him back, to wrench his silly gun from his grasp, to push him back down into the soil and hold him there with a strength she is suddenly sure she has.

But he is bent over, an arm wrapped around his stomach. When he raises his head she sees that his face is glistening and sickly white, and she takes hold of him not to push him back down but to hold him up. He is frail and ill. There is no harm that he can do to anyone now.

"Can't you see her?" he gasps. "There—up ahead. Beckoning to me."

Weiwei turns, but sees only the narrowing tunnel of greenery behind her. Grey squeezes her arm. "Thank you," he says, his eyes red and watery, fixed on the carriage ahead. "Thank you." Then he lurches away, holding on to drooping branches as he goes.

"We should follow him," says a voice in her ear.

Weiwei closes her eyes. She feels Elena's breath on her cheek. "What's wrong with him?" she asks.

Elena emerges into the greenish light. "He's dying," she says, and there is a sadness in her voice that Weiwei hadn't expected. "There is a wound inside him. It can't be healed."

"Elena," she whispers, "you have to go. The train won't pass the Vigil, not after all this. It will be sealed up. Do you understand? You're the only one who can slip out of the skylight without being seen. We don't have time to follow Grey, there's nothing you can do for him. You have to leave now."

The stowaway's eyes gleam in the dim light, as though she is underwater. "Not yet," she says. "Not yet. Just a little longer." She takes Weiwei's hand and pulls.

"No," says Weiwei.

"But the train will help us."

The vines around them shift and curl.

"We will look for Henry Grey," says Elena. "We will play our game."

The rules of the game are different now. It is a test of speed, and observation. They twist their way back through the ferns and the hanging branches. They creep through the broken web of threads across the door to the infirmary. The changes have spread through every carriage. There are shapes in the darkness that do not seem human; women with wings and men with antlers on their heads. There is a figure with a crown of twigs and leaves who holds out their hand to Weiwei, and resting on their palm are little white mushrooms, juicy and plump.

"I wouldn't eat them," says a voice at her side. Alexei, his pupils huge and black. "Not if you want to keep your feet on the ground."

"You lose a point," says Elena, appearing out of the undergrowth. "Two points."

"Did you find Grey?" asks Alexei, as he escorts them through the Third Class sleeping carriages, making a channel for them through the undergrowth; past a priest counting off shining berries through his fingers like prayer beads; past the boy Jing Tang, leaping from bunk to bunk.

"We are still looking," says Weiwei. Alexei doesn't ask anything else, but joins them, wordlessly.

Passengers have spilled out into the next carriages, and she sees stewards and porters and passengers from First, all distinctions blurring. Dima stalks beside them, a gray shadow, his eyes like lanterns. "Perhaps he is remembering his ancestors," says Elena, crouching down to run her fingers through his fur. "Perhaps he is walking through their dreams."

They see a stumbling figure in the distance, then lose him again. They plunge deeper into the rustling green.

5

BIRDS OF ILL-OMEN

Marya is hunting for Crows. She walks the train, trailing her fingers over night-blooming flowers and delicate, dripping fronds. The lights outside seem to cast moonlight through the carriages. She sees the Professor among the crowd in the Third Class dining car, scribbling on pieces of paper that are already dappled with soil. He is changed from the frail figure she had seen in the infirmary, as if the weight of the years has fallen away. There is an odd asymmetry to their situations, she thinks—by putting on the guise of Artemis, he has become more himself; he has stepped into the person he really was, all along, while she has shaken off her borrowed skin, stepped back into her real self. *But no,* she thinks, *that's wrong.* She has lost the old Marya along the way, and here, in this suspended time, she is someone altogether new.

"Ah, my dear, my years have been long, but yours . . ." The Professor trails off.

What would she have done with all the years she should have had? Seen the sun rise and fall along the Neva; opened her windows to the smell of the sea, walked and walked among endless birches, a hand entwined with hers; yes, this could have been a life—for her, and for a man with no nation. Its loss overwhelms her.

"Here," the Professor goes on. "The last testament of Artemis. When the train is finally unsealed, it will be read. People will know your name, and your father's. They will know us all."

And in how many years might that be? she thinks. Not until what is left of them has long turned to dust. But she says, instead, *"Through glass we see the truth,"* looking around at the vines winding themselves around the iron piping; at the clusters of bright-yellow flowers bursting from the floor beneath the table.

"The truth!" He bangs the table, causing a cloud of pollen and dust to rise up around them. Someone gives a cheer, and she thinks, *Do they really know? Do they truly understand what is happening, or are they trying not to see? Not this truth, not when it is so painful.*

"Thank you," she says, squeezing the Professor's hand. But there are still things for this new Marya to do, in what little time is left.

In the whispering, moving wildness, the old order is falling apart; the lines between Third and First, passengers and crew, are blurring. Shadows up ahead. There—*Birds of ill-omen,* she thinks. They move with a sense of purpose missing among the rest of the passengers and crew, and she wonders where they are flying to. She could almost swear that under their coats she catches a glimpse of dark feathers. Through the Third Class sleeping carriages and toward the crew carriages, and they are secretive, furtive. They look over their shoulders, and she presses herself into the shadows. She has grown furtive too. She has learned to keep secrets.

As she follows them, the carriages lose their definition. The blooms of mold and webs of pale-white threads block the light from the windows in the crew mess. There are rustles and sighs from the leaves in the silence. She takes off her shoes and places them tucked into an alcove made by two intertwining saplings. After a moment's thought she takes off her stockings too. There is cool moss beneath her feet, and she splashes at times through what seems to be a stream.

It is not until she has followed them into the service carriage and watched them stop beside one of the doors to the outside that she realizes what the Crows are going to do.

They are going to leave the train.

Crouching unseen among the ferns, she feels as if she is watching them from very far away. *They seem to be waiting for a signal of some kind,* she thinks. They have opened the first of the two doors to the outside, and they are staring intently out of the window. One of them takes a pocket watch out of his coat, tapping the case and frowning. Of course—of course they have thought to bribe their way out. They have taken all they can from the train, and now they have given themselves a way out. "*Move*," she tells herself, but she can't seem to force herself out from the shelter of the ferns. Is this really how it will happen? All their money and power, protecting them still.

Without really thinking about it, she has been running her fingers through the water that is bubbling up from the floor like a spring, glad of its coolness. When she looks down there is something in her hand, something slim and pointed, as if water has turned to glass; strong, and hard, and sharp. She raises it to the light. It is beautiful; as clear as the water itself, catching the greens and golds around it.

She steps out toward the Crows. The blade feels solid in her hand. The two men spin around.

"Where are you going?" she asks, pleasantly.

She remembers that evening in Beijing, the way they spoke to her father, the dispassionate sympathies they conveyed to her mother. They look behind her, to see that she is alone, and Petrov says, in a desperate attempt at authority, "As Company representatives we have special dispensation to leave the train early. We will of course be wait-ing at the end of the Vigil, but we must ask that you return to the in-firmary, madam, for your own health." He tries to pull himself up to his full height, but he is more stooped than she remembers—smaller.

"You will be *waiting*?" she says. "How long your patience must be, to wait for a train that is to be sealed up."

"There will be time to—"

"To what? There is no time left, my father knew that. Anton Iva-novich Fyodorov warned you. He warned you this would happen, yet you did nothing."

For the first time, they notice the glass blade in her hand, and she sees them step backward.

She steps closer.

"Madam, we must ask you to stay back—"

The glass blade seems to sing beneath her touch. How easy it will be. How powerful she feels. An instrument of justice. But she feels herself waver. Among the creeping tendrils and ferns, the growing wilderness, there are still decisions she can make.

And she opens her hand and watches the glass blade turn back to water, spilling out onto the floor.

A voice beside her says, "I think it will make you happy, to know that they were afraid."

Elena isn't wearing her veil of moths anymore, though she has a dusting of fine golden pollen over her shoulders, and trickles of water are running from the ends of her hair. *She looks,* thinks Marya, *as if she is shining.* Behind her, in the shadows, Marya can see Weiwei and the young engineer.

"I already knew," says Marya, and glancing down, sees pale tendrils appearing from the floor, snaking toward them, pausing for a moment, as if they are sniffing the air, then moving again. *Hyphae,* thinks Marya. That's what Suzuki had called them. Connecting everything.

The Crows try to speak again, but no words come out. They can't see the tendrils because they're clutching at their necks, but the pale threads have reached their feet, they are winding up their legs, and the noises the men are making are bird-like, inhuman; their fingers are cracking, compressing, twigs breaking out from where their nails should be. Marya wants to look away, but she can't. She watches as their throats spasm, and the smooth shapes of eggs form beneath the skin, emerging from their mouths, bluish-green and hollow, shattering into fragments of shell between their teeth. She watches as they come apart, piece by piece, and she doesn't move until there is nothing left of the Company men but a little collection of feathers and bones, of shining coins, of bright black stones, of the detritus that might be found in a long-abandoned nest.

She takes a long look. Then she turns back to Elena. "You did this."

Elena shrugs, in a way that reminds Marya exactly of Weiwei, and she sees the train girl hovering in the shadows, her eyes fixed on what remains of the Crows.

"I did nothing, Marya Antonovna," says Elena. "I did not need to." She pauses. "And neither did you."

A sound from outside makes them both turn. It has been so long that it takes Marya a moment to understand what it is. Rain.

Elena looks out, an odd expression on her face, and Marya thinks, *There is no mimicry now.* This is her real face—happy and sad at the same time. The girl is pressing herself to the glass, as if she can feel the rain through it, as if she could drink it down.

"*Glass is controlled,*" Marya's father had said; "*it is time, suspended.*" But she imagines it all turning to water—unstoppable. She imagines the Wall tumbling down, the Wastelands pouring out. She feels it filling her up with unimaginable joy.

6

THE END OF HENRY GREY

He sees it all, from the shadows. Sees the Company men transformed. A just punishment, he thinks. She is good and fair, his new Eve. How had he ever thought she was ethereal? She is of the water and the earth.

Outside the window, rain has started to fall, and he sees her raise her hands to it, her eyes turned toward Heaven.

"And so reveal in water and in sky," he murmurs. *"The mirror of the Heavens and the window of His eye."*

He has to lean against the trunk of a tree as pain roars through him, radiating out from his stomach. There are thorns growing inside him. His heart is beating so fast that it could burst from his chest, red and wet, another bloom in the darkness of the forest around him. His legs weaken and he lets himself sink into the deep green moss on the floor. This is what he has always wanted—to feel the life beneath his hands; the quickening heartbeat, the slow pulse of the earth. To follow a line back to its source; to read the maps of creation. Here he is, at the beginning and the end.

"Dr. Grey . . ." He opens his eyes. It is the young widow, kneeling beside him, and behind her, the train girl.

"This is Elena," she says.

And she is here, looking down at him. She shines.

"Elena . . ." Names are important. He has always felt the satisfaction of knowing, classifying, writing down. It is an act of faith, to make sense of God's creation. "You saved me," he says. "Outside, in the water. Why?"

"Once, there was another man," says the girl, says *Elena*. "He was like you, a little. He wanted to know the truth of things. He wanted to understand. He was looking for . . . communion."

"Yes . . . Yes. I have always endeavored to . . . My life's work . . . Did you save him too?" He tries to keep his eyes open, to keep her in his gaze, but it is hard. He is so tired.

"He was not saved. And I am sorry for it."

Henry Grey nods. "I understand what you are," he whispers. "You are what I have been searching for, all these years." The end of the line he has been following. *A new Eden.* Now he has found it, there is nothing to do but rest. "A more perfect form," he says, or perhaps he just thinks it. Within all things, a striving to achieve a more perfect form.

"You can sleep," he hears her say, "if you are tired," and the pain that has accompanied him for so long has vanished, leaving a space inside him that feels like the wide, clear halls of a palace of glass.

He closes his eyes. There is nothing more he needs.

7

DECISIONS, RISKS

He looks like he is sleeping, thinks Weiwei, cushioned by moss and leaves.

"He wasn't well," says Marya Antonovna. "There was nothing we could do for him." She folds Henry Grey's hands across his chest. Elena is blinking rapidly, her forehead creased into a frown. Weiwei and Alexei stand like mourners looking down into a grave.

"I should have done something," says Alexei. "Even in Beijing he wasn't well—there was something wrong with his stomach; the doctors told him to be careful."

"I'm not sure he would have listened," says Marya.

No, thinks Weiwei. *He wasn't that kind of man.* Too certain in his own beliefs, too sure of his own place in the complex machinery of the world.

She nudges what is left of Mr. Petrov and Mr. Li with her foot. Amidst the pile of feathers and twigs and stones, bright shoe buckles clink. Train justice. *But is it enough,* she wonders, *for Marya Antonovna?* The glassmaker's daughter has the stunned, bewildered look of a survivor of an accident, who has unexpectedly found herself saved. Weiwei is trying to find something to say when Suzuki enters and, to her amazement, takes Marya into his arms.

"I know I said I would not follow," he begins, but Marya just shakes her head and smiles, and there is some unspoken communication between them that Weiwei can't understand but that feels too intensely private to watch, and she turns away, quickly, only to see that Elena has no such qualms and is staring at them with interest.

"Come," says Weiwei, pulling her away. There is so little time left.

They leave Grey already cradled by roots and tendrils, pulling him down into the earth. They enter the crew mess, where the musician stands on a chair, playing a waltz in a minor key that is happy and unbearably sad at the same time. Vassily is pouring drinks from bottles turned silver and gold by the light filtering through the trees, and the passengers are dancing, First Class and Third Class together, in fine silks and rough cloth, all divisions forgotten in this suspended time. Weiwei sees Sophie LaFontaine, dancing by herself, her eyes closed. She sees the scientific gentlemen and the traders dancing together, arms around each other. She sees the brothers from the South raise their glasses and empty them in one gulp. She sees branches of ivy curl their way around the lamps, sees lichen creep across the ceiling, silver and brilliant blue.

Elena does not hide anymore. She is part of the changes and the passengers seem unafraid of her. She offers her hand to the Countess, who throws back her head in a peal of laughter and says, "I am too old, young woman, but Vera will take up your offer." The maid's face is uncertain as Elena takes her into the waltz, but the music transforms into a jig, fast and merry, and her expression turns to exhilaration, and Elena is moving from passenger to passenger until she reaches Weiwei, who thinks of the girl rising from the water. Coming back to life.

"To our journey's end!" cries a voice, and glasses are raised, and someone is weeping, and the cleric Yuri Petrovich is intoning a prayer but he is drowned out by the musician, who plays faster and louder, and Weiwei lets herself be whirled into the dance by Elena, around and around until she is laughing and dizzy and it feels almost like they are up in the open skylight again, that feeling of glorious release.

"Look!"

A string snaps on the musician's violin. The dance ends with a sudden, jarring chord. The dancers move apart.

"What are they doing?" Alexei has cleared one of the windows and is pointing outside, at the guards running back from the train, their guns on their shoulders, at others massing beneath the spotlights, the rain making their silhouettes flicker. It is churning the Vigil grounds into mud.

"Twelve hours have not passed, surely?" Weiwei says, still breathless.

Alexei looks up toward the water clock and she sees his back stiffen.

"What's wrong?" She follows his gaze. "That's not—" The basin the water pours into is far fuller than it should be.

"They've sped up the clock," he says. "They've poured away the hours. The Vigil is ending."

The train is about to be sealed up.

Alexei slams his palms against the window. There is uproar in the carriage. Weiwei feels her chest constrict, as if the air is already growing stale.

"You have to go now, Elena, now!" she says, shouting above the noise. She takes the stowaway's hand; she will drag her to the skylight if necessary; she will not allow her to stay entombed with them, not after everything. The urgency sets off a humming beneath her skin, a humming in her bones, as though the train is alive again, as though its heart has started beating.

"Weiwei," says Elena, and it is the first time she has used her name, though she is pulling away from her, standing her ground. "Listen."

"There's no time—"

"*Listen!*"

Elena's voice silences the carriage. And Weiwei feels it. She feels the pull of the furnace, its mouth hungry for coal and heat, the wheels hungry for the miles to come, for the rail stretching ahead. She feels the train waking up.

The Cartographer and Marya appear.

"Something is happening," Suzuki says, rolling up his sleeves and holding out his arms, and Weiwei sees that there are marks, almost like the tattoos that the engineers give themselves after each of their crossings. Yet these are different—thin lines and markings like a map. She sees Alexei staring as well.

"It's *pulling*," says Suzuki, and they watch as the map on his skin seems to shift, just a fraction, as if a photograph has slid just out of focus. "Can you feel it?" he says to Weiwei, and she can, she can. She can feel the train and the earth and the earth and the train, all connected. She can feel the humming in her bones becoming a roar.

"It wants to go," she says. "It wants to be moving." She turns to the rest of them. "And what is stopping us? Are we not stronger than anything out there?" She gestures at the guards and the Vigil yard. "We boast that we are the biggest, the strongest train ever built. What can stop us if we wish to go?"

"The gates can stop us," says Alexei. "If we were travelling at our full speed, perhaps we could break through, but it would be impossible now."

Elena taps her fingers on the window. "But if the gates were open?" she says.

They find the Captain where Weiwei was sure she would be—in the cab, where the walls gleam in iridescent greens and blues, shot through with seams of orange, as if heat pulses through them. Dry, sharp fingers of pale lichen encircle the furnace itself. The Captain sits on one of the stokers' stools, staring into the coals, just as Weiwei has seen her do on quiet nights on earlier crossings, as if searching for messages in the flames. But the coals are silent and cooling now, and the Captain's shoulders are slumped in defeat. She doesn't raise her head as their little group enters.

"Captain?" She feels a stab of doubt, then sees Elena gazing around the cab in delight, and the walls shimmering, and the faint glow of embers in the darkness of the furnace. She stands to attention before the Captain, and she tells her their plan, and as she comes to the end, the Captain raises her head, looks around and stands, as if she is waking from a dream. "If I understand you correctly, then what you are proposing is . . ." She shakes her head. "Even if we could do it, we would be changing the course of . . . everything. It cannot be our decision to make."

"Then whose decision should it be?" Marya's voice has changed, thinks Weiwei, now that she is not pretending anymore. She looks at Elena. "What do you think?" she says.

"I can help," says Elena. "I can open the gates, I know what to do. Remember that I was the garrison ghost. I watched and learned, I can give you time." Her eyes are bright, unquestioning, and Weiwei realizes that it is not only Marya who has changed. There is something different about Elena. She is more certain, more present. As if a weight has been lifted, a decision made. "I will hide behind the rain, they won't see me." Elena turns to Weiwei. "You know what I can do. Please, let me help."

They are looking at the Captain. Alexei, Suzuki, Marya—they are all waiting for her judgment. Such is her power, still.

The lines on the Captain's face deepen. She leans against the wall, as if asking the train to hold her up, for just a little longer. *She has finished defying the Wastelands,* realizes Weiwei.

"Is this truly a risk you would take for us?" says the Captain to Elena.

"Yes," says Elena. She looks at Weiwei. "Yes," she says, again.

8

AWAKENING

Here, then, the great train, awakening. Here the rising glow of the coals, the roar of the furnace. Here the spit of the rain on hot metal. The stokers have returned to their posts, the drivers beside them. The stewards are buttoning up their collars, brushing the dust off their lapels. The porters are fastening up the luggage racks. The clockwork of the train is set going again and the passengers too play their parts. The Countess presides over the saloon car. She has thrown off her shawls and is crowned with a wreath of birch leaves. The Professor comforts the timid and scared. The pious pray to whatever gods might be listening. The impious pray to the gods of the rail—to the furnace and pistons and power. *Let the great gates open, let the guns of the guards be no match for the train, let the world forgive us for what we are about to do.*

"When you come back you must run for the last door on the train," Weiwei says. "I will make sure it is open for you. As soon as you can, you must run faster than you have ever run before."

"I will run faster than ever before," says Elena, and it is the repetition of the words that makes Weiwei realize what is truly different about her—she is no longer mimicking. Her gestures and expressions belong to her, only her.

She steps backward, holding Elena at arm's length, just like some of the passengers used to do with her when she was little, exclaiming over her precociousness, her tiny Company uniform. She doesn't want to let her go. "What has changed?" she says. "Why are you different? Is it the rain?" She wants to cry but she will not let herself. *It will work.*

Elena smiles. "Are you not different too?"

Weiwei manages something between a laugh and a sob. "I don't know what I am anymore."

Elena steps backward, holding out her arms just as Weiwei had done, examining her. "Not just one thing," she says, with a little nod. "Many things." Then, after a moment's hesitation, Elena throws her arms around her in a fierce hug. She doesn't smell of damp and rot anymore but of green, growing things, of the soil after the rain. Weiwei wants to hold on to her, to tell her she doesn't have to take the risk. She wants time to turn on its axis, for the water in the clock to pour upward, for the wheels of the train to follow the rail back, for a child of the train and a Wastelands girl to be playing games of stealth in the dark, to be telling stories, to be raising their faces to the sky. She wants to stay right here.

"It will work," whispers Elena. "I will see you again."

And she is gone, scrambling up into the ceiling of the storage carriage and out of view, and Weiwei runs into the corridor to the window and presses her face to the glass, but all she can see are the clouds of steam from the undercarriage, swallowing up the shadows of the guards.

In the watchtower Oleg the gunner stands with his eye to his rifle and the Captain stands watching the gates. In her hand is the brass speaker. "*Hold fast*," she says to the drivers in the cab. The train is pulling against its stillness; Weiwei can feel its complex machinery moving into place.

"*Hold fast.*"

She looks back down the train and sees Suzuki and Marya Antonovna in the opposite tower, watching through their telescopes. But the Vigil yard is still.

"I can't see her," Weiwei says, looking through one of the lenses, a tight, sickening feeling in her stomach. "I can't see her anywhere."

"Then neither can they," says the Captain.

Oleg has the sights of his rifle trained on the yard. "There," he says, just as Weiwei sees the faintest ripple in the rain. Elena is at the gates.

"*Stand by*," says the Captain.

The great iron gates are beginning to open.

The guards erupt into life and Oleg fires into the yard, drawing them away from the gates. They return fire, though they may as well be throwing pebbles at the train.

"*Stand by.*"

The gates have opened far enough to reveal the rail stretching ahead, but it is a slow, ponderous process, and more guards are pouring out of the watchtowers.

She watches for Elena but there are too many figures; they are lost in the steam and the smoke from the guns. The train is poised, all of its joints straining, but the gates have fallen still.

"What's happening?" She presses her eye so hard to the scope that her eye socket aches, but she cannot make out the scene below. "Can you see her?"

"*Hold fast.*" The Captain's voice is strained. Weiwei feels a wave of despair sweep over her.

"Captain—"

The hesitation in the gunner's tone makes Weiwei look up. She follows his gaze to a patch of ground near the main building, but can't understand at first what he has seen. Then she sees it too—out of the churning mud, slim green shoots are growing. They vanish in a burst of gunfire, but more grow before their eyes, ragged and determined. They curl around ankles, they hold the guards tight in their grip.

"Look . . ." Weiwei watches as trickles of mud creep up the walls, as if long fingers are questing to find a way in. The muddy ground is turning to liquid, the weeds growing faster than they can be shot down.

"The river!"

The gunner's shout sends her running to one of the far scopes, looking back the way they have come, and her breath catches in her throat. The river has broken its banks. It is rising up, impossibly fast. "Like Rostov's dream . . ." That final, famous vision of apocalypse.

How it had thrilled her, as a child. How she had urged the water to rise up, each time the train crossed the river. And now the waters are coming to meet them.

"We're finished." There is despair in the gunner's voice. "After all this . . ."

"No, they're helping her. The soil, the river . . ." *There is nothing that can hold them back anymore.*

The iron doors are moving again.

"*Now.*" At the Captain's command, a burst of power, and the scene outside is hidden by a cloud of gray, as the train starts to move. Weiwei is already running for the stairs. She pushes her way back through the forest of the train, passing through each carriage as they emerge through the gates, running backward as the train runs forward, the familiar rhythm of the rails beginning beneath her feet, though the water is rising, it has broken down the far walls, it is surging forward in waves. Alexei is waiting at the final door, his hair and uniform soaked with rain.

"Can you see her?" she yells.

"Keep back—" He pulls her away from the door as muddy water gushes over their feet, and she feels for a moment that they are waterborne, sailing weightless through the great gates, carried onward by the flood.

"Where is she?" She grabs the doorframe and leans out. "We have to wait for her, we have to tell the Captain to wait." She is sure she will rise out of the water, any moment now she will come splashing toward the train, arms outstretched.

The rain and the floodwater chill her skin but she leans out further. They are picking up speed, they are outrunning the flood.

"Weiwei, we can't stop!" He has to shout over the roar of the water.

"But she's the reason we're through! It's all because of her . . ." Her voice cracks. "We can't leave her behind, we can't."

She can feel the rhythm of the rails. Insistent, familiar. She can feel the power released as the train picks up speed, and there will be no stopping now, no waiting for what they have left behind. She looks up at the Wall and sees that cracks have appeared, water and weeds pushing their way out of the stones, as if the Wastelands are escaping, as if the Wall itself is weeping.

Part Seven

Days 21–23

The traveller may experience a peculiar phenomenon—a dread of arrival. This may manifest in a dangerous lethargy; the traveller sits by the window, unable to tear their gaze away. They await the sight of the station with anxiety; they do nothing to prepare their luggage or their dress. After all their days and nights onboard, they are afraid of what it means to be still.

The Cautious Traveller's Guide to the Wastelands, page 240

1

ONWARD

They cannot be stopped. They eat up the miles between the Wall and the first cities of the Russian Empire, their passing marked by the ringing of bells in wooden church spires and by glimpses of pale, frightened faces in the windows of watchtowers. They plunge through the barricades set up across the rail—through iron bars and barbed wire and the bullets of the soldiers. They cannot be stopped.

What happens next? They are past the point of knowing. They have left Rostov and his guide behind, they have traveled off the map, staying away from the cities where the might of the Russian army and the Company forces will be mustering. Here are places they do not know. Small stations with fading signs, priests standing on the platforms, holding up crucifixes; women dressed in black, their hands together in prayer. But others reach for the train as it passes, dangerously close to the platform's edge. They stretch out their hands, pull at the vines that hang around it, as if they want to take its strangeness for themselves.

Where are we going? They do not know. Only forward, forward. Weiwei can see them watching her, the passengers and crew, as if she has the answers they need. Even the Captain, hesitating before giving an order, is waiting for her word. "But I don't know anything," she tells them, "I don't know what we should do." Not without Elena, not with the line back to her lengthening, minute by minute, hour by hour. *Stop,* she wants to say. *Go back.* She watches the rail from the observation car, she turns at every flash of blue inside the train, as if she might see her stepping out from the shadows of the undergrowth, giving a bow—*For my latest trick . . .* Hasn't she always been adept at vanishing and reappearing? But there is no sign of a not-quite-girl.

The passengers gather together. They sleep where they want, on the moss-covered floor or on bunks where willow branches hang down like curtains. The Professor and Marya are collecting their stories—writing them down on sheets of paper that will become the next column by Artemis. A final outing for the old Artemis, says the Professor. Or the first outing for the new. They don't know anymore. All they know is that they have to keep moving.

Weiwei stands in the watchtower in the evening light. And she can feel the train, pulling them onward. She knows where it wants them to go.

2

THE GLASS PALACE

The palace of the Great Exhibition. Rising from the earth and emerging from the sky at the same time, light caught in its two thousand panes of glass, as if it is made out of air itself.

Enough glass to bridge the Neva three times over, Marya's father had said. Glass made in their Petersburg works and shipped by barge to Moscow where all the world would come to gaze and wonder at it, where the Fyodorov name would be celebrated and admired. She has never wept for her father. Only now that she sees this building—this beautiful, ingenious, useless building—only now does she wish to stand and weep at what she has lost. She takes out his letter to the Company, retrieved from where it had been buried in the saloon car, creased but safe. Proof of what he tried to do, evidence enough to clear his name, even if no one else is to read it. Evidence enough for her, alone.

They are slowing down. For the first time since the Wall, since they outran the flood, they are slowing down.

"Surely they will be waiting for us," Marya says to Suzuki. "The Company, the military." All the might of an empire afraid of what lies beyond its walls, waiting with guns and cannons. "Surely we cannot think that we will . . ." she trails off.

They are travelling on the new rail, built for the Exhibition itself. On either side, there are the well-dressed and the poor, the young and the old; children scampering ahead, pointing in merry delirium at the train and the palace in turn, as their mothers and nurses grab their hands to pull them back. Some stand stock still and stare. Others turn on their heels and run. *We are bringing terror with us,* she thinks. *We are bringing tainted Wastelands air, that's what they think. The Company has taught them to be afraid.*

Surely the train must be stopping soon. The palace is rising above them, and she has a dizzying vision of the train barreling straight ahead into the glass, the sound of a thousand shattering panes, all coming down around them. But no, she realizes that they are not simply riding up to the palace but *into* it, under a high, curved doorway, and with a scream of brakes and clouds of steam they come to a halt in the very center of the astonishing edifice of glass and wrought iron and air.

Through the steam Marya sees the scarlet of the soldiers' uniforms, the gray of gunmetal. But in front of them are the crowds lined up behind the railings surrounding the platform, applauding, staring, pointing, recoiling—at the train transfigured; turned into an exhibit, a monument to the glory of the Trans-Siberia Company. How her father would have hated it.

Further into the hall, she can see other machines; instruments of industry, of science, of military might, their metal arms raised as if to greet the coming century, proud and satisfied and sure.

"So this is what it feels like, to be a marvel of the modern world." The Professor has come to stand beside them, turning his latest pages over and over in his hands.

Alexei has his face pressed to the window.

"I think Dr. Grey would be pleased that we are here," says Marya, putting a hand on his arm.

"Look," says Suzuki.

In front of the glass cases holding machinery and models of the train, unmistakable in their dark suits and grim expressions, stand the representatives of the Trans-Siberia Company.

3

THE CHILD OF THE TRAIN

Weiwei steps down onto the platform into a sudden hush. There hadn't been a discussion—the Captain had simply nodded to her, and the passengers and crew gathered by the windows had parted to let her through. She feels very small, and the expectant silence of the crowd makes the exhibition hall seem impossibly huge, far bigger than any building she has ever been inside. Rows of balconies run along the walls. Mechanical contraptions the size of trees stand high up on plinths; a statue of the Russian Emperor on his horse, many times larger than life, frozen as though galloping into war; and row upon row of tall glass cases stretch out as far as she can see. In some there are lifeless creatures, eyes unseeing. In some there are things that climb or crawl or fly, bumping furred bodies against the glass. This is what the Exhibition is saying—*Look at our achievements, look at what we have made. Then look at what we are not.*

She reaches for the train, places her hand on its warm, overgrown side; feels its power, beating like a pulse, as if it is as alive as those creatures trapped behind glass. *The spectators can feel it too,* she thinks, as a wave of murmurs fills the hall, and she is aware of an uneasy, mistrustful attention; a thousand pairs of eyes, all fixed upon her.

But here come the Company representatives, hurrying along the platform, hands clenched by their sides. Men in dark suits like the Crows; men just as formless and nameless, molded by the Company into its own image. Behind them come the soldiers, the insignia of the Company on their uniforms and rifles in their hands. Countless soldiers, as if the military might of an entire nation were pouring onto the exhibition floor, their boots shaking the ground. They place themselves between the spectators and the train. They raise their rifles to their shoulders. And Weiwei sees, in a glimpse of one possible future, the train tamed by guns and rules and timetables. She sees order brought about again, the Trans-Siberia Company triumphant, the old century folding neatly into the new. She sees the men in front of her, unshakeable in their self-belief.

"Where is the Captain?" It is the Chairman of the Board of the Trans-Siberia Company, tall and gray-bearded and bristling with righteous fury, though the soldiers behind him make him seem smaller, more diminished than Weiwei remembers. "We must speak with her immediately. And our consultants, where are they?"

Gone, she wants to say. *Turned into pebbles and twigs and bone, and there is nothing you can do about it.* But before she can speak, a flash of blue catches her eye and she crouches down, ignoring the thump of boots and metal, the gasp from the crowd, the sudden shout from Alexei behind her. There are rifles, readied, trained right at her— she knows this, but she cannot seem to take her eyes from where a small patch of brilliant-blue lichen is growing, silver veins among the overlapping scales. When she touches it, with the very tips of her fingers, she feels—

—*Here.* A presence. A beating heart. *Here, and here, and here.* A thread stretching back toward the Wastelands, back toward Elena— *Here*—and pulling toward something new. The earth alive with anticipation, with change. It makes her feel as if there are sparks bouncing from her skin.

"Miss Zhang, we asked you a question," says the Chairman of the Board in an outraged tone. Two of the soldiers step closer; close enough for her to smell the metallic tang of their guns, the polish on their heavy boots, but then the Professor is beside her, raising her up gently and turning his back on the soldiers and the Chairman of the Board. "You appear to be worrying these gentlemen," he murmurs.

"But there is something I think you should see." He passes a sheet of paper to her, an odd expression on his face.

This is the last testament of Artemis, she reads, before the words begin to move and uncoil in front of her, like the thin threads that snaked through the train.

"An interesting phenomenon, is it not?" The Professor peers at it over his glasses, and Weiwei watches, fascinated, as the spirals of the Cyrillic letters unfold themselves and weave their way toward the edges of the paper before spilling onto the floor, onto the scales of lichen, turning them a deeper, inky blue.

"Are you listening? Do you have any idea—" But the Chairman's words are lost among a growing rumble of sound from the crowd. Weiwei follows the fingers pointing upward, the raised heads and wide eyes and open mouths, and she sees the glass *changing*. A ripple passes through it, like water, like the silvery-blue scales of lichen—like ink, and there are words forming within it, moving across the walls of the palace, across the ceiling, and with the words comes a swell of confusion and panic and fear. Some of the spectators turn and run, pushing past anyone in their way to reach the doors, causing a swell that makes her fear that the fragile control of the crowd is about to break, that the railings holding them back are about to come crashing down. But the railings hold, though some in the crowd weep, some scream, some faint right away.

And some simply stand, and read.

I, Artemis, set down these words, for whoever may find them . . . Though my voice is small, against the might of the Trans-Siberia Company, I hope that one day it will be heard and that you, my loyal readers, will know of the greed . . . of the endless arrogance . . . of the lies the Company has told you.

"Slander!" shrieks the Chairman of the Board, as the other Company men are shouting that it is sabotage, it is nothing but a trick. His face crimson, the Chairman dives for the paper that Weiwei still holds, and rips it into tiny pieces, letting them fall and stamping them underfoot.

"It's too late," she says, calmly. "The words are already gone, they are all up there, for everyone to see."

. . . the glassmaker Anton Ivanovich Fyodorov risked his own reputation and livelihood . . . finding proof that in the Company's determination to increase crossings and revenue . . . they ignored the evidence of changes to the Wastelands caused by the train itself, and the danger to . . .

She turns away from the furious Company men to see Marya Antonovna stepping down from the train, Suzuki beside her. There are tears in her eyes and a smile on her lips. The Professor bows to her. "It is little enough justice," he says.

"No," says Marya. "It is a lot."

It is the Company's greed that harmed the train, that harmed the landscape itself. This is the truth. I do not presume to understand the meaning of the Wastelands . . . or to propose, indeed, that there is meaning to be found . . .

The crowd has quietened. All the passengers from the train have stepped down onto the platform. All have their heads raised to the words in the glass. They are all waiting. Like the glass and the iron, the vines and the flowers and the bark. Watching. Waiting.

. . . but the Society has theorized and argued for long enough. The doors are open. The end of the Company is here. It is time to see what has been kept hidden.

Weiwei feels the hum in her bones. She feels the train and the lichen and the glass. She feels change thundering through the exhibition hall. Rust prickles along the metallic bodies of the looms and weapons and presses, then ghostly lichen blooms and vanishes, pale threads reach into machinery and clockwork to set them running. Glass cases shatter into droplets of water, rising again into fountains where birds and insects drink in their freedom. The Emperor's horse picks up its hooves and gallops out of its palace, leaving the Emperor cracked in pieces on the ground.

The Chairman of the Board screams at the soldiers to fire, but they have already lowered their rifles. They are falling back, leaving the Company men exposed to the growing jeers of the crowd, to the pieces of food and rubbish thrown down at them from the galleries just as flashes of light herald the arrival of the newspaper men and their photographic apparatus.

Weiwei turns back to where the Captain is stepping down from the doorway behind her. "They weren't just helping Elena, at the

Wall. The water and the soil—they were helping us too. They want us to go on."

The Captain hesitates. Then she gives the smallest of nods.

Weiwei looks at the faces of the passengers. At the spectators, as hushed now as if she were a priest performing a rite on sacred ground.

The soldiers have left the exhibition hall. The Company men have been swallowed up by the crowd.

She looks back toward the train, seeing it fully for the first time; wild and overgrown, part forest, part mountain, part machine. Full of the crossings it has made. Full of the crossings yet to come.

She hears its engine roar into life.

EPILOGUE

From *The End of the Cautious Traveller*
(Preface, pages i–iv) by Marya Fyodorova
(Mirsky Publishing, Moscow, 1901)

You will know us, of course. The train travels through myth, through the stories that have proliferated as fast as the seedlings that burst up through the paving stones of the cities. You will have seen us caught in the camera's eye, pinned to the pages of the broadsheets or plunging through flickering light on a screen. You will have traced our path across the continents, stopped in your tracks at the sound of rails in the night, listened to all the tales told of us, not knowing what to believe.

It is time for us to tell our own story.

I remember those first months only in a whirl of wonder and horror and disbelief, certain that we would be stopped; just as certain that we were unstoppable. Terrified of what we had released. What would we do, we asked ourselves, when we ran out of rails? But we never did, the earth beneath us made sure of that, we never have, and the new Captain drove us onward, through Europe, into the famous, glittering cities and through fields of lavender and golden wheat. And when we reached the edge of the land we turned to travel a different route, the rails rising up before us, plotting a path across the continent.

I don't pretend to understand what it is we do; I leave the investigation of our many mysteries to the scientists, who study them through the microscope's lens, and to Suzuki Kenji, who maps the changes we bring, though even they have not come close to understanding the rails themselves, in part because they do not last but crumble behind us like bones collapsing into the earth, to be born again, elsewhere. The changes, though, remain. We leave new life in our wake; young vines curling around ancient houses; new shoots stirring in the soil; flora and fauna not found in any of the natural histories so far written. We leave you to find ways to live alongside it, to make the choice that faces us all—whether to turn away from the changes, to fight, to flee; or whether to welcome them in.

It has become part of our legend, that all of us who made that last crossing remained onboard, but that is not quite true—there were some who chose to leave, whose ties to family, land, duty were too strong. Those who were unwilling or unable to give themselves to the train. And there were those whom it tore apart; the wife who hesitated at the door; who, when her husband turned to help her down to the platform, shook her head and said that her place was here, with us, and when her husband raged and tried to reach for her the branches and leaves stopped him, and the train would not have him back. And the previous Captain, who had ridden the train all her life, daring the Wastelands to rise up against her, she stayed with us for a while, then became one of those who settled in Greater Siberia, after the Walls came down, searching for the home her ancestors had lost.

But it is true that many remained, and that more come, every year. Some ride for days, weeks. Some never leave. We grow and change, as everything must.

———

Of course, there are those who fear us. There are those still loyal to the Company, though it has been broken down, its ruins fought over in the courts and the banking houses. There are those who blame us for the nightmares we released; for the wings and claws and teeth that demand new ways of coexistence. The cleric Yuri Petrovich follows us like a malign shadow. We see his picture in the papers, see him preaching fire and brimstone in city squares and on isolated station platforms. He is indefatigable, and I suppose I admire him for it. His own followers call him a prophet; they flock to him, fearful and eager, longing to believe that he can make sense of a world changing beneath their feet. It is against God, he says. It is an abomination, this train, it must be stopped. The changes must be turned back, the creatures hunted down. And they listen. Young men with their faces hidden behind masks throw burning bottles at the train as we cross over borders; beacons are lit as we pass, to tell the faithful to ready their traps, and there are plenty who heed the call. These Petrovites, as they have come to be called, have tried it all—blockades and dynamite and bullets, and yet the train endures. And yet the creatures they hunt flourish.

I should speak of our Captain. The child of the train, as she once was, as she is still. Those of us who knew her before still see the young girl she was: watchful, clever, always poised for flight. She is different now, of course.

For months, she searched. Everywhere we traveled she watched for signs of Elena, the Wastelands girl she had left behind. This is the part of the story you will not know; that it was because of a stowaway that all this happened, that everything changed. Because of a friendship.

When we first traveled back across Siberia she barely slept, spending her time instead at the windows of the watchtower, certain Elena would hear the call of the train, as she had done all that time ago. We travelled far into the places that no human had seen since the changes began, where eyes opened in the trunks of the birches and shadows moved in the rib cages of fallen animals, as tall as church steeples. We crossed into regions where the land all but sank into water and the rails carried us above glassy surfaces, and in certain light we thought we saw her reflection in the shallows.

There was a longing, a desperation in the Captain in those days. But as the months passed, and we travelled into the new century, we saw a change come over her. She lost the hungry expression we had come to know; she stood taller, at ease in her own skin. She learned to read the land before us, knowing where to guide our path, where the sweetest fruits grew and where clear, pure water rose up from the ground. We would see her, at times, stretching her arms out of the window as if to greet someone waiting on the air. We began to understand, then, that she had found what she was looking for after all; that the Wastelands girl we had known is as much a part of the landscape as the Captain is of the train. We understand that they will never be parted.

I write this at my desk in the Cartographer's tower, my hand long accustomed to moving my pen to the rhythm of the rails. It is morning, and the train is full of life. We picked up new passengers in Nanjing and now we are heading south. The Countess and Vera are preparing the soil in the garden carriage for what new seeds we may find. The Professor is at his printing press. Alexei is teaching the children the workings of the brakes and gears. And Suzuki is at work with his lenses and charts, moving quietly from scope to scope, passing by with a touch on my shoulder or to place a cup of tea on my desk.

Beside me as I write is Valentin Rostov's famous guide. I keep it open at the author's portrait, so that he might see the world he once described now loosened from its bindings. It seems only right that he travels with us, and I believe he understood that it is no longer possible for us to be cautious note spelling, only curious ones. I like to think that he would be proud.

All summer we keep the windows open. We breathe in transfigured air. It is not only the landscape that has changed; our own bodies are alive with transformations. I watch as the sunlight catches the new silvery scales on my skin. I lick salt from my lips. I write this book as a way of remembering what we have been, and of finding a way through this new world to what we will be.

Where will the great train take us? We stand at the open windows and we watch the horizon approaching.

ACKNOWLEDGMENTS

I owe an enormous debt of gratitude to the following people and organizations:

My incredible agent, Nelle Andrew, for her belief in this novel from a very early stage and for her patience and enthusiasm, as well as the whole team at Rachel Mills Literary—Rachel Mills, Alexandra Cliff and Charlotte Bowerman.

My editors, for their insight, kindness and unstinting support—Caroline Bleeke at Flatiron Books, and at Weidenfeld & Nicolson, Federico Adornino, who acquired the book, and Alexa von Hirschberg, who took it on. I feel so lucky to have had three such amazing champions for this story.

The whole team at Flatiron, especially Malati Chavali, Sydney Jeon, Christopher Smith, Maris Tasaka, Emily Walters, Jeremy Pink, Eva Diaz, Tania Bissell, Flatiron president Bob Miller and publisher Megan Lynch. Also Chloe Nosan, Claire Beyette and Isabella Narvaez for their work on the audio production, and the team at W&N and Orion in the UK.

Emily Faccini for her beautiful train map, and Will Staehle and Donna Noetzel for their gorgeous cover and interior designs, as well as Keith Hayes and Kelly Gatesman as art director and designer.

The Lucy Cavendish Fiction Prize, for playing such an important role in the life of the book, and especially Gillian Stern, for being a staunch supporter through it all.

New Writing North, for granting me a Northern Debut Award in 2021, which provided vital encouragement, as have Harminder Kaur, Rob Schofield and Gareth Hewitt.

The Leeds Writers' Circle, who, apart from being (possibly!) the longest running writers' circle in the country, are an incredible fount of knowledge, advice and friendship. (And I did indeed cut the first paragraph.) And especially Suzanne McArdle, who gave me confidence and inspiration at a vital time.

The Northern Short Story Academy and SJ Bradley and Fiona Gell, for the incredible amount of work they do for writers in Leeds.

My brilliant Clarion West class of 2012, and the organizers and tutors. This story wouldn't be here without you, and those early handwritten comments have travelled with it all the way. And to Laura and Greg Friis-West, for the ongoing conversation about books, writing, and life.

Interzone magazine and editor Andy Cox, for publishing the short story that grew into this novel.

Friends and colleagues in Leeds and at the university, especially Frances Weightman and Zhang Jianan.

In St. Annes, Mr. Walker, Miss Yeadon, Mrs. Houghton and Mr. Birch, who unwittingly set me off from a small seaside town to adventures on the other side of the world.

And last but very much not least, my family, for the books and for everything else: my parents, Chris and Linda; my brother Michael; Jerry and Celia; Dan and Annette and Willow. And Calum, for his unfailing belief and many, many cups of tea.

ABOUT THE AUTHOR

Sarah Brooks is a writer living in Leeds, England. She won the Lucy Cavendish Fiction Prize in 2019 and a Northern Debut Award from New Writing North in 2021. She works in East Asian studies at the University of Leeds, where she helps run the Leeds Centre for New Chinese Writing. She is coeditor of *Samovar,* a bilingual online magazine for translated speculative fiction. *The Cautious Traveller's Guide to the Wastelands* is her debut novel and will be published around the world.

Recommend
The Cautious Traveller's
Guide to the Wastelands
for your next book club!

Reading Group Guide available at

flatironbooks.com/reading-group-guides